THE GIRL WHO WOULD LIVE FOREVER

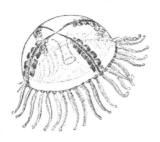

REBECCA CANTRELL

1

ALSO BY REBECCA CANTRELL

Yuletide Thrills (standalone short story collection)

Award-winning Joe Tesla thrillers

- *The World Beneath*
- *The Tesla Legacy*
- *The Chemistry of Death*
- *The Steel Shark*

Award-winning Hannah Vogel mysteries

- *A Trace of Smoke*
- *A Night of Long Knives*
- *A Game of Lies*
- *A City of Broken Glass*
- *Cigarette Boy (novella)*

Sofia Salgado comedy mysteries (co-written with Sean Black)

- *A is for Actress*
- *B is for Bad Girls*
- *C is for Coochy Coo*
- *D is for Drunk*
- *E is for Exposed*
- *F is for Fred*
- *G is for Groovy*

Gothic thrillers in the Order of the Sanguines series (co-written with James Rollins)

- *Blood Gospel*
- *Innocent Blood*
- *Blood Infernal*

Young adult novels in the iMonster series (written as Bekka Black).

- *iDrakula*
- *iFrankenstein*

THE GIRL WHO WOULD LIVE FOREVER

REBECCA CANTRELL

COPYRIGHT INFORMATION

DEDICATION

For Max, Toby, and Jim for hanging in there all
these years

TABLE OF CONTENTS

CHAPTER ONE

The scold's bridle is an iron cage worn on the head. When locked in place, it secures a spiked bridle bit over the tongue. From the 1500s to 1800s, this form of painful public humiliation was designed to punish and silence the wearer, usually a woman. Want to step back in time and see how it felt?

The ting of Ivy's pen against the iron bridle echoed through the empty exhibition room. She slipped on the virtual reality helmet, settled the disposable tongue depressor in her mouth, and stepped back in time. Tallinn's Town Hall Square, just on the other side of the museum's thick stone wall, bloomed to life. Winter there, too, and snow dusted cobblestones and wooden market stalls.

The flat iron band that ran down to the bridle bit obscured her view of the scene and the steel bead glued to the tongue depressor dug painfully into the top of her tongue. The taste of metal filled her mouth. Not nearly as uncomfortable as the real thing, but enough to remind her constantly of its presence.

Medieval craftsmen in woolen capes and pointy shoes hurried from the cheese stall to the sausage stall. She did a slow pan around the busy square, studying each stall and actor. All clear. Then the scene jumped a little. A quick jerk to remind her that her husband held a leash connected to the back of the cage and he determined what she should see.

With measured steps, she walked through the square ahead of him. Snow and straw squeaked under her boots. Voices filled the air. A woman stopped in front of her and glared with cold, contemptuous eyes that tried to hide a spark of fear. After all, it could be her in that bridle next time.

A man in a hat spit on Ivy, the sound so clear she flinched away. And then the narrator read the words that she had written to put the device into historical context. They told how similar devices were used in Britain, Europe, America, China, and Japan. Usually, the husband requested the bridle for his wife, but other male relatives could too. When not doing chores, she and the bridle could be chained to a hook on her wall. The voiceover actress's strong performance carried her along.

In the real world, a hand tapped her shoulder and she jumped, winter scene bobbing. With an exclamation, she spit out the tongue depressor and yanked off the helmet. She felt lighter and calmer instantly. The exhibit was too immersive, but that was a good thing.

"Sorry to bother you." Liilia's lips pursed in annoyance. She handed Ivy her cellphone with a significant look. "Your phone is buzzing a million times a minute."

Ivy looked down at the screen. Twitter. Why was she tagged in a hundred tweets?

Her heart rose. Today was the release date for her first novel. Clearly it was getting a lot of press. Maybe people were buying it and reading it and liking it and she wouldn't have to spend her life designing museum exhibits about public shaming and other tortures. Maybe this was her big break.

Liilia cleared her throat.

"I'll turn it off." Even though she ached to read the notifications, Ivy held down the power button. Liilia had a strict policy about phones on the job. She had a strict policy about nearly everything, and Ivy wasn't sure enough that her book was going to break out to risk losing this job.

"The final run through?" Liilia looked at her watch. She belonged to the era of wristwatches, and kept to her schedule like a Japanese train conductor.

"I'm on fifteen of sixteen. Everything looks good." The exhibit, which aimed to give attendees a virtual experience of torture and public shaming in the Medieval era, was solid. "The motion glitch over by the cheese stall is fixed and the audio syncs perfectly."

She itched to pull out her phone.

Liilia nodded. "Good."

"The Iron Maiden is all that's left." Claustrophobic and dark, she'd left it to last. The sense of being shut in alone to die felt too powerful there. Ivy had insisted they add a trigger warning to it and, over Liilia's protests, she'd won.

Liilia cracked a smile. "I'll take it. Go to your signing."

Ivy stared at her. "I---what?"

"You heard me. It's a big night. You've done good work here. Take off a half hour early."

"Thanks." Ivy pushed down the urge to hug her and fast walked toward the door in case this was a trick. She passed the rack, the Judas Chair, the Iron Maiden. Each lurked in its own stone alcove, artfully lit. Visitors could touch and interact with these replicas. The original devices were in another room next to Medieval-style sketches of them torturing hapless victims.

"You feeling ok?" asked Lucas at the front desk. The tips of his white linen coif bobbed when he spoke. All the reception staff had to wear period garb.

"Liilia let me go early."

He rocked back in his battered wooden chair, eyes wide. "Wow."

"I have to get out of here before she changes her mind."

Lucas jumped up and raced to the coat check. He returned with her hat, scarf, and leather jacket and thrust them into her hands.

"Good luck tonight," he said. "I'll come by for your reading."

A jolt of fear shot through her at the thought of reading her book in front of people. "Did you know that some people fear public speaking more than death?"

"Go before that sinks in," he said.

She hurried through a heavy wooden door hung before Columbus stumbled on America. When she stepped into Town Hall Square, the cold hit her. Her jacket wasn't warm enough, but she hated to let it go. It had been her mother's. She stamped her boots against icy cobbles, took a deep breath, and turned on her phone.

While she waited for it to boot, she gazed at the towering pine decked out in golden lights and red hearts. The center of Tallinn's Christmas market cheered her every time she saw it. Sixty feet of Christmas joy was about enough. With a cup of mulled wine.

Her phone binged to life and she logged in to get to Twitter. She must be missing the excitement generated by her little book, and she wanted to savor every word. She bet that her interview on that book podcast had gone viral. Before she could read a single message, the phone rang. Rita at Apollo Bookstore.

"I've got everything set up, but I can't get the connection working. Are you sure your publisher sent the right link?"

Ivy wasn't sure about that at all. She talked Rita through the setup process, verified the link in her own email, and put in an emergency call to her editor. All the while, she hurried toward the bookstore, going as fast as she dared on the ice. It was a couple kilometers away and she was out of breath when she arrived.

Rita met her at the door and pulled her into the warmth and light. "I rebooted. It seems OK."

Ivy's phone buzzed. She touched it in her pants pocket then rubbed her cold hands together.

"Come see the setup." Rita herded her deeper into the store. "I'll take your coat."

Ivy peeled off her coat, gloves, and scarf and Rita grabbed them and hung them over one arm. Ivy's phone buzzed in her pants pocket, again and again. Her book must be blowing up. Even though she'd waited for this moment since she was a little girl hiding under her bed reading while her parents screamed at each other, she couldn't believe it. Today she officially became an Author. She might never have to see Liilia's smiling face again. She might be able to hunker down in her apartment and write. She was already casting the movie by the time Rita stopped walking.

"Here's the display." Rita pointed to a veritable shrine to Ivy's book. Seven copies propped up on a luxurious spread of dark green velvet. "Green because of the cover. I know space is black, but black doesn't grab you. The book got lost, and I wanted to pick out the green in the spaceship lights. And it matches the store more. Plus Christmas colors."

"It really pops." Ivy had never seen her book in the wild before. She'd received a few advanced reader copies but they had black and white covers, like generic soup at the store. But this. This looked resplendent. Her day had arrived.

"I set up a table in the science fiction section." Rita dragged her across the green carpet. "For the signing."

Ivy's phone buzzed again and her hand twitched toward her pocket.

"I borrowed a rope from a friend who does events," Rita said. "You'll be at the lectern."

Green velvet draped the lectern. Next to it a stack of books and a poster of Ivy's author photo rested on the table. Her head had never been that size before. She was glad she'd paid extra for a professional photographer.

"I got an easel for the photo," Rita said. "Maximum visibility."

A line of wooden folding chairs faced the lectern. Ivy's friend Anu already sat in the front row. She waved urgently and mouthed "Now."

"Could I have a minute?" Ivy asked.

"Let's check the lighting and the camera. You're livestreaming on the internet and I want to get everything right. The store must look good for your first worldwide appearance."

Worldwide. Ivy's knees wobbled. Across the room, Anu texted into her phone. Ivy's phone buzzed again.

Rita had already maneuvered her to the lectern. "Stand right there."

Ivy stood. Anu looked worried, and nothing fazed Anu. She must be happy for her friend. Well, this was a big deal. After a lifetime of obscurity, Ivy's first novel had emerged into the world and clearly the world was paying attention. Her phone buzzed again. Anu didn't look happy. Ivy's bubbling excitement fizzled, but only a little. It was her night.

"I don't like that light." Rita adjusted it and moved to the camera. "Still not right."

Ivy stood, not sure what to do with her hands. She pulled out her battered Advanced Reading Copy and touched the black and white cover. She'd put a yellow sticky note on the page she intended to read after she'd marked it up with a blue pen to remove sections with spoilers before practicing it in front of her bathroom mirror.

Her editor had told her not to read from the beginning, because that was already up for free on Amazon. She needed to hook them with something later in, a passage that made the stakes clear. Had she chosen the right one? It was her first time reading, ever, and she didn't want to mess it up.

"Say something into the microphone," ordered Rita.

"Something," answered Ivy. "Something. Something."

Anu smiled, but Rita shook her head. "Let me adjust this."

Ivy's phone buzzed again. Not Anu. She'd stopped texting and sat like a runner about to jump off the blocks at the start of a race.

More people filed in. Lucas and Liilia from the museum. Her writers' group. The four of them looked even more nervous than Anu. Did everyone think she'd blow it up here? They waved frantically, and she waved back. She gave them a thumbs-up sign. Nobody gave her one back.

Between the lights and the microphone and the internet, Ivy never left her place at the podium before the event started. Before she knew it, Rita stood in front of her and introduced her, reading advanced rave reviews so hyperbolic Ivy blushed.

Then her turn came and Ivy talked about her inspirations. Her worries about climate change balanced against the hope that the world would go on, and that humans would one day colonize space. About how huddling inside in the cold dark of a Tallinn winter made her think about living in a space station. How snowsuits felt like spacesuits. How the long dark of a northern winter mirrored the vast emptiness of space.

When she wound down, Rita called out. "Please read us a section."

Ivy took a deep breath and opened the book.

Captain Jasper smiled as air hissed into the airlock, equalizing pressure between the shuttle and the Curie. The airlock reeked of gunpowder, like Luna, and she drew it deep into her lungs. She'd been on medical rotation on Earth for the last six months, building up her bones, and the smells there were overwhelming—salt from the Southern California ocean, rain against hot asphalt, exhaust, and the musk of humans stewing in the heat. The simple scents of Luna were perfume to her now.

Ivy cleared her throat, dropped her voice from the nervous squeak, and continued.

Jasper rubbed the stubble on her scalp. She kept her hair shaved close for spaceflight. One less thing to fuss with. When she'd captained her first voyage it had been black and shiny, like a mink. Now she saw as much white stubble as black. She'd grown grizzled and old in the service.

The Curie had carried survey teams from Earth to Luna, Mars, and Enceladus. But this was her most important mission of all. She bore within her hull a pilot, an engineer, and four scientists who worked feverishly with data they'd received from probes exploring their destination planet. A botanist. A biologist. A geologist. And a doctor. If all went well, they would remain on the planet's surface to make it fit for human colonization. Then the women who slept in the cryogenic bays below would be revived in their new home. If they failed, the last vestiges of humanity would live out their lives closed up in metal coffins. They'd suffocate in the ship's hull or die under vast domes carved by the robots they'd sent ahead.

Ivy felt the rhythm of it now. She read another page, closed the book, and looked up at her audience. Scattered applause. Everyone looked worried. Even Rita's good cheer had vanished.

Ivy went cold. She had humiliated herself in front of the world, streaming live, and she struggled to keep her face calm.

Rita spoke into the silence. "Now we'll take questions from our online audience."

Anu jumped to her feet. She pointed to her phone, then to Ivy's pocket. Ivy took out her phone and it buzzed with a text from Anu. Other texts too.

Online trolls attacking your book. I'll feed you questions on your phone

All those tweets were from people who hated her book?

Anu texted again. How does faster-than-light travel work?

Ivy gulped, repeated the question for the audience, and answered. "The ship uses something called Alcubierre drive that's been posited by a theoretical physicist in Mexico named Miguel Alcubierre. The drive contracts spacetime in front of the spaceship and expands spacetime behind it, basically folding spacetime around the ship's hull. The Curie has two parts: living quarters in the middle and a ring around the living quarters that holds the drive."

She usually had a longer answer and demonstrated it with a folded piece of paper and a pen, but she'd been thrown off. Trolls attacking her book. Had they moved to attacking her personally?

Anu texted. Can they communicate with Earth?

Ivy repeated it and answered. "Some of the time. The Curie follows a preset route where previous drones have set up quantum entanglement buoys after each fold. Electrons in those buoys are entangled with electrons back on Earth. So, messages are sent by changing the state of the electrons in the buoy. Those changes are mirrored by the electrons back on Earth, which results in instantaneous communications back and forth. This only works when they're near a buoy though. Folding takes time, so they're out of communication most of the time."

Part of the audience looked interested, and the rest looked blandly polite. Anu fired her another less nerdy question and Ivy answered it. Her phone didn't let up with the buzzing from Twitter, but Ivy focused on Anu's questions. Across the room, Rita's shoulders went down a notch.

Ivy's answers got longer and people in the bookstore started asking questions, too. And then it was over and she still didn't know what was going on. She smiled and signed books and drank wine and cut up a giant cake with the cover of her book printed in the frosting on top. She'd worked toward this night for years and she wanted to savor it. But her stomach roiled with existential dread.

CHAPTER TWO

Anger and fear accompanied Ivy through the winter forest. Her boots crunched through a thin crust atop the snow and squeaked when they settled against the snow beneath. Cold and clear, usually a good night for a walk in the woods. Tonight was different. She'd finally read the tweets on the drive over. So many people hated her book. So many people also hated her personally. Her life's work had been dismissed, trampled, and bombed by one-star reviews on the day of its birth.

Someone named @barryfightsformen89 had kicked it all off with a tweet that read @IvyCorvaAuthor says men are useless and the future is female only. Tell her why we're necessary!

Boy had they ever told her. She'd sent an email to her editor for advice, but didn't expect to hear back. Maybe ever.

"It's so peaceful out here." Anu's breath puffed out in tiny clouds. When she pulled her pink beanie over her ears her hair crackled with static electricity.

"The internet is a foul and treacherous place," Ivy said. "Teeming with demons and worms."

Anu rolled her eyes. "Drama."

Although not given to drama herself, Anu had no trouble identifying it in Ivy. They'd been friends since Ivy arrived in Estonia, and Anu had identified plenty of drama.

"Was there a time when the internet wasn't awful?" Ivy had no intention of being sidelined.

Anu shrugged and nudged her onto the river trail like a helpful herd dog. They often ended up at the Pirita on their after-work walks. In summer, the river burbled and the breeze cooled their cheeks. In winter, the river sometimes froze and the wind across its surface strafed their faces. Ivy liked it best then. The pain felt honest.

Ivy kept going. "Take Facebook. It started as a way for the Zucc and his classmates to rate women as hot or not. Annoying if you're hot. Cruel if you're not. And a reduction of you in front of all your peers either way. It's not like they had a feature to rate the guys. Did he create a dick measuring site? Someplace where women rate men's dicks as puny or adequate? Is there one anywhere on the internet?"

"Probably," Anu said.

"Maybe." Ivy's inherent honesty made her pause. She stomped a few minutes before winding back up. "Even so, that hypothetical dick site isn't on par with Facebook for popularity. Plus, who wants to be the guy who has to hold the tape measure?"

"#NotAllMen." Anu sounded winded and Ivy slowed down. "#MenAreVictimsToo."

"Some are, and that's wrong, too. But the balance skews toward women as victims. Do you know how many dick pics I've gotten today?"

"More than you wanted."

Ivy tucked her hair behind her cold ears. "Fifty-one before we got out of the car. At least one more lonely little penis is waiting in the ether, waiting to surprise me when I look at my phone again."

"That's a whole deck of cards," Anu said.

"The dick deck."

They both laughed.

"You know," Anu said. "You'd be prettier if you smiled more."

Ivy groaned.

"And make me a sandwich, Miss Novelist," Anu said.

"A dick sandwich," Ivy answered.

Anu snorted and Ivy grinned at her.

They walked for a few minutes in silence. Ivy tightened her scarf.

"Lots of people are defending your book, too, you know," Anu said. "It's easy to miss."

"It's a science fiction world," Ivy pointed out. "An intelligent spaceship going to the colonies using Alcubierre drive. It deals with quantum entanglement across space and time. Colonization in the future."

"I know." Anu had read Ivy's novel before publication, offering calm and sensible advice then too.

"No one has a problem suspending disbelief for the made-up science. Instead, they have a problem because the crew is all female and the colonists too. How many all-male crews have we seen in science fiction?"

"10,874," Anu answered.

Ivy broke stride to look at her. "Really?"

Anu's lips quirked into a tiny smile.

"Even so—" Ivy stopped. "Do you hear that?"

Anu tilted her head and lifted the beanie off one ear.

"It sounds like a little kid," Ivy said.

She sprinted toward the river with Anu close behind, listening. Ivy's feet crunched too loudly for her to hear anything over her own racing heart.

In a few minutes, she reached the frozen bank. Night came early here and it was too dark to see much. Unbroken snow-covered hummocks ranged in front of her. The snow leveled out where it covered the ice at the edge of the river. Dark pines and spruce loomed from the bank.

On cold nights, a skin of ice formed on top of the water, thin as a pane of glass. Sometimes, it froze through, but the soft sound of water trickling told her that underneath, the river was free.

Ivy stopped to listen. No whimper. Wind stung her cheeks. She tugged her own beanie down to cover the tops of her ears.

"Too much imagination?" asked Anu.

Ivy ignored her and turned on her phone's flashlight. Snow glittered blue-white at the river's edge. Ice extended about ten feet from the bank and dark water flowed beyond. She knew from summer swims that the river got deep there. At the edge of her light a shadow moved.

"A dog," Anu said. "He's stuck in the ice."

"But—" Ivy cut off her protest. She'd wanted to ask how Anu knew the dog was male and then realized that the question was absurd. It was that kind of a day.

Instead, she walked to the edge of the river. The toes of her boots broke through the ice and she retreated a pace.

She tried again with her phone. Light reflected off a pair of half-closed eyes and a soft whimper cut her heart. "We have to get him out."

"It's not safe," Anu answered. "We should call for help."

When they checked their phones, neither had any bars. One of the reasons they'd chosen this spot was so Ivy wouldn't be interrupted by death threats on Twitter. Now, she regretted it.

"I had reception back at the parking lot," Ivy said. "My phone buzzed as I got out of the car."

"Probably that last dick pic."

Ivy shifted from foot to foot. "What if you go back, call for help, and lead them here?"

"And what do you do?"

"I stay here with the dog. Try to keep him calm."

"Right here on the bank, where it's safe?" Anu asked.

"You have to be the one to go," Ivy said. "My Estonian isn't good enough."

They both knew it was, but Anu's was inarguably better. Anu sighed. "Promise you'll stay here?"

"Sure."

Anu gave her a sour look before sprinting back into the trees.

"Hey, pup," Ivy called low across the water. "We'll get you out."

The dog whined.

They carried on a conversation like that for a while. Ivy used reassuring words and the dog answered with soft whimpers. Until the dog went quiet.

"Come on, pup," Ivy called.

No answer.

She lifted the light up over her head. The dog's gray form lay motionless, front legs and head above the ice, haunches and part of his belly in the water. He must be freezing. Maybe to death.

Ivy listened for Anu returning with help. Only the burble of water and the wind in the pines. She glanced around as if the answer waited for her to find it.

And she did.

One long branch of a nearby pine dangled over the river, probably cracked by a recent windstorm. Ivy hurried over and yanked on the branch until it broke loose. The sharp scent of pine pitch perfumed the cold air. "Sorry, tree."

Returning to her post at the water's edge, she knelt and slid the branch as far as she could across the ice. It fell several feet short of the dog's still form. "Pup?"

No answer.

Ivy swore and stomped up and down the bank. "ANU!"

No answer there either.

Then the damn dog whimpered again. Still alive.

But not for long. Somewhere, a little girl stood in her backyard in a thin nightgown and boots, calling for this dog. And the dog would never come home. He'd freeze into the river and, come spring, he'd be carried to the sea. Fish would eat his furry ears. And the little girl would never know. She might think he'd left her because he didn't love her. Right before Christmas, too. Practically a whole country song of woe.

Ivy gritted her teeth. Little girl or no, the dog really was dying a few meters away. While she stood safe on the bank, he was freezing to death. This wasn't a cyberbattle. This was real and the stakes were immediate. All the dog had going for him was her stupidity.

Swearing at the top of her lungs, she stomped into the water. The thin ice broke and she crashed through to her knees. Water filled her boots, soaked her socks, and wicked up her jeans. Her feet ached and tears sprang to her eyes. She swore in an unbroken stream.

But she pushed the branch ahead of her and plowed on. Water hit her crotch with another wave of cold and pain, then her waist, her nipples. She said a silent prayer that her phone case was really as waterproof as advertised.

Finally, the branch reached the dog. He leaned forward feebly and bit down on the end. She hauled him back, hand over hand, like a fish on a line. The dog held on.

When he was close enough, she lifted his furry body. He smelled of wet dog and snow. She tossed him over one shoulder. Fireman's carry. Remnant of a high school first aid class.

As she slogged to shore, she imagined the little girl's face lighting up when her pet came home. Her little arms around his chest. His tail wagging a greeting.

A rock rolled under her boot and they both went down in the icy water. With the dog curled around her shoulder, she reached out with her free hand to keep from being swept under the ice. She struggled to get both numb feet onto the riverbed but they were clumsy and slow, like a glitchy robot.

And still the current dragged her forward.

One boot wedged under a rock. It was enough. She got both feet situated on the ground, like feet were supposed to be, and splashed toward shore. The dog lay still. Either it was dead, it had given up, or it trusted her. All bad choices.

By the time she reached the bank, her teeth chattered so hard she thought they'd break. How would that dental conversation go? At least there'd be a warm office and gas. It'd be nice.

She shook her head. Not right. She looked over at her hands. They were frozen into claws, pink, and marbled. Bad statue hands.

The best thing to do was to run. She was sure of it. Except she couldn't feel her feet or see the path. Didn't matter. She hefted the dog, tightened her claw hands, and shuffled forward like a character in a bad zombie movie. Except she was the zombie and, if she fell, she'd die for real.

Eventually, blue light strobed from the darkness. The light at the end of the tunnel everyone always talked about? Was she actually dying? Because of some stranger's dog? Was the dog dying and seeing the light, too? Did that happen for dogs?

She hit the parking lot and someone took the dog and lifted her into the warmest ambulance in the world. He had crystal blue eyes, tousled blond hair, and a jawline to die for. She gazed up at his face silhouetted against the ceiling of the ambulance as he wrapped a heated blanket around her shoulders and cut off her wet jeans with giant shears. He touched her black leather sleeve and she pulled away.

"Not the jacket," she said.

Or at least that's what she tried to say. With her chattering teeth it barely sounded like words.

Then Anu climbed into the ambulance. She held up a hand and peeled off Ivy's jacket and boots. Then she nodded to the hunky EMT, and he cut off the rest of her clothes. So, the hottest guy she'd seen in a while had undressed her and it wasn't sexy at all. Just her luck.

The guy eased her down onto a gurney and piled up more blankets, the top one blue with white Nordic stars.

"I'm Toomas," he said. "How are you?"

"Ivy," she said. "C-c-cold."

Toomas piled on more blankets. They were the best thing ever. Warm and soft and they smelled of lavender and pine.

He dried her head with a towel, which seemed weird because she didn't remember when her hair got wet. The rock. The slipping. The going down. It came back to her.

He put a dry cap on her head, then held a cup of warm something to her mouth. She shivered too much to hold it herself. When he touched the cup to her lips, she sipped. It tasted like sugary tea. She warmed up.

Now everything prickled and burned. Warming up was worse than freezing. but she wasn't going to cry in front of this guy and Anu. Anu's eyes were huge, and her eyebrows looked angry. Crying would just piss her off.

Toomas put a warm gel pack behind Ivy's neck. It felt like Christmas already back there. She closed her eyes for a while and tried to pretend she wasn't part of her body. That this pain was all a dream. A dream where she chattered her teeth out and shook her skin off.

"The dog?" she asked.

"A veterinarian is here for the dog," Anu said. "They're taking care of him."

"Good." She sipped warm sugary tea. "Tastes like nectar. Like a hummingbird."

Anu looked at her like she was nuts.

"Except hummingbirds never get this damn cold. They know better," Ivy continued.

"Hummingbirds can get really cold safely," Anu said. "They can lower their body temperature to 48 degrees, which would kill a human."

"Fun facts about hummingbirds." Ivy raised the tea in a salute. Now Toomas looked at them both like he hadn't expected any of this.

"I knew you would do a very stupid thing." Anu trembled. "That's why I called the ambulance."

"You cold?" Ivy lifted one blanket-clad arm and Toomas pushed her arm down and tucked her in like a little kid. She didn't mind. That guy could tuck her in any time.

"I'm not cold." Anu glared at her. "This is me when I'm pissed off."

A drop of water trickled down Ivy's cheek. "This is me when I'm pissed on."

Toomas thought it was funny too. He and Ivy had a good laugh and finally Anu joined in.

Then they all sat around and waited for Ivy to warm up. It took a while and it hurt. Toomas kept it up with the warm packs and new blankets and took her temperature a lot, which was getting sexier.

Someone rapped on the back of the ambulance, and Toomas opened the door. A man with an impressive brown beard clambered in. He had on a yellow jacket and reminded Ivy of Paddington bear.

"My name is Peet," he said. "From the dog rescue."

He looked so serious Ivy clenched her jaw. "Is the pup OK?"

"Oh yes," he said. "His blood sugar is a little low and he's tired, but he's warm and eating and they come to pick him up."

"His family?" she asked, thinking again of the girl with the shining eyes who would be reunited with her beloved pet.

Peet stroked his beard and looked uncomfortable. Anu said something sharp, and he shrugged.

"The dog you rescued is not a dog," Peet said finally.

Ivy figured the hypothermia must be messing with her hearing. "So, it's a monkey?"

Peet smiled. "It's more like a wild animal."

"A feral dog?"

"Did he bite you anywhere?" Toomas asked.

Anu went pale. "Rabies?"

"I don't think so," Ivy said.

Toomas had already taken the warm blankets off and there she was naked in the back of an ambulance in front of two guys and Anu. Nobody else seemed to think it was weird so she decided to view it like a sauna. Everyone was naked in the sauna, not just her, but it was the best metaphor she could come up with right now.

Toomas ran firm hands over her face, ears, arms, back, neck, legs, even under her pink goose-pimpled breasts.

"Nothing," he said, which she found a little insulting.

"No bites," clarified Anu. "That's good."

Toomas wrapped her up again, quick and efficient. The blankets felt better now. She was pretty sure she was going to live. And she had to use the bathroom. Did hummingbirds pee in the air?

"If it had bitten her." Anu shuddered. "What would you do next?"

"Kill it and test its brain," Peet said. "And give her shots."

"Kill it!" Ivy glared at him. "I worked hard to rescue that dog.

"That dog is no dog," Peet said again. "That dog is a wolf."

Anu slid down the side of the ambulance and sat on the floor with both legs sticking in front of her like a doll.

"I think she needs you more than I do," Ivy said to Toomas. To Peet she said, "So what happens to him?"

"Once he's fattened up a bit, they will give him his shots. Then put a radio collar on him and let him go."

"In Tallinn?"

"Down south." Peet smiled at her. "You did a foolish thing. Brave, yes, also foolish."

"More foolish than brave," Anu put in. "Because it could have killed you in a couple of ways."

"He who saves one wolf saves the world entire. Or the pack entire. Or something like that," Ivy said.

"You give her the good drugs." Peet told Toomas before he hopped out of the back of the ambulance and the darkness swallowed him up.

Ivy couldn't decide if that was an order to Toomas or an assessment of her current mental state. Not that she cared. She'd saved a freaking wolf. Easily the most badass thing she'd ever done.

And for the last hour she hadn't once worried about internet trolls finding her and killing her.

CHAPTER THREE

Back in her apartment, Ivy perched on her broad wooden windowsill. She'd taken a warm bath, put on polar fleece pajamas, and now she sipped a cup of hot mulled wine Anu had made before leaving. More simmered on the stove and the scents of wine, cloves, and lemon drifted through her apartment. Outside her window a street lamp lit ancient cobblestones golden and snowflakes whirled in the circle of light. It was like being inside a cozy snow globe. Safe until she looked at her phone.

She glanced around her darkened apartment. The building was a couple hundred years old and right on the edge of Old Town, close to her favorite Cafe Caffeine and a stone's throw from the gothic St. Nicholas Church. Her walls were so thick she could sit on the windowsills and read or write on her laptop. Bright rugs covered wooden floors battered by a century of trauma. The mismatched furniture was cast offs from Anu's family and IKEA pieces she'd carried home on the ferry from Helsinki.

Her phone bonged.

"We aren't friends," she told it. "I know we used to be close, but now you're only the bearer of bad news."

Still, she couldn't resist checking. She received her fifty-second dick pic and a picture of a plunger.

The poster had painful ideas about what to do with it. She shuddered.

Then her phone rang. Still suspicious, she checked the caller ID. Shelby Linton.

She and Shelby had been college roommates. Shelby had lost her mother; Ivy was a full-on orphan. Shelby had majored in biochemistry. Got a PhD in record time while Ivy looked at trees, worked on her novel, wrote help systems, and edited little printed cards at the torture museum. Someone on Yelp had said the previous cards were too pro-pillory. They weren't wrong, so Ivy had fixed them. That led to a gig working on the exhibit, struggling to put humanity's cruelty against each other into a historical context as if it helped to know that humans had always been assholes. In between, she piled up words in her novel. And now her hard work got her attacked by trolls while Shelby had become the rich and famous CEO of her own biotech company, Nyssa. Don't major in English, kids, it's a trap.

Anyway, Shelby wasn't likely to threaten to defile her with a plunger.

"Poi," Shelby said. She always called Ivy Poi, because Poison and Ivy. "Gratz on the book."

"Reviews have been mixed. Praise and pricks."

"You got your words out there. Nobody can take that away."

"I've been getting emails from guys straight up telling me how they're going to rape me with a broom or a knife or with their own tiny little dicks and then set me on fire or make me eat my own entrails or make me pregnant and then make me eat the baby when it's born."

"Nine months for a pregnancy to play out," Shelby said. "That's commitment. Hard to find guys who'll commit like that these days."

"And they doxed me." While she'd rescued the wolf, her name and address had landed on Twitter. They'd even helpfully included a picture of her apartment building. Thanks, Google Earth.

"Do you think anyone is going to fly to Estonia in winter to mess with you? What an ego!"

Ivy wasn't sure if she should feel reassured or offended. She sighed.

"What's the worst that can happen?" Shelby asked.

"Literally one minute ago a guy online threatened to rape me with a plunger."

"Which end?" Shelby asked and they both giggled at the absurdity of the question. Ivy laughed so hard warm tears ran down her face.

After they finished laughing, Ivy dried off her cheeks with the back of her hand. "I rescued a wolf from a frozen river tonight."

"Is that a metaphor?"

"Actual wolf." Ivy summarized the story and Shelby was, uncharacteristically, impressed. Ivy toasted her reflection in the window.

After making sure she was warm and safe and well and pointing out that the wolf could have been rabid and killed her, Shelby turned the conversation to her favorite subject—her biotech company. For once, Ivy was glad for it.

"We're close on another round of VC financing, 93 million." Ivy knew from previous conversations that VC stood for venture capitalists and they were a source of endless cash to finance Shelby's plans. Even so, Shelby sounded like a teacher checking a lesson off her list, not someone who'd received a windfall.

"Gratz." A little more momentous than Ivy's travails with the trolls and the wolves. She sipped her wine, but it had gone cold so she headed for the kitchen. "That's...huge."

"It's the last round. We start clinical trials next and that'll show the doubters. It's almost ready to sell."

Shelby had been moments away from releasing her drug for years so it was hard to fake enthusiasm, but Ivy tried. "Great!"

"It's expensive work stopping the bony hand of death from choking out the life of everyone on Earth." Shelby's tone said she'd sensed Ivy's lack of fake cheer and took it personally. "Bottling immortality."

"Won't that lead to overpopulation and world hunger?" Ivy poured the cold wine back into the pan and ladled out warm. It smelled amazing.

Shelby chuckled. "It's not like everyone will be able to afford it. Those who can won't be worried about contributing to world hunger."

Ouch. Shelby's cynicism ran deep. Still, according to her press releases, she had accomplished the impossible. She'd invented a drug to roll back the ravages of aging. If it worked, she'd be the most important scientist of the century. And one of the richest. Maybe eventually the benefits would filter down to the average person like Ivy.

Ivy padded back to her window seat and needled her anyway. "Immortality for the highest bidder."

"Capitalism, baby. Survival of the fittest."

"Survival of the richest," Ivy corrected. Capitalism had always worked for Shelby because she'd had the foresight to be born to a rich father. Sure, she also worked hard, but her father's money and connections meant that she was a tourist who could leave the working world whenever it ceased to be fun. Not like Ivy. Ivy reminded herself to be fair. The trolls must not be allowed to make her bitter. "Truly a gift for all mankind."

She wasn't going to win an Oscar for that statement.

"Is that howling in the background a wolf or actual wind?" Shelby asked.

Ivy listened. "Wind."

"Do you know it's seventy degrees here right now? Sunny and bright and a palm tree is waving in front of my office window."

"Sounds like a movie set." She took another sip of warm wine. Anu's recipe was perfect.

"Are your dick pics and frozen rivers making you happy, Poi?"

"It's a complicated happiness."

Shelby took a deep breath. "Why not use your skills somewhere warm and safe?"

"California?" Ivy watched snow swirl around the streetlight. Shelby had never offered her a job before. Was this a new high or a new low?

"I need a writer," Shelby said.

"No one needs a writer." Ivy took a long drink of wine. "People need doctors and plumbers and farmers and magical immortality drugs. Writers are froth."

"You're not enough fun to be froth," Shelby said.

Ivy snorted wine out her nose and coughed.

"And the drug isn't magic," Shelby continued. "The FDA is strict about that."

"Sure," Ivy said.

"Nyssa needs a writer," Shelby persisted. "Seventy thousand a year, plus benefits."

Ivy almost dropped her phone. "How much?"

"To start," Shelby said. "We can bump it up later."

Bump it up? Ivy set down her wine so quickly the cup cracked against the windowsill. "What would I have to do?"

"Talk about how much good we're doing. How we're going to change the world. How we're already helping get people off the streets with outreach programs."

"I don't have any experience with that kind of stuff."

"Sure you do. Talk about people who are homeless and not spaceships full of wombs hurtling through the black. Your book was snarky, but warmhearted. Nyssa needs that voice and tone."

"You read my book?" Ivy imagined herself with a wide-open jaw and a square mouth, like an anime character.

"I started it," Shelby said. "It's good."

"Read the jacket copy and page one, maybe flipped to the end in case there's a quiz?"

"See? That's the kind of humor we're looking for."

Ivy looked out at the snow globe and tried to imagine trading it for palm trees and sunshine. "Could I do it from here?"

"Wouldn't it be nice to be somewhere warm where life is simple and you can do good without taking shit from everyone?"

"Like you do?"

"Plus, you've been doxed there. My apartment has great security. Have Christmas in California. Do a three-month gig and be back rescuing wolves by summer."

"I have book things to do." Nothing she hadn't planned doing remotely at Cafe Caffeine with European pop songs in the background and warm chai in her hand. But California must have chai and music, too.

"It'll be like college. Roomies again." She sounded too serious.

"Why me?"

"I need someone out here I can trust. Someone fun."

"Aren't you supposed to be the fun one?" Ivy asked.

"You'd be surprised." Shelby's voice wavered.

That brought Ivy up short. "Are you OK?"

"You're the one being attacked by angry trolls and wolves in a frozen wasteland."

"Wonderland. Winter wonderland. And the wolf was kind. Cuddly even."

"You'll come, right?" Shelby asked. "Promise me you'll think about it? And bring that salted licorice I like."

Shelby was gone before Ivy could promise.

Her inner Stoic said she should stay here and work on the sequel to her first book and get more trolls worked up into a froth with the knowledge that wombs were more valuable than sperm.

She finished her wine and watched the wind chase snow across the cobbles. Mesmerizing, but cold. Was Shelby trying to help her escape the torture museum and wolves and trolls? Or maybe she'd made the offer because she wanted a friend close now that her company had started to take off. Ivy had read the stories about Shelby online. Lauded as a genius on most business and tech websites where the writers always sounded starstruck by her drive, her youth, and her brilliant formula. But they also said she was aloof, distant, and alone. Shelby didn't make friends easily. Maybe it was true that she needed someone to trust.

Maybe it would make more sense in the morning when she wasn't buzzed on wine. Without checking email or Twitter, Ivy went to bed to dream of immortal wolves. The dream wolves devoured her and left her bones to float out to sea.

CHAPTER FOUR

The next morning, she woke up to a headache. When she groaned and stretched, her shoulder twinged and her feet throbbed. She wondered how the wolf felt.

It took a few minutes to talk herself into getting out of bed. She teased felt slippers over her swollen feet and shrugged on a thick robe before heading to the bathroom for a long, hot shower. She checked every inch of her body for bites or scratches, but the wolf hadn't hurt her. That knowledge, plus a few ibuprofens, and she was ready to make tea and contemplate the new day.

The sun hadn't come up yet, because winter in the north, so there wasn't much new day yet. She munched a stale piece of gingerbread from the Christmas market and checked her phone while the hob heated.

She read one ranting email threatening to kill her. Then she selected fifty more that looked similar and moved them to a newly-created Trolls folder. She wanted to have a record of them somewhere in case she ended up dead with a mouth full of entrails. Hiding them in the Trolls folder felt like stuffing troll shit under a bridge, but better under a bridge than in her inbox.

The hob clicked off and she poured water over a teabag. A strong Russian tea, the kind that leeched enamel off your teeth. Hearty and good for headaches. She dumped in milk and sugar.

Now that she'd de-trolled her inbox, she looked at the remainder of her messages. She had a few emails from kind people who defended her and wished her well. That was nice. An email from someone named Olivia Ajak at Nyssa. It had been sent a few minutes after her call with Shelby last night. Olivia, it turned out, was Shelby's executive assistant, and she'd booked Ivy on a flight to California the day after tomorrow for an interview. Olivia's number was listed at the bottom of her signature. Ivy noted it, but called Shelby first to see if she had thought better of this job idea. She didn't answer. Probably working or sleeping or blowing her off. Shelby was often hard to reach.

Then Ivy tried Olivia's number, expecting to get a work number and leave a message.

"This is Ivy Corva. I—"

"Ms. Corva, I'm delighted you called." Olivia sounded too chipper for the time it must be there.

"I'm sorry it's so late—"

"I'm on call for Nyssa twenty-four hours a day. Don't give it a second thought."

"I'm not sure I can fly out to California so soon." Or ever. In the painful almost-light of day, she was sure she'd been wrong about Shelby's mood on the phone.

"The flight is at Nyssa's expense. I hope that was clear."

"I'm not even sure what position I'd be interviewing for." She massaged her shoulder on the side where she'd carried the wolf.

"Details about the position can't be posted." Olivia sounded so earnest. "Nyssa is cautious about the release of any private information."

"A job description is private information?" All her other jobs had been as public as the internet. Given her current experience, maybe that wasn't the best thing.

"I'm not at liberty to tell you details about the job. I don't even know them myself." Olivia paused. "Ms. Linton can tell you everything after you've signed an NDA."

"An NDA?"

"Non-disclosure agreement stating what you can and can't legally talk about. The project we're working on is sensitive."

The secret to immortality ought to be public domain, not a trade secret, but Ivy held her peace. "I have other priorities right now."

"Your book release," Olivia said. "I absolutely adored Lessons from the Curie."

"You read my book?"

"Ms. Linton loaned it to me. It was so witty and on point."

Ivy had never spoken to anyone outside of the book community and the troll community about her book. "Th-thanks."

"I'm so sorry how you've been vilified on social media," Olivia said. "You and Captain Jasper don't deserve it."

Tears welled up in Ivy's eyes like a tragic anime character. Olivia was the first person to say that. She blinked them away and thanked her again. Maybe hypothermia recovery made her weepy.

"Let us spoil you. Even if you're not interested in the job, it's a free trip to San Francisco. Business class. I know Ms. Linton looks forward to seeing you."

Again, Ivy wondered if that was true. Shelby didn't often call or even respond to texts. Most of the time she was caught up in her own obsessions. "I'd have to check my calendar."

"Please do." Olivia sounded far more worried than the situation warranted. "I can wait."

Busted. Ivy's calendar was a vast expanse of emptiness. She tidied away the tea things while counting to ten, then said, "I can move things around."

She hung up on a grateful Olivia. Based on the response, Ivy had the feeling Shelby would have fired Olivia if Ivy didn't go. Which made her even more worried about Shelby. She called again, got her message again. Texted her and got nothing.

Well, she was going but she worried about the trip. A little bit of Shelby went a long way and the thought of living with her, working for her, and being financially dependent on her was a little frightening. Not like being raped to death with a plunger frightening, but still.

Then she read an email from her editor where she asked for an essay for the publisher's website about biological reasons to send women on a potential colony ship. Five hundred words about how it took nine months for a woman to grow a baby or two, and how sperm from a thousand men could be frozen in a Pringles' can with room to spare for chips. Not that she'd want to eat chips from the sperm repository. Ivy smiled. At least that was a hook.

49

She got to work.

CHAPTER FIVE

And so Ivy arrived at the San Francisco Airport two days later and faced the Christmas music. She'd been underway for twenty-four hours straight and in all that time she hadn't written a word on her new novel, barely managing to write about writing for the blogs and interviews her publisher had sent her. Online the anti-Ivy furor continued apace.

Anu had told her not to engage, not to feed the trolls. Let the book stand on its own. But it wasn't only her book that they were insulting. Wasn't just her life's work they were putting down. They threatened her body with rape, her psyche with suggestions of suicide. They derided her for everything she'd ever said or written or posted. Someone attacked a photo of a baby squirrel she'd posted weeks ago. Things didn't get any more innocuous than a baby squirrel. One of her anti-fans wanted to eat it. They'd exchanged recipes and posted pictures of a skinned squirrel, hopefully not killed just for the post.

True, she had her defenders too, but they were getting attacked in turn and she wanted to protect them, too. And she couldn't. It felt weird walking around after reading all that drama, but she did.

She hadn't spoken with Shelby again either, but she wasn't surprised. Shelby was busy curing death and spending $93 million. One had to work overtime to accomplish that kind of thing. Or at least Ivy imagined one did.

At least she was off the plane. Everyone around her spoke English with an American accent like a giant tour group straight off a cruise ship. At home, if she walked a few yards away someone would be holding an umbrella and everyone would be speaking Japanese or German or Russian. Here when she kept walking, she heard English all around. It felt alien after her years away.

She brushed at a spot on her jeans. She'd planned to change into an interview suit in the airport, but her suitcase hadn't gotten on the plane in Riga. So she gave the airline Shelby's address at Millennium Tower and wondered if her suitcase would ever turn up there. Maybe a troll had stolen it and was doing unspeakable things with her underwear right now.

Instead of putting on a business outfit and walking around like a grownup professional, she hunted up a restroom in the terminal where she swabbed herself with a wet wipe that smelled like rubbing alcohol and swiped on another layer of deodorant. She went out of the stall, brushed her teeth and hair, washed her hands, and checked herself out in the mirror. Terrible.

The woman standing next to her gave her the kind of encouraging smile you give people who look like they need validation. And Ivy needed validation on so many levels today. She gave the woman a thumbs-up. Neither of them seemed encouraged and the woman hurried out.

Not her best look for meeting the people she might interview with. At least she still had her jacket and her backpack and laptop. And the weird

Estonian salted licorice Shelby'd asked for. She'd almost forgotten it, then bought it at the airport and tucked it into her backpack. Licorice was everywhere in the Nordics.

As she descended the escalator, she looked for Shelby or someone who looked like an Olivia with a sign with her name on it. Limo drivers in caps held signs with other people's names on them, including a large one for a Mr. Carver. A couple dressed in Christmas sweaters came together for hugs and enthusiasm. A man in uniform swung a small child up in the air. Nobody waited for her. But at least there wasn't some guy with a plunger.

Olivia had assured her she'd send a car and she'd seemed so sincere. Ivy tried to call, but her Estonian phone didn't work. She hunted up a store and bought an overpriced SIM card, wondering if she could expense it to Nyssa, and tried again. Olivia still didn't answer and neither did Shelby.

Sure, they wanted to hire her. For a second, she wondered if this was a prank, but couldn't come up with a rationale and told herself to stop being paranoid about every. Single. Thing.

She couldn't exactly stay in the airport, so she used her Uber app to call for a ride. A black Nissan Leaf was seven minutes out. She used that time to get a coffee so she'd at least look conscious when it arrived. The coffee came in a red cup that looked festive against the green and white logo and the caffeine helped.

The Uber driver's name was Karlo, and he was a solicitous guy. He pressed cold water and chewing gum and wet wipes on her. She accepted them all, because it was nice to think someone cared. Then she gave him the address from Olivia's email. While he drove and played easy listening music, she finished off her coffee and started in on the water. It was like being in a fancy elevator on wheels.

"Did the water help?" he said. "You're looking refreshed."

"Thank you," she said. "Five stars."

He smiled at her in the rearview mirror, face earnest above the pine tree air freshener. "It really helps."

"I live and die by the star rating system myself." She realized she hadn't checked her Amazon reviews or her Twitter feed in almost an entire day while she'd traveled. She logged on and gave Karlo his stars. A quick scan of her email showed more troll messages, but nothing from Olivia or Shelby.

Her editor had sent her a long email telling her this attention was a good thing for sales and a good thing for her long-term career. All publicity is good publicity. Easy for someone who wasn't worried about ending up on the wrong end of a plunger to say.

And the editor also said that she should finish the second book while attention was so high. But every time Ivy started, she second guessed every word and every idea, terrified they would rain doom upon her too. Then she argued with herself about not letting herself be silenced, about forging away to write her own truth. And then her writing time ran out and she had written and erased paragraphs all day.

She'd forwarded her the flight info before she left, and the editor told her that she'd booked a reading at Kepler's Bookstore, right in the heart of

Silicon Valley. Right into the mouth of Troll Cave. It would be a good turnout, her editor promised, with a sympathetic crowd. Sure.

On Twitter, the hate continued. Hard to believe so many people hated her little book so much. But Ivy stood by the logic that had set them off. It was unassailable. If you wanted to colonize a new world, you'd send women and sperm, not men. Ten women could have 100 children in ten years. If you had sperm from 1,000 genetically diverse men, none of those kids would be true siblings. That was more than what scientists calculated as the minimum to rebuild a population. If those women kept going, they'd have 200 offspring, more than twice the necessary amount to be self-sustaining in a single generation. Or, if they were busy building the colony, two generations. Biological math valued wombs over dicks.

What she'd never calculated was how much her biological math would prove incendiary to random men on the internet. The thought of their entire essence reduced to a couple of ounces of goop ready for insertion into a much more valuable womb broke their angry tiny brains. And they weren't shy about voicing their displeasure. She scrolled until she realized she was hyperventilating. Then she forced herself to stuff her phone in her pocket.

She took off her jacket and stared out the window. The internet wasn't the real world. This was. Even though it was overcast, the morning light was too bright. Sun glinted off windshields and hurt her eyes and all the cars crowded too close and moved too fast. Jetlag? Or was she really out of sync with this bright, fast world? She bet there weren't as many cars in all of Estonia as in this one city.

Karlo drove expertly through the glare, really earning those stars.

She took a deep breath, inhaling the fake scent of pine. Not exactly the forest. She let it out. Closed her eyes and did it a couple more times.

They exited onto a city street where the cars were slower, but crowded up closer. An accident here would give her whiplash, maybe a minor concussion, but not the kind of thing that would call for the jaws of life to pull her out of shredded metal. The kind where everyone could get out and yell about it after. Until someone noticed her name and refused her medical treatment for the crime of angering the internet.

"Which business you going to?" Karlo cut the wheel to the side to avoid a cyclist. "That address is an industrial park."

"Nyssa," she said. "My friend works there. I know it's Saturday, but she'll be there."

"Nyssa?"

She spelled it, like it mattered, and glanced at her phone. Another dick pic. This one had lipstick on it, presumably applied by the owner in a yogic feat she didn't even want to think about.

"Sure that's the name?" Karlo sounded uneasy.

"Why?" She stopped messing with her phone and looked at him.

"I thought I heard something about them on the news. I must be mixed up."

"What did you hear?"

"I must be mixed up. I'm sorry." He turned the radio to a classical station and didn't look at her in the rearview mirror. She didn't rescind his stars.

"Something about VC funding?" she said like she knew what that was.

"That must have been it. That."

She wasn't sure she believed him. "Was it something bad?"

"I don't remember," he said unconvincingly.

He pulled into the parking lot of a glass and block office building and up to a section painted half pale blue and half white. Nyssa's corporate colors. Shelby had a color theory behind it, but all Ivy remembered was that the pale blue matched a certain species of jellyfish because Nyssa's logo was a stylized jellyfish. Allegedly, those jellyfish were immortal and aged normally, then returned to earlier life cycles again and again.

Ivy sighed. The thought of regressing to any earlier life stage was too damn depressing to even think about. She stuffed her empty coffee cup into the garbage bag Karlo had thoughtfully provided in the back seat. She didn't feel properly caffeinated for a job interview.

"We're here, ma'am." He was already out of the car and pulling her backpack from the trunk.

Shrugging back into her leather jacket, she climbed out to take the backpack off him. She didn't like people touching her stuff. He smiled, glanced worriedly at the building, and drove away. She'd figure out what he'd been so worried about soon enough. She'd had enough bad surprises lately and wasn't eager to run right into a new one.

Instead, she took a long look at the waves rolling in all green and pretty and with no chunks of ice on them. Shelby was right about the weather. Even overcast, it was better here. The air smelled of salt and fish and waves broke clean against the rocks.

She was surprised Nyssa's office was so close to the sea. Shelby used to have a terror of the ocean. Back in college, she hadn't even watched movies with the ocean in them. Maybe she'd had therapy for it. No time for crippling phobias in her new life.

As Shelby had promised, a row of palm trees lined one side of the building. Presumably, her office was behind one of them. Ivy sketched a wave in the direction of the window.

With a tired sigh, she hoisted her backpack onto her good shoulder and hiked to the front door. The office had opaque windows, like a sex toy store. Anything at all could be going on in there. Immortality, apparently, was murky.

Ivy opened the door and stepped into an empty lobby. An aquarium on one wall faced a shining high-tech desk clearly designed for aliens. Chairs in the same pale blue as the Nyssa logo clustered around a coffee table holding an illuminated jellyfish sculpture. The whole place felt like a spaceship. Not the kind of spaceship she'd designed in her novel with algae tanks and mushroom farms. More like the first-class section of a luxury liner.

She put her backpack next to a chair and stood, afraid if she sat she'd fall asleep, maybe snore, and jinx her chances of getting the job. She pretended not to notice that she was putting a lot of mental energy into a job she didn't want.

"Hello?" she called. No answer.

Two closed doors flanked the desk. Like the windows that faced the street, the glass in the doors was opaque. She tried to push the first one open. Locked. The second one too.

So she retreated to the aquarium and checked it out. Jellyfish. Tentacles swayed and bells rose and fell as the jellyfish paced inside their illuminated prison. Too big to be the immortal ones, so they must be a metaphor for show. Slick and soothing to watch. Five stars for the keeper of the aquarium. She rubbed her gritty eyes.

"We're not open to visitors today." A woman spoke from behind her.

Ivy turned to face her. The woman was short and freckly, with earplugs and a nose piercing and a tattoo of a mandala on the back of her left hand. Her fiery red hair matched her outfit. She had a mood going.

"I have a meeting with Shelby Linton today," Ivy said.

"It's not a good time." The woman started toward her like she intended to herd Ivy right back out the door, one hand raised in a shooing motion.

Ivy didn't budge. "I've traveled all the way from Estonia, so it has to be a good time. Shelby asked me to come."

"When did you last speak to Shelby?" the woman asked.

Unlike Olivia, she didn't call Shelby Ms. Linton. "Last Tuesday. She asked me to come for an interview today."

"Tuesday?" she said. "How did she seem?"

"That's your business, how?" Shelby wouldn't want her telling some random woman about their conversation. "I'd like to speak with Shelby now."

59

"That's going to be a little hard." The woman wiped her hand on her pants and held it out. "Wendy."

"Ivy Corva." Ivy shook her hand. Her grip was intense, like a tiny chihuahua picking a fight.

"So, about Shelby." Wendy smiled and Ivy's stomach dropped. "She had an accident, probably not long after she called you."

"What kind of accident? Is she OK?"

"She's not."

"Where is she?" Ivy moved closer to Wendy. "Take me to her. Has someone called her father?"

"He knows." Wendy looked like she was enjoying the conversation. "The funeral is today."

Ivy's knees gave out and she fell into a hard chair. Jellyfish rose and fell, living with no idea of the wider world in a state of blissful ignorance.

Ivy gulped. "Was there a note?"

"Interesting," Wendy said. "Should there have been?"

"In college." She took a deep breath. "What happened to Shelby?"

"She jumped off the Golden Gate Bridge. It's a long way down."

Ivy shuddered. Shelby would never have wanted to die in the water, pulled down into the cold and dark. Ivy had been to the Golden Gate Bridge once. It had a fence with high railings. No one fell off it, not without trying. Shelby must have been motivated.

"That doesn't make sense," she said. "Not for Shelby."

Wendy glanced at her phone. "I have to go."

"There's a funeral already?" Ivy asked.

"I know it's fast," Wendy said. "Her father insisted."

When Shelby's father insisted, things happened. She remembered her words from a long moment ago: Shelby insisted. Not anymore.

"I don't have any other clothes," she said, because Shelby cared about fashion. "For a funeral."

"You don't have to come."

"I'm coming." She could insist, too. She glared. "Would Shelby want me to take an Uber there?"

"Maybe." Wendy said. "Is this you asking for a ride?"

"Thank you." Ivy's tone was the fakest one she could muster.

She followed Wendy out the door into the bright parking lot. Everything looked like a movie set now, unreal and remote. The sun was a giant floodlight. The ocean CGI. Somewhere, beyond her visions, cameras recorded a story. Just a story.

The sound of a car door opening brought her back. She sat in Wendy's Prius. It had that new car smell, like probably everything she owned, and it made no noise as she started it and drove, too fast, toward Shelby's funeral.

Ivy leaned her forehead against the cool glass of the passenger-side window and closed her eyes against the movie world outside. Shelby hadn't been immortal after all. Ivy inhaled the twin scents of new car and licorice and remembered the time she'd been able to save her friend. The time when she hadn't been too late. She closed her eyes and remembered their first year at Carnegie Mellon.

CHAPTER SIX

Freshman Ivy had finished her shift at the computer science center in Wean Hall at midnight and had hurried across campus to her dorm at Morewood Gardens. Fall air bit her ears and fingers, and she shivered in a leather jacket that had once been her mother's, or so her aunt said. Ivy's parents died when she was fifteen, and she never saw her mother wear it. But Ivy wore it everywhere.

She checked in and took the elevator to their floor. The hallway was well lit, but all the room doors were closed. Late on a school night, after all. The space between her own door and the frame was dark, meaning Shelby was probably asleep inside. Following roommate etiquette, she eased open the door and walked carefully across the carpet.

She glanced over at Shelby's bed, lit by the streetlights outside. The bed was empty so all the quiet had been in vain. Ivy wasn't sure why the empty bed made her uneasy, but it did. She tried to argue away her feeling. Shelby had a boyfriend. Some nights she didn't come home at all. Not a big deal. Only Ivy slept at the dorm every night. Everyone else was out having fun.

But Shelby's empty bed was made and Shelby never made her bed.

Ivy clicked on the desk lamp. A bright white envelope rested atop Shelby's pillow. No name. Sealed. Pushing down a feeling of dread, Ivy tore it open.

Dad,

I'm sorry. I didn't mean to let you down.

Shelby

Ivy's heart raced and she ordered herself to calm down. Why would Shelby leave a note to her father on her pillow? Ivy looked around the room for answers. Shelby's boots were gone, along with her coat. So, she'd dressed to go outside.

Her gloves lay on the floor next to her desk. The gloves were expensive, a present from her father and made by a famous designer whose name Ivy forgot before Shelby finished the sentence. One glove probably cost more than Ivy's entire wardrobe. Shelby wore them everywhere, sometimes even in the drafty lecture halls, and definitely when going outside on a cold night.

Still no reason to panic. A freshly made bed, a weird note, and a pair of gloves weren't compelling evidence of anything.

So she called Shelby's cellphone. When something buzzed in the room, she opened the desk drawer and stared at a vibrating phone. The screen displayed the word Roommate. Not even Ivy's name. Ouch.

She hung up and activated the screen. It displayed a picture of a much younger Shelby. She and her father wore matching tweed coats and a pumpkin patch filled the background. Ivy closed the drawer.

Any way you looked at it: Shelby would never leave her phone. Time to panic.

Ivy ran to the resident assistant's room and banged on the door until Deepa opened. Deepa wore pajamas in Carnegie plaid and her long dark hair fell down to her waist.

"What's up, Ivy?" Deepa said with a giant yawn.

Ivy explained the situation and handed her the note. "Found it on Shelby's bed."

Deepa's eyes widened as she read. "Do you know where she might have gone?"

Ivy barely knew Shelby. They had different majors and schedules and treated each other with formal politeness when they overlapped. Up till now, that had seemed enough for both of them.

"Boyfriend?" Deepa asked.

"Gerald something or other. Electrical engineer."

"Do you know his last name? Could she be there?"

Ivy pulled out her phone and checked Shelby's social media. Gerald's picture had a weird emoji next to it. "McGuire. I think they broke up."

Deepa glanced at the page. "Her last post is a dolphin jumping into space."

"Crap." Ivy hadn't noticed.

"What does it mean?" Deepa furrowed her brow, like she was trying to answer a question on a test and Ivy realized that Deepa wasn't much older than her, just a few years. She didn't have all the answers.

"It's from The Hitchhiker's Guide to the Galaxy," Ivy told her. "It's what the dolphins do before they leave Earth forever."

"I'll call Campus Security." Deepa started to close the door, then beckoned Ivy inside. "Wait here with me."

As Ivy paced Deepa's tiny single room, she tried to assemble the facts in some kind of order. That's what had gotten her into college: facts and logic. What facts did she know? Gerald and Shelby had broken up. She was distraught (odd, because she hadn't even seemed to like Gerald). Where would she go? The dolphins had leapt straight up into space in the movie and winked out of existence using trans-dimensional travel in the book. Not useful. Or was it?

What if Shelby intended to jump out of the world like the dolphins? CMU's campus had plenty of options. Buildings. Stairwells. They'd never find her and stop her. But if it was about Gerald, maybe she'd pick a place that would wound him.

"Schenley Bridge," Ivy said.

Deepa stopped talking into the phone and looked at her.

"The bridge. Send help." Ivy sprinted out of the room.

Down the elevator, out the front door. Past the lights on at the fraternity houses and the empty front lawns. She jaywalked across Forbes Avenue and ran onto campus and down the Cut. Past the Fence. Between Baker Porter and the glass monstrosity of Hunt Library. Ivy had run in high school as a way to burn off her grief and anger and now she made good time.

Down Frew Street to the bridge. Leaves shattered under her boots. Her breath leaked out in jagged spurts and her nose ran. Her legs flagged, but she kept pushing until she reached the bridge. A small figure stood in the middle of the walkway. Shelby?

Ivy ran like that figure was the finish line.

Breathing hard, she stopped next to Shelby.

Shelby faced away from her with her fingers interlaced in the chain link fence that ran along the side of the bridge. Bright love locks hung near her hands. Ivy knew one of those locks had been put up by Shelby and Gerald. She'd overheard them talking about it a week ago and tried not to roll her eyes.

She looked past Shelby's fingers at Hamerschlag Hall, lit up golden like Shelby's hair. At least Shelby hadn't decided to jump off that. She'd never have found her there.

"Hey," Ivy said awkwardly. "I found your note."

Shelby's fingers curled closed. Ivy remembered she'd been a gymnast in high school. Climbing something like this fence wouldn't be a problem for her. But she hadn't. Yet.

"It wasn't for you." Shelby glared at her.

"Is this about Gerald?" Ivy looked down at the concrete far below. Not a survivable fall.

Shelby crouched to spring. Ivy stepped close and grabbed her belt. An overpriced designer thing, it felt sturdy.

"Don't try it," Ivy said. "I'd hate to pull you down and kick your ass in front of the police."

"Police?"

67

"Deepa called." Or at least she hoped Deepa had.

Shelby took her hands off the fence. Red lines crisscrossed her palms from the chain links. Ivy didn't let go of her belt.

"Don't give that worthless shitbag the satisfaction," Ivy said.

"Your language is straight from the ghetto." Shelby tossed her hair in a motion Ivy could only describe as prissy.

"I'm straight from the ghetto," Ivy answered. Not strictly true, but her parents had never, even combined, earned as much in a year as tuition cost. Ivy was the poorest person at this school, and it wasn't even close. So, compared to Shelby, she was from the ghetto.

A car roared by behind them and Ivy's back muscles tensed like she expected it to jump the curb and smash them against the fence. It passed. Still not the police.

"What did your father like best about you?" Shelby asked.

Ivy let go of the belt with one hand and wiped her nose on a ratty tissue from her pocket. "He didn't give me a ranking system."

Shelby twisted the belt out of Ivy's fingers and Ivy didn't grab it again. "Try."

Ivy tried. Her parents had been way too busy fighting and drinking to notice her, so she had to work to pull up a good memory. She shivered. "My fierceness. He said I was relentless."

"Hard to imagine," Shelby said and Ivy recognized the sarcasm.

Easy for Shelby to say. Ivy's family wasn't rich. This college was her one chance to get away from grinding poverty. If she messed this up, she had no net. She had to be relentless.

Instead of arguing, she asked the question she knew Shelby wanted her to ask. "What does your father like best about you?"

Shelby slid down the fence and leaned her back against it, feet pointing to the remorseless traffic. Tears glistened on her cheeks. "That I'm his little girl."

Ivy was so far from anyone's little girl that she didn't know what to say. She crouched next to Shelby, ready to jump up and pull her off the fence or out of traffic. Where were the campus police? Or the real police?

"Smart and pretty and precious," Shelby said. "That's me."

"Not the worst qualities for a dad to admire." Ivy was failing a test here. She had no idea what to say. Down here the air reeked of car exhaust and she worried it was poisoning their lungs.

"Sure," Shelby said.

"Are you pregnant?" Ivy went for the obvious.

"What? No!"

"Sorry." It did happen. Two girls from Ivy's high school class had gotten pregnant before the end of senior year. That kind of thing was probably taken care of more discreetly in Shelby's world. Ivy put on a knit beanie she kept in her pocket and blew on her hands.

Shelby wiped her cheeks with the back of her hands and tucked her perfect hair behind her ears. She didn't even look cold.

"Then what is it?" Ivy asked. "I can't see you jumping off a bridge because Gerald dumped you."

"I dumped him," Shelby said. "Clear?"

"Whatever." Ivy looked down the bridge to where she hoped the campus police would come from. Lots of cars, but nothing useful.

"I dumped him because he's an overbearing asshole."

"Since Day One," Ivy agreed.

Shelby dropped her head into her hands and cried. Her thin shoulders bobbed up and down.

Ivy patted her awkwardly on the arm and watched the cars. Where were the adults to fix this? Nowhere to be found, as usual. Ivy had no experience with breakup bonding. And how did Shelby's father fit in? "Did your dad like Gerald?"

Shelby shook her head. Ivy patted her on the back. Her coat felt soft, probably cashmere or something. Ivy wasn't surprised that the father didn't like Gerald either. Anyone could see that Gerald was a tool. All Ivy's pats didn't slow down the gulping and the tears. No more answers from Shelby.

Ivy tried to put the facts together on her own. Shelby was suicidal. It had something to do with Gerald because she ended up next to their love lock on the bridge. But not because he'd dumped her. She'd dumped him. And dumping Gerald wouldn't disappoint her father. And Gerald was a tool. And she wasn't pregnant.

Ivy handed her a tissue from her pocket and Shelby blew her nose, the sound louder and less ladylike than Ivy'd expected.

So what did any of this have to do with her father and how he thought she was his little girl? Ivy was afraid to ask for more clues. Shelby sat with her head bowed, gulping and crying. And Deepa and the cavalry didn't arrive.

Ivy's phone dug into her leg and she moved it to her jacket pocket. A picture flashed in her mind of Shelby's phone. A few weeks ago, it had sat in an empty water glass, camera pointed at Shelby's bed. At the time she'd wondered why Shelby would keep her phone in a glass. Now she had a good guess. Gerald was more of an asshole than Ivy'd thought.

"Revenge porn?" she asked.

Shelby's shoulders flinched as if against a blow. She whimpered, which Ivy took as a yes.

"You can ask for a takedown. You're still seventeen, a minor," Ivy said.

"Nothing ever comes back down off the internet."

"You don't know that," Ivy said. But they both did. The chainlink rattled when they rested their heads against it together.

"It's there forever. And my dad will see it and then he'll know I'm not so precious."

"Your dad hangs out on revenge porn websites?"

Shelby snorted. "No!"

"Well, you have that going for you."

71

"He'll be disappointed." Shelby's voice was so tiny Ivy strained to hear.

Ivy's parents had never noticed her enough to be disappointed. She tried to figure out what a normal friend would say. She still hadn't found the words when a campus police car with a flashing lightbar stopped on the street in front of them. Thanks, Deepa.

"Our ride's here." Ivy stood and held out her hand to Shelby. An officer piled out of the car and ambled toward them. Despite the light bar, he wasn't in a hurry.

Shelby placed her icy hand in Ivy's and Ivy hauled her to her feet.

Shelby leaned in and whispered. "Thanks."

"We'll come back later with bolt cutters for the lock," Ivy said. "And if they somehow slip and cut off Gerald's tiny dick, I'd be OK with that."

Shelby squeezed her hand. "Deal."

And that was the first day of their friendship.

Sadly, Gerald's dick wasn't removed. Yet.

CHAPTER SEVEN

Wendy's car stopped. Ivy rubbed her eyes with her knuckles and sat up. They were parked next to a crowd of shiny Priuses, a Tesla, and a Smart car. Silicon Valley mobiles. Estonian tech worker cars were cheaper and splashed with mud and dirty snow this time of year.

Ivy grabbed her backpack and got out. Then she stopped and looked back at the car. She caught a glimpse of her reflection in the window. A pale face with unwashed black hair, dark circles under bloodshot eyes. She raked her fingers through her hair and zipped up her leather jacket. At least it was black, like her sneakers. In between was a pair of grubby jeans she'd worn for thousands of miles. Still, better than showing up naked.

Her battered backpack was completely inappropriate for a funeral but Ivy didn't want to be parted from it. It held everything she owned on the continent—laptop, pens, paper, phone, chargers, wallet, passport, wipes, and Shelby's licorice. But she was already underdressed. Lugging her backpack around would make that worse. Shelby's father would be horrified. He cared about protocol and proper dress.

Wendy appeared over her shoulder in the reflection, shameless in a red suit. But Wendy clearly wasn't a mourner.

"I have a long coat in the trunk. If you're cold. It's black so that's something."

She wasn't showing up wearing some random angry chick's trunk clothes. "No, thanks."

Wendy shrugged and they set off at a quick trot through a field of brilliant green grass dotted with headstones toward a distant crowd gathered around what looked like a marble hut. A crypt. Of course Shelby had a family crypt.

"It reminds me of Arlington," Ivy said. "So many headstones."

"Colma has more headstones than living residents. They call it the City of the Silent," Wendy said. "A good place to rest, in the end."

Shelby would never want to be in a silent city. She loved action and movement and energy. And immortality. Ivy dried her eyes on her sleeve and hurried to catch back up with Wendy. Wendy marched ahead like a tank.

As they neared the group, Ivy recognized Shelby's father, Arthur Linton, by the crypt's open door. He wore a black coat over a bespoke suit and hunched forward as if into a bitter wind. She noticed his tie—blue and green with red lines. Carnegie plaid. She'd been with Shelby when she'd picked out that tie in the bookstore. Father's Day, end of freshman year.

In front of him a golden urn gleamed in the sunshine. Shelby. All that was left of Shelby and her golden hair. Ivy looked away.

A priest with a tombstone-white collar faced Mr. Linton and about fifty other people who stood in a ragged group. Most of the mourners were young, some dressed in black, one in Nyssa blue. A

74

group of women stood apart from the rest. A few nodded at Wendy. Nyssa employees? She also noticed a thin man dressed in an ill-fitting suit next to a blond woman in a black dress with a veil so thick you couldn't see her face. They didn't fit in.

She recognized an Indian man in an impeccable black suit from her job research. He fit in perfectly and his suit made her aware of her grubby jeans again. Timothy Shah, CFO. He glanced over at her and she was struck by his chiseled jaw and perfect hair. She bet Shelby had been inside that suit.

She followed Wendy over to the group. No introductions which was fine because she hoped never to see any of them again. Mr. Linton looked at her and gestured that she come stand next to him. She complied. He was the only person she knew.

The priest spoke about death and God and resurrection and eternal life, but Ivy couldn't listen. Whatever he said wasn't enough to describe the enormity of a world without Shelby in it. She inhaled the scent of crushed grass as mourners shifted around her and looked everywhere but at that urn.

Head bowed, the muscles in Mr. Linton's jaw jumped, otherwise he might have been cast in stone. Wind ruffled his white hair. When had his hair turned white? He'd been hot when she was in college, more of a player than a father in her mind, but not anymore.

Timothy seemed sad, but the others didn't. Whispers drifted through the group like wind through leaves. Impossible to make out the words, but they sounded almost gleeful. A voice whispered, "Ding dong" and hummed a melody.

The words cut through the numbness and made Ivy angry, although she didn't know why. The cadence sounded familiar. She craned her head to look for the speaker. It sounded like a woman. That left her with three nearby options. A stylish woman wearing the suit Ivy should have worn who seemed to be paying attention to the priest: Ms. Alert. An older woman with streaks of white in her hair and bright red glasses: Ms. Scarlet. And Wendy. She'd catch up with them later and find out what ding dong meant.

For now, she turned back toward Mr. Linton and confronted the pictures set up on easels in front of the crypt, flanking the urn. She'd been avoiding the pictures, too. The images were ephemeral, harsh, and modern compared to their weathered marble backdrop. Her eyes caught random details before jumping away—Shelby as a baby in the arms of a beautiful blonde woman—her mother before cancer took her. Shelby in a cap and gown with one arm thrown around her father's shoulders and the other around a similarly gowned Ivy, golden tassels caught in a breeze that blew them to the side like an arrow pointing to their futures. Shelby in a white blazer and Nyssa-blue shirt in front of a tank of jellyfish, perfectly composed, from a magazine cover. The jellies' tentacles floated to the side like the tassels, the bells facing Shelby's incandescent face. Shelby laughed in a long white satin dress with a tattoo running along her bare side and her bell-shaped birthmark peeking out from the edge. The tattoo was of a molecule with interlocking hexagons and pentagons and letters that represented chemicals on the sides.

The priest's voice stopped and everyone stood blinking in the sun. Ms. Alert stepped through the crowd to hand Ivy a tissue. "I'm sorry for your loss."

Ivy recognized her voice. "Thank you, Olivia."

Olivia drew in a quick breath. "Ivy?"

"I got in today."

"I should have sent a car." Olivia looked stricken.

"I ubered to the office and Wendy was there and gave me a ride here."

Olivia shot a surprised glance at Wendy. Apparently Wendy didn't help out stranded mourners in her regular life. Ivy was unsurprised to find this out.

The priest cleared his throat and they faced him again. Mr. Linton picked up the burnished urn and carried it into the crypt. Ivy stayed outside and breathed in the cloying reek of lilies. Shelby had hated lilies.

In the distance, another black-clad party approached another grave. Death on a conveyor belt in the City of the Silent.

A rail-thin man with huge hands approached Timothy whose back stiffened. The newcomer fiddled with a dark green tie that didn't match his outdated suit. He looked rough and tired, not perky and wealthy like the rest of the mourners.

"Ms. Linton saved my life, Mr. Shah," he said. "Her outreach program helped me find my way."

"She'd have been glad to know that." Timothy smiled, and the smile never reached his eyes.

"I was close to Ms. Linton. We talked about a lot of things." The man stepped closer, leaning toward Timothy. "What happens to Margie's Second Chances now? Will we be taken care of?"

"Nyssa intends to honor our agreements going forward and carry out all of Ms. Linton's wishes." Timothy took a step away.

"God bless you." The man didn't sound grateful. He gave Timothy one final glare and marched across the grass away from the crypt with the woman in the black dress limping at his side, veering neither right nor left. They never looked back. The first to leave. Ivy fought down her temptation to run after him, both to get away and to find out more about whatever Shelby had talked to him about. It sounded like more than how to write a resume.

Another woman caught her eye. She didn't fit in either. About Ivy's height with spiky dark hair. She wore a suit, like a few in the crowd, but it looked like she spent a lot of time in it. Mirrored sunglasses covered her eyes and her head followed the man who'd talked to Timothy. She stood positioned on the edge of the gathering and faced the crowd more than the crypt. No one stood near her. Her erect posture made Ivy wonder if she was former military, or if she had back problems. Either way, not a techie. Maybe a bodyguard. Mr. Linton probably had a bodyguard. Or maybe his girlfriend. He probably had at least one of those.

Olivia broke into Ivy's thoughts. She spoke in a low voice. "My apologies again for not notifying you. Things happened so quickly."

"I understand," Ivy said.

"Shelby would have wanted you to be taken care of." Timothy patted her shoulder. "She was the most amazing woman. Her clarity of vision was extraordinary."

"Will the product come out without her?" Ivy asked.

"She was meticulous about documenting her vision, so we have a strong blueprint to follow. She always said that we were like a train and she was dragging us along to her promised land. So many cars, and I was the caboose." He smiled. "Not the most flattering metaphor, but she was a driving force. Unstoppable once she'd started."

"Turned you into roadkill if you got stuck on the tracks," Wendy put in.

"It's the only way to create something so rare and precious," Timothy said. "She didn't have time for social niceties. None of those rules applied to her."

"Maybe a few should have." Wendy scowled.

"Do you have a place to stay?" Olivia asked Ivy.

"I planned to stay with Shelby."

"Let me get approval for a hotel," Olivia said.

"We can put her up at an airport hotel," Timothy said. "And alter her ticket to send her home right away. She doesn't need to be here."

"She'll find her own hotel," Ivy said. And decide on her own when she flew back.

Mr. Linton emerged from the crypt. He looked across at Ivy. "You'll stay at Shelby's as planned. Like when you were girls."

Timothy looked affronted, but said nothing. Mr. Linton was always in charge.

Mr. Linton turned to Olivia as if she worked for him and said, "You'll see to it."

"Of course, sir," Olivia responded.

Mr. Linton took Ivy's elbow and guided her toward the crypt. Out of the corner of her eye, she watched Olivia take out her phone and text, presumably seeing to Ivy's lodgings as ordered. Did Mr. Linton know her, or had he ordered around the first person he saw? Tough to say with him.

Ivy paused before she stepped over the threshold and into the darkened crypt, her boot scuffing against the marble. She didn't want to go inside, but she didn't want to make a scene. And Mr. Linton needed her. They looked like the only ones there who had loved Shelby.

She let him draw her inside where the scents of stone dust and lavender filled her nose. She bent to sniff a sprig, remembering Shelby stopping the car to sniff a stranger's plants in a yard near campus.

"Her favorite flower," Ivy said.

"Her mother's too," Mr. Linton replied.

Nameplates for a century of distinguished Lintons lined the walls. Ivy recognized the nameplate for Anna Nurmi Linton, Shelby's mother. Next to it a brighter one shone in the gloom. The letters engraved on the front spelled out Shelby Rose Linton. With a death date. Ivy's eyes blurred. She hadn't ever expected to see that.

"I'm sorry," she said. "Your loss."

She had blown even the most basic and trite response. She tried again. "I'm sorry for your loss."

"If it hadn't been for you, she might have been here a few years ago. Different bridge." He touched the nameplate with his index finger. The urn must be behind it, hidden away.

"She told you?"

"The university told me."

How much did he know? Had Shelby ever told him about the revenge porn? Shelby had used the family lawyer to send threatening takedown notices to the website and the video seemed to have disappeared. Hopefully, he'd never seen it. Shelby deserved to take that secret to her grave.

"I'm sorry I didn't get here sooner." The weight settled on Ivy.

"I was here, and it wasn't enough." He touched his tie. "Did you know her mother died by suicide?"

"I thought cancer?"

"That's what I told Shelby. But the cancer wasn't what killed her."

He'd been through this twice. Women he loved who couldn't stand to live anymore.

"Do you think it was in her blood?" he asked.

"That's not how it works." Or was it? Shelby had always said we carried our secrets in our blood.

Echoing her thoughts, he spoke. "Maybe that's what she was really searching for, the cure for her own tainted blood."

"I think she was searching to make the world a better place," Ivy said. "Give people extra years of life."

"Sell them, you mean." Mr. Linton shook his head. "It was always a far-fetched idea. That's why I

81

never invested. I thought she'd give up on it before it cost the family our reputation."

"Your reputation?" Ivy hoped he wasn't as bitter as he sounded.

"That didn't work out for me, did it?"

"Sir?" Ivy asked.

"I'll take a shellacking in the press for a while," he said. "But I'm still sorry she's gone."

"Still?" Ivy asked.

"Always," he corrected himself. "When we brought her mother here, Shelby took my hand and led me out of this crypt. A little slip of a girl."

"She had a strong will."

"Even then. I always thought she wanted to create this drug to save her mother, or at least keep me from dying so she wouldn't be alone. She pulled so many people into her idea of a new world. It was a good fantasy."

"It wasn't a fantasy," Ivy said.

"We'll never know, now."

"Timothy says they can carry on without her."

Mr. Linton shook his head. "They can't. She was the genius with the vision and the drive. Sixteen-hour days. Relentless belief in herself. Without her their little train will stop within a year."

They stood there awkwardly. Ivy wanted to cry, but not in front of Mr. Linton. Technically, he was the chief mourner. But right now she wondered if she was the only person here today who really missed Shelby and mourned her absence.

When they came out into the sunlight, only Olivia waited. Ivy's backpack crushed the grass at her feet.

"I'll drive you to Millennium Tower," Olivia said.

Mr. Linton handed Ivy a business card. "Call if you need anything."

Ivy fished the package her new SIM card had come in and handed it to him. Not exactly an elegant business card, but it had her phone number on it. "You, too."

A slight smile lifted the corners of his mouth as he slipped the bulky piece of cardboard into the inside pocket of his suit jacket. He nodded to her and Olivia and walked away. In the distance, a chauffeur waited next to a silver SUV. The woman she'd thought was his bodyguard had already left. Maybe she hadn't been his bodyguard after all.

Ivy hefted her backpack with a sigh. It seemed weeks since she'd packed it. Back in her cozy apartment on a dark morning on a continent far away. When Shelby was still alive.

"I can carry that." Olivia gestured to her bag.

"I got it." She'd carry her own burdens.

They hiked across the lawn of death toward a blue Prius huddled alone at the edge of the lot. Far away a bird twittered and another answered.

"Who was the man who talked to Mr. Shah before I went into the crypt?" Ivy asked.

Olivia took a few steps before answering. "Probably part of a foundation Nyssa funds to help homeless people. Funded."

"They're not going to fund them anymore?" In spite of Timothy's words.

"The new CEO might have different priorities."

"Who's that?" Ivy stepped to the side to avoid a headstone with a lamb carved on the top. A child's grave.

Olivia shrugged. "The board'll bring someone in."

"Not Timothy?"

"Mr. Shah?" She looked surprised. "He's the CFO. They'll want someone with a biotech background to be the new CEO."

Someone like Shelby. Probably older. Not as visionary, but poised to reap the rewards of Shelby's brilliance and drive.

They reached the Prius and Olivia stowed the backpack in the trunk. Ivy closed the door with a thunk and swayed in the seat, light-headed.

"When did you last eat?" Olivia asked.

Ivy tried to remember. "Yesterday is a long blur."

Olivia turned on the car. "How about we get something to eat on the way?"

"And something stronger?"

"I know a bar with pretty good food." Olivia eased out of the cemetery and onto the freeway.

She was a much more calming driver than Wendy, precise and careful. In the distance, the rolling hills of graves changed to houses, and the movie in Ivy's head rewound. Late afternoon sun slanted across the highway. Her first day in California.

With a quick flash of turn signal, Olivia darted across the lanes to a freeway exit and Ivy caught her breath. A few blocks later she pulled up in a front of a bar named Murphy's.

"There's one of these in Tallinn," Ivy said. "Not a chain, a coincidence."

"They have a hearty shepherd's pie," Olivia said.

"Our own little Irish wake."

Olivia was already out of the car and probably hadn't heard.

Ivy followed her inside. A long bar dominated the middle of the room, but Olivia chose a table near the door. Cleaner and shinier than Tallinn's Murphy, this room was hundreds of years younger and felt almost sprightly. Holly and pine boughs decorated the bar and the Christmas tree in the corner sported straw ornaments. Ivy looked around for mistletoe and found it in the hall that led to the bathrooms. The Pogues sang that Christmas song Ivy hated. Even so, it felt like a relief to step outside of California for a minute.

When the professionally helpful server appeared, Ivy was struck by the difference between American and European waitstaff. The server seemed impossibly perky and extroverted. Because she had to live on her tips.

"Know what you want?" Olivia asked.

For her friend to be alive. She looked at the menu, and the words swam in front of her. "The shepherd's pie you mentioned earlier. Guinness and a shepherd's pie."

"I'll take a coffee," Olivia said.

The server left without writing anything down.

"I'll book a flight out tomorrow." Olivia looked down at her phone. "Mr. Shah's right. You don't need to hang around here."

"What happened to Shelby?"

"Why does anyone do something like that?" Olivia didn't seem particularly curious.

"I want to know the details," Ivy said. "I want it clear in my head."

Olivia sighed and looked at her for a long moment before speaking. "Ms. Linton went out for an evening run. Her doorman saw her leave. After she left him, she apparently ran to the Golden Gate Bridge."

The server arrived with her beer and Olivia's coffee. Ivy breathed in the malty scent of Guinness, a scent from a different era. "What happened then?"

"Halfway across the span, she climbed the railing." Olivia cleared her throat.

Shelby hated the water. She wouldn't have wanted to stay there long. It was still hard to imagine her jumping toward the waves. Maybe the darkness helped. Maybe she couldn't see it at night. "How long was she in the water?"

"Mr. Shah called 911. An accident on the bridge stopped his car and he saw someone climbing up. He thought he recognized her at the time. The police found her about a half hour later. They said she died instantly."

Wendy hadn't mentioned that. Ivy took a long sip of the dark beer and the bitter taste of hops rolled down her throat. She sucked in her lip and set the glass back down on the coaster.

"Are they sure it was her?" Ivy knew the answer, but the question slipped out anyway.

"Her father identified her body. And the dental records matched. And her tattoo."

"Why would they need to use dental records?"

"Her face was damaged. A pylon or something on the way down." Olivia winced. "Anyway, they're sure."

Ivy didn't say another word. The server brought the shepherd's pie. Ivy looked down at it, trying to remember what it was like to feel hungry. Aesthetically, the pie was well put together with the mashed potatoes formed into intricate waves and chives sprinkled on top, a veritable pie sculpture. But it didn't make her want to eat it.

"Tell me about your book." Olivia was clearly steering the conversation to safer ground. "How did you get the idea for it?"

"I've always loved haunted house stories, and a haunted spaceship felt like the next step." Ivy's stomach unclenched and she ate a bite of mashed potatoes. Carbs were supposed to be comfort food. "And being in the long Estonian nights got me thinking about outer space."

She never had a good answer for the 'where do your ideas come from' question. The air, like breathing? No one wanted to hear that one.

"The quantum mechanics were over my head," Olivia said. "But I loved the characters, especially Captain Jasper."

"Jasper's been getting a rough reception."
Understatement.

"Undeserved. That's the internet for you. And a colony spaceship full of women? Our uteruses would plumb fall out at those speeds."

Ivy smiled.

"Did you ever read about how during the Victorian era they were worried women's uteruses would fall out because train travel was too fast?" Olivia asked.

"I did," Ivy said. "But I never met anyone else who has."

"Now you have," Olivia said. "So far, my uterus hasn't fallen out despite train, plane and automobile travel. Maybe I'm hardy."

Ivy took a small bite of pie. Lamb and salt. Her stomach told her this was a bad idea and she put her fork down with a clink. "I can't finish it."

"Maybe in a minute," Olivia said.

Ivy took another sip of beer, reassured by the bitterness. Her head felt heavy. "How did the Nyssa employees feel about Shelby?"

"Feel?"

"Was she well liked?"

"Respected, certainly," Olivia said. "She did brilliant work. Her theories about reducing mutational load factors are groundbreaking."

"Liked," Ivy repeated.

Olivia took a long sip of coffee. "Shelby wasn't there to make friends. She was there to bring the drug to market."

"So, she wasn't well liked?" Another Gaelic singer sang a tragic and sad ballad. Ivy toasted them and drank.

Olivia spoke. "She's your friend. I'm sure you know she had a challenging personality."

"Diplomatic," Ivy said. "I noticed that the team didn't seem to be mourning."

"I can't speak for the team, but I'm sorry she's gone."

"Also not the same as mourning." Ivy realized she was picking a fight and changed her tone. "Was Mr. Shah upset about her death?"

Olivia reached across the table and put her cool hand on top of Ivy's. "Shelby was your friend, and I think that's what you should hold onto. No matter what else happens, hold onto that."

"She's already dead. What else might happen?"

Olivia took her hand back. "When do you want to head back to Tallinn?"

"I have publication events here." Ivy said it like they hadn't been booked a few days ago and couldn't be canceled.

"I'd love to attend one," Olivia said. "Where?"

"Kepler's." Ivy was glad she hadn't been bluffing. "Day after tomorrow."

"Wonderful," Olivia said. "I'll book you a ticket back to Tallinn for the next day."

"Let's see." Just because Ivy had a ticket didn't mean she had to use it.

"Let me know the dates when you want to travel. You still have my number, right?"

"It's in your email." Ivy looked down at her plate. "Shelby and Timothy? I see the attraction now."

"She told you?" Olivia looked surprised. "They were being discreet."

Ivy had suspected as much since she'd seen Timothy looking sexy in his fancy suit, but she was relieved to have it confirmed. One predictable thing about Shelby anyway. "I don't think she thought I'd come out here."

"Your pie is getting cold," Olivia said.

"I can't eat it." Ivy poked her fork through the mashed potatoes down to the bottom of the dish and turned it over to reveal the meat and vegetables jumbled together.

"Then let's get you to the tower. You probably need to rest."

Rest in peace. Ivy sighed.

Olivia signaled for the server and snagged the check. "I'll put this on the corporate card."

Ivy was ready to argue until she saw the price. Let Nyssa spend some of that 93 million on her lunch. "My last meal on Shelby and I didn't even eat it."

"Do you want to take it to go?"

Ivy's stomach heaved. "No."

Olivia paid and they zipped right back onto the freeway. They talked about science fiction for the rest of the trip. Olivia was well read and Ivy thought they would have formed a book club under different circumstances and seen each other once a week over wine and literature, instead of whatever this was.

"Is Shelby's building still tilting?" Ivy asked when they got to the city. Shelby had complained about it for years. The engineers hadn't anchored the base properly and one corner was sinking into the San Francisco sand. It had already sunk more than a foot and a half. The outside glass cracked on one side and they'd had to block off the street below to protect pedestrians. A glitzy multimillion dollar skyscraper built on a shoddy foundation. That was a Silicon Valley metaphor if she'd ever heard one.

"Are you worried about staying there?" Olivia asked. "I can book you a hotel."

"I'm fine." Ivy wasn't worried about the building collapsing and killing her. Much.

Ivy saw more people without a place to live in a few blocks of San Francisco than she'd seen in years in Tallinn. Blue tarps formed tents with shopping carts. People in hoodies slept under bus stop benches. An old man with no teeth and three coats shuffled along carrying a tiny black dog. These people could never afford Shelby's immortality drug. And would they even want to live forever like this?

"There it is!" Olivia pointed at a glass skyscraper that reflected the last rays of the sun. It looked like the towers of Emerald City in Oz. The wealth in the midst of squalor was jarring.

At fifty-eight stories, it was higher than the tallest building in Tallinn. Of course, the tallest building in Tallinn was St. Olaf's Church, constructed in 1549, so it wasn't exactly a fair comparison. Ivy missed the old church and the cobblestones and her life of a few days before. She wanted to go back inside that snow globe.

Olivia stopped next to the building and turned on her hazards. They ticked in the background. "I called ahead."

"Thanks for everything," Ivy said.

Olivia was already out of the car and getting her backpack from the back.

Ivy followed, exhausted. Her limbs dragged down like someone had turned up gravity and her backpack straps cut into her shoulders. She wanted to curl up in a ball and sleep for a week. Jetlag and grief were a brutal combo.

"Are you all right on your own?" Olivia asked.

"It's a way of life," Ivy answered.

CHAPTER EIGHT

Ivy hefted her backpack higher on her back and looked at the glass status symbol reaching up into the clouds, the top obscured by fog. The fog seemed to seep into her bones. A wind knifed down the street right through her jacket. It felt colder here than in snowy Tallinn. She'd better get inside before she shivered herself unconscious like a Victorian matron laced into a too-tight corset. Then her uterus would fall out into noisy traffic.

She hurried toward the front door. The man standing next to it looked like a retired professional wrestler except he wore a doorman uniform, something she'd only seen in movies.

"I'm sorry, ma'am." He moved to block her way. "Who are you here to see?"

"I'm a friend of Shelby Linton. I'll be staying in her apartment."

He didn't look convinced. And he didn't move. He crossed thick arms and glowered down at her. Way down at her. His head looked like a basketball on top of a wall.

She searched for something polite to say. "Olivia called ahead. I'm Ivy Corva."

He looked at her grimy jeans, ancient jacket, and shook his head. "You're press."

"I'm a writer, yes," she said without thinking.

He stepped forward and she took a step back, closer to traffic. "You vultures have been circling all day. I won't let you pick over her life."

"I'm an old friend from college. Not a vulture."

"An old friend. A colleague from work. You need to go up to get something." He herded her toward the street. "I've heard it before."

She lurched back a step, off balance, and almost fell off the curb. An SUV swerved and beeped. That pushed through the numbness and the grief.

"Listen up," she said. "Ms. Linton's executive assistant, Olivia Ajak, called the building about an hour ago to set things up. March your ass in and check."

His eyes narrowed. His ass did no marching.

"If not, I'll call Mr. Linton, Shelby's father. He owns Shelby's apartment and another one here besides, and he won't be happy to be disturbed on the day of his daughter's funeral."

He glanced back at the front door.

Ivy drew Mr. Linton's card out of her pocket and held it up.

She flipped it over so he could see, then turned it back over so he had no time to read the number. No point in giving Mr. Linton's number to this stranger.

"Stay right here," he said. "If you're lying, I'll call the police."

"And what would they cite me for? Flashing a business card?"

Behind her, a car beeped. Ivy jumped and took another step onto the sidewalk. The doorman's face had brightened, so Ivy turned to see why.

Olivia to the rescue. She must have circled the block.

"Hi, Stephen." Olivia beamed through a rolled-down window, all teeth and eyelashes. "I see you've met Ms. Corva. She's an old friend of Ms. Linton and a famous writer. Mr. Linton insisted she stay here for the next few days. She's been given the keys and alarm codes. I know you'll take good care of her, Stephen."

"Thanks for clarifying the situation," Stephen said.

"Indeed." Ivy clamped her lips together before more came out.

Olivia waved and pulled back into traffic.

"Nice to meet you, Ms. Corva. May I take your bag?" Stephen's lips tilted into a facsimile of a smile.

"I got it." Ivy gripped her backpack strap and headed toward the door. He hurried ahead.

"Welcome to the Tower." He held open the door and gestured her inside, the model of restrained courtesy. And, to be fair, protecting Shelby from reporters was what she'd have wanted. He'd been doing his job.

"Thank you." Ivy unfroze enough to give him a smile. She glanced back to where Olivia had stopped. Had she called ahead? Or had she set her up for a confrontation?

Then she stepped through the tall glass door and into Shelby's lifestyle. In here the air was warm and smelled like a pine fire. Soft piano music played in the background. Light-colored stone ran across the floor and along the walls. Leather chairs beckoned. A pair of Christmas trees decorated in gold and red anchored both ends of the lobby and a wreath bigger than a tractor tire covered one wall.

Shelby must have walked by all this at least twice a day. She probably barely noticed it, just part of her background. Ivy was tempted to collapse into one of those cushy chairs, then call Olivia and ask to be taken straight back to the airport, but she steeled herself and took the elevator to Shelby's floor. Twenty-five.

When she opened the apartment door, she didn't know what to do. She stood alone in the hall, as if waiting for Shelby to invite her in with a laugh and a glass of wine. Shelby didn't. Well, Ivy wasn't a vampire, so she could go right in without an invitation. With a sigh, she stepped over the threshold.

A beep from the alarm startled her. She took the disarm code Olivia had given her out of her pocket. It worked and the alarm turned off with a chirp. Easier to deal with than Stephen.

First crisis averted, Ivy looked around. Everything expensive and cold. Gray buffed concrete floors, gray stone counters, white carpets, gray furniture. A modern kitchen with stainless surfaces that looked more like a commercial kitchen than a cozy one. She shivered.

The art surprised her. Giant canvases displayed red blotches on white backgrounds. Abstract, maybe red poppies, like the Brits wore on VE day? She studied one until the red blobs resolved into giant blood cells pinned on the white canvas like specimens trapped on a microscope slide. The answer to everything, Shelby had often told her, was in our cells. Each cell held the secret to its own immortality or its own senescence. Ivy wondered where these particular cells were on that journey.

She ran an index finger along the edge of the canvas. Shelby had chosen this. Not an amorphous, graceful jellyfish; not candid family portraits; not still photos of the cityscapes around her. Blood. The image of Shelby's blood blooming into the dark ocean under the Golden Gate Bridge sprang into Ivy's mind and she shook her head and left the living room.

She ended up in Shelby's bedroom. It smelled of lavender like the crypt where her father had seemed more irritated than grief-stricken. Ivy blinked and backed out, closing the door. She never needed to go in there again.

Further down the hall the second bedroom was as nondescript as an upscale hotel. Again with the gray. Gray sheets and a dove gray comforter, gray walls. Another blood canvas above the bed. It felt morbid—everything gray and lifeless except for blood cells magnified a thousand times. In Shelby's world, only blood mattered.

The art on the back of the door held a surprise—a giant poster for the anime 'Cells at Work.' A spiky-haired ghost-white man in a military uniform stood behind a perky girl with a bloodred jacket and cap. Ivy was surprised that Shelby had seen the show. Ivy had seen it too. It was about the inside of a human body with the cells represented as anime humans fighting the good fight to keep the body alive.

Was Ivy the invading infection or the helpful blood cells?

Maybe she'd taken the metaphor too far. But at least the poster was there. The first bit of whimsy she'd seen in the apartment and it cheered her. At the moment that Shelby had bought and hung this, she'd been thinking about something fun and, well, not gray.

Ivy dropped her backpack in the closet and took a deep breath. She'd come here to see Shelby, to help her, to have time together before success launched Shelby into a higher orbit. To be someone who Shelby trusted. To be the fun one, the froth. Too late. If she was a cell at work, she had failed in her job.

Or, looked at another way, while she'd been saving that wolf, no one had been saving Shelby.

Enough self-pity. What was the next thing to do? Shower. It had been a long time since her last shower, hours since her quick wipes in the airport bathroom. A hot shower later, where she learned to appreciate Estonian water pressure, she smelled like rosemary and lavender and her hair was better conditioned than it had been in years. She smelled of affluence. Organic goopy affluence.

A thick gray terry cloth robe was laid out on her bed like Shelby had expected her arrival before she'd left the apartment to end her life. Ivy touched it with one finger. She and Shelby had often spent hours in bathrobes, eating pizza and solving the world's problems. After the bridge, they'd become friends, and Shelby had been the one person she trusted with everything. Clearly Shelby hadn't trusted her back or she'd have waited before she jumped off that bridge. She'd have let Ivy's plane land and they would have gotten metaphorical bolt cutters to cut off the metaphorical dick of Shelby's problems.

Ivy tightened the belt on the robe with a hard jerk and loaded her dirty outfit into Shelby's washer. It already held a pair of socks and panties. She'd probably changed out of them before she left to go jogging on that last day. Pushing that thought aside, Ivy started it up. She might only have one outfit, but at least it would be clean tomorrow.

Here in sunny California, she felt colder than at home watching the snow. Exhaustion, grief, or genuine cold. Ivy didn't even know anymore.

Her stomach rumbled. It didn't know when it last ate something. A bite of shepherd's pie. Gum in the Uber. Coffee at the airport.

She rummaged through the kitchen. Shelby clearly didn't spend much time cooking, but eventually she found a so-called pizza in the freezer. While the label said pizza, since it was topped with chicken, green stuff, and a white sauce, Ivy didn't count it as such. It was exactly the kind of pizza she'd never eat in Tallinn. A California pizza. Shelby had been a pizza snob back in Pittsburgh too, but clearly California had changed her.

Better than the vinaigrette dressing and butter in the fridge though. Ivy popped the pizza into the oven. While it baked, she tried to figure out how to raise her own temperature. She found the thermostat next to the alarm and jacked it up.

When her phone timer dinged, she lifted the pizza out of the oven with pristine gray oven mitts. The kitchen smells of warm pizza dough and garlic were comforting. She left the pizza to cool on the counter while she made an espresso with Shelby's state of the art machine. Good to see that, even if she'd compromised on pizza, Shelby's love of coffee had stayed true.

Coffee made, she put a slice of pizza on a gray plate and took a bite. Her throat closed up and she set the plate aside. Here she stood in Shelby's kitchen, baking her pizza, wearing her robe, and smelling like her soap. Her stomach was having none of it.

Wiping her face with the back of her arm, she plopped the pizza back in the oven and placed her dishes into the dishwasher. It already held one small plate, one cup, one glass, and one knife. Shelby's last breakfast, probably toast and coffee and orange juice. Perfectly ordinary.

She sat on Shelby's gray couch and braved the internet while she sipped the coffee. Her own death threats seemed tame and distant now. Juvenile fantasies removed from Shelby's brutal death. These notes were men masturbating murder fantasies onto the internet. It barely seemed to have anything to do with her, even if she was the target. Without thinking, she moved the emails to the Trolls folder. Her new ritual. None of her other messages seemed important either. Nothing seemed important.

She slipped down to the floor, leaned against the couch, and closed her eyes. Her head thrummed with adrenalin and exhaustion. Once that wore off, she'd sleep for days under Shelby's soft cotton sheets. Or at least she hoped so.

The window beckoned. The city outside glittered like hard jewels. In the distance, a red light blinked through the fog from atop a bridge. How often had Shelby stood here and enjoyed this view?

Had she thought of herself as an eagle in a nest or a princess trapped in a tower? Knowing Shelby, neither. She wouldn't have wasted her time daydreaming while looking out the window. Shelby got shit done.

Ivy would, too. If she got up early enough, she'd walk around the city and say goodbye to her friend. Then, she'd get through that Kepler's event somehow and take the offered ticket home to Tallinn. Shelby was beyond her help now.

Her phone pinged and Ivy sat back on the floor before answering it. She'd turned off her Twitter notifications after the wolf rescue, so it had to be someone she knew.

Anu: Landed ok?

Ivy: Flight fine

Anu: And? Did you get the job?

Ivy: No job

Anu's three reply dots bounced and stopped and bounced again. She was thinking what to type. Ivy put her out of her misery.

Ivy: My friend died. Just back from funeral

Her phone rang. Anu, calling. Ivy appreciated the thought, but declined the call. She was too tired.

Ivy: Can't talk now

Anu sent a GIF of a cat hugging the camera.

Anu: Ready when you need me

Ivy sent a thumbs-up. It struck her as ridiculously short and optimistic, but she didn't have energy to look for a better one or heaven forbid type a word. She hoped Anu would understand.

She slipped further down on the carpet. Her bones seemed to be liquefying. It had been a long time since she'd been this tired. She ought to get up and go to bed before she passed out on the floor. That coffee had been useless.

The red blood cells in the painting on the wall vibrated when she blinked. Clever design or exhaustion? She scrubbed her aching eyes. The right thing to do was to go to bed and let her eyes rest before they hallucinated red blood cells coming off the wall to attack her like angry red UFOs.

Or got to thinking about a timely car accident on the bridge that had kept anyone from seeing Shelby, maybe stopping her. Or that kept anyone but Timothy Shah from watching what actually happened. She should go to bed and think about it all in the morning.

Instead, she went back to her phone and Googled shelby linton.

Headlines splashed across her browser. Shelby's death was big news. Pieces in all the tech magazines, newspapers, everywhere. She clicked over and read one on Wired. Shelby was under investigation for defrauding investors. The alleged cause of her suicide was listed as fear of criminal charges. The piece gloated about it. Shelby as a fallen Icarus. Young, beautiful, and brash, she'd flown too close to the sun. She deserved her fall from grace and presumably, the reader was left to assume, her fall from the Golden Gate Bridge, too.

Mr. Linton's words in the crypt made more sense now. Shelby had disgraced his family name. Had he read them before the funeral? She checked the dates. Some were a few days old. Some had been published while her father had been at the funeral putting her ashes behind that shiny brass plaque.

Was this investigation what Olivia had hinted at when she'd said 'no matter what else happens?' The revelation that Shelby had played fast and loose with money and expectations. That her legacy wasn't going to be what she'd have hoped. Like Ivy gave two shits about that. She wanted her friend back.

Her phone rang again. Not Anu. A 415 area code. Shelby'd had a 415 area code. So, the call was from San Francisco. She took a deep breath and answered it, worrying at the last second that it might be press or one of her trolls.

"Todd from the front desk," a cheerful male voice said. "I'm sorry to disturb you."

"OK," she said, relieved it wasn't someone worse. "How did you get this number?"

"Ms. Linton's assistant called with it," he said.

Olivia had called to arrange things. One point for her. "Why are you calling?"

"The airline delivered your suitcase. Should we bring it up?"

"I'll come down." She hung up and that was when she realized all her clothes were spinning in the washer. She wandered into Shelby's room and spent an eternity staring at her closed closet door. She was never going to be able to open it up and wear anything in there.

Whatever. She'd go down naked if she had to.

She clutched the robe more tightly, gathered up the alarm code and keys and padded to the elevator on bare feet. Cold from the floor seeped into the soles of her feet, but it still felt warmer than the Pirita river. Not that picking up a suitcase was worth the same discomfort as saving a wolf. If she was going to come up with a ranking system for reasonable discomfort, she had those two data points and a lot of space between them.

When the elevator opened, Stephen stood next to the desk at reception. She recognized the wall of his back. Parked next to his massive leg was her suitcase. Next to him stood about five guys. One was in the burgundy uniform of the building, presumably the Todd who had called her. The others looked like tenants—well-groomed, designer clothes, and a strong sense of entitlement. She was going to have to get her suitcase while wearing a robe in front of all these guys. One looked about her age, two younger, and one the same age as Mr. Linton. A couple of them laughed in a way that made the hair stand up on the back of her neck.

But she wasn't going to wimp out now. As she got closer, she saw that they were gathered around a young guy's phone. Stephen glanced at the screen, and looked uneasy. She wondered what it was. Maybe someone was stealing an expensive car from the garage. Or having sex in the other elevator. She glanced over at the elevator hoping naked people would tumble out to take the pressure off her in her robe out in public. They did not tumble.

Her feet made no sound as she hiked across the lobby. She held her robe closed around her neck with one hand, but the men were too occupied by the phone to notice her anyway. Maybe she could snag her suitcase and get out of there without having to talk to them. A tiny scrap of luck on a terrible day.

Then, she glanced over and saw a naked woman on the tiny screen. The few bites of not-pizza thought about coming up, but she forced them back down.

She remembered the pinstriped sheets from their old dorm room. Red and white, like a Christmas mint. Shelby lay, naked, splayed across those crisp sheets. Ivy wished Gerald a million painful deaths. His ancient revenge porn had returned to haunt Shelby after her death. The digital vengeful spirit was finally released.

Even worse than the public humiliation, Mr. Linton would know. He'd see it. She remembered Shelby, stricken, on that long ago bridge, terrified to disappoint him. Another shame for him to bear, another way his daughter had failed him.

Not just Mr. Linton. This was what the world would remember of her friend—a fraud, a failure, and a leaked sex tape. The ding dong from the funeral echoed in her mind. This time she knew where it came from. The Wizard of Oz. The song the munchkins sang after Dorothy's house landed on the Wicked Witch of the West. Ding dong. The witch is dead.

Shelby's legacy.

Shelby had lived her whole life for her legacy. She'd labored to bring something into the world that no one else had ever created. She'd wanted to stop death. That was supposed to be what the world knew her for.

Not for this.

One of the tenants let out a wolf whistle and Ivy walked forward. She wasn't going to let this be how Shelby ended. She'd tell Shelby's story. Not just the lurid and shameful parts. She'd reconstruct Shelby's last days, the days Ivy had arrived too late to see, and the days before. Then she'd show the world true pictures of her friend. Ambitious, yes, but in the pursuit of a goal to help all mankind. She'd fallen far because she had dared much. She had been extraordinary.

And Ivy would show the world.

"What the hell!" she yelled. All of the men jumped and looked guilty. A young guy with curly hair clicked off his phone display, like it wasn't already far too late.

"I didn't see you," he said. "I'm sorry."

"But you saw Shelby," she said. "You saw plenty of Shelby."

"This is Shelby's college roommate," Stephen said.

At least a couple of the guys looked embarrassed, but the rest didn't.

"We didn't realize—" The curly-haired guy held his hands up at shoulder level, like she'd ordered him to drop his weapon and wait to be arrested. He still held the phone.

"You realized. You knew. You just didn't care."

"It's not like that. I liked Ms. Linton. I—we—respected her," Stephen said.

Curly nodded furiously. "We did."

"And you thought the best way to show your respect was watching an illegally leaked sex tape recorded when she was a minor?"

"She didn't look like a minor," the jumpy older guy said.

"Do you have a lot of experience watching minors having sex?" Ivy asked him.

He reddened. "No. I don't. I didn't mean it like that. Miss..."

Ivy accepted no apologies. She grabbed her suitcase and snapped out the rolling attachment.

"I can help you with that." Stephen reached for it.

"Don't. You. Dare." She glared at them as a group, grabbed her suitcase, and fast walked to the elevator on her bare feet.

Behind her the lobby was so silent she wondered if the men were holding their breath.

They'd better be.

CHAPTER NINE

The next morning Ivy woke in a dark room. Disoriented, she tried to remember where she was. Tallinn? Her bed smelled like lavender and the sheets felt oh so soft. Shelby's. And then everything else came back in a rush. Her friend's death. The allegations against her. Gerald's humiliation.

Ivy gritted her teeth against it all and listed things she wouldn't do. She wouldn't let them put a scold's bridle on Shelby and drag her through the town square. She wouldn't let their vision of Shelby be the only one in the world. She wouldn't give up on her friend. Not ever.

And that thought led to her new plan: create an online memorial for Shelby. Her life had ended tragically. She'd made mistakes. The world would vilify her mistakes, but Ivy's memorial would showcase Shelby's ambition and her accomplishments as gifts, not as factors that led to her death. As gifts that might keep thousands or millions of people from dying at all. Ivy was a writer and this was the one thing she could do for her friend.

That and find out what had really happened on that last day.

Decision made, she sat up in bed and glanced out the window. The dark sky wasn't unusual for a Tallinn winter morning, but she suspected it meant she was up way too early in California. Still, it wasn't wholly pitch-black—skyscrapers and streetlights and a few headlights and taillights far below made it feel like the world was slowly waking up. And so was she.

As she lathered up with Shelby's expensive products, she made a list. First, she was going to have to learn more about Shelby's work. For that she needed verifiable facts, not her own memories of their phone conversations. The steamy shower filled with the scent of lavender and she breathed it in. It made her sad, but she'd harness that to do right by Shelby.

She'd start at Nyssa. They must have nonconfidential information that she could use for the memorial, like a full set of articles written on Shelby since she founded the company or details about her work with people who were homeless. They'd be sure to have specifics about her vision to fight back against the ravages of aging since that was their vision too. Maybe they'd have quirky stories that would tell the other side of Shelby's life.

Feeling cheered, Ivy dried off, opened her suitcase, and looked at her clothing options. Already better than yesterday. She decided to wear a nice pair of jeans, a white button-down shirt, and a blazer Anu had persuaded her to buy. Green, like poison ivy, with a Baltic amber brooch shaped like a spaceship. In Tallinn, this was business casual. Not that it mattered, as she wasn't interviewing for a marketing writing job anymore.

Since it was too early to do anything else she made herself a deluxe coffee, bitter and strong, and drank it while she de-trolled her email, which was likewise bitter and strong. Even reading the hateful subject lines was exhausting. And scary. Death threats. Suggestions that she kill herself. Rape threats. A lot of punishment for writing a novel that pointed out that women's bodies spend nine months and ten minutes longer growing a baby than men's do.

She took another sip of coffee and wondered: if they didn't like it, why did they read it? She didn't read things she didn't like and after not reading them never felt obligated to go on the internet and threaten to kill the authors. She looked away to calm herself back down. Breathe, drink a sip of coffee, close her eyes and center herself. Meditate on calming drifts of snow and starry skies.

But even with all the meditation in the world, it wore on her. She wasn't ashamed of what she'd written, and she didn't think she was in the wrong. Her research on public shaming told her that this might protect her from the worst of this shaming event. But it didn't make it easy. Or fun.

Even ignoring the trolls, her editor hadn't answered her last two emails, and she wondered if her publisher had abandoned her. Was this the only book she'd ever be able to write under her own name? A lifetime of working on her writing craft and she was being condemned to fail based on two paragraphs in 350 pages. Like Shelby, she was being marched around the public square. And she had no idea when it would end. Or if it would end with her own death. And then she'd join Shelby in being two women that the world had destroyed. Whee.

She heard Anu's voice saying "drama" in her head and smiled. Ivy's experiences were nothing compared to Shelby's. Her own attackers were random trolls, not news sites and TV shows. Ivy would come out the other side of this. And she could stand up for herself. But no one could speak for Shelby but Ivy.

Back to her real emails. The last one from her publicist was a reminder about the Kepler's event. If it went well, they might book another at Mysterious Galaxy bookstore in San Diego. If not, they'd cut their losses and keep her doing online publicity. A lot depended on a good reading at Kepler's, and it was only the second one she'd ever given. This time she wouldn't have Anu to feed her questions.

Also, she was afraid to meet her readers. After all the hate against her book, it was hard to imagine how she'd face them. But, presumably, at least some of them didn't want to kill her. Was that enough to count as a success in her publisher's eyes?

She sent off a quick email confirming the Kepler's event. She'd stacked up interviews she'd written on the plane, so she sent those along too. She wondered if they'd ever appear online or if they'd be consigned to the one space worse than the sucking black hole of internet irrelevance: they'd never be published at all. Everything about her book would disappear. The book itself would vanish. She'd be digitally erased.

She'd seen it before. It would be like the book itself had never existed. The only things to read about her book would be the ranting of trolls who'd never even read it. That thought hurt more than she wanted to think about.

She didn't even look at Twitter. She didn't want to know.

Anu had sent a few worried emojis while she slept, and she gave her a quick call.

After a quick round of pleasantries, Ivy said, "Nyssa has offered to buy me a ticket back."

"I hear a but in that sentence." Even over the phone, she saw Anu's skeptical raised eyebrow.

"I have a book event tomorrow and I want to do a little digging into Shelby's life."

"Why?"

"Google her. I'll wait." Ivy paced and waited. Shelby hadn't skimped on her coffee beans. Anu's keyboard clicked in the background.

"Wow," Anu said. "That's a lot. They even pulled her off her company's website."

"They did?" Ivy looked. Shelby wasn't listed as the CEO or founder or at all. Her pictures were gone. Her bio taken down. Her erasure had begun. "As if the company popped into being entirely without her."

"Damage control," Anu said. "It's not personal."

"It is to me. Her work made them famous."

"Does it matter to her now?" Anu asked.

"Yes." Ivy struggled for the right words to explain. "Legacy."

Silence stretched out between them.

"Anyone can get the old links and files off the Wayback Machine," Anu said. "Nothing is really gone."

Ivy thought about Shelby's sex tape. So true. "I want to build a memorial site for her that highlights the good things she did. For her father to remember. For me to remember."

Anu's fingers tapped on faraway keys. "Looks like shelbylintonmemorial.com is available. How about I buy it? Set up a template and you drop some pages and links in there?"

Ivy was so grateful she had to sit down. "I'll pay you back. Thank you."

"No big deal," Anu said. "An hour's work, tops. Worth it to be able to tell that wolf story for the rest of my life."

Ivy laughed. She thought she'd forgotten how. "Do I come off as heroic?"

"Idiotic. But committed."

"I can think of worse things to have on your tombstone."

"How about we don't talk about your tombstone quite yet?" Anu asked.

"Someone posted my tombstone on Twitter. According to the date on the tombstone, I have two days to live."

"I saw that. They misspelled your last name. So, maybe they're wrong about the date, too. I don't think they did much fact checking."

Ivy changed the subject. "Thanks for calling for backup so I didn't die when I stumbled into the parking lot with a frozen wolf."

"Really, I did it for the wolf."

"Have them put that on my tombstone," Ivy said. "And make sure they spell it right."

They chatted while she finished her coffee and she remembered what it was like to have a normal conversation with a friend again. Anu was no Icarus. She was more like Atlas—patient and kind and quietly saving everyone's ass.

After the call Ivy emptied her backpack onto her guest bed. When she'd packed it, Shelby had already been dead, but she hadn't known it. She lifted the packet of salty licorice to her nose and inhaled the sharp scent. Unlike Shelby, she hated licorice in all its forms, and the smell took her back to Shelby eating black licorice on her dorm room bed, letting inky drool run out of her mouth and lisping "I'm a squid!" That wasn't going on the public memorial website.

She carried the bag of imported licorice into Shelby's bedroom and set it on her nightstand. She'd delivered it, if too late. "Here you go, Squidward."

Backing out of the room, she wiped her eyes and reloaded her backpack with supplies for the day. Basics attended to, Ivy went to the table by the front door and looked at the gray bowl, hand-thrown, which contained Shelby's keys. Ivy passed up a Tesla fob that looked like a tiny car and grabbed the motorcycle keys. Years ago, she'd taught Shelby to ride on her battered little Kawasaki Ninja. Ivy could never afford anything better than that, but Shelby could. And she wanted to drive it.

First, she had to trick someone into granting her access to the parking garage. Olivia had mentioned that she didn't have the access to grant. Someone must and she had to find them and convince them she was supposed to go down and drive Shelby's expensive vehicles. Otherwise she'd be at the mercy of California's terrible public transit system.

Swinging on her backpack and stepping into her boots, she made for the elevator. A lot more comfortable than taking the elevator wearing panties, she noted. But a letdown to see that now that she was fully dressed, the lobby stood empty. Her timing was, as always, bad. Still, when she made for the front door, her boots felt better against the floor than her bare feet had the night before.

Outside, fog blanketed the street and the air settled cold against her face, an aggressive damp cold with a nasty wind that wanted to hurt you. She zipped her leather jacket and walked over to Stephen. He looked tired, and she wondered if he'd worked all night. She remembered him watching Shelby's revenge porn and pushed down her feelings of fury. She needed to get information out of him and shouting at him probably wasn't the best way.

"Good morning, Ms. Corva." He gave her a slight bow. His nose was pink with cold.

Definitely more cordial than yesterday. "You work here twenty-four hours a day?"

"Marco called in sick," he said. "I'm glad I got to see you again. I wanted to apologize for what you saw yesterday."

"Not what you usually watch in the lobby?" She had a tone and she didn't care.

"I liked Ms. Linton. She was a nice lady."

Shelby had once given her an entire lecture on the overuse of the flaccid word 'nice.' "Was she?"

"She was kind to all the service staff, and she tipped at Christmas." He wound down. Again, not much of a legacy. Cars beeped and glowed in the foggy dystopian street. Who knew that dystopia would be so cold and clammy?

"You saw her that last day," Ivy prompted.

"She was dressed to go jogging."

"How could you tell?"

He gestured down at his front. "She had on running shoes and a white sweatsuit with green and red stripes on the side. Gucci, I think."

Shelby did like her designers. "How did she seem?"

He shrugged. "In a hurry. Weird because she never jogged. Besides that, she looked a little better than usual."

"Better how?" Ivy perked up. It didn't make sense that she'd looked good on her night of deepest despair. Or maybe Stephen wasn't observant.

"She'd gotten skinny the last few months. Maybe the stress of her big job, I don't know. But on that last day she looked like she'd gained a little weight back." He shook his head. "Not that she was fat or anything. Just not so thin."

"Did she say anything?"

"To me?" He looked surprised at the thought.

"Did she seem depressed?" Ivy asked.

He shook his head. "Definitely not. She seemed happier than she had in a while. Had a bounce in her step. When she looked back at the building, up to where her apartment is, she smiled before she ran off into the fog. She looked like someone who was going to have a good day."

"She was depressed before that day?"

"Don't know if I'd call it that. Droopy. Distracted. And she kept getting skinnier."

That was twice he'd mentioned her weight. "Was she ill?"

"Maybe?" He stepped past her to open the door for a woman in pink yoga pants leading a shivering little dog. Maybe it needed a thicker dog sweater.

He turned back to her. "She hadn't been normal for a while anyway."

Ivy filed that away. "Normal?"

"Charging around talking on her phone looking like she'd eat you if you crossed her."

That did sound like Shelby on a normal day and Ivy felt a little more sympathy for him. At least he'd paid attention.

"How long had she seemed not normal?" she asked.

"I don't know," he said. "It kind of crept up on me and then one day I noticed but I think it had been going on for a while. A few months, maybe?"

"Do you think you were the last person who knew her to see her alive?" Ivy asked.

He didn't look happy at that thought. He glanced down at his hands, past her shoulder at traffic, and then back to her forehead. "I don't know."

Actually, that must have been Timothy, but Ivy didn't correct herself.

"Did you wonder why she didn't come back after her run?"

"I figured she caught an Uber to work or something. She worked all the time."

"Kind of like you?" she asked.

He laughed. "I think she got paid better."

Ivy held up the key to Shelby's motorcycle. "How do I get into the garage?"

He paused, like he wasn't sure whether to give her access. Which meant it wasn't an oversight that Olivia didn't have it and it wasn't routinely granted. Ivy's brain worked overtime on excuses.

"We'd agreed I'd borrow the motorcycle while I was here. Before." They hadn't, of course, but he couldn't possibly know and Shelby couldn't contradict her.

"The Ducati?" he said. "She never lets anyone drive that."

"I taught her to ride my motorcycle back in college." Ivy smiled her sweetest smile.

Stephen struggled with his conscience, but she already knew how flexible his conscience was. Eventually, he realized that too and went inside to print her a keycard for the garage. She followed and huddled next to the stylish burning rocks that stood in for a fireplace while he got the card. How could San Francisco possibly feel colder than snow-swept Tallinn?

He handed her the card like an apology. "Swipe it in the elevator and you can go down to the garage floors."

When Ivy finally got down to garage level, she understood the reason for the security. The place

118

was flush with luxury statement cars. Bugattis. McLarens. Ferraris. Enough horsepower down here to power a thousand Mongolian hordes. These cars represented more wealth than she'd ever make in her lifetime. And they were so shiny and clean.

It didn't look like any of them had ever been driven. She spent a few minutes walking around gawking before she remembered that Stephen probably was watching her on a security feed. She waved.

Then she looked for Shelby's spaces. Shelby's little red Tesla roadster looked dowdy in this luxurious company with mud on its tires and bugs on its windshield. This car drove around in the world, running errands and taking people to work and back. Unremarkable in this space, but not cheap either.

The Ducati held its own. It glowed a fierce bright red, like arterial blood, and every curved surface promised speed and death. If Ivy had to die young, she'd want it to be quick and on this bike.

She ran a finger along the soft seat where Shelby must have sat, slipped on the blood-red helmet, and started it up. The bike's throaty roar echoed in the garage, a lion proclaiming dominance to the concrete world. She laughed inside the helmet. Those rich fools could have their four-wheeled luxury statements. This bike was enough for her.

Once she was out of the garage and on the street, the handling was so superior to anything she'd ever driven before that she realized at once that Shelby would never have trusted her with it. Good thing Stephen hadn't known her that well.

The streets of San Francisco morphed into a glorious Christmas video game. Dodge. Accelerate. Near miss. Straight ahead under white lights. A battle of speed and maneuverability vs. hapless drivers and bicyclists. It required every ounce of concentration. She took the long way to Nyssa and arrived at the blue-and-white building by the ocean happy for the first time since she'd heard the wolf would live. Adrenalin sang in her veins. The air smelled briny and clean.

She recognized Olivia's Prius from the funeral. Two other cars sat next to it in the morning sun. No early risers at Nyssa? Then she realized that today was Sunday. Probably not the best day to get answers, but she was already here so she might as well poke around.

Carrying Shelby's helmet, she entered the blue-and-white sanctum and nodded to the jellyfish. At the front desk, Olivia stared at a monitor. Ivy hoped she wasn't watching the sex tape. Just in case, she cleared her throat.

Olivia sat up quickly, looking guilty enough to have been watching that video, but when Ivy angled her head to look, she saw a spreadsheet. At least not every single person she ran into would be watching the sex tape.

"Good morning?" Olivia turned the words into a hurried question.

"I'd like to talk about that organization that helps people experiencing homelessness." Ivy decided to start there because it was clearly for a good cause, something Shelby would want to be remembered for. And learning about it was supposed to have been her job. Shelby must have wanted her to know.

"It was more Ms. Linton's thing." Olivia's eyes wandered back to the spreadsheet. "She worked with them directly."

"What was the name of the organization?"

Olivia whipped out her phone. "Let me send you the contact information."

Ivy's phone pinged with the contact. Margie Stich.

"I'm sorry," Olivia said. "But there's no PR job here anymore."

"That's not why I want to talk to them. Or to you."

"No?"

"I suppose you've seen the bad press about Shelby," Ivy said. The jellyfish rose and fell like they didn't care about the press.

"It must be difficult for you," Olivia said.

"And I noticed her name and bio are already gone from the Nyssa website."

"The board is sensitive to bad press," Olivia said. "I'm not surprised they made that decision."

"I am," Ivy said. "Without her, none of this would exist. None of you would have jobs."

Olivia glanced down at her phone like she expected a call.

Ivy hurried on. "I'm pulling together old articles, writing down details about her everyday life. Things like that." A shadow passed over the window as a car parked behind her. "I want to show the good things about her too. Create a memorial for her online. For her father."

Olivia's face softened. "Oh, Ivy. I'm so sorry."

Ivy didn't want her pity, but she'd take it if it was useful. "I plan to talk to this Margie Stich about the good that Shelby did for them there. Plus other people who remember her more fondly than the internet seems to think right now."

Olivia shook her head sadly. "It's going to get worse before it gets better."

"You think she did the things they're talking about?" Ivy tightened her hands on the motorcycle helmet. "That she was a fraud and a cheat?"

"The truth will come out, Ivy, and it might not be what you want it to be."

"What's that supposed to mean?"

Olivia sighed. "I have a document full of the URLs for articles about Shelby. How about I email you that?"

"Thank you," Ivy said. "It would help a lot."

Timothy Shah opened a side door and strode in. He looked as immaculate as yesterday, this time in a navy-blue suit and a red tie. She didn't know why she'd expected him to be in black, mourning. But she did and she was annoyed at him before he said a word.

A woman from the funeral came up behind him. The one with the mandala on her hand. Wendy. She looked smug and she stood a little too close to Timothy. Asserting ownership? If so, it hadn't taken him long to move on after Shelby's death.

Ivy whistled the tune to 'ding dong the witch is dead' and the woman's chin rose defiantly.

"So that was you." Ivy's voice was what Anu called low and deadly.

Timothy looked between the two of them like a man who had never seen The Wizard of Oz, but Olivia sucked in a quick breath and came out from behind the desk.

"This is Wendy Hank," he said. "She's chief biochemist here at Nyssa and she'll be carrying on Ms. Linton's work. Wendy, this is Ivy. She's a childhood friend of Ms. Linton's."

"We've met," said Ivy.

"I'm sorry for your loss." Wendy's words rang with insincerity and Ivy wanted to smack the smug smile right off her face.

"Are you, though?" Ivy took a step toward her.

"Ms. Linton and I weren't close." Wendy smirked.

"Ding dong. The witch is dead." Ivy sang the words.

Olivia looked at Wendy and shook her head like a disappointed parent.

"At her funeral," Ivy said. "With her father right there."

"I'm not quite sure—" Timothy said.

Wendy cut him off. "I stand by it."

Ivy shifted the helmet to her right hand and hefted it like a bat. "Cold."

Timothy took a step back from Wendy like he'd finally figured out what the song meant or maybe like he didn't want to be on the business end of Ivy's helmet. Smarter than he looked.

"I'm not shedding any tears for her," said Wendy. "She endangered a lot of people by cutting corners. Made my life a living hell."

"The kind of person you'd want to toss off a bridge?" Ivy asked.

"She tossed herself off the bridge and saved me the trouble." Wendy shrugged. "I know you were her friend, but you didn't really know her."

Ivy held her breath and counted to ten. She wasn't here to make trouble. She was here to find out about Shelby. "What didn't I know?"

Olivia looked between them like she was unsure how to intervene.

Timothy gaped at Wendy. "A living hell?"

Clearly he was going to be a couple of beats behind everyone else in the conversation. Ivy stayed quiet to hear the answer.

"The animal testing results." Wendy paused. "You know I filed a written letter of formal protest, and I can't get into it here in front of her."

"Me?" Ivy said. "In front of me?"

"You're not an employee. You never signed an NDA." Wendy pursed her lips in disapproval. "I'm not allowed to talk to you at all."

"Except for about how much you hated my friend."

"The NDA is vague on that kind of disclosure," Wendy said.

"What kind of formal protest?" Timothy asked, still behind. "Why haven't I seen it?"

Now it was Wendy's turn to look surprised. "You've seen it. I cc'd you."

Timothy looked bewildered and Olivia furrowed her brow.

"Did you get a promotion after she died?" Ivy asked.

Wendy glared at her. "One that's long overdue."

"Motive," Ivy pointed out.

"You think I drove her to suicide?" Wendy scoffed. "With my whistling?"

Ivy hefted the helmet again.

Olivia looked toward the door. "I think we'd better calm down."

Ivy turned to ask her why, and the front door slammed open. Two burly men dressed in suits walked in, followed by two smaller men in suits who looked like accountants. All four were grim, purposeful, and out of place. Even Ivy could tell they didn't work there.

Wendy looked pleased, Timothy surprised, and Olivia only vaguely annoyed. Did this happen every day here? Attack of the angry accountants.

"Mr. Shah?" said one of the suits. "I'm Ivan Pavlova from the FDA."

Timothy paled and Wendy's eyebrows rose. Olivia checked her watch.

Olivia gestured to Ivy. "This is Ivy Corva. She's here for an interview as a PR writer. The interview was booked a few days ago, before the news broke. She's not an employee here, nor has she been informed about anything or ever signed an NDA."

Ivy realized Olivia was trying to help her, but didn't think this was the right time to thank her.

"Could I see some ID?" asked a guy who looked like he could bench press more than Stephen. "Maybe a driver's license?"

Ivy realized she didn't have a US driver's license, even though she'd been driving around all day. Was that legal? She dug out her passport and handed it over. When he entered her name in his tablet, her stomach wasn't sure it liked this.

"That'll do," he said. Then he opened the door for her. "Let's go, ma'am."

"What's going on?" she asked him as she walked out.

He stopped in front of the closed door. "We're shutting this place down."

"Down? Why?"

A van screeched to a halt a few yards away. It had KGO painted on the side in blue letters and a satellite folded over on the top. A news van. More bad publicity for Shelby.

"It'll be in the papers tomorrow, I don't doubt," the FDA guy said. "We'll contact you if we need more from you."

He turned away to go back inside, clearly finished with her.

A guy with a camera piled out of one side of the van and sprinted toward Nyssa's front door where the other burly suit opened the door and led Timothy out in handcuffs. The news photographer snapped pictures with a long lens as they tucked Timothy into the SUV. Whatever was happening, Mr. Linton would see it soon too.

Another car arrived, a black SUV predictably, and more law enforcement got out. This was a big event. The KGO photographer snapped more shots.

"Move along," said the guy who'd led Ivy out, and she decided that was pretty good advice.

Not quite ready to leave altogether, she walked over to the news van.

"Do you work here?" A man in a white tie with candy canes on it held a microphone toward her face. Blond and conventionally handsome, he reminded her of Toomas, but without the sincerity.

Ivy glanced back at the guy who'd led her out. He watched her. "Nope."

"Lucky for you," he said. "They're wrapping up a multiyear investigation. Financial fraud. Medical fraud. Jail time for some. That Shelby Linton was a piece of work. Damn lucky she jumped when she did."

Ivy tightened her hands on the helmet. "And a jackass like you knows that?"

"Watch for it on the news tonight." He jogged toward the building with his microphone held like a tennis racket ready to swat away any truths he encountered.

Ivy was tempted to follow, yank that microphone out of his hand and shove it down his candy cane hole, but restrained herself. Instead, she hung out by the empty news van and waited to see what else would happen.

Men and women in suits trotted out of Nyssa's front door carrying cardboard boxes. Ivy couldn't see what was inside, but the sheer number surprised her. Who kept paper records anymore?

They filled up an SUV and it drove away and another arrived. Whatever was going on, it was big. If Shelby had been alive, she'd have needed someone in her corner. She still did.

Ivy was regretting her large coffee and thinking of asking to use Nyssa's staff bathroom when Wendy came out alone. Even across the parking lot Ivy recognized the glee in her bouncing steps. The news reporter must have seen it too, because he headed straight for her. So far, no one had given him more than a sentence.

Keeping an eye on the guy who'd told her to leave, Ivy edged closer. When the reporter reached Wendy and asked her a question, she fiddled with her right earplug, then shook her head. But when the reporter held out a business card, she snatched it up and tucked it into her pocket. Then she turned away and got into her Prius.

Ivy scrambled for the Ducati. By the time Wendy pulled out of the parking lot, Ivy was ready to follow. She let a few cars get between them as she tailed Wendy out of San Francisco. Wendy was a careful driver—she signaled well in advance, made precise turns, and stuck to the right lane. Clearly someone who followed the rules. Grateful for her predictability, Ivy let a few more cars in between them.

When Wendy got on the Bay Bridge, Ivy followed and hung back. The Ducati wanted to go faster. It wanted to tear by her and all the other cars and be free and alone on the bridge. But Ivy kept it reined in and poked along behind Wendy's dutiful Prius.

Cars passed, because it was a freeway and you weren't really supposed to go fifty-five, but Wendy did so Ivy had to, too. She tried to enjoy the free open ocean on the sides and the giant dome of the sky. All the buildings in downtown San Francisco had penned her in.

As they neared the end of the bridge, Ivy closed the gap, following Wendy onto 580 headed for Oakland. Even lab directors couldn't afford San Francisco rents. Wendy took the Grand Ave/Lakeshore Exit and the Ducati followed. Now that they were on city streets, it was tougher to keep an eye on her. She could turn anywhere. Reluctantly, Ivy got so close that only two cars separated them.

They passed a lake with grass and giant Canadian geese, which seemed like an odd thing to have in the middle of a Californian city before Wendy turned off onto a side street and parked. A pretty neighborhood. Ivy saw why she'd chosen it and was irritated at herself for liking anything about Wendy.

Ivy quickly found parking for the Ducati, secured it, and sprinted over. She got there while Wendy stood fumbling with her house keys.

"Yo," Ivy said.

"This constitutes harassment," Wendy said. "I should call the police."

"I'm standing on a public sidewalk talking to a colleague at a company I'm thinking of working for." Ivy gave her a fake smile. "Imagine meeting you here."

Wendy pocketed her keys and stepped away from the door, probably afraid Ivy would force her way into the building. She might, too.

But Wendy was a source. Ivy had interviewed reluctant people for stories before. And Wendy, Wendy drove like a control freak. The kind of person who liked to control the narrative.

"Don't you want me to know your side of the story?" Ivy asked. "You know everyone else is going to mess it up."

Wendy weighed that for a few seconds. Ivy held her breath, hoping the scale came down in her favor.

"Somebody needs to tell you before you do yourself damage blundering around defending your poor, sad, pathetic little friend."

She spit out the word friend like an obscenity. Not the kindest offer Ivy had ever received, but better than she'd hoped.

Wendy walked them to a nearby diner advertising egg creams and hot dogs. With its old-fashioned red pleather booths and yellow shaded lamps, it should have looked retro, but it just looked old. Tired red and gold tinsel garlands draped the walls and a fuzzy red bell hung by the cash register. 'Twas the season to be depressed.

The waiter wore a sailor's hat and nodded to Wendy like she was a regular. She ordered a chocolate egg cream and Ivy ordered one too, even though she had no idea what that was. Maybe a custard?

"What do you think happened to Shelby?" Ivy emphasized the word you, so Wendy would know it was all about her.

"Nyssa was shut down for breaking the law. Financial fraud and not passing their lab inspection," Wendy said.

"I heard that from the newsguy. Tell me about Shelby."

"The story will be all over the news," Wendy said. "I'm not going to tell you anything you won't hear on the news, but let's at least get it in order."

As she'd guessed, Wendy liked to control the narrative. Since she actually had a narrative, Ivy was willing to let her, but she already knew she wasn't going to like the process.

The waiter set tall glasses in front of them and gave Wendy a concerned look. Ivy smiled in what she hoped was a non-threatening way. Neither Wendy nor the waiter looked convinced.

Wendy took a sip of her chocolate drink and smiled at Ivy. Her smile won the Smuggest Smile of the Year award.

Ivy tried her drink. It looked like a milkshake but was the consistency of milk and carbonated. Unexpected. Still, it tasted like chocolate, so she considered it a win.

"So it's all Shelby's fault?" she asked.

"Did anyone else cultivate a culture of fear and paranoia? Burn folks hotter than a California wildfire?"

"Drama much?" Ivy asked. Too bad Anu wasn't here to see someone way more dramatic than Ivy. She'd never believe her if she told her.

"It's all documented in black-and-white," Wendy said. "This train took a long time to wreck in full view of lots of witnesses."

"What does that mean?"

"Look," Wendy said. "I'll tell you whatever I can without violating my NDA if you promise to leave me alone."

"Sure." Ivy had no intention of following through on that promise.

"Have you worked on biotech?" Wendy asked.

"Tech-tech," Ivy said.

"OK, then you know how it goes. The mice run through the maze and management tries to make them come out at the same exit. More or less."

"Usually less." Ivy took another sip of her carbonated chocolate drink. Still weird, but it was growing on her.

"Shelby sent all the mice in different directions. She siloed us off in our own little cages. Your NDA kept you from talking to employees even in other parts of Nyssa, which I've never seen before."

Ivy hadn't either so she pasted a mildly surprised expression on her face.

"If she caught you hanging out with mice in other groups, she fired you," Wendy continued. "Like you were fraternizing with the cats, but these mice were actually in the same lab as you, eating the same cheese."

"Maybe she worried about trade secrets." Ivy was getting sick of this mouse metaphor.

Wendy snorted. "Everyone worries about trade secrets. All the time. But not like this."

Ivy wasn't conceding the point, but she wasn't slowing her down either. "And then what?"

"She started pushing me, probably others too but I don't know because I couldn't ask. She wanted deadlines moved up. Data to be massaged."

"Wanting it done faster? That sounds like every tech company I've ever worked at." Ivy noticed the waiter wiping a table over and over at the next booth and leaned back like a friendly person would.

"Some things you can't rush. These are biological processes. Mice take time to mature. Pathologies take time to manifest. It's not like telling a programmer to code faster. Organic things grow on their own schedule."

"You think Shelby didn't know that?"

"You'd be surprised. Her background in biochemistry was as deep as—" Wendy dripped egg cream onto the table and pointed at the smallest drop. "That."

Wendy was kind of an asshole. But that didn't make her wrong about everything. "But you knew better?"

"Of course I did. Everyone does. Anyway, I had data from the mice about effects on the pancreas, and Shelby wanted to tank them. They weren't even necessarily statistically significant."

"Seems like that's not a statistically significant crime either."

"It needed to be reported and tracked. That's how science works. It's how safety works." Wendy shook her head like an angry librarian.

"I'm sure Shelby cared about safety too." Ivy finished her egg cream.

"You bet she didn't," Wendy said.

Ivy bet she did, but she kept that to herself. "What about Timothy Shah?"

"You're mad because he's throwing Shelby under the bus in the press?"

Ivy hadn't even read those articles yet. "Because she's not here to defend herself. She gets the blame and he gets the company."

Wendy slurped the last of her drink. "Like there's a company anymore. Timothy will be lucky if he ever gets out of jail. The investors are furious. They may go after him in civil court, too. He's going to lose everything."

"It seems to me that Shelby lost everything."

"That was her choice though, wasn't it?" Wendy said. "Nobody else got to choose."

"Well, you can always make that choice too," Ivy fired back. "You know how to get to the bridge."

"That's not my point." Wendy sucked in a deep breath. "I know you were friends and I imagine it must be hard for you to hear this stuff."

"Wow. You sound almost like a human with human feelings." Ivy knew she ought to suck it up to get more information, but she couldn't.

"Look. I'm sorry you're upset. But my career is dead. And your friend killed it."

Wendy fished a ten dollar bill out of her pocket along with a business card, probably the one she got from the KGO newsguy. She dropped the bill on the table, tucked the card back in her pocket, and walked out.

Ivy didn't follow. She sat in the red booth and tried to fit what Wendy had told her into everything she knew about Shelby. It didn't fit. Shelby wanted to discover the secret of immortality, not hurt people. She wanted to be remembered as the person who gave the world an incredible gift. Maybe she hadn't been the best manager, the best people-person, but that didn't mean she was a bad person.

Wendy was probably bitter and angry all the time. And today she'd lost her job and maybe her new boyfriend so she wasn't exactly at her kindest. The mouse pancreas thing sounded trivial. Keeping employees from gossiping to each other didn't sound like that big a deal either. Not that those were the crimes that Shelby would have been charged with anyway.

Eventually, Ivy gave up on figuring it all out, went to the bathroom, got on Shelby's motorcycle, and left Oakland behind. Cars flashed by in a blur. She pushed the bike hard so she couldn't think about anything beyond the next turn, the next stop, the next obstacle. The adrenalin wasn't fun now. It was a tool.

CHAPTER TEN

Eventually, Ivy fetched up in the parking lot at the south end of the Golden Gate Bridge. The orange span popped against the blue sea. Iconic. And one of the last things Shelby had ever seen. Ivy took off the helmet and wiped her cheeks. She hadn't realized she'd been crying. She hadn't even been here for twenty-four hours and Shelby and everything she'd worked for had been destroyed.

Swallowing hard, she rooted around in her backpack and found a tissue to clean the inside of the helmet. Shelby's suicide made a lot more sense now. Had she known about the investigation? That she'd have been arrested? She must have.

Olivia had known. That's why Olivia had been warning her since she arrived. Why she'd tried to ship her back to Estonia before the news hit. And why she'd protected her and gotten her away before the questions started. Chalk one up to Olivia for kindness.

If Olivia knew, then Shelby must have too. Or had she? Olivia had seemed in control, unsurprised when the authorities arrived. And she hadn't come out in handcuffs either. Had she been working with the police? Had it been Olivia who betrayed Shelby, not Wendy? One quick minute from protective hero to undercover cop. Ivy was letting everything run away with her.

She sighed. If Shelby had committed medical and financial fraud, then maybe she deserved to be arrested and hounded by the press. But she didn't deserve to die and anyway Shelby wouldn't have done the things they said. Ivy could see her being optimistic about schedules and results, maybe even crossing the line into fraud. Not padding results, but maybe pretending future results were closer than they actually were. Fake It Till You Make It was the mantra of Silicon Valley. Everyone did it. If they started arresting people for that, when would they stop?

Medical fraud was something else entirely. Fudging test results on rats. Even Wendy had said that whatever was wrong wasn't statistically significant. Shelby had said herself that the drug wasn't approved for testing on humans, so how bad could Shelby's actions be?

Ivy didn't want to know the answer.

Instead, she locked up the bike and helmet and walked to the bridge. In spite of the sunshine, wind cut through her jacket. Shelby had lied about how warm it was out here.

Ignoring the wind, she walked out onto the span. A suicide fence loomed above, much taller than the one on Schenley Bridge. A friendly blue and white sign told her to text for help and there is hope. Not, apparently, for Shelby.

Ivy leaned her head way back to see the top of the fence. The determination Shelby must have had to climb so high, flip over, and let herself fall into the cold water far below. The despair. Pain knifed through Ivy's stomach, so sudden and intense that she doubled over.

"Are you OK?" asked a woman in yoga pants pushing a jogging stroller. She wore rainbow earmuffs and a look of concern. Even her baby looked concerned, its little eyebrows lowered over its round brown eyes.

"I'm fine," Ivy lied and straightened up. "Your baby is adorable."

The woman didn't look convinced, but her watch beeped and she gave Ivy one last look before jogging away. Would this stranger's concern have been enough to stop Shelby? For all she knew a stranger had tried. Maybe fifty people had tried to talk her out of it. Or maybe none had.

Ivy stood and threaded her fingers through the cold chain link fence, as she'd seen Shelby do all those years ago on Schenley Bridge and as Shelby must have done a few days ago. How long had she gazed out at the city lights? How many times had she looked down at the black waves before she started her climb? If Ivy had come running up, would she have been able to stop her like she had before? Not that she'd ever know, now.

"What the hell, Shelby?" Ivy asked. "What the actual hell?"

She stared across the bay toward the prison island of Alcatraz, past Alcatraz to Oakland where Wendy lurked, and over to the hills beyond. A flock of pelicans flew low over the waves looking like dinosaurs. So much of the world was spread out right there in front of her. But it was all behind Shelby. She'd never feel the salt air on her cheeks, watch the birds, or experience the sting of a friend's betrayal.

Ivy shivered and walked further along the span, following the concerned mother. She stopped next to a bouquet of white roses leaned up against the railing. Were these flowers for Shelby?

A woman in a bright orange vest came over and scooped up the bouquet. She looked tan and windblown and healthy.

"Hey!" Ivy said. "Put that back."

"You're not allowed to leave anything on the bridge," the woman said. "Since 9/11."

"Really?" Ivy had never heard that. "But isn't this a memorial?"

The woman looked up. "Probably. Somebody jumped right here a few days ago. It's the only blacked-out spot on the damn bridge. Anyplace else, we could've stopped her."

"Right here?" Ivy put one hand on the orange railing.

"Yeah. We gotta send someone up to fix that camera." The woman shook her head and then glanced back at Ivy. "You want the flowers?"

She held them out stiffly.

Ivy didn't want to steal flowers from Shelby's memorial. That was even worse than having them taken away by a bridge employee. "No, thank you."

The woman shrugged, looked up at the broken camera again, then tucked the bouquet under her armpit and walked off with the thoughts and grief of the person who'd left the flowers.

Ivy stood there for a long time with the cold briny wind blowing against her face. She held onto the fence where Shelby must have stood. A blonde woman in a white tracksuit with a stripe on the legs ran by and Ivy ran after her. She looked so much like Shelby. Then the jogger turned and it wasn't

139

Shelby at all. Of course not. It would never be Shelby again.

Grief and jetlag and Ivy's own imagination were running away with her. She walked to the north end and looked back across the bridge, down at the pylons that supported it. One of those had killed her friend. Or at least, she hoped it had. She hoped Shelby hadn't gone into the water alive. That she'd been spared that, at the end. Mr. Linton probably knew, but she couldn't imagine asking him.

Out of all the people on the bridge that night, she'd been seen climbing up to jump by Timothy Shah and only Timothy Shah because a broken camera didn't film the spot where she'd stood. That was two coincidences too many.

What could it mean? That Shelby hadn't really jumped from the bridge? She couldn't picture someone killing her elsewhere, hauling her body onto the bridge, dragging it to the top of the chain link fence, and tipping it over the edge. Not even counting the logistics, wouldn't someone have seen them somewhere along the way, including on the other video cameras? Even moving a body underneath the bridge undetected seemed like an impossible task.

A tour group surrounded Ivy, speaking German, and she made way for them to take pictures and smile and be overjoyed that they were here, in this place, looking at the bridge. A special moment for them.

"Can you?" A tall man with a bushy red beard that made him look like a Viking held out his phone and gestured toward his two friends, another man with a much sparser beard and a dark-haired woman with piercings.

Ivy took the phone, framed them in the lens with the bridge behind them, and snapped three pictures.

"Many thank you," he said. "Isn't it wonderful?"

"My friend jumped off this bridge," she said. "A few days ago."

His eyes widened. "That is very terrible."

He reached out and grabbed her hand and shook it, the German equivalent of a bearhug. "Are you OK here?"

Tears jumped into her eyes. She was a weepy damn mess is what she was.

"Where is your car?" he asked.

She pointed back along the bridge. The wind tore at her hair.

"We bring you back." He yelled to his friends and they came over. The woman touched Ivy's arm and they walked back along the span.

Ivy felt oddly comforted by their gesture.

"It's a beautiful bridge," she said, almost apologetically.

"What is that color name?" the woman asked. She had a different accent than the man.

"Vermillion orange." Ivy knew from a previous visit. "Also called international orange."

"I am sorry for your friend."

"Thanks," Ivy said inanely. The tour guide in her wanted to spout all the facts she'd read on

Wikipedia since Shelby's funeral. That this bridge was the most used suicide site in the world. That more than 1,500 people had died here. That 95% of people died on impact, but 5% of them survived to drown or die of hypothermia. That Shelby couldn't have been one of those 5% because she'd hit that pylon and wasn't that comforting? Ivy curled in her lips and bit down to keep anything from spilling out.

"My mother suicide," the woman said. "She cut."

She pantomimed slashing her wrists.

She put an arm around Ivy's waist. "It's no good."

Ivy dropped an arm over the other woman's shoulder and together they walked behind the German Vikings and off the bridge. Ivy spotted a man in a dark blue suit sitting in an SUV not far from her bike. Did he look familiar?

"My bike." Ivy pointed. The man in the SUV didn't seem to care.

The German who had shaken her hand let out a surprised whistle. He and the other man walked around the Ducati, talking over each other in excited voices like children. Ivy didn't blame them. The bike had that effect on her too.

"Be safe driver," the woman said. "Especially right now. Too easy to make mistakes when sad."

She tightened her hand on Ivy's waist and the two embraced. These three complete strangers were more sympathetic about Shelby's death than everyone at her funeral.

Ivy thanked them and said her goodbyes. As she drove off, she realized she didn't even know their names. Maybe just as well. Maybe they wouldn't have been so sympathetic if they'd known who she was or who Shelby had been.

When she pulled into traffic, the black SUV slipped in a few cars back. Maybe a coincidence, but also maybe not. After all, she'd followed Wendy to Oakland and Wendy hadn't once looked back.

She opened up the bike and put space between them. A little voice in the back of her head reminded her that her Estonian driver's license might not even be valid here and it was a bad time to get pulled over, but her self-preservation instinct shouted it down.

She cut between two cars to pass, slid in front, and made an illegal left turn. The SUV couldn't follow. She drove aimlessly until she was sure it wasn't behind her. Then she went back to the leaning tower of Shelby.

When she pulled up in front of Shelby's building, a black SUV lurked half a block away. Was it the same one? Maybe San Francisco was thick with black SUVs. Or maybe not.

Feeling eyes on the back of her neck, she zipped into the parking garage and fast walked to the elevator. Nothing to see here except for one freaked-out woman and a fleet of expensive cars. Presumably she was safe. That's what the expensive building bought: security. Plus a wine cellar, a pool, a gym, and who knew what else. But it didn't buy you everything. Shelby was still dead.

Since she took the elevator from the parking garage, she managed to bypass the front desk which was good because she only had enough energy to worry about one thing at a time and right now it was that black SUV. Was it the FDA or some other law enforcement agency seeing if she was involved with Shelby's mess? If so, they'd lose interest because she was a sweet little cinnamon roll who lived on snarky words and Estonian chai and had no idea what Shelby had been up to. But what if it was someone else?

She ordered Chinese for delivery and watched the news from the gray couch. Shelby led the segment. They showed about three seconds of Timothy being walked out in handcuffs, two minutes of vague allegations, and ten minutes about the sex tape. That's what Shelby's life and even her scandal had been turned into—a salacious story about a sex tape. So far, no one had identified Gerald as the man in the video. She wondered if he was sorry or glad. She was tempted to send in an anonymous tip, but wrecking Gerald's life didn't feel like the right thing to do either.

So, she opened up a bottle of Shelby's wine, ate Mongolian beef and dry braised string beans and somehow ended up on Twitter. She was tired of soaking up punishment, of hearing herself slandered, of quietly waiting it out. After a couple glasses of wine, she fed the trolls. She responded to tweets. She defended her book. She took up space. She asserted her right to know what she'd actually written herself. She fought back.

It didn't go well.

She had just sent off a long angry tweet when Shelby's front door opened. Someone had found her. One of the guys yelling on Twitter was here with a plunger.

She jumped up and ran for the kitchen. A knife snicked free of the knife block and she turned, holding it high. They weren't taking her without a fight.

"Back the fuck off," she screamed.

A surprised Mr. Linton stood next to the counter. He held both hands in front of him in a shushing gesture.

"I'm sorry." He backed slowly down the hall. "I forgot you were here."

She dropped the knife on the counter and it rang against the surface.

Heart still racing, she put the pieces together. He'd come here to mourn his daughter on the night after her funeral. And she'd nearly stabbed him.

"It's OK," she said. "You can stay."

He stopped, swaying. His eyes were bloodshot, his shirt half unbuttoned. He wasn't even wearing a tie. And the smell of alcohol radiated from him.

"How about you sit down?" She led him into the living room and watched him collapse onto the couch. She perched next to him on the arm. Weird to see him undone like this. He'd seemed so together at the funeral.

"I didn't mean to intrude." He paused and looked toward the kitchen, probably thinking about that knife. "Who were you expecting?"

"About a million men on the internet are threatening to kill me right now."

"That seems excessive." He blinked a few times. "What did you do?"

"Blame the victim," she said. "Thanks."

He raked one hand through his hair. "Apologies."

She spun her laptop around and handed it to him.

His eyes jumped as he skimmed through the tweets. "Is this one yours?"

"Which one?"

He read it aloud. "When you write YOUR homoerotic male fanfic version of my novel, you can have exo-wombs and frozen eggs and the colony can be all men and you can drone on about their biological superiority all you want."

She winced. "I may have had a lot of wine."

"Me, too."

She plopped down next to him. "You OK?"

"Is this normal?" He gestured to her laptop, clearly not intending to answer her question. Like an answer existed.

"This week it's normal," she said.

"I read your book and I wasn't mortally offended."

She heard Anu saying #NotAllMen. Aloud, she said, "Thanks?"

"I quite liked it. Jasper never gave in to the horror, even when she thought she was losing her mind. It was a stunning portrayal of strength under adversity."

He had read the book. For a moment she was shocked into silence. He buttoned up his shirt and tucked it in, pulling himself together.

"Not losing your mind," she said, "is easier when it's on the page and not your own life."

He sighed. "You saw the news?"

"Not all news to me."

"The tape?" He paused, looked like he was going to say something, stopped, and tried again. "That was made in college?"

"It's why she wanted to jump off that first bridge."

He closed his eyes for a long moment. "I thought it was grades."

"Nope." Shelby's grades had been nearly flawless.

He picked up her wine glass and drained it. Not that he needed it. "Still poor judgment on her part."

"Also on Gerald's part to upload it onto the internet. But he got off scot-free. They still don't know who he is, because no one cares. Because he's the guy and not the girl."

"I care," he said. "My lawyers will be contacting him about uploading pornographic material containing a minor. What's his name?"

"Gerald McGuire." Turns out she was willing to get him in trouble after all. "Same year as us. I'm sure he's easy to find."

Her laptop bonged.

"You got a response to your tweet." Blue eyes so much like Shelby's skimmed along the words. Then he closed the laptop. She wondered what the tweet said.

"Do you need additional security?" he asked.

"I guess that wasn't from a true fan?"

"I can assign you some of my protective detail while you're here."

She gaped at him. "You'd loan me a bodyguard?"

"Reassign," he said. "If you're feeling unsafe. You could work with the team Shelby used."

"Shelby had a security team?" They sure hadn't done a good job.

"For events," he said. "And to manage threat assessment."

"She got threats?"

"Not like the one I just read." He gestured at her laptop. "That one was pretty graphic. It involved an empty barrel and lighter fluid."

"Shelby got serious threats?"

"They didn't kill her," he said. "We looked into it."

He refilled the wine glass and drained it again. She patted his arm awkwardly, reminded of failing to comfort Shelby on the other bridge. She hadn't learned any comforting skills in the intervening years.

"How about I make us tea?" She picked up the wine bottle and scooted off to the kitchen. When she came back to the living room with a teapot and cups on a tray, he'd recovered himself. His shirt was tucked in, his hair neater, and his expression calm. She envied him his return to composure.

"Chamomile?" she asked.

"I sent an email to Tristan," he said. "He's trained in threat detection. Lawyer. Degree in psychology too. Works with a lot of celebrities. He can go over those tweets and see which ones are dangerous."

"And emails," she said. "And handwritten letters to the publisher."

"Your book has only been out a week!"

"I really appreciate this." She poured him a cup of tea.

"Of course." He looked annoyed. "Do you think I'd do nothing?"

"Everyone else is doing nothing," she said. "It's super trendy right now."

He took a sip of tea and made a face. "Shelby would have wanted you to be safe."

Maybe, she thought, but she didn't lend me her risk assessment dude.

They drank tea in silence, looking out at the city lights.

"Isn't it weird that Timothy Shah saw her climbing the fence that night?" Ivy asked.

"She'd called him to pick her up at the other end of the bridge and drive her back to the office."

"Why would she do that?" Ivy didn't believe it.

"She was tired, he said. Phone records verify that they spoke for a few minutes. He was at the office when he got that call, and came straight over, according to cellphone record pings."

She wondered how he got that information. "But no one knows what they said."

"He didn't leave his car when he saw her. I've seen the security footage. He calls 911 without ever getting out."

Well, he hadn't climbed up after her either. Ivy would have climbed up there, grabbed her, and dragged her back down and sat on her until she thought better of her decision. "Why didn't he get out of his car?"

"I'd like to pin it on him," Mr. Linton said. "But Shelby threw herself off that bridge while he was several feet away. She did it to herself."

He drained his tea like he was hoping it was wine.

"Why did you come down to the apartment?" she asked.

"I thought I would sit here and pretend that she'd be coming home from work and we'd get dinner." He looked around the living room. "I know how that sounds."

Before tonight, she wouldn't have believed it of him. He was a complicated dude.

Ivy bit her lip. She hoped she wouldn't regret this. "I ordered Chinese."

"I failed her," he said as if she hadn't spoken. "All my risk assessment people and they never even saw the real risk."

"I didn't see it either."

"You knew about Gerald," he said. "She never trusted me with that."

"You're the last person she wanted to know about that."

"Turns out I was the last person who did."

"What about the Amish? They don't even have TV. They have no idea."

He grimaced. "The Amish don't know. Comforting."

She handed him a takeout container and an unopened pair of chopsticks. He looked at them like he hadn't seen something like that in a long time.

While he ate, they talked about everything except Shelby. Then he left her alone with her thoughts and her laptop. She didn't open either.

CHAPTER ELEVEN

A buzzer rang. Ivy's head rang in sympathy. She sat up, regretted her decision, and rolled off the bed onto the floor. The floor was no better for her headache than the bed had been and it felt colder. The damn buzzer rang again. It didn't seem to care that she had a headache. Nasty-ass buzzer.

She looked at her phone on the nightstand. For once, it was innocent. No alarm clock either. That left? Buzz. The front door.

"What the hell?" she asked and winced. Who would bother her here? And at whatever time this was.

She stumbled to the front door and looked into the camera feed at a complete stranger. How did he get past Stephen? Or did Stephen's protection only extend to Shelby?

The guy outside her door wore a well-cut suit and carried a leather laptop case. Was this how the trolls looked in person? Not how she'd imagined them. He seemed so put together. And so early. And also a little bit cute.

As if he sensed her looking, he stepped forward, rang her front doorbell again, and then held a business card up to the camera.

Tristan Walsh, Threat Specialist

The night before came crashing back and she groaned. She held down the button to talk. "Can you come back in half an hour?"

"Good boundary," he said. "Don't make it a question."

She flipped him off through the door, which he sadly couldn't see. "Forty-five minutes and I meet you downstairs in the lobby."

He cracked a smile.

Forty-five minutes later, to the minute, Ivy walked into the lobby. This time she was awake, showered, dressed, had eaten a piece of toast and clutched two cups of coffee. She was adulting. Her head still hurt though. A good reminder that she hadn't been adulting so well last night. She spotted the security guy standing underneath the giant wreath.

"Thank you for coming, Mr. Walsh."

"You can call me Tristan," he said. "Shelby insisted on first names."

"Ivy Corva," she said, letting him figure out which name to use.

On this side of the camera, he was tall, with freckles and a cleft chin like Dean Winchester. She wondered if Shelby had been inside that suit. The concierge behind the reception desk was someone she didn't know, but he checked out Tristan like he wanted to get inside that suit too. Tristan's look crossed boundaries. Then the concierge caught Stephen's eye and smiled. Interesting.

Tristan shook her hand, firm, not too crushing. "Mr. Linton mentioned that you were receiving unwanted attention online."

"Explicit death threats in email, Twitter, and on paper," she said.

"That sounds unpleasant." He had a smooth, reassuring voice. She wondered if he took vocal lessons for that. "What's your goal for me?"

"Make sure I don't end up dead on a public street, naked, with my intestines stuffed in my mouth."

He chuckled. "That's specific."

"I brought you coffee." She gestured to the leather chair next to her and they sat. This was going to take time. She pointed to her laptop bag. "I have sugar in here, but no cream."

"Black is fine," he said.

She gave him the cup and opened up her laptop and logged in so he could see tabs for her email and Twitter. She hadn't checked either today. After what she remembered from last night, she suspected she ought to never go on there again. She took another long sip of coffee.

He asked for some time and so she went to the corner of the lobby where she could still keep an eye on him and called Anu to talk about the memorial website. It looked great on her phone. Anu had disabled comments and stuck to reposting positive stories that were being buried. Shelby had a small tribe of women entrepreneurs who still believed in her and Anu was spreading their stories. The site was classy and kind. Ivy forwarded a link to Mr. Linton and thanked him for loaning her Tristan.

"Now that's done, tell me about this threat guy," Anu said.

"I googled him. He looks legit. And he looks like his picture on their website."

"Mm-hmm." Anu's keyboard tapped in the background. She was checking too.

"I think I trust him," Ivy whispered, in case he might overhear and take advantage. Across the room he scrolled through Twitter and took notes on a yellow legal pad and didn't seem to notice what she was doing or saying.

"You do?"

"Don't sound so surprised. I know it's weird. Maybe he's using some kind of trust pheromone?"

Anu laughed. "Maybe it's associative trust because you trust Shelby's father?"

"Or maybe he's actually trustworthy?" Ivy sighed. "It can't be that easy."

"I'd say you're overthinking it, but you never do that."

"Ha ha," Ivy said. "Overthinking things is good."

"Because...?"

"I'm always prepared."

"True," Anu said, dryly. "So, Mr. Linton walked right into your apartment yesterday?"

"He has keys and the alarm code and, no, I'm not happy about it either," Ivy said.

"Who else has keys and the alarm code?" Anu asked.

"Scary thought, isn't it?"

Tristan turned and waved at her.

"I gotta go," Ivy said.

She walked across the lobby to see what he had to say about her tweet storm. The lobby was empty, so no one would witness her shame, except for the concierge and he clearly wasn't looking at her.

Tristan sat with one leg crossed over the other. He looked calm and thoughtful, not like someone who had actually read her tweets and emails. Maybe he'd been taking notes on his new novel or something.

She plopped onto a chair. "What's the verdict?"

"I've done a quick assessment," he said. "I'll need to follow up on a few of these folks."

Folks. He sounded sixty years old, but he wasn't that much older than Ivy. "Am I in danger?"

"Impossible to say for sure, but most of these folks are more bark than bite."

"Their barks are pretty toxic."

A man jogged into the lobby and she jumped. Tristan, she noticed, had uncrossed his legs and was ready to stand. They both relaxed when the man kept jogging to the elevators. Tristan wasn't as calm as he seemed either. So, that was her life now. Heightened risk perception.

"The explicit nature of their comments is disconcerting, but the worst offenders seem to attack someone online, then move on within a few days. That's based on their past behavior with other celebrities. It doesn't look personal to you."

"It feels personal," she said. "Especially the ones that use actual pictures of me in graphic scenarios. They're surprisingly good with Photoshop."

Tristan looked concerned, a professional caretaker expression. "A lot of research talks about the connection between public shaming and depression or suicide. How are you handling this emotionally? Because we have folks to help with that, too."

"Emotionally? I'm pissed off about it and grieving the death of my oldest friend." She took a deep breath. "I understand public shaming and shunning are damaging to the victims. I literally spent the last year researching torture and public shaming. But I'm not ashamed of my book. Not one damn bit."

"Good to know," he said. "And if you need any emotional support later, please call, because knowing something intellectually isn't always enough to armor one against these kinds of attacks. We're here to help."

Not going to happen. She'd deal with her shame privately, or call Anu. "What's the next step? Send out nasty letters on fancy lawyer letterhead?"

He shook his head. "The best course is to watch and wait."

"That sounds both boring and ineffectual."

"What these people want is engagement. Like last night." He tapped her Twitter feed onscreen.

"There was wine involved," she said, like that helped her case.

"On the bright side, #exowomb trended on Twitter." He chuckled.

"Did it?" She wished she'd checked. "Can I see?"

He took a sip of his coffee, which had to be cold by now, and didn't hand over the laptop. "The less you engage with them, either positive or negative, the better."

"Don't feed the trolls." Anu's voice echoed in her mind.

"We'll issue a statement saying you appreciate the passion that's been brought to your work—"

"I don't appreciate the violent passion. At all."

"...And that you hope everyone enjoys the novel."

"But they're trashing my work. They're trashing me. They're threatening my life, my damn unborn children." Ivy scowled. "I want to fight back."

"How?" he asked.

"I get that it's hard." She mulled it over and searched for a metaphor. "It's like how a great big caribou can be killed by a cloud of tiny mosquitoes. All the caribou can do is run away and hope the mosquitoes give up and then they don't and it dies. They're the mosquitoes and I'm the caribou."

"I got the metaphor," he said.

"The mosquitoes are pegging my anxiety meter."

"Let's work on reducing your anxiety," he said.

"Doesn't seem likely, but let's run with that." Her anxiety was getting in the way of figuring out Shelby's story. And sleeping. And writing. And functioning.

"Here's my contract." He held out a piece of paper. "It states that, although I'm paid via Linton

Enterprises, my loyalty is to you as my client. Anything you say to me is covered by attorney client privilege and I cannot divulge it to anyone."

She read through the contract and that was pretty much what it said. Tristan had already signed and dated it. She signed it, too. "Is this really accurate? Mr. Linton is obviously a valuable client and I'm just a random writer."

"My loyalty is absolute to every client." He looked dashingly sincere.

"And if there's a conflict of interest between them?"

"I keep everyone safe," he said. "Are you concerned for your safety from Mr. Linton?"

"If I said yes, what would you do?"

"I'd recommend that you leave the building. We have various lodgings you could choose from. After that, we'd put together a threat profile and see where to go from there." He returned the contract to his briefcase. "Do you want me to get started on that?"

"Just checking," she said.

"You sure?" He looked at her closely. "Even if it's a little feeling. Your gut feelings are powerful indicators of your fears. Always listen to them. It's more important to be safe than polite."

"Good advice," she said. "And I'm pretty sure."

"OK, then let's get back to the internet trolls. But tell me immediately if that changes."

First, she posted the bland and cheery statement he suggested on her social media platforms while biting her tongue. Clearly, defending herself after drinking too much wine wasn't helping make things better. And she couldn't fight the whole internet. So, maybe trying to de-escalate would work.

Then he got into the emails. She agreed to have all emails with certain code words forwarded to his office and then automatically filed into her Trolls directory so she didn't have to see them if she didn't want to. She was to forward him any threatening emails that got through those filters and store them with the other troll stuff, too. He'd do threat assessments on the lot and tell her if any concerned him. Hopefully, he'd have a better way to deal with them than she did. That part felt like a pile of trolls had moved underneath someone else's bridge.

Next up: Twitter. He suggested turning her social media account over to his office for the duration and she balked. No one was posting as her but her. He cautioned her to post only bland, pre-canned stuff sent by her publisher about reviews and events and not to respond to any tweets, good or bad. She didn't like that, but she said she'd give him a week.

The other platforms were easy after that.

Her anxiety meter did feel better. But she was also muzzled. She had put the scold's bridle over her own head, choosing silence to avoid the pain of more public shaming. It didn't feel right. She tried to convince herself that it was a tactical retreat before a final victory but she didn't believe it.

Also, she was also a little pissed off that her publisher hadn't offered to help with any of this. She'd assumed they could do nothing. It turned out they could do plenty. Maybe only if they could afford someone like Tristan. Which they probably could.

Mr. Linton had arranged for Tristan to go with her to the Kepler's event too. Tristan didn't know what to say about the black SUV from yesterday, but promised to get video footage.

That taken care of, she got back to the part that had interested her when he first arrived.

"Tell me what you know about Shelby's death. Beyond what's on the internet. Are you sure she jumped of her own free will?" Ivy knew what she'd heard, but part of her couldn't believe Shelby would end her life in the water. A drug overdose, maybe.

"We obtained security footage from the Golden Gate Bridge. She walked across the span alone until she passed into the zone with no camera coverage. That's where she jumped." His eyes were compassionate. "I reviewed it myself. And we have an eyewitness backing that up."

"Timothy Shah. But don't you think it's weird that she jumped in the only place that isn't covered by a camera?"

"It seems like a coincidence," he said. "We checked all the footage around that part of the span and found no indication anyone was with her or in any way threatening her."

"Did you see her call Timothy Shah?"

"We saw her make a short phone call, yes."

"How did she seem?"

"She seemed tired," he said. "But as someone who doesn't jog regularly and had walked all that way from her home, that's not unusual."

Ivy swallowed hard. "Who benefited from her death?"

"No one, much." He shrugged. "Shah's in jail. If she were here, she would be, too."

"And that would be a bigger story. Because she's a woman."

"Because she was brilliant, telegenic, and the face of the company. Mr. Shah is an accountant who eschews the spotlight. Also, because she was a woman."

"Eschews?" she said. "If I put that in a book, they'd make me take it out."

"I think you'd hold your own with the editor," he said with a smile.

"Won't Nyssa fold up without her?" Ivy hoped so. They didn't deserve to profit off Shelby's brilliance.

"Tough to say. Either way, they probably have key man insurance on her, enough to bring in a replacement if they're permitted to reopen their research facilities."

"Key man insurance?"

"A special kind of insurance that pays out when key people within a company die."

"Could that be a motive?" she asked.

"She wasn't murdered," he said softly. "She jumped off that bridge of her own free will."

Ivy pulled her sleeves down over her hands. "I'd like a copy of the reports you wrote plus the autopsy report."

"Mr. Linton has to authorize that," he said. "It's pretty gruesome. Why do you want to see it?"

"Closure," she said.

"It's often best to let things be." He set down his cup. "You have a lot on your plate right now."

"One more thing," she said. "Could you give me the name of the police officer in charge of the investigation into Shelby's death? It's public record."

He hesitated. "Detective Juanita Rodriguez."

She wanted to know more about Shelby's death than the versions she'd heard. Maybe they were shielding her. Or maybe they hadn't noticed something.

He turned toward the door. "I'll pick you up here at six for your event. I'll coordinate security arrangements with the store before I come. In the meantime, be aware of your surroundings. Trust your instincts. And call 911 and then me if you feel at all threatened. We can get a team to you quickly."

She didn't know what to say. It was the first time someone had ever lectured her on personal safety. Her parents had never bothered and after that no one dared. Even if he was paid, it was caring by extension from Mr. Linton. That counted for something.

CHAPTER TWELVE

As soon as Tristan was gone, she called the police station and set up an appointment with Detective Rodriguez at the San Francisco Mission Police Station. Thinking about the parking situation and how much sympathy she'd get if she rolled up on an expensive motorcycle, she took an Uber. No black SUV followed her.

The station was an unimposing brick building with a green door. Inside, she walked past a guy dripping blood onto the floor, a woman who wore so much makeup her face looked like a mask, and a young girl with a chicken tucked under one arm. No chairs, only a dilapidated Christmas tree and a long line of people waiting for help with their dilemmas.

When she got to the front of the line, she looked through a thick glass window at a blond guy in uniform. His hair short, his posture erect: he looked like he'd stepped off a TV set.

"I have an appointment with Detective Juanita Rodriguez." She stayed away from the stainless-steel counter in front of the window. "In 15 minutes."

He looked at a wall clock behind a battered cage. That clock had seen things. "I'll call her."

After a quick confirmation, he ushered her down a brown corridor with a low ceiling that housed fluorescent lights and acoustic panels. It had the charm of a Greyhound station but without the hope of boarding a bus to get away.

"Hello, Ms. Corva," said a woman with dark hair spiked up like a hedgehog. She was about Ivy's height, but seemed taller and bigger and altogether more imposing. She didn't open any of the doors, so they stood awkwardly in the hall. The guy from the front desk strode away, his duty done.

"I remember you from the funeral," Ivy said.

"I'm sorry for your loss," Rodriguez said flatly. She didn't sound like it.

"Thank you for taking the time to see me," Ivy said, trying to sound more authentic than Rodriguez but also falling flat.

"I have ten minutes." Rodriguez glanced at another battered clock and smoothed her suit jacket.

"I have a few questions about my friend's death. Shelby Linton."

Rodriguez compressed her lips. "The evidence points overwhelmingly toward suicide."

"Right," Ivy said. "How?"

"You're not a family member, are you?" Rodriguez looked like she knew the answer.

"We were friends. Since childhood." College was practically childhood.

"I'm sorry for your loss." Her expression didn't change. "I can't help you."

"Was there a note?"

"There isn't always." Rodriguez said.

So, that meant no. Which didn't mean anything.

"And the identification was positive?" Ivy leaned forward as if she could will the truth out of the detective.

"I know you need to work through your grief." Rodriguez crossed her beefy arms. "But I don't have time for it today. Your friend died by suicide. That's it. No special circumstances to warrant an investigation."

"Shelby was a human being, the same as everyone else." Ivy's voice rose.

"Really?" Rodriguez cocked her head. "Because I get the feeling she was more special than everyone else."

"Everyone should be special," Ivy said. "Of course."

"They're not though, are they?" Rodriguez gave her a flat stare. "I've had a rash of homeless deaths in the past few months. No one called about them. No one talked to the mayor. No one even claimed most of the bodies."

"My problem is my friend," Ivy said. "Shelby Linton. And you haven't told me anything about her."

"Look." A muscle twitched under the detective's eye. "I can't tell you anything more because you're not a family member. If you want to know more, get a family member to come in and ask."

She couldn't see Mr. Linton coming in here to ask for anything. "Wouldn't you want to know, if it was your friend?"

"Sure, I would. And I'd find out through regular channels." Rodriguez walked her toward the exit. "Sorry again for your loss."

And on that insincere note, she opened the door to the waiting room and pushed Ivy through it. A battered guy cradling his arm like it was broken gave her a sympathetic look.

Out on the sidewalk, Ivy didn't know what to do next. She wasn't going to get any more information until Mr. Linton told her, or authorized Tristan to tell her. She hoped for the latter as she'd rather hear the grim details from Tristan than from Shelby's father.

A few steps from the door, she stopped and examined her surroundings. Nobody stuck out, so either nobody was tailing her, or they were good enough at it that she couldn't spot them. Which was probably about anyone, realistically. But at least no black SUV.

What was her next step? She had hours before her Kepler's event and she didn't want to go back and wait in Shelby's apartment. Out of ideas, she decided to do the job she'd almost been hired for: go to the shelter, interview those using the service, and write up a piece about Shelby and all the good she'd done. She could post it on the memorial website. And, remembering Detective Rodriguez's comments, she'd tell their story too. Shelby wasn't the only one with a story to tell.

A quick Google later, she'd found Margie's Second Chances. It was close, and she decided to walk. Being outside in the sunshine would help with her jetlag. Or something.

But the walk didn't help her at all. First, the streets were full of humans in various states of misery and, as the detective pointed out, they lived and died unremarked. Had there been this many homeless people when she left the United States after college? She didn't think so, but maybe she'd been used to it back then. Now, compared to what she was used to in Europe, it was overwhelming.

All around them expensive cars drove by—sportscars, limos, and shiny SUVs. The sidewalks also held people in suits and studied business casual that was equally expensive to pull off. They gave off a vibe of wealth and indifference. The city was full of people with money, shiny and clean.

All around the wealthy and the tech workers were people who had no place to sleep, to shower, or to eat. She passed twenty in a few blocks. More on every block. And she was the only one who seemed to see them. Everyone else avoided eye contact, stepped out of their way, and paid them no more mind than if they were trees or bus benches.

By the time she reached the shelter, she was chilled from the cold wind and conceded Rodriguez her point. Her streets overflowed with people who would never get the kind of attention Shelby got every day. Even Ivy the orphan had people who'd take her in if she lost her home and who would miss her if she died. These people on the streets were on their own.

No one was going to spend time verifying their cause of death, insisting on a quick burial, and questioning everyone involved. No service, no fancy crypt, no expensive risk assessment team going over all the details. Just gone.

Margie's Second Chances was housed in a building in the exact shade of hopeless gray as the cleaner parts of the sidewalks. After all the grays in

Shelby's apartment, Ivy felt like a connoisseur. Margie seemed to know it was bleak, as she'd hung a bright purple awning above each window. A line of people exited a purple front door. Some carried paper plates filled with meat, potatoes, and corn. They wrapped ragged coats around themselves and wandered off down the sidewalk.

Ivy must have missed lunch. She waited for things to slow down, then went inside. Rows of long tables were empty and a food serving counter in the back looked empty too. The smell of beef stew and freshly baked biscuits made her stomach rumble.

A plump woman with short brown hair wearing glasses with clear frames bustled up. "Are you here for lunch? You missed the sitdown, but we can fix you up a plate."

Ivy warmed. "I'm looking for Margie Stich."

"You found her, first try." Margie shook her hand. Margie's hand was warm and damp. "I have dishes to load. Talk while I work?"

"Sure." Ivy followed her past tables being wiped down by a couple of teenagers in dark beanies.

Back in the kitchen, Margie sprayed white bowls with a wand and stacked them into an industrial dishwasher. Her movements were quick, efficient, and practiced.

"How about I rinse and you load?" Ivy was sure Margie had a system for loading that she might not understand, but spraying water on a bowl seemed just her speed.

"Do you need an apron?" Margie pointed down at her own purple apron. "I have extras."

169

Ivy looked at her jeans. "Nope."

She rinsed a bowl and handed it to Margie. Margie placed the dish on a kind of Tetris-stack. Ivy was glad she was rinsing.

"I'm a friend of Shelby Linton, from Nyssa." Ivy handed her another bowl.

Margie took it and patted her arm. "I'm so sorry about your friend."

"Thank you." Ivy rinsed a couple bowls to get her composure back, glad to be doing something useful. "What kind of work did she do here?"

"All sorts. She was more hands-on than most of our supporters. Most give money, and we do sorely need it. But Shelby gave money and got to know people. She'd cook and clean on Thursdays."

"Really?" That didn't sound like Shelby. Ivy had never seen Shelby voluntarily cook or clean.

"She had a group of folks she mentored after dinner that day. She tutored some and helped them to fill out job applications. She even pressured her friends to hire them on and hired a few for odd jobs herself."

"Really?" Ivy hated to repeat herself, but this didn't feel like Shelby either.

"Of course she did. How did you say you knew her?"

"College roommate." It seemed like a million years ago now.

"Ivy Corva?" Margie asked.

"She talked about me?"

"She was so proud about your book coming out. Said you'd worked so hard."

Ivy dropped her bowl and it clattered into the sink. Margie patted her arm again. Ivy thanked her and got back to work.

After that, they fell into a good working rhythm and the dishes moved quickly between them. While they worked, Ivy interviewed Margie for background information on the shelter, on its program with Nyssa, and general information.

"Have many of your clients died recently?" asked Ivy when they finished the dishes.

Margie dried her hands on her apron. "Even one is too many."

"But more than usual?"

"What have you heard?" Margie asked.

That wasn't the response she'd been expecting. "I talked to a police detective this morning and she mentioned a rash of deaths in the population of homeless people."

"It's hard on people, living on the street. And lately fentanyl is making the rounds." Margie sighed. "It's tough to get out in front of that."

"So, more people than usual have been dying?" Ivy felt guilty that no one else seemed to care. Margie was doing a lot.

"It goes in waves sometimes," Margie said. "But this is a wave."

"All overdoses?" Ivy asked.

"I don't really know," Margie said. "Sometimes they disappear and you never know. But your friend Shelby was looking into that, too."

"She was?" Ivy asked.

"She cared about them," Margie said. "And she wanted to know what happened to them. I think she was going to have Nyssa follow up on deaths for a study to show how vulnerable the population really is to bring attention to it. But then she died before she could."

That would make a good story—Shelby cared about people who had lost their homes.

"I have administrative work I have to do now," Margie said. "But come back any time."

Ivy wrote her new phone number on a flyer and gave it to Margie. "If you do remember anything more about Shelby, can you call me?"

Margie folded the flyer carefully and put it in her apron pocket and then she waved to a man standing outside the front door smoking. "There's Jacko!"

Ivy recognized him from the funeral. The rough-looking man with the giant hands.

"He worked with Shelby," Margie said. "Why don't you scoot and ask him about it? Don't let him hurt your feelings. He's sharp since Pat passed, but he means well."

"Pat?"

"His girlfriend," Margie said. "Pretty blonde. He has a thing for blondes."

Ivy remembered the blonde at the funeral. "How did Pat die?"

"Don't know. She stopped showing up. I asked around and someone said she OD'd. That gets a lot of them. It's why programs like Shelby's are important. Preparing people for a job and giving them hope for the future. It's so important.

Anyway, Shelby's detective probably talked to him about Pat's death."

Ivy dried her hands and hurried to the front door, but by the time she got there, Jacko was gone. A smoldering cigarette butt rested on the sidewalk where he'd stood.

Already composing the story, Ivy walked back to Shelby's apartment. She looked for Jacko along the way, but didn't see him.

Once inside her gray cocoon, she managed to write up a decent piece about Margie and her work and peppered in good quotes too. She was glad to have something to add to the memorial website. Shelby had helped people when there was no profit in it. She had been a good person, too. Despite what the press and Wendy said, Shelby had cared about the greater good.

And then Ivy tried to work on her next book. But every time she tried to type, the screen morphed into hateful tweets and pictures of herself being tortured. She knew she was letting them in her head. She knew better. But it didn't make the words come.

CHAPTER THIRTEEN

Eventually, she gave into her rising sense of dread as the time to speak at Kepler's approached. She imagined trolls attacking her with plungers, bats, and guns. She didn't have to work too hard at it either, because they'd kindly posted pictures of themselves doing those things. They'd photoshopped her head onto crime scene victims and porn stars. Even though she hadn't checked Twitter or her email since this morning, yesterday's images were stuck in her head and they popped up whenever she let her guard down.

She dressed in the blazer and jeans combo she'd worn to Nyssa the day they were raided. Anu had declared the outfit fine for a reading. She imagined Shelby would have disapproved of the informality and tried to loan her something fancy. It would have been a familiar conversation.

But it looked like Shelby had given up on trendy fashion. In recent online pictures she usually wore the same thing: a long white tailored blazer that hinted at a lab coat, loose white pants, and silk shirts in all the colors of blood—burgundy and crimson for mammals, purple for some marine animals, green for certain worms, and bright blue for horseshoe crabs. Shelby had explained the reasons for her color palette to Ivy in a long-ago conversation.

In some pictures, Shelby wore jellyfish earrings, and Ivy remembered when she'd bought them.

Midterms had been brutal and Ivy was lying on her bed staring at the ceiling and regretting her life choices when Shelby bounced in. Midterms never bothered her. She sailed right through them. Of course, she didn't have to worry because her financial aid wasn't linked to her grades. Which meant that her whole future wasn't linked to her grades.

"Get up!" Shelby yelled like a football coach.

Ivy flipped her off and closed her eyes. She wanted to be miserable in peace.

"Do you know what today is?" Shelby asked.

"My first day of intellectual freedom in weeks."

"It's the first day of the new jellyfish exhibit at the aquarium."

"It's like you're on acid," Ivy said. "And spouting random words at me. Is my face melting?"

"Listen up, Poi. This will do you good."

When Shelby was in football coach mode, it was easier to go along than to argue with the perkiness. But the problem was that this aquarium thing probably cost money Ivy didn't have. Her diet was down to one meal a day at the dining hall and one packet of oatmeal. Her budget was tapped out.

"I hate jellyfish," Ivy lied. "They float around like plastic trash bags and sting you if you touch them."

175

"Floating around like ocean blimps," Shelby corrected. "And they'll never sting you. They'll sense your innate hostility and keep their distance."

"Nature is wise," Ivy said. "Be more like nature."

"Come on!" Shelby grabbed Ivy's hand and hauled her into a sitting position. "My dad's a member and I have free tickets and I don't have anyone to go with because it's kind of for kids but also cool."

Ivy opened her eyes. Free tickets sounded promising. "Do we have to take a bus?"

"One bus and I already have two tickets. Get up! I haven't seen you anywhere but in this bed or in a study carrel for days."

"Study carrels have walls. They're very freeing." But Ivy was already standing up and getting her jacket and shoes.

Shelby pulled out the tickets and handed her one. "It has a jellyfish printed on it."

"I recognize that."

They headed down the elevator and across the quad. Shelby led and chattered away about fall break, when she was going home to California and Ivy was staying on campus and getting some extra hours of work in to pay for her fall textbooks. Shelby was going to San Francisco first and then she and her father were flying to Tokyo, which didn't even seem like a real place to Ivy. She'd never even left the state of Pennsylvania, except once to go to Ohio to pick up alcohol and fireworks.

Shelby presented their tickets and they jogged past the other animals to go straight to the aquarium. Shelby dragged her past fish and penguins until they entered the darkened world of the jellies.

"Wow," Ivy said without thinking. Giant glass tanks formed pillars in the dark room, each illuminated a different color. Jellyfish swirled in blues, lavenders, and pinks. One entire wall was given over to a single tank. Ivy stood next to it and imagined herself inside, rising and falling and at peace. It was the most beautiful thing she had ever seen.

"They're like stars," Shelby said.

"Forming endless constellations," Ivy agreed.

Shelby laughed and took her hand and tugged her deeper into the room. "There's supposed to be a tunnel."

Ivy let herself be pulled forward. Together, they stopped inside a thick plastic tunnel. Clear water surrounded them and it was full of round jellyfish drifting in an invisible current. Blue light fell upon their faces and it felt like they'd entered another world.

"They're moon jellies," Shelby said. "Not really stars."

Ivy's eyes slid from jellyfish to jellyfish. Her heart rate slowed. Her breathing slowed. She'd never felt so calm. Shelby drifted off, finding new jellyfish to name and count, but Ivy stayed in the same place, slowly turning. She tracked a smaller jellyfish as it rose toward the top of the tank, accompanied by two others. At a signal she didn't understand, the jellies stopped swimming and let the current pull them over the top of her tunnel and down the other side. She placed her palm against the curved plastic and watched them glide through her fingers.

"I knew you'd like it." Shelby was back. "I found something really special. Come on."

Ivy glanced dreamily up at the jellyfish surrounding her. "Better than this?"

"Much." Shelby hurried through the tunnel, then turned and beckoned to Ivy.

"I'll be back," Ivy told the moon jellies and then followed her friend.

Shelby stopped in front of a smallish tank with circles embedded on the sides. Inside the tank floated jellyfish smaller than a grain of rice.

"See?" Shelby asked.

"It looks like a snow globe." Ivy got closer and put her eye to one of the circles. It was a built-in magnifying glass and when a tiny jellyfish swam in front of it, it trailed tiny white threads from a translucent bell. A red blob was in its middle. "Not as cool as the moon jellyfish."

"Wrong!" Shelby said. "These are Turritopsis dohrnii. They're immortal."

"Like vampires?"

"Like for real. What we're looking at here are the full grown medusae. They swim around and eat and reproduce, but if they're injured or starving or otherwise stressed out they can transform back into polyps and then grow back up into medusae. Over and over, maybe forever."

Shelby watched a tiny jellyfish swimming across the magnifier, rapt. "Imagine if we could figure out how to do that for humans? Our lifespan is about eighty years, given our birthdate, and most

178

of it will be healthy if we're lucky. Imagine if we could go back to earlier physical stages when we were hurt? We could let our own bodies heal us and then start again."

"Imagine how much we could overpopulate," Ivy said.

"So, we move around like jellyfish. Live a few years on Earth, a few on the moon, a few on Mars, a few who knows? But if we could gather knowledge and participate in society for all that time, everything would change."

"Imagine all the time spent working minimum wage jobs," Ivy said.

Shelby laughed and the jellyfish swirled around in their globe. "Even so, that's what I want to do with my life. I want to give everyone more time to be with their family, to pursue their interests, to travel the world."

"Big dreams." Ivy never gave herself permission to dream like that. She hoped for a time when she didn't worry constantly about money. When she could buy food, see a doctor, maybe buy a new pair of shoes. Her dreams suddenly felt small.

"Why not dream big? We're young and tough and smart and we can do things that were unimaginable for our parents' generation."

"Maybe."

"Maybe nothing. What's your big dream?"

"Get through life OK, without worrying about money."

Shelby's face fell. "But suppose you never had to worry about money again. What would your dream be then?"

"To sit around and read all the time. Write books that make people think."

"Dream about that, Poi."

And then Shelby went back to staring at the Turritopsis dohrnii and Ivy returned to the tunnel to watch the moons rise and fall. And think about dreams.

On the way out Shelby had purchased tiny jellyfish earrings and worn them every day until graduation.

Ivy smiled at the memory. Shelby had started her off on her road as an author. And, no matter how difficult it was dealing with the trolls, she had made people think. Sure, some were thinking of creative ways to send her pictures of their dicks, but others were thinking about how powerful and important women were. About the possibilities of travel to the stars. About human footprints on other planets.

She was ready to go to the event when Tristan rang her bell. Even though she knew him now, he held up his badge to her surveillance camera, then stepped back so she could get a good look at him. Probably a habit to keep his customers feeling reassured.

"Hello, Ms. Corva," he said after she opened the door. "Are you ready to go?"

She wasn't, really, but she came out anyway, with her battered ARC tucked under her arm. "Did anything weird come up today in my emails? Or on Twitter? Or at the event?"

"I've worked with Kepler's and the event is well planned. I'm not expecting any trouble." He walked ahead of her to the elevators. He had a brisk walk and she hurried to keep up.

"That answers the third question," she said.

The elevator arrived and he paused a second before he stepped in, eyes flicking from side to side. His situational awareness reminded her that her own was inadequate.

Once inside, he said, "Twitter is calming back down. About 20% fewer tweets than yesterday, so it's on a good curve. You're getting lots of positive responses in there, too. I've reached out to your publisher and told them not to pile on defending you and that should help."

"I like being defended." She looked up at him. Still devastatingly handsome and still not listening.

"It's all fuel to the fire," he said. "The goal is to choke out the fire and wait for them to move on to their next target. The more we engage, the more they respond."

She didn't have an answer that didn't make her sound like a petulant child. "And the emails?"

"Reducing too. I forwarded a few positive ones back to you, in case you'd like to answer those. The review blogs are almost uniformly positive."

"Almost?"

He smiled. "Sounds like you're getting greedy."

"Anything else?"

"There is one account that concerns me: @allspermmatters. He's made specific threats. He knows you're in California, and he's fixated on you."

Her stomach gave a little twinge of panic. "Do you know who he is? Or what he looks like?"

"I don't. We're working on that."

"Is it safe to go to the event?" she asked.

"There are no guarantees."

"That doesn't sound reassuring."

"My job is to keep you safe. Not to reassure you. But it's also to help you continue your normal life." Tristan gave her a smile that looked textbook reassuring, which Ivy thought was in direct contradiction to his words. "In my judgment, you can safely attend the reading, but we need to stay alert."

"So, that's a long way to say 'yes'?" she asked.

"Technically, I said a lot of other important things." Tristan smiled. "But also yes."

The elevator opened to the parking garage, but not the good level with the fancy cars, the ordinary level with regular cars. Ivy found that reassuring.

"I'm going to ask Mr. Linton for permission to view the video and the files about Shelby's death," she said as they walked a few steps to a blue sedan.

"OK," Tristan said, opening the door for her.

She waited until he got in on his side before getting in. "Has he seen them?"

"I made him a high level report." Tristan buckled up. "He didn't want to see the photos or the autopsy report."

"I do," she said, although she really didn't. But she had to. She had to see it to believe it.

"As soon as he gives me clearance, I'll show you what we have."

Tristan pulled out of the garage and the gate arm came down behind them. He was a good driver, safe and competent. All part of the bodyguard personae. They got onto a freeway and drove between rolling golden hills dotted with trees.

"It's prettier here," she said, thinking of the smell of downtown San Francisco and the amount of human misery she walked through every time she left Shelby's apartment.

"In the rainy season those hills are green like Ireland."

"Shelby and I were going to do a biking tour of Ireland after we graduated." Shelby's treat, of course, since Ivy could never have afforded it.

"But?" Tristan asked.

"Stanford had a job for her." Ivy had hung around Pittsburgh, met a cute Estonian guy and ended up following him home. She'd never been to Ireland, even though it was a pretty cheap flight from Tallinn. But she still had a chance to go, unlike Shelby.

Tristan exited the freeway and they drove through bland city streets adorned with Christmas decorations. All the buildings were short and boring and modern, completely unlike Tallinn and San Francisco. A lot of suburbs all laid out in a line. She wondered why they didn't build tall apartment buildings here. They clearly had people who needed homes.

"Did Shelby ever hire you to look into deaths of homeless people?" she asked.

"I'm not qualified to do that kind of investigation."

"Not a no," she noted.

"She didn't ask me," he clarified. "No."

"Do you know if she hired anyone else?"

"It seems like an odd thing for her to do."

"It's because she knew them from her work with Margie's Second Chances."

"I see," he said with a tone that seemed to indicate he didn't see at all.

Before she could figure out how to respond, they pulled into an underground garage and walked out to Kepler's. Noise and laughter rang from the cafe next door. People on metal chairs drank frothy drinks. It looked jovial and peaceful, like a place she would have sat the summer before. But now she eyed the patrons nervously. Were any of them there for her reading? For her?

She studied her book in the window. Several copies were arranged around a review quote '...controversial and brilliant...'

"I never read that," she said.

"It came out yesterday in the San Francisco Chronicle," he said. "It's a great review."

"You read it?"

"I subscribe to the Chron," he said.

She stuffed down resentment that he'd known before she did. Staying off the internet meant missing good things like this. But she was also missing pictures of people torturing her. Wouldn't it be grand to get the good stuff without the bad?

The door opened and a woman with light brown hair pulled up into a messy bun bustled out. She wore jeans and a brown turtleneck. "Ivy Corva. I'm Haven. We just love your book here!"

"I—thank you," Ivy said.

"We have a good crowd here tonight. And I have stock for you to sign after." She looked up at Tristan. "Provided that's OK with your risk expert."

"It's OK with me," Ivy put in before he could say anything. He wasn't in charge of her.

"Great!" Haven opened the door. "Come on in!"

Ivy entered and walked past a giant shrine to her book—copies artfully displayed on a table by the door. The scents of books and pine and cinnamon lingered. Pine boughs decorated one wall and red and green posters advertised various books. Festive.

"Everyone's ready for you," Haven said.

Ivy avoided looking at her phone to check the time. She didn't think they were late, but maybe Tristan had timed it that way.

Haven hurried to a podium at the back of the store and Ivy followed. About fifty people sat in folding chairs facing it, including Olivia. She nodded to Ivy and Ivy gave her a quick wave. One friendly face anyway.

Tristan stationed himself next to the wall near the front, half-facing the audience. His eyes ranged over everyone and his hands were loose at his sides. He looked like he was on guard to protect her against a rogue plunger attacker. She did appreciate that.

Earlier in the day, she'd changed the part she wanted to read, choosing a passage about the trip and the goals and the frozen women and the rows of tubes of sperm. It seemed like a good idea to face the controversy head on, and also a chance for the audience to hear the controversial parts, instead of reacting to an interpretation of them on the internet.

Haven launched into an introduction even more flattering than Rita's a few days before. She had quite a few more quotes and she read the entire review from the San Francisco Chronicle to the audience. Ivy didn't think her editor had liked the book as much as this reviewer and those kind words lent her strength.

When Haven finished, she gestured toward the podium and Ivy walked over amid a comforting round of applause. If someone hated her here, at least they were keeping quiet so far.

She thanked Haven and the audience and talked about the book for a few minutes. Then she said, "I'm going to read to you now. You might have heard about some controversy associated with this book." She tried for a wry smile.

The audience laughed.

"I'm going to read the section that's got everyone so fired up so you can make up your own mind." Afraid to see their responses, she kept her eyes glued to the page while she read. This wasn't comfortable and easy like the Tallinn reading. But she wasn't backing down. This passage had gotten her into trouble. She'd chosen to read it so they would know exactly what it said and could make up their own minds. When she closed the book and looked out at the audience, she heard only applause. Her stomach unclenched.

She fielded a few questions about where her ideas came from and whether there would be a sequel and then a man in the back raised his hand. Tristan shifted slightly and her heart sped up. She wasn't sure why.

"Yes?" she said.

"Is it true you think men are worthless sperm receptacles?" He glared at her and pushed his glasses up on his nose. He wasn't so big. She could take him if he wasn't armed with a knife or a plunger. Olivia craned her head to see him, and Tristan was already moving.

"This event is about Lessons from the Curie," Ivy said. "Do you have any questions about the book?"

"So, you're refusing to answer?" He laughed snidely and the audience shifted in their seats. Ivy hoped it was an uncomfortable and sympathetic shifting and not one that showed agreement.

"I've never said anything derogatory about men," she said. "I pointed out basic biology. How you feel about that isn't my problem."

Tristan stopped next to the man and gave Ivy a disapproving look. So, apparently that wasn't the response he'd hoped for. Tristan turned back to the man and said something in a low voice. Ivy wasn't sure what he'd said, but the guy argued and waved his arms. That sure didn't look like the kind of de-escalation stuff Tristan talked about either. Still, she was glad he was here.

Then she saw a flash of silver and the man was on the ground with Tristan's knee in his back. Ivy flinched back and caught herself.

"It's OK," Tristan called out.

A knife sat on the floor not far from his knee. Her mouth went dry.

Tristan dragged the man to his feet and walked him out of the building. She watched him frisk the man through the window.

Haven looked at Ivy like she ought to know what to do.

"As you can see," Ivy said into the microphone. "The controversial nature of the book hasn't been exaggerated."

A scattered wave of chuckles encouraged Haven and she asked Ivy about faster than light travel and Ivy was ready with a long answer. She kept talking about it until her heart slowed. Someone asked her for her favorite authors and she gushed about Becky Chambers and Connie Willis and Naomi Novik and Martha Wells. She had tons more, but she stopped there. She could talk about books all day.

Outside, a police car pulled up in front of the bookstore and they loaded the man in the back and drove away. Tristan came back inside, straightening his tie. He looked much more put together than Ivy felt.

A woman in a tweed jacket with her hair pulled back in a ponytail asked, "Are you involved with Nyssa?"

"No," Ivy answered. "Let's talk about the book."

The woman persisted. "So you're not friends with disgraced CEO Shelby Linton?"

"We were college roommates," Ivy said. "Now back off."

Tristan shot her a placating glance that begged for de-escalating strategies. She felt sympathy for him. He probably didn't want to take down someone else again so quickly. She wasn't going to change, but she could see how it made his life harder too.

"What do you know about Nyssa's criminal financial fraud?" the woman asked.

"Not a damn thing." Ivy yanked out the microphone and stepped from behind the podium. "And you don't either. You're all ready to tear her to pieces, but you didn't know her. She was a brilliant woman and she wanted to change the world."

"Or did she want to abscond with investor money?" the reporter asked.

"So you think she absconded with it right off the Golden Gate Bridge?" Ivy'd had enough.

Tristan shook his head like a disappointed parent. OK, that had been over a line.

Haven hurried forward. "Let's form a single line along the wall and get those books signed!"

Tristan came over to stand next to the signing table.

"Thanks," she said.

He nodded and kept scanning the crowd like he expected someone else to pop out. That didn't make her feel calmer.

She sat at the table, wiped her sweaty hands on her jeans, and got ready to do her job. Haven shooed people into a line running along the wall and handed Ivy a Sharpie pen. It felt weird to be asked to sign books for strangers.

Olivia was first in line. Ivy smiled at her and wrote The future is female. Reach for the stars! and signed her name. "Thanks for coming."

"I enjoyed the reading," Olivia said. "And I'm glad to have my own copy of the book."

"Thanks."

"Do you need a ticket back to Tallinn yet?" Olivia asked. "Just let me know."

"I'll email you when I'm ready," Ivy said. "I really need to get through this line."

In the next book, Ivy wrote Raise your voice! Don't let them silence you. The woman looked pleased. Tristan must have been reading over her shoulder, because he sighed. She ignored him. She was the author and she was going to sign these books however she wanted.

Then the reporter got to the front of the line. She had not, Ivy noticed, purchased a book.

"You were seen leaving Nyssa on the morning it was raided," the reporter said.

"This is the signing line. Do you have a book for me to sign?" Ivy asked.

"If you step aside, Ms. Corva will talk to you after the signing," Tristan said.

No, she won't, Ivy said silently. But putting off the reporter seemed like a good strategy, so she nodded. She could fight this battle later. The reporter stepped out of line, but she didn't move too far. After putting the other guy on the floor, Tristan clearly had some credibility here.

A man approached the table. "Can you sign it Stay out of my #exowomb?"

Ivy gave him a long look. He had his hair up in a man bun, pants that looked like they were made out of hemp, and a faded blue t-shirt. He didn't look like a right-wing internet troll.

"Happy to," she said.

The rest of the signing went quickly as she chatted and signed and posed for pictures. This was the author life she'd dreamed about. Signing books for readers who wanted them, ones who were friendly and kind. At least in this room, right now.

A few feet away, the reporter checked the wall clock obsessively. Presumably, she had a deadline and this wasn't her dream reporter life. Tough. Ivy slowed down to put off their encounter, but eventually she ran out of readers.

"OK," the reporter said when no one was left in line. "My turn."

"I have stock for you to sign," said Haven. "I'll bring it right out."

And off she went, abandoning Ivy to the reporter. Tristan stayed put and didn't relax his posture at all. Ivy was starting to like him.

"Were you aware of financial fraud at Nyssa?" the reporter asked.

"Of course not," Ivy said.

"Why not?"

Ivy ticked the reasons off on her fingers. "I live thousands of miles away. I don't work in biotech. I

191

didn't review Nyssa's balance sheets. I'm not a criminal fraud investigator. Do you know what your newspaper's accounting department is doing right now?"

The reporter pursed her lips.

Haven hurried back with about a hundred books on a cart. Ivy had never seen so many copies of a single book in one place in her entire life.

"Are these already sold?" she asked.

"You bet!" Haven beamed. "You're our book club selection for this month."

"Wow." Ivy smiled at her. "Thanks."

"Our pleasure," Haven said.

"What about your relationship with Shelby Linton?" The reporter must have been feeling neglected.

Ivy picked up a book. "I've got to get back to work."

The manager opened and flapped each book and Ivy signed her name. In spite of all the drama around the book and Shelby, this part was really cool. Even if she did get canceled, these paper books would still exist in the world, sitting on bookshelves and in libraries. Some of them were sure to get read. That might be enough.

"You have to give me something," the reporter said as Ivy finished the last one.

"Do I?" Ivy stood and thanked Haven.

Tristan positioned himself between her and the reporter and edged her toward the door.

"You must have known something," the reporter said.

"Why?" Ivy asked. "Because you need a quote? Do you know the accounting regularities and irregularities of your college roommate? How would you feel if she were being publicly humiliated like Shelby is right now?"

"My roommate was studying to be a zookeeper."

Ivy stopped, looked her up and down and said, "I'm not surprised."

CHAPTER FOURTEEN

Ivy woke early the next morning. Time change, jetlag, whatever. She was tired of being up so damn early all the time, but she wasn't going back to sleep, so she brewed coffee and found a packet of oatmeal in the back of a cupboard. Probably expired, but did oatmeal really go bad?

She decided not and added hot water. It smelled fine, and it tasted like cardboard and sugar, which she was pretty sure was how it was supposed to taste. She took another bite, since it had the added attraction of being the only breakfast food in the apartment since she'd finished the bread yesterday. She ate her oatmeal standing up and staring out the window at the fog. Everything was so socked in that she could barely see the building across the street.

Changing up her usual routine, she didn't check her email or Twitter or any of her portals. She was going to try to shift her focus away from the internet to the real world. Tristan had filed a restraining order against the guy from the reading. She tried not to think about what he might have done if Tristan hadn't been there. That wasn't going to lead anywhere good. Tristan wasn't sure if he was @allspermmatters, so maybe that guy was out there still too.

What should she do next to help Shelby and take her mind off things?

She'd said goodbye to Shelby on the bridge. She'd filled out the memorial website with articles and her own stories. She'd survived her reading. She should go back to Estonia and get back to her regular life. Based on the reactions of her editor, regular life was going to include working on more museum exhibits, editing, and maybe a little technical writing the same as it always had.

Her book wasn't going to rise up and become the kind of runaway bestseller that would let her quit her day job. It might not even do well enough for her to publish the second one. Even so, after a few days in Shelby's world, getting back to her own boring life seemed like a great idea.

But what about the pieces that didn't fit? Was it a coincidence that Shelby had jumped from the only spot on the bridge with no video coverage? Had she really called Timothy to come pick her up? Had she wanted him to see her jump, for whatever reason?

She didn't have the answers she needed. She googled timothy shah. He'd been denied bail. The pundits said he'd be in there a long time. That's where Shelby would have been, if she hadn't jumped. She had to have known that too. Was she afraid to face it? Ashamed? Ivy didn't know enough.

Maybe Tristan had more answers. She sent a text to Mr. Linton.

Ivy here. Could you give Tristan permission for me to see his reports about the investigation? I want to know more about what happened

He responded immediately. Why?

She answered. It might help me to accept things and move on

He texted back. OK. Take care of yourself.

She answered with You too

After a few seconds of deliberation, she added a heart emoji.

A full minute later Mr. Linton sent back a heart emoji himself.

She wondered if he'd been sitting there staring at his phone deciding whether to send it or if he'd gotten distracted for a minute or if he'd decided not to send it and then felt guilty and sent it after all. Which was a ridiculous amount of thought to give to a single emoji.

Mercifully, she was out of oatmeal. She rinsed the bowl and put it in the dishwasher next to Shelby's last day dishes and the few she'd used since she arrived. Their dishes sat together, lonely in the dishwasher. The last thing they had in common.

The doorbell jerked her out of her reverie. She went over and checked. Tristan. She'd texted Mr. Linton like five minutes ago. Tristan must live right around the corner. Or maybe he had a secret bodyguard teleportation device.

Even though she wore only a robe and her hair looked terrible and she smelled like coffee and oatmeal, she dragged the chair away from the door and pulled back the chain to let him in. It wasn't the best alarm system, but better than nothing.

"Good morning," he said. He wore his regular suit and shirt and both looked immaculately pressed. Did he ever sleep? Maybe he slept standing up in a closet so he didn't get rumpled.

"Thanks again for last night," she said.

"Just doing my job."

"And I appreciate that," she said. "Do you know if he was @allspermmatters?"

"I believe so, but we're double checking."

"Is he still in jail?"

"Yes." He lifted his laptop bag. "Are you sure you want to see this?"

"Don't want to. Have to."

He went into the living room, sat on the couch, and plugged in his laptop. He seemed pretty comfortable here. Had Shelby had him over often?

"Would you like coffee?" she asked.

"Had some already, thanks." His laptop bonged when he started it up. "You're authorized to see these files, but not to keep them, print them, or forward them to anyone."

"Do you need me to sign something? Maybe in blood?"

"I think it'll be enough if I keep an eye on you," he said with his eyes on the screen. She couldn't tell if he was joking or not.

He pulled up a file and held out the laptop. "This has the summary."

She took it and sat on the couch to read. As promised, Tristan stayed close by, watching her every move. Apparently this trust thing didn't go both ways.

Looking at the dates, Mr. Linton had ordered an investigation as soon as he heard Shelby had jumped, before he'd even gone to identify the body. She guessed he didn't have a lot of faith in the police. Or maybe he always used his own people for everything. If Tristan was any indication, they were pretty competent.

His team had tracked Shelby's whereabouts on that last evening—work, home, out for a jog and then the bridge. Somehow, they'd gotten her cellphone data. All the phone data was marked on a city map in 1-minute intervals. Clear, easy to see.

The pings showed how her little phone ran slowly from her house, across the city and ended up at the Golden Gate Bridge. It stopped a few times, but never for long, like she was out of breath and taking a break. Ivy imagined Shelby, in her white tracksuit. How she'd stopped to rest, maybe sat on a bench for a few minutes before running again. Did she know even then what she was running toward?

"Is it legal to have this data?" Ivy pointed at the cellphone information.

"It's a gray area," Tristan answered, which meant no. He rubbed the dimple in his chin like he knew that.

Ivy went back to the report. Shelby walked out onto the span, which they'd verified with surveillance footage from the cameras that did work. She walked along steadily, close to the orange railing. Ivy imagined the dark ocean far below, cars driving by on the other side, and the well-lit concrete span in front of her.

Then she stepped out of view of the last surveillance camera and into that dark spot with the broken camera. While she stood in that spot where no one could see, only her phone records told the story. They showed that she'd called Timothy and they'd spoken for one minute and seven seconds. Not long for her last phone call to anyone ever. Had she known then that she intended to jump? Was she calling to say goodbye? If so, she should have tried Ivy's number or her father's. She hadn't seemed that close to Timothy, or at least not from what she'd told Ivy. But Olivia had said that they were involved.

No more pings after that last call ended. Maybe she turned her phone off because she didn't want another call. Or she threw it off the bridge, slotting it between the chain link fence and dropping it into the water, too far away to hear the splash when it landed. Or maybe she jumped with it in her pocket and carried it down to the ocean with her.

The next page of the report showed Timothy's data. His phone took Shelby's last call and they talked. After he hung up, he and the phone went from Nyssa's office straight to the bridge. Faster than Shelby had walked, stopping where Ivy assumed traffic lights must stand. Eventually, it went on the bridge, then stopped near that blackout spot. Shortly after, it called 911. Like everyone said.

"How'd you get the surveillance footage from the bridge?" she asked.

"Mr. Linton has a friend." Tristan touched his chin again, his tell for when he was uncomfortable about something. A man with a conscience. So, Mr. Linton had probably pulled strings or bribed someone to the data.

"Did you get surveillance footage for her walk to the bridge?" she asked.

"I'm still trying," he said. "It involves talking to individual businesses and trying to get their footage. Most erase it pretty frequently."

"Can I see the video footage of her walking onto the bridge?" She kept her voice even and casual, like the thought of watching Shelby walk to her death didn't terrify her.

"I don't think this is going to help you feel better," he said.

"Mr. Linton said I have access," she reminded him, hating that she argued for something she didn't even really want to do. But she had to.

He moved to another tab and pulled up a video file. Taken from a high location on the bridge, the black and white footage showed a woman dressed in a white tracksuit with a stripe on the pants who walked from darkness into the brighter pools of light cast by the streetlamps. Car headlights brightened the scene as they passed. She walked quickly and steadily, like Shelby did when she was on a mission.

"That could be anyone." Ivy pointed out. Even as one of Shelby's oldest friends, she couldn't be sure this was her friend.

"But it isn't just anyone. It matches the cellphone data perfectly," he said.

Her stomach clenched and she took a few steadying breaths. "I want to see the autopsy results."

He moved to another file and opened it up.

She read the report at the beginning. "Malnourished?"

"I know it sounds odd." He hesitated. "But she had recently lost weight and she may have been using drugs. The toxicology results aren't back yet."

Ivy remembered Stephen telling her that Shelby had lost weight. Of all the people around her, he seemed like the only one who had noticed. "What kind of drugs?"

"Meth is the suspicion. But, as I said, this is unverified." He looked sad, so she suspected he thought it was true.

"Shelby never used drugs!" She caught herself. "Maybe Adderall in college."

"Adderall?" he asked.

She shivered, cold in this gray room with the blood pictures on the walls. "Lots of Adderall."

"It can be a gateway drug to meth," he said. "I'm so sorry, Ivy."

She hated to think of Shelby buying meth, doing meth, losing weight because of it. If so, Shelby had been changing for longer than she'd thought. She hadn't been there for Shelby for a long time.

"We can stop now," he said. "Nothing in there will make this easier for you."

Ivy clenched her jaw and went back to reading about the weight of each of Shelby's organs, which didn't tell her anything, except that her pancreas was inflamed. And then came the pictures.

Shelby's head had struck the pylon and it looked like a horror movie, not her friend. Ivy's stomach heaved and she closed her eyes. Tristan touched her arm, but she shook off his hand and opened her eyes again. She looked at each picture, pausing at the picture of the tattoo, a defiant reminder of what she had sought to accomplish. Ivy traced the chemical structure with one finger, slipping through each hexagon and pentagon. She hoped that someone, someday, would call Shelby's dream into existence.

She took a deep breath and finished the report. Its conclusion was that Shelby had sustained blunt force trauma to her skull. Ivy flashed on the orange pylons holding up the bridge and disappearing into the green water. But Shelby had salt water in her lungs, so technically she had drowned.

Ivy closed her eyes. She'd drowned after all.

Tristan closed his laptop with a click. They sat in silence. She tried concentrating on her breath, counting to four on each inhale, hold, exhale, hold.

"Are you OK?" Tristan asked.

She was very much not OK. "Been better."

"I'm sorry for what happened to Shelby." His eyebrows were drawn down in concern, his eyes worried. He reminded her of the woman with the stroller on the bridge.

"Did you see this coming?" She pointed at his laptop. "In your threat assessments."

He winced and covered it up, a man attacked. Ivy didn't care.

"I didn't work with her directly often. I mostly handled threat assessment for her communications."

"Who worked with her directly?" Another person to talk to.

"No one," he said. "She didn't want that."

"How do you know?"

He sighed and looked at his closed laptop. "She was specific about what she did and didn't want."

Something in his expression made her ask. "Did the two of you ever hook up?"

"She was a client." He sounded outraged by the mere suggestion.

"Evading the question," she said.

"No," he answered. "We didn't."

He didn't touch his chin and he met her eyes when he said it with a hint of irritation in his voice. So, he was probably telling the truth or he was a good liar. Really, it could be either. She filed it away as a possibility anyway.

"So nobody had any idea she was going to jump?" she asked.

"I don't know what idea anyone else had." He looked past her at the canvas pulsing on the wall. "I didn't."

"What anyone else?" she asked.

"Mr. Linton, I guess. I worked with her more than anyone and I didn't see it. I've been over the last few days of her life in my head a hundred times. What did I miss? How did I fail her?"

Ivy pulled her sleeves down over her hands. "I'm familiar with those questions."

"A lot of suicides don't broadcast their intentions, or even have intentions until the minute they do it. We couldn't have followed her every second. We couldn't." It sounded like he was trying to convince himself more than her.

"Maybe not every second, just that one." She regretted her tone.

"How do you know which second to watch for?" he asked. "Out of all the seconds in a life, how do you know which ones are going to matter?"

She didn't have a good answer. She didn't have a good answer for any of it. Shelby using meth. Shelby lying about test results. Shelby taking money for a product she knew wasn't going to be ready any time soon. Shelby jumping off that bridge.

Ivy stared out at the city lights glowing in the fog. Thousands of people going about their lives like Shelby never existed. "I should go home."

"You can't change what happened to her," he said. "Not here or anywhere else. Maybe it's time to get back to your own life."

If he spouted out a single platitude, she didn't know what she'd do, but it wouldn't be kind and he had been nothing but kind to her. "I need to be alone. Please."

He slipped the laptop into his bag and stood. "If you need someone, you can call me anytime, day or night."

Like Shelby hadn't.

"You don't sleep?" she asked.

"I'm a light sleeper," he said. "I can be here in a few minutes."

What woman wouldn't want to hear Tristan say those words?

"Thanks," she said. "You're kind."

"It's no problem," he said. "You're going through a lot."

"Not as much as Shelby did." She stood and walked him to the door, feeling like a bitch for her words. He had done his best. He'd been prepared to take a knife for her and he was clearly even more attached to Shelby. Whoever had failed her friend, it hadn't been him.

After the door closed behind him, she turned on the security alarm and put the chain and chair back, like they would save her. But the worst demons were inside her head. Shelby was dead. She'd suffered for months. Then she'd chosen a different path. She'd drowned. And the world hated her memory.

Ivy got out her phone and prepared to send a text. Her thumb hovered over the keyboard for several seconds before typing.

I'm ready for that ticket back

Bouncing dots indicated the recipient was typing. Olivia was on top of her messages.

Olivia: I'll book it and email you the details

And just like that, her trip to California was over. She hadn't arrived in time to save Shelby, probably not by months, and it was too late to help her now. The best thing she could do was go home and mourn her in peace and try to hold on to her old memories of a girl who wanted to help everyone to live forever. That girl had been wonderful.

Decision made, Ivy found a can of beans in the pantry and ate it cold, straight from the can. Feeling like things couldn't get worse, she checked her email. Another troll mail that she needed to forward, and an email from her editor. Maybe they were going to book her another event. Or extend the deadline for her next book because of everything she'd been dealing with. Miracles could happen. She clicked the email.

After the violence at your last public event, where a knife was drawn and police were called, we have decided to cut short your book tour.

Ivy's stomach clenched. Her editor didn't usually refer to herself in the plural. It sounded like it had been drafted by a lawyer. Trying not to hyperventilate, she kept reading.

We don't feel that we can guarantee your safety or the safety of the attendees and the bookstore employees. We have even received threats against our publishing house and its employees and we are concerned for their safety as well.

They hadn't worried about her safety back when they were saying all publicity is good publicity. Apparently, it was only good publicity when Ivy was the only one in danger. She read the next paragraph.

Although we realize that the controversy surrounding Lessons from the Curie is not your fault, it has affected expected book sales for your thoughtful and well-written book.

Sudden empty flattery ramped up her worries.

Considering the new sales figures, and your own tardiness in delivering the manuscript for the sequel, we will be canceling your contract to allow you to shop your second book at a house that may be more equipped to deal with contentious issues. No payment will be forthcoming for the second novel.

It ended with a sincerely. They sure did sound sincere about sacrificing her books and her career to save themselves. She read it again. Her writing career was over. The trolls had won. And she was broke. She slumped against the wall, wishing she could go back up and undelete this reality before reading it.

But it wouldn't change anything. She was still screwed.

She texted Anu: u up?

I am now

Ivy called her and caught her up on recent events, ending with the cancellation of the contract.

"That sounds like a lot," Anu said.

"Cautious as ever," Ivy answered.

"I'm sorry about your friend and I'm glad you're coming home." Anu was good about making her feelings clear.

"Me too." Ivy watched the fog suffocating the street below. "I knew about Shelby, but it was hard to see. And I knew that the troll attacks were bad, but I didn't expect them to just ditch me."

"Can you sue them?" It felt like Anu was leading her away from talking about Shelby and the bridge.

Ivy let herself be distracted. "The trolls?"

"The publisher," Anu said.

"That would cost more than the advance, and even if I won, they could just refuse to bring the book out or print five copies or something."

"At least you got the one book," Anu said. "And plenty of people liked it."

"I can't believe they won," Ivy said. "That the AllSpermMatters movement ruined my life."

"Not just the trolls," Anu said. "Lots of other bad stuff is happening to you, too."

Ivy laughed. Anu always made her feel better. "Thanks."

"It's not your whole life ruined," Anu said. "Come back home, grieve, and rest. There's more to your life than this moment."

Ivy sighed into the phone.

"Drama?" Anu asked.

"I wish there was a way to turn their rage and power into something useful."

"A power station that runs on rage?" Anu asked.

"That describes Twitter. And Facebook." Ivy sunk onto the couch.

"There are more good people out there than bad ones," Anu said. "Even if it doesn't seem like it right now."

Ivy closed her eyes. "Sure."

Anu started reading her positive tweets. By avoiding the negative ones, Ivy had missed all these. "Love your book...Sorry this is happening to you...Jasper is a badass."

Anu drew in a quick breath.

"What? Don't read it if it's bad."

"This guy named @drmanbun has a great idea!"

"Dr Man Bun?"

"Shush," Anu said. "He says 'I love your book and hope you write more. Have you thought of starting a Kickstarter so those who support you have a place to help out?' That's it!"

"A Kickstarter?" Ivy asked.

"It worked before. Gamergate," Anu said. "You must do this."

"Must I?"

"It's not just fighting with them or putting a scold's bridle over your head. You can take control of the narrative."

A tiny flare of hope bloomed in Ivy's belly at the thought of taking control of anything. "Maybe. Maybe we could do it."

"It might not work," Anu pointed out. "Don't get your hopes up."

"Weren't you just trying to convince me?"

"Convince you, yes, but keep your expectations reasonable also."

Ivy smiled. "That does sound like you. But even if it doesn't work, I don't see how I'm worse off."

"OK," Anu said. "Let's get to work."

And so they did. By the time they were done, Ivy's energy had drained away and she was falling asleep over her keyboard. She didn't tell Anu, but she had started to doubt the entire idea. Things could always get worse. But at least she'd done something new. She decided to ignore the little voice of worry and went to bed.

CHAPTER FIFTEEN

Ivy's ringtone woke her up. The room was pitch black and she had no idea where she was. Her phone rang again and she groped blindly for the sound.

"Tristan?" she said.

"It's Stephen at the front desk."

She sat and rubbed her eyes. She remembered where she was. Grief, jetlag, despair, hope. It was all wearing her down. "What time is it?"

"It's 9:15 at night," he said.

She'd slept the day away. She wondered what time it was in Tallinn, but couldn't bring herself to even try the math. Her stomach rumbled.

"Why did you call?" she asked.

"I know it's a little late," Stephen said. "But a man here says you'd like to talk to him. He said you'd want to be disturbed."

Ivy yawned and tried to wake up. "Mr. Tristan Walsh? Send him up."

Stephen cleared his throat. "He says his name is Jacko, and I think it's best if you meet him down here."

She stumbled into her clothes, fingers clumsy on the buttons and zippers. She was so tired that she felt nauseous. But if she didn't go talk to Jacko right now, he might disappear forever. Maybe he'd have answers about Shelby that she liked. Maybe he'd seen a softer side to her. She'd helped him look for a job, after all, and Margie spoke highly of her. Shelby was more than the dark pieces Ivy had been given. Light and kind pieces existed too.

When she got to the lobby, Stephen stood behind the front desk in his uniform. She was glad he got time off from standing outside. It looked cold and miserable out there. Rain sheeted down onto the street.

"He's outside." Stephen pointed toward the front door. His expression made it clear he'd never allow Jacko to wait inside the lobby, even on a miserable night like this. Before she judged him, she reminded herself that he'd probably lose his job if he did.

When she got outside, Jacko puffed on a Marlboro three steps from the door. He cupped his hand over it to keep it dry and rain ran down his knuckles. He looked even more gaunt than he had at the funeral. His shoulders were soaked dark from the rain.

"I'm a friend of Shelby Linton." She stood under the overhang by the front door, a space Stephen had probably chased him from, and held out her hand. "Ivy."

When he shook her hand, his was cold and wet.

"Jacko," he said and the tang of alcohol accompanied his words. "Saw you at the funeral. You looked rough."

"We were friends a long time."

He blew out a cloud of smoke. "I heard you were doing an article."

"From Margie?" she asked.

"Doesn't matter where I heard it from. Are you?"

"I am," she said. "About the people Shelby worked with at the shelter."

"What's it worth to you?"

Ordinarily, she wouldn't pay a source for information, but she paused before giving her standard answer. It wasn't going to be a real journalistic piece. She wanted to know, had to know, that someone remembered her friend fondly. "Twenty bucks."

He eyed her for a second and took another long drag on his cigarette before answering. "Two hundred."

She stepped away, back toward the door. "Wasn't she your friend?"

"I need money more than I need dead friends."

She couldn't argue with that. "A hundred bucks."

He pushed off the wall. "My first offer was my final one."

"Fine," she said, although it was all the money she had left. She was leaving tomorrow anyway. "I'll pay you after."

"And dinner," he said. "At a diner around the corner."

He dropped his cigarette on the sidewalk and crushed it with the heel of his raggedy tennis shoe.

She followed him down the street. Rain soaked her jacket, her pants, and her hair. It ran down strands of hair and dropped onto her cheeks like cold tears. She missed honest snow.

He walked steadily, like someone who didn't care about the rain, turning right and then left. Everything looked the same. She got lost and knew she'd have to use her phone's GPS to get back.

Finally, they ended up in front of a twenty-four-hour diner. Clean and shiny inside, it looked more like a movie set than a place where people sat and talked and ate, tastefully decorated for Christmas. But people were in there eating and looking mercifully dry. Ivy followed him in and took off her jacket by the door. She shook it out and water scattered.

Then she draped it over her damp arm and followed a waitress with bright green hair to a leather booth by the window. The waitress poured them both coffee and Ivy wrapped her hands around the warm mug. She was cold and miserable and still so tired she was nauseous. Jacko better have some good stories.

He ordered the bacon and egg special and a piece of apple pie. Ivy, craving sugar, ordered a piece of pie, too. Even though she wasn't having real food, it was going to cost more than an expensive dinner for two in Tallinn. Way more. Not that it mattered. She had to pay to find out more.

"Let me see the money first," he said.

She opened her wallet and counted bills out onto the sparkling table. Who knew having a rich friend could be so expensive?

He reached for it, but she pulled it back and shoved it in her pocket. "After."

He poured packet after packet of sugar into his coffee. She sipped hers. Surprisingly good, and it chased away the chill.

"Start talking," she said. "Margie said you and Shelby worked together. With someone named Pat."

He tensed. "She 'mentored' me."

His tone worried Ivy. "In what?"

"Supposed to be job hunting." He took a pull on the coffee like it was whiskey.

"What kind of job?" And what did he mean by supposed?

"Construction. I used to work construction before."

"Before what?"

"Life hit me," Jacko said. "Like a ton of bricks."

"How'd she help?" Ivy drew warmth from her coffee cup and wished for that pie to hurry up.

"Resume stuff. She helped me put together a resume. Like anyone is going to hire someone who looks like me for a real job." He gestured to his emaciated frame.

"You look fine," Ivy lied.

"I wouldn't hire me," he said.

She sipped her coffee. "Did she ever get you work?"

"She paid me to do odd jobs for her."

"What kind of odd jobs?" She couldn't picture Shelby working with this guy, but she was proud of her.

He sipped his coffee and dumped in four more packets of sugar. It must be more sugar than coffee by now. "Moving boxes at her work. Dealing with the mice."

"Mice?" She thought of Wendy and her mouse results.

"She worked with mice. I cleaned out cages, killed mice, and took it all to be incinerated. Refilled the cages with new bedding and new mice."

A tiny little alarm rang in her head. That seemed like something the lab techs should be doing and counting and not a random guy off the street. But what did she know about mouse testing protocol? "Did that seem weird?"

"It was weird that she drug-tested me first."

"As an employer, maybe that was standard?" She had never heard of anyone asking for drug tests for someone who did random odd jobs.

His laugh turned into a cough. "Every week? Brought her own needles and kit and everything. She used blood tests because she didn't trust us to give her real urine samples."

She tried to imagine the conversation that had led up to Shelby talking to this guy about his pee, but she couldn't. This was so far from Shelby's regularly pampered life that she couldn't picture it at all. Especially now that she knew that Shelby would have failed those selfsame tests. "She knew how to take blood?"

He stirred his coffee and the spoon clinked against the side of the mug. "She said she did and she did fine. It was a condition of getting the jobs."

Ivy wasn't touching that. "Did you work for her often?"

"We were out once a week for a couple months."

"How many of you?"

He shrugged. "Do you know what was weirder?"

She hated to ask, but she did. "What?"

He clicked his spoon against the coffee cup again. "She used to inject us, too."

"With what?"

"She said it was B12."

Ivy thought about that.

The waitress arrived with three plates. Jacko dug into his bacon and eggs. He was a neat eater, but he could definitely put away a lot of food quickly. Ivy took a bite of pie. Sweet and tart, the way pie should taste. Estonia didn't have American-style pie and she'd missed it. She took another bite and discovered that she was hungry.

"Could you give me the names of the others Shelby helped? I want to write a piece about it, to show that side of her." She took another bite of pie and thought about ordering another piece. Pie was her Death Star exhaust port.

"I don't think so." His words were flat and final.

"Why not?"

"If they want to come forward, they can contact you."

She took a long sip of coffee. It would wake her up. Or at least she wanted it to. "How many?"

"At least a dozen. That I knew about. Probably more."

"Who would know?"

He shrugged again. "Leave a notice at Margie's. They can come forward if they want."

She didn't like leaving a loose end, but she let it go. "Did you notice anything unusual about her before she died?"

"Like what?"

"Anything. Was she depressed? Anxious?"

"Same as always. Busy. Impatient and rushed." He shoveled in his breakfast with quick methodical movements. "We weren't close friends or anything."

She'd agreed to pay all that money and she still didn't have an answer about who Shelby had become. She wasn't even sure what she wanted or needed to hear. "Were you surprised to hear that she died by suicide?"

"People die all the time," he said. "Pat didn't give me a note either."

"Margie mentioned that your friend died. I'm sorry."

"She say it was an OD?" His hand closed into a fist around his fork.

"We talked about a lot of people." Ivy wasn't going to say yes and get Margie into trouble. She realized then that she wasn't any more likely to tell him unpleasant truths than vice versa. Which made this whole breakfast a waste of time and money.

She ate more pie. Might as well at least clean her plate.

"She had cancer," he said. "Wanted to go out on a big high. I never saw her after she told me. She's probably dead, but I don't really know. Maybe she went home to see her daughter."

An alarm rang deep in her foggy brain. "What kind of cancer?"

"Pancreatic. Doctor said from years of alcohol and drug abuse." He ate a strip of bacon. "If an OD doesn't get you, something else does."

She thought about what Wendy had said about the mice. Coincidence. Unless it wasn't. "Tell me more about the B12 shots."

She held her breath as she waited for his answer.

"She said a lot of druggies were deficient and she had it through her lab. She'd give us shots of that. It used to pep me up for a few days after."

"B12 is supposed to be healthy," she said.

"It wasn't B12." He put down his fork.

"What else would it be?" she asked.

"Don't know." He mopped up the last bit of egg yolk with his toast. "The box had that jellyfish on it from her company. She said it was leftovers from a company wellness event."

"A what?"

"Yeah," he said. "I didn't believe it either."

Ivy had a sick pit at the bottom of her stomach.

"I figure there's money in it," he said. "If it was something else."

"Of course it wasn't something else!" she answered indignantly. Shelby would never do that.

"Who would pay?" He leaned in close. "That company has a lot of money and they don't want to get in trouble. Who should I talk to?"

"I don't know," she answered. "Nobody. The company is shut down now."

"Everyone she injected is homeless. They're alcoholics or druggies so they think nobody cares," he said. "Pat's dead."

"Did any of them see a doctor?"

"We're all in and out of the clinic. I have some sores on my legs. Do you want to see?" He pulled up a pant leg to reveal a grotesquely swollen leg with a red, pus-filled sore on his shin. A diner at the next table looked at it in fascination, Ivy with what she hoped was well-disguised horror.

"Is that the injection site?" she asked.

"Maybe," he said, like he'd just thought of it. "The stuff inside was blue, not red like regular B12."

"How do you know what B12 looks like?"

"They give it to you in recovery all the time. It doesn't look like that."

"If you thought it wasn't B12, why'd you let her inject you?" Ivy asked.

"She paid me," he answered. "And I think there's more where that came from."

She pushed her plate away. She didn't want the rest of her pie.

"You going to eat that?" he asked.

She pushed it toward him and he ate and washed it down with the last of his coffee.

Her brain felt fogged up, like the city. She tried to put his words into a context, but she couldn't. She must be missing something. She was too tired to put it together, but everything had a simple explanation.

"Give me a name," he said.

"A name?"

"Someone I could talk to at the company about getting paid for my troubles. Who was that Indian guy at the funeral?"

"He's in jail," she said. "Financial thing."

"Give me another name."

"We could go to a doctor and have you tested."

"I don't want to be tested. I want to be paid." He clenched his fists and glared at her.

She leaned back in the booth. "I can only pay you for your story."

He leaned until his chest touched his plate. "You going to stiff me for that, too?"

"Let's get you tested," she said. "Get evidence to back up your allegations and see where that leads."

"Allegations?"

Diners at nearby tables glanced over at them. The conversation was getting out of control and she didn't know how to bring it back.

"The things you just told me."

"I know what allegations means." He stood and loomed over her. "It means you don't believe me."

221

"I believe in evidence."

"Pay me." He leaned close, face contorted in anger.

"But first—"

And then he punched her in the face.

CHAPTER SIXTEEN

Her head slammed back against the booth. He reached into her pocket, lightning quick, and grabbed the money he'd seen her put there.

She kicked him in the knee and struggled to stand. Blood ran out of her nose and her cheek throbbed.

He ducked to the side and came back for another round. Restaurant patrons jumped from their tables and a glass crashed to the floor.

She brought up her hands to guard her face. She hadn't been in a fight in years, but she still had instincts.

"One name," he said, and swung again.

She blocked it with her forearm. It hurt, but she ignored it.

A waiter came up behind her. "We don't want any trouble."

Jacko's eyes flicked over to the waiter. He patted the pocket where he'd stashed his payment and glared at her. "This isn't over. We're not done with you."

We? Then, he ran toward the door.

She sprinted after him. She wasn't sure what her goal was. She had agreed to pay him the money so he wasn't technically stealing. But she wasn't going to let him get away with punching her.

She was halfway to the door when the waiter grabbed her sleeve and yanked her back.

"Are you OK?" he asked. "Have you paid for your food?"

She pulled her arm away and swept the back of her hand across her nose. Blood streaked up to her wrist and her nose throbbed.

"I can get you ice," said the waiter without moving from his position between her and the front door. Jacko was already outside.

She watched him through the diner window. He crossed the street without looking. A car slammed on its brakes and almost hit him but he kept running. She stood, shaking, in the warm restaurant, and watched his olive-green coat cheat death twice more before he vanished in a crowd of people at a bus stop. She'd never catch him now.

"I have a credit card." She handed it to the waiter and swabbed at her nose with a napkin, then she scooped ice out of her glass and wrapped it in a couple of napkins. Not the best ice pack, but better than nothing. She stuck it on her nose. She'd entered this restaurant as a reporter on a puff piece about her friend and here she was bleeding into the remains of her pie. She pinched the bridge of her nose to stop the bleeding. The worst part was that the punch wasn't the worst part of the meeting.

Another waiter came back with her credit card. This one was bigger, clearly the one they sent to deal with trouble.

"Do you want me to call someone?" he asked.

"Like the police?" Even Ivy didn't think the police would do anything useful.

He handed her a baggie full of ice. "Someone to pick you up, maybe?"

She couldn't think of a single person. "I'm fine on my own."

She waited while he ran her card, going over the steps of the conversation in her mind, trying to see how she could have reached a different outcome. Jacko had clearly expected her to help him in his blackmail threat against Nyssa, and he'd also thought she was going to stiff him for the interview. She should have paid him when he started escalating. And there she was, blaming herself for getting punched in the face.

"Here's your card." The waiter handed it back.

She resisted an urge to overtip, then walked out into the rain and headed back to the sinking tower. The rain didn't bother her anymore either. As she walked, she searched online. Raindrops ran down her phone while she read. Injectable vitamin B12 was a thing that people used. As Jacko had said, alcoholics often had a B12 deficiency. It was a reasonable thing to inject. You stuck the needle right into the muscle. No training necessary. Maybe Shelby had been doing them a favor.

But Ivy didn't believe that. She'd never heard of a corporation having a wellness day where employees got injected with B12. And, if they had been, the box would have had the logo of the drug company that made it, not Nyssa's. Yet Jacko had said the box had the jellyfish logo on it.

Unless he'd lied. He was angling for a payout from Nyssa and Shelby injecting him with her drug would definitely get him one, assuming Nyssa had money left to be sued for.

And Shelby shouldn't have been injecting him with anything. Ivy hid from the rain under an awning and popped over to images to see what injectable B12 usually looked like. It was bright red. Not blue like Jacko said.

She stood for a long moment with the ice against her nose, trying to come up with a reason for Jacko to be wrong. Maybe he was color blind. People were color blind. A quick web search revealed that no kind of color blindness would make someone see red as blue. As usual, the internet was not her friend.

She didn't know what else to search for to prove that Shelby had injected Jacko with B12 like she said until she remembered an article she'd seen while constructing her memorial website. It showed Shelby injecting a mouse with Nyssa's formula. It was easy to find using the links she'd set up and she scrolled through the article, then zoomed up the pictures. The liquid in Shelby's syringe was unmistakably pale blue.

Maybe Jacko hadn't been lying. Or maybe he'd seen this picture too. All that assumed that he'd been injected with anything at all. He could have done the web search, the same as she had, to make his own story stronger and to earn a payout from Nyssa. A few weeks ago, they might have paid him to avert a scandal, but right now they probably had so much scandal it wouldn't matter to them. But it mattered to the people who were injected, if they even existed.

She jammed her phone in her pocket, then stepped back into the rain. For the first time, she realized that Jacko could be out there watching, waiting to get her alone and beat a name out of her or maybe someone in the "we" he'd mentioned would do it for him. Someone she wouldn't even think to suspect.

She walked faster until she was jogging and then running. She wove around people on the sidewalk and nearly ran into a shopping cart. So many invisible people here. So many people that no one would notice if a few were missing. Including her.

"He's lying. He's lying." She repeated the phrase as she ran. It was something to say to stop the other voice in her head, because she couldn't bear what it was saying. It couldn't be true.

Shelby would never do that. But then she reminded herself that she was saying that a lot lately about things Shelby had actually done.

But injecting people with her drug before it was ready? Her vision of Shelby was flawed. But not that flawed. Never that flawed.

If Shelby had experimented on homeless people, why had she hired Ivy to interview them? Why had she wanted to bring Ivy out at all? She was letting her imagination run away with her because she'd read too many mystery novels. The real world wasn't full of dark killers.

Shelby wasn't evil. Shelby was the girl who stood in the midst of the dancing jellyfish and recognized that their beautiful secrets might save everyone.

If she saw Jacko again, she'd see if she could get a blood sample. Maybe he'd let her if she paid him. Surely someone from Nyssa could check it out.

She found herself, wet and shivering, in front of Shelby's apartment building without any idea of how she'd found her way there. The building loomed above her in the darkness and the fog. That's when she remembered that she could have called Tristan. This was exactly the kind of thing that Mr. Linton paid him to deal with, and she hadn't even thought of it once.

She stepped through the door and into the warmth, light, and Christmas decorations. Back through the looking glass.

Stephen came out from behind the desk. "Miss Corva?"

"I'm OK," she said. "I'm OK."

Neither one of them thought that was true.

He handed her a towel with the building logo on it.

"It's from the gym," he said. "It's all I have."

Then he herded her toward the fireplace where she stared into the flames, towel clasped in one hand.

"Let's dry you off," he said gently. He took the towel out of her hand and wiped off her face and ran it over her hair like she was a toddler.

She took the towel back and patted her face. Her nose still hurt, but not as much as before. Maybe Jacko had pulled his punch.

"What happened to you?" he asked. "Should I call someone? Is your nose OK?"

She took out her phone, opened the camera, and reversed it to look at her face. Her nose didn't look too bad. Not broken, barely swollen.

Stephen looked around the lobby, then pulled a leather chair right up next to the fireplace and sat her down. She brought the ice pack up to her nose again and leaned toward the flames. He left and came back, then tucked a sweatshirt around her and put a cup of hot coffee in her free hand.

"This'll warm you up," he said. "I don't think you should go upstairs on your own just yet."

She didn't want to go up there either. She wanted to get on a plane and forget she ever came here. She didn't owe Shelby anything. Not a Shelby who had done these things.

"Take a little sip," Stephen said.

The moment reminded her of sitting in the ambulance with Toomas and Anu and she smiled at the memory.

"I saved the wolf," she whispered and took a sip of coffee.

"Sure you did," said Stephen.

Together, they watched the fire and she warmed up. She finger-combed her hair into a more reasonable state and concentrated on box breathing. In for a count of four, hold for a count of four, out for a count of four, wait for a count of four. Start over. It got her heart rate back down too. Stephen looked less worried.

And then Mr. Linton showed up.

"Thank you for calling," he told Stephen. Stephen stood and nodded to him.

Stephen had called Mr. Linton. It irritated her, but she supposed that was the only person he could think of to call. And he did live in the building.

Mr. Linton took the chair next to Ivy's. Stephen hovered, then returned to his position at the desk.

"What's going on?" Mr. Linton asked. "Stephen said you met a man and then came back in a state."

"I'm not in a state," she said. "I met a man who knew Shelby for a story. He said she used to work with him at the clinic."

"Did he hit you?"

"Sucker punch to the nose," she said. "I blocked the second one."

"Do you want me to call the police? To press charges?"

She shook her head. "More trouble than it's worth."

"Why did he hit you?"

"Victim blamey," she said. "Again."

"So he hit you for no reason?"

"He wanted me to give him the name of someone at Nyssa."

Mr. Linton looked puzzled. "Why?"

"He wanted a payout. Said that Shelby injected him with something."

"What?" Mr. Linton's solicitous manner disappeared.

She told him that Shelby had given this man weekly drug tests.

"Probably a good precaution, considering."

"Maybe a good precaution, but I'm not sure that's even legal."

"You're upset because Shelby gave drug addicts a drug test?" His eyebrows raised. "I don't think that's illegal. Employers do it all the time. I bet Stephen over there has random drug tests."

She looked over at Stephen. He typed into the computer and didn't look up. One good thing about writing: no random drug tests. But how was Shelby's testing any different?

"And the B12?"

"That's a healthy thing, right?" he said. "She must have been trying to do them a kindness."

"Maybe." She had to admit he might be right. But all she could see was the jellyfish logo on the B12 box and the blue liquid Jacko had described. And the pancreatic cancer his girlfriend had been diagnosed with. That a few of Wendy's mice had pancreatic cancer. That Jacko had killed Nyssa's laboratory mice and replaced them. And the fact that, the deeper she delved into Shelby's affairs, the worse everything looked.

"Did he say it was something else?"

Mr. Linton was the most likely person to try to get money out of, so Ivy reasoned that he ought to know. "He implied that it was Nyssa's drug."

Mr. Linton hesitated, then threw back his head and laughed. "That's the most ridiculous thing I've heard all week."

His response made her feel better. "It is?"

"She started on the mice recently. The drug wasn't anywhere near ready for human testing." He shook his head. "I wasn't following it closely, but I know that much."

"That's the part that worries me," Ivy said. "That it wasn't authorized."

"Shelby would never take a risk of accelerating the timeline outside legal boundaries. Any data she produced would be unusable. All her work would be discredited. She knew that."

Of course she did. It would be a ridiculous thing to do. Ivy let out a shaky breath. "You're right."

"Of course I am. She wasn't a Bond villain," Mr. Linton said. "She was your best friend and my little girl. This man is trying to get quick cash. He's an addict, right?"

"I think so."

"If she gave this man B12, she must have thought he needed it. Shelby was working to help people. She wanted to give the world immortality."

Ivy took off the ice pack and touched her nose. She winced.

"Did you tell anyone about this man's allegations?" Mr. Linton asked and the hair rose on the back of her neck. "Post it on the internet?"

She lied without thinking. "I told a few friends, but I trust their discretion."

"That's good," he said. "The last thing we want is for more people to pile onto the attack against her work, her character, her gender, and everything that she stood for."

The heat in his voice put her on edge and she remembered his bitter words at Shelby's crypt. The family reputation was important to him. Who knew what he'd do to protect it. Or what he had done.

"I know," she said.

"Do you really?" He gripped her elbow hard and his fingers dug into her bone.

"Of course I do." She yanked her arm free. "Of course."

She clamped her lips together until she thought of the right words. She'd revealed too much and she'd learned nothing in return. She pulled Stephen's sweatshirt closer against the cold. "Did you read my story about Shelby's philanthropy? I sent you a link."

"I didn't see it." And he didn't look like he wanted to.

Glad to have something else to look at, she took out her phone and scrolled through the messages. She pointed to the message she'd sent him. "I think you'll like the story."

"What's the name of the man who hit you?" Mr. Linton asked. "I'd like to have Tristan run a check on him in case he harasses you again."

His words sounded kind, but his tone didn't.

"I don't know his last name," she lied. "Jay something."

"We can't have someone like that running around making wild accusations."

Her elbow throbbed where he'd grabbed it. "It's the twenty-first century. Wild accusations power the internet."

"Even so," he said. "He needs to be stopped."

Although she wasn't feeling too kindly toward Jacko, she didn't like the implications. "Stopped how?"

233

Mr. Linton clenched his jaw. It looked like he was counting to ten. At about eight, he said, "Explain to him the consequences of his words."

That sounded menacing and vague. The kind of thing to say to achieve plausible deniability if Jacko accidentally stepped in front of a bus. And a reminder that she didn't want to get on Mr. Linton's bad side either.

"It's kind of you to worry about me," she said and stood.

He stood too. "How about I escort you up to the apartment? To get you home safe."

Her elbow throbbed again and her heart sped up. The thought of being alone with him in Shelby's apartment didn't make her feel safe at all. "I'm fine on my own."

Before he could argue, she walked to the front desk and handed Stephen his sweatshirt.

"Thanks," she said to Stephen. "I'm sorry I got it wet."

Mr. Linton loomed at her back.

Stephen looked between them. "No problem."

"Ready?" Mr. Linton asked.

He clearly intended to escort her up to Shelby's apartment no matter what she said and she had no intention of letting him. The guard that she'd let down before Jacko punched her in the face was back up now.

Another doorman entered the lobby. He nodded to Stephen and she seized her moment.

"Are you going off shift?" she asked.

"Yes, ma'am," Stephen said. "It's been a long day."

"Could you show me that Irish bar you mentioned?" She hoped he'd play along. "Please?"

Stephen blinked. "Umm...sure."

"Great!" she said brightly. "I think I need a drink and something fun to cheer me up."

"Everybody does, sometimes," Stephen said.

Mr. Linton looked between them. His eyes narrowed suspiciously, but he didn't say anything. "We can discuss this more later, then, Ivy."

That's when she remembered that he had the keys and alarm code to her apartment.

CHAPTER SEVENTEEN

She hung around the desk while Stephen talked to his replacement so she could watch as Mr. Linton walked briskly over to the elevators and presumably headed up to his penthouse apartment. After the doors closed, she dragged up her sleeve and looked at the bruises forming where he'd grabbed her elbow.

"Could you come help me bring my suitcase down?" she asked Stephen.

"You're leaving the Tower?"

"Flying back to Estonia," she said.

She led him across the fancy lobby to the elevators, got in, and pressed the button for Shelby's floor. "Do you take random drug tests?"

Stephen raised his eyebrows. "Do you?"

"I was wondering how common they are." She glanced at the elevator doors. "And, no, I don't."

"I do," he said. "Building management requires it."

"Do you take vitamin B12 shots?"

He looked over at her. "No."

That was the extent of her curiosity and her small talk, so they stared at the doors in silence until they reached Shelby's floor where Ivy let them both into the apartment. It took a few seconds to unlock the door and disarm the alarm system. That's how long it would take Mr. Linton too.

With an uneasy glance back at the door, she hurried to the guest bedroom. Stephen was better than nothing, but she wasn't sure she could count on him hanging around if Mr. Linton ordered him to leave.

"Wow," Stephen called from the living room. "This isn't how I pictured Ms. Linton's apartment."

Ivy tossed her clothes in her suitcase like the apartment was on fire.

"What's up with this art?" Stephen asked.

"It's blood cells," she said.

A quick tour through the bathroom, nothing to see there, then out into the living room to pack up her laptop.

"You can slow down," Stephen said. "I don't mind waiting."

"I hate to put you out." She did a quick sweep and dragged her suitcase to the door.

She dropped the Ducati keys in the bowl and pulled out the Tesla's. Technically, she was stealing the car, but she didn't like to think about that. Shelby would have wanted her to be safe. Maybe.

"Did Mr. Linton give you permission to use that?" Stephen seemed to have read her guilty thoughts.

"You bet," she lied. "I'm going to an airport hotel tonight and he said he'll send someone to pick it up tomorrow."

Stephen tilted his head like he was confused, but thinking hard.

Before he could reach any conclusions, Ivy opened the door and tossed her crap into the hall. She almost handed him the house key. Instead, she crammed it in her pocket. She could always mail it back.

The elevator was empty when it arrived and she let out a breath she hadn't known she was holding. With Stephen and the bags safely inside, she pressed P1. As the doors slid closed, she heard a ding. Another elevator had stopped on Shelby's floor. It could have been anyone.

Down in parking, she fast walked to Shelby's Tesla and popped the trunk.

"Do you need a ride anywhere?" she asked. "I can drop you off on my way."

Stephen gawked at the expensive cars. Clearly, he'd never been down here. Under normal circumstances, she'd let him look at all he wanted but she beeped the horn, and he jumped.

"In the car," she said and he got in.

She put it in gear and drove out.

"Buckle up," she said. "Where do you live?"

"Daly City." He looked toward the closing garage door like a kid being dragged away from the swimming pool on a summer afternoon. "What about the bar thing?"

"Changed my mind. I'll drop you off."

"I'm not stupid," he said. "Why'd you tear out of the apartment?"

Stephen noticed things whether you wanted him to or not. "I have a plane to catch."

"Sure," he said. "And that's all?"

She grimaced and plowed on. "It's been a shit trip. Between Shelby's death and the threats on my life."

"Someone's threatening your life?" Stephen sat straighter.

"Internet trolls," she said. "That threat guy, Tristan Walsh, says it's fine."

"Tristan knows what he's talking about," Stephen said.

Something in his tone caught her. "You know Tristan?"

"He's...uh...in and out of the building a lot."

She remembered the guy at the concierge desk checking out Tristan when they'd first met and how he'd looked over at Stephen.

"You're dating!" she said.

Stephen didn't answer. She was debating whether to ask again when his phone rang.

"We were just talking about you!" Stephen said.

"Is it Tristan?" she asked.

"—drop me off at home," Stephen said.

Ivy waited.

"But—" Stephen stopped. He glanced over at her. "OK."

She kept driving. "Well?"

"Tristan says we're to meet up with him at this Irish bar near my apartment."

She didn't like the sound of that. "Why?"

"I trust him," Stephen said. "I know you don't trust Mr. Linton, and I wouldn't trust him either if money were involved. But Tristan's not like that."

The car headlights glittered in the raindrops on the windshield and Stephen gave her directions for her next turn. He looked puzzled, but not worried. If Stephen trusted Tristan, could she? After all, Stephen noticed things. Surely he'd notice if Tristan was trustworthy. And Tristan had been nothing but trustworthy to her. He'd even made her sign that contract which had sounded like a loyalty pledge. But Mr. Linton was paying him, not her. Mr. Linton was probably his biggest client.

Coming up on the right, she saw a bank branch with an ATM right next to an electronics store. Perfect. With a sigh, she pulled over. Better to be too paranoid than not paranoid enough, right? "Wait in the car."

Stephen looked at her like he was trying not to argue and then shrugged. "OK."

She went into the bank's ATM lobby and took out her daily account limit.

Then she went to the electronics store and bought a burner phone with cash. Mr. Linton wasn't going to be able to track her phone the way he had Shelby's. Before she did anything else, she imported her contacts into the new phone. Then she had to figure out how to get rid of the old one.

Decisions made, she went and got her suitcase out of the trunk. She dropped her cellphone inside next to the spare tire. She wouldn't be seeing that again. It felt like losing a friend, even if they hadn't gotten along recently. But the phone needed to go to the Irish bar in case it was being tracked, and she didn't. She closed the trunk as Stephen got out of the passenger side.

He stood next to her in the rain. "What're you doing?"

She handed him the car keys. "Take the Tesla to meet Tristan. Tell him I'll call in ten."

"I can't leave you alone on a street corner in the middle of nowhere," he said.

"I'll be OK."

He took the keys. "Do you need money?"

She shook her head. "I'm OK."

She didn't see any point in telling him that she was broke and couldn't afford to pay next month's rent. That was a problem for later.

He clapped her on the shoulder. "Good luck."

CHAPTER EIGHTEEN

She watched the Tesla carry him and her phone into the night. Once he was out of sight, she turned and walked to the BART station and caught a train to SFO. According to her new phone, she had eleven minutes till she got there.

Positioning her wet suitcase next to her, she set up the new phone to block her outgoing number, then called Olivia, who answered, even though it was the middle of the night.

"Are you ready for your flight tomorrow?" Olivia asked.

Ivy told her what she'd learned from Jacko. Olivia was a patient listener and asked intelligent questions.

"That's a lot of supposition," Olivia said.

"Wendy Hanks should know how long it remains in tissues or hair or whatever," Ivy said. "Maybe she can test for it, if you can find him."

"Why are you telling me?" Olivia asked.

"Because you're not Shelby's assistant. Or at least that's not all you are."

Olivia chuckled. "I'll see that it gets to the right people."

Ivy bowed her head in relief. "Can you find out if Shelby could have gotten doses of the Nyssa medication out of the building?"

"Yes," Olivia said. "She could have."

"Isn't it tracked?"

Olivia hesitated. "The amount produced and used is carefully tracked."

"And?" Ivy expected more.

"And it has a short shelf life. A few weeks. Then it's discarded. That's logged too, of course, but it might have been possible to swap out the bottles at that point and use them."

"So, she may have injected people with expired medication?" That made it worse.

"I can't say," Olivia said. "It's the only way I can see how she could have gotten it out."

Ivy let out a long, shaky breath.

"Where are you?" Olivia asked.

"Doesn't matter."

"What are you going to do next?"

"I'm going to try to find Jacko and get him to help you." And to warn him. Even though she still owed him a punch in the nose.

In the international terminal at last, she let herself relax. She repacked her suitcase in the bathroom, transferring basic toiletries and clothes to her backpack and putting everything else in the suitcase. Then she stashed it at the storage lockers. Feeling lighter, she called Tristan. Let him hear the airport announcements and think she was leaving.

"Are you in a safe location?" he asked without even saying hello.

"Yes."

Behind him music grew quieter and then cut off. He must have gone outside.

"Where is your phone, the one you called me from before?"

"In the trunk of the Tesla," she said.

"Good thinking." He sighed with what sounded like relief. Maybe he was on her side after all.

"What are you going to do with it?" she asked.

"Stephen will drive the car to the airport, then back to the Tower. He'll put the keys in Shelby's mailbox. After that, leave it alone. That car is too easy to track."

"What about my phone?" It shouldn't sit in the garage, pinging till it ran out of batteries.

"I'll mail it to Estonia from the airport. I have your address from the contract."

"You do think of everything," she said. "Thank you."

"It's my job," he repeated like someone who was tired of saying it. "If you're really going back to Estonia, I think that's a good idea."

"I need to figure out what happened."

"Do you?" he asked. "Some things are better left unknown."

"Curiosity killed the cat," she said. "I get it."

"OK," he said. "What can you tell me?"

Once again, she summarized her suspicions. Tristan waited until she got to the end. She was getting better at it.

"I'll forward this information to the authorities," he said. "And cc you on those emails so you'll know it's been done."

He knew how much she trusted anybody right now, even him. "Thanks."

"Is there anything else I can do for you?" he asked.

"Why are you being so helpful?"

"You're my client," he said.

"Mr. Linton is your client."

"He has my company on retainer," Tristan said. "But all decisions about your personal safety are between you and me. It's in the contract you clearly signed without reading."

"How much danger do you think I'm in?" Might as well get an expert opinion.

He was silent for a long moment, presumably calculating the odds.

"If you had to guess?" she asked.

"I don't see how your internet trolls can find you, since you've ditched your phone and you're outside your usual patterns."

"And what about people related to what happened to Shelby?"

"That's a known unknown," he said. "On the one hand, it seems to have been her own decision to take her own life."

"On the other?"

"The act always felt out of character to me and the circumstances since are definitely odd." He cleared his throat. "And I'm concerned about the rumors that the US government is preparing a secrecy order for Nyssa's work."

"A what?" That wasn't in the news.

"It's when the government declares a product as dangerous to national security and stops further research."

"They can do that?" It made sense, Ivy supposed, for things like creating patents for chemical and nuclear weapons, but for immortality research it seemed wrong.

"They can and do. And that would have ended the company even faster than the fraud allegations."

So Shelby's company had been facing yet another threat. "Did Shelby know?"

"She was the one who told me," Tristan said. "I've never seen her so dispirited."

Dispirited was another Tristan word. "Enough to...you know?"

"I wouldn't have thought so." He sighed. "If I had, I'd have taken different actions."

"Did Stephen tell Mr. Linton the name of the man I met?"

"Just a minute." Irish music and shouts nearly drowned out his voice. He must be back inside.

While she waited for him to ask Stephen, she wondered about the order. Why was Shelby's drug so dangerous that the government took such drastic steps to shut her down? If it didn't work, wouldn't they deny her application to bring it to market? Ivy knew that was just a guess because she knew nothing about the process of bringing a drug to market.

Then things got quiet again on the phone. Then Tristan said. "He told him the name."

Her stomach sank. While she might be dangerous to Mr. Linton, Jacko was even more so. It was like the wolf, except this time she'd thrown him into the icy river herself.

She thanked Tristan, took the last BART back into the city and fast walked to Margie's Second Chances. It was late, but she might get lucky.

When she peeked in the door she saw Margie alone at one of the tables staring at a laptop. She knocked and Margie hustled to open the door.

"We're closed for the night," Margie said as she opened the door. "We don't have beds, but maybe I can find you—"

"It's OK," Ivy said. "I'm not here for that."

"Are you back for a story? It's awfully late." Margie pulled her in out of the rain. "Let me get you coffee and maybe something to eat?"

"That would be great." While she waited, Ivy scribbled a note asking Jacko to call her on her new phone about the B12 and stuck the paper on the bulletin board. She didn't leave her name, but she figured he'd know. She wrote out another flyer asking anyone who had received B12 injections to contact her and put down her email address. It was all she could think of.

Ivy looked at the wall clock. Almost midnight.

Margie came out with a bowl of goulash and a cup of coffee.

"It's decaf," she said. "And the goulash is from yesterday, but it's still good."

Ivy scarfed it down like a wolf and took a long sip of coffee.

Margie waited until she slowed to speak. "Everything OK?"

"Have you seen Jacko?"

"Yesterday. He usually comes in for lunch."

"Do you know where I might find him?" Ivy asked.

"Right now? Why?"

"He told me things in an interview tonight and I wanted more information."

"Must have been pretty important." Margie looked over at the clock.

"I'm leaving soon," Ivy said. "And I wanted to wrap things up."

"What things?" Margie took a sip of her own coffee. She looked tired and who wouldn't be, sitting at work after midnight?

Ivy tried to decide if Margie was safer not knowing and decided she wasn't. She might know who else Shelby had dosed, so she told her everything.

"I don't believe it," Margie said. "And I can't believe you do either. Shelby was helping people here. Some of the people she helped got real jobs and got off the streets. She pulled people back from death's door."

"Like who?"

"Camilla," Margie said. "She was so ill. I tried to get her into section 8 housing, but the lists are so long. I knew she'd die before they got to her. Breast cancer. But your friend stepped in. She got Camilla into a nice one bedroom and gave her a job as a procurement clerk at her own company. And Camilla made a full recovery, too. It was only a few months ago, but she looks fantastic. That's what Shelby was about. Not whatever nonsense Jacko is trying to sell you."

Ivy was starting to think that wasn't all Shelby was about. "Can I have her contact info?"

"Camilla's?" Margie crossed her arms. "I'll take a message and have her contact you."

Ivy sighed. "Thank you for the coffee. Can you tell me how to get to the airport?"

Margie gave her directions to the SamTrans station so Ivy could catch a night bus.

"Walk fast and look sharp," Margie said.

Ivy jogged the whole way there, took the slowest bus she'd ever ridden, and slept on the airport floor.

CHAPTER NINETEEN

Ivy woke up decidedly unrefreshed with a crick in her neck and a sore nose. An email from Camilla asked her to lunch not far from Nyssa's office, which Ivy's new phone told her was a bus ride away. Nobody had answered her flyer, but it was early. Beyond that, she had angry trolls that she directed over to Tristan's bridge. An email from Mr. Linton wishing her a pleasant flight so she assumed he must've talked to Tristan or Stephen or Olivia and they'd all said she intended to leave. Which she did, eventually.

Missing Shelby's luxurious bathroom, Ivy wiped down and changed in an airport stall. She'd definitely come down in the world in the last twenty-four hours. Her nose was a little swollen but basically looked ok. It was sensitive to the touch, so she resolved to stop touching it. Jacko's punch must have been more of a warning than an attempt to really mess her up.

"That's the kind of thinking that leads to Stockholm Syndrome," she told the mirror.

The mirror was unimpressed. It had definitely seen worse.

She packed up her stuff, grateful to have that international flight or they wouldn't have let her in here to sleep and use the free water. She rebooked her flight for tomorrow and left the booking fees on the Nyssa credit card. This was their mess she was trying to clean up.

Clutching a scone and a large coffee, she tried to write. Nothing came. She reread the pages she'd written before her book came out. They seemed flat and uninspired, but she imagined they were full of innocuous sentences that would restart the rape and death threats. That wasn't going to help inspire her to keep going. She decided to do a five-minute timed writing exercise, using a prompt of two random things in her surroundings. Kid with teddy bear. Pilot with a tiny rolling suitcase. Plus setting it on the space colony. Even that didn't work.

Giving up, she headed out in search of the bus to meet Camilla.

On the bus ride, she checked in with Anu, who sent her a GIF of a cat with big eyes asking her to come home. She pictured Anu in her apartment, ready to go to bed, sighing worriedly. The image made her feel better, because someone cared. She knew the cat was probably right, but she sent back a sad Pokémon shaking its head.

Foolishly, she checked her email again. More hate mail for Tristan's files. Notices from Kickstarter. And a woman named @planula. The email trashed Jacko and also said that B12 wasn't harmful. She must have seen the flyer at Margie's. Ivy remembered vaguely that a planula was an item in a video game, but didn't bother to look it up.

She sent back a long email explaining that she was writing a story on Shelby and added a link to the memorial website so @planula could see what she'd already done. Then she asked if they could meet to discuss her experiences.

She spent the rest of the bus ride worried about Jacko and Shelby and her own pathetic inability to write pages. The trolls didn't have to kill her off. She was doing that to herself.

Camilla had chosen a Chinese restaurant near the bus stop on El Camino Road. The broad street and low buildings looked like every movie she'd seen about California. Generic, but quirky.

She found the restaurant easily because her phone maps knew their stuff. Because she was early, she went in to get a table alone. The smell of garlic, soy sauce and spices made her stomach growl. She asked for a table facing the window and ordered a jasmine tea while she waited.

Then she played "Is this woman Camilla?" which was a harder game than she'd expected. A single young woman in leggings and a bright red top wasn't Camilla. Another older woman in jeans and a sweater likewise. She was starting to wonder if she'd been ghosted like a Tinder date when a black woman in a business suit stopped at her table.

"Ivy Corva?" she asked.

Ivy held out her hand and they shook. Camilla was thin, with short hair, and she glowed with health. Her skin was flawless and her eyes seemed preternaturally bright. She looked to be in her early twenties.

"Thanks for meeting with me," Ivy said as they both sat down.

"Anything I can do to help Shelby, even now." Camilla glanced at the menu and then back at Ivy. "She saved my life, you know."

"How did she do that?"

Camilla shuddered. "About a year ago, I got breast cancer. The aggressive kind."

"I'm sorry to hear that."

Camilla waved her hand. "Not gonna lie. It was awful. I had chemo and I could barely stand up and I couldn't work and I lost my job."

The waitress came and enthusiastically asked for their orders.

"Spicy dan dan noodles," Camilla said. "And a custard tart. And green tea."

Ivy ordered pot stickers.

"So," Camilla continued. "I couldn't pay my bills and I ended up on the street."

Ivy wanted to tell her about medical leave and all the benefits in Estonia and why that should never have happened in a rich country like the US, but she kept quiet.

"It was grim." Camilla took a sip of green tea and winced. "Hot. I was living in my car and the chemo was making me sick and I lost all my hair. I thought I was going to die in a crappy 1995 Ford Taurus."

Ivy nodded in what she hoped was a sympathetic way and tried to keep a horrified expression off her face.

"I ended up getting dinner at Margie's every day. She's really kind. She found special cancer lady hats and cooked me super bland food and gave me a Thermos so I could eat some later, too."

An entire government safety net replaced by a kind woman with a Thermos and hats. Margie was doing a lot.

"Anyway, I met Shelby there and she got me into section 8 housing and then she got me a job at her own company and gave me health insurance there, too."

Ivy wished she'd met Camilla yesterday when she was less cynical. "That was wonderful of Shelby."

"She didn't have to do it." Camilla sipped her tea and looked at the door to the kitchen. "And once I was in a house and had medical and a stable job. Well, I got better."

The waitress arrived with their food and Camilla dug into hers right away.

Ivy hated to ask the question. "Did Shelby ever inject you with something?"

"You mean the B12? The cancer doctors said it wouldn't hurt and might help, so we kept at it and then my cancer went into remission."

"That's great!"

"It's a miracle is what it is. One of my doctors is writing up a paper. Said he's never seen cancer shrivel up and die like that. And I owe it all to your friend."

"So, they didn't expect your cancer to go away?"

Camilla drew a finger across her throat. "Death sentence. Six months, three months without the chemo. Same kind of cancer that killed Shelby's mom."

"And it's all gone?"

"The tumors started shrinking like ice cubes in hot tea until they disappeared." Camilla beamed and finished off her noodles.

Ivy hadn't even had a single pot sticker. She ate one now. Garlic and meat and soy sauce and the perfect fried shell. "Wow."

"This place is amazing," Camilla said. "Only the best for any friend of Shelby's."

"Do you know if Shelby injected anyone else with the B12?"

"Lots of folks. Moms and kids, too." Camilla smiled. "I know that's not what cured me, but it's the thought that counts. And the job and the housing."

"Moms and kids?" Ivy's voice squeaked.

"Sure, but it was just B12. Kids need it too. No big deal."

What if it wasn't B12? What if Shelby's formula had cured Camilla? "How long after you started taking those B12 shots did you improve?"

"It wasn't the shots, you know," Camilla said. "When the stress went away, the healing could begin."

Ivy studied her. She was the picture of health and calm and confidence. Shelby had done that. She'd found a woman living in her car and dying of cancer and she'd reached out to help with her formula and with more pragmatic help. Either way, it was a good thing.

"Do you have a job now, since Nyssa?" Ivy wasn't sure how to finish the sentence.

"Switched over to one of their suppliers to keep up my health insurance." Camilla sighed. "I was sorry about Nyssa folding. Shelby believed in it so much. One time I asked her to a movie and she said she hadn't seen one since college. Or gone on a real date. Or taken even a single day off."

"She barely did those things in college either."

"No days off?"

"When we were roommates I used to have to remind her to eat. I was gone one weekend and on Sunday she fainted in the library from low blood sugar."

"At Nyssa she had a timer on her watch," Camilla said. "It told her when to eat. She mostly lived on energy bars she kept in a drawer in her office. We called her the Cliff Queen."

"Yet she still had time for homeless outreach."

"Your girl was a saint. A driven, hangry saint."

They both laughed.

"Do you know the names of other people Shelby helped?" Ivy asked.

"I was kind of balled up inside myself back then, waiting to die. Margie might know some. But Shelby worked with people right on the street, too."

"So Margie won't know them all?"

"Probably not. Probably impossible to know how much good Shelby shared in this world." Camilla beamed at her and ate her custard tart.

Ivy wondered why it was easier for her to believe the negative things that Jacko had said than it was to believe the positive ones that Camilla had. She felt like it was a character flaw she should work on. While Camilla talked about her job ordering things for the business, Ivy finished her dumplings and ruminated.

Camilla insisted on paying for lunch and then suggested they take a walk. She led them out of the restaurant and in the direction of Nyssa. Once on the road, she walked at a good clip, like a woman with a limited lunch hour.

In a few minutes they arrived at a rocky beach where long green waves rolled in and retreated. The kind of ageless scene that usually made Ivy happy.

"I come here most days to watch the cormorants." Camilla pointed to a pair of black birds standing with their wings spread. "I love how they dry their feathers. Like they're posing for a calendar."

"Shouldn't their feathers be waterproof? Like ducks."

"Their design seems flawed, doesn't it?" Camilla said. "They live on saltwater fish that they have to dive to catch, but they don't have oil glands so their feathers get waterlogged."

Ivy watched a newly-arrived bird shake till droplets flew. "So they're in the wrong place?"

"It seems like it, but they're not. They can dive deeper than other birds because their feathers get waterlogged. I used to look at them and hope that I had cancer for a reason, a reason that made me stronger like these birds, even if I didn't know what it was."

"And?"

"I'm still looking," she said. "But at least I'm out of the car."

"Feels like progress." Ivy realized that she didn't have a home right now either. Or even a car. She had the airport until Nyssa figured out what

257

she was doing and stopped letting her change her ticket.

While they strolled along the shore, Camilla watched the birds and Ivy the waves. Camilla bounced with each step like a teenager, making Ivy feel impossibly old. Camilla slowed when her phone rang.

"Who?" She stopped walking altogether and Ivy wasn't sure if she should step away to give her privacy, but decided to stay and be nosy.

"Where?" Camilla asked. The person on the other end, who sounded pretty upset, seemed to be giving directions.

"I know that spot," Camilla said. "I'll be there in a couple minutes."

Ivy looked at her expectantly.

"A guy I used to know OD'd not far from here," Camilla said. "I have to go."

She jogged away and Ivy followed. She'd learned basic CPR in high school. Maybe she could help.

She was out of breath too quickly, a reminder that she'd sat around too much the past couple of weeks. Camilla bounded ahead like a marathoner out for a stroll. Ivy reminded herself that she liked Camilla. She sure did.

After they'd jogged a couple kilometers, Ivy was considering giving up and letting those who weren't out of breath do first aid when Camilla stopped next to a couple by the road. Thin to the point of gauntness, the woman kept hugging herself with her bony arms, her hands fluttering like skeletal butterflies. The guy stood still as stone, staring at a rock.

"Where?" Camilla asked and the woman pointed.

Ivy followed her indication and picked her way across the rocks to where a man lay crumpled against gray stones battered smooth by waves. His pale abdomen gleamed in the sun and she wondered what had happened to his shirt. As she neared, four black cormorants took flight.

She studied the man. Rubber tubing encircled his thin arm and a needle rested at the crook of his elbow. The bruise on his bare forearm must have been from where she'd blocked his punch.

Without his jacket, his ribs jutted out painfully. She reached around his oily hair to search for a pulse in his neck, but she knew already that there would be none. She stumbled to the ocean and threw up her potstickers in the water. Even after there was nothing left, her stomach still heaved. She spat into the water.

"I'm sorry," she said and walked back over to Camilla and her friends.

"Is he dead?" Camilla asked. The woman hugged herself tighter.

"No pulse," Ivy said.

Camilla nodded and pulled out her phone.

"How do you know him?" Ivy asked.

"He ate at Margie's, too," Camilla said. "Lots of nice people on the streets, but he wasn't one."

"He came into money," the thin woman said. "We came down to see if he'd share."

Came into money. Into Ivy's money. Her nose throbbed.

"Why here?" Camilla asked.

The woman shrugged. "Not the first place we looked. We come up here sometimes because Jacko got paid by a business lady near here."

"Do you remember her name?" Ivy asked.

The woman wiped the back of her hand across her nose. "He never said."

Camilla handed the woman a tissue. "I'm calling 911."

Ivy barely listened as Camilla described their location and what they'd found. Camilla sounded calm and matter of fact, like she found bodies every day. Ivy couldn't even look in his direction.

"Be about a half hour," Camilla said after she got off the phone. "Faster than usual."

"Usual?" Ivy asked.

"Not my first rodeo. Not even my first one on this beach." Camilla fished around in her purse and handed Ivy a mint. "Peppermint calms your stomach."

Ivy popped it into her mouth. Her stomach didn't improve, but at least her mouth didn't taste so gross. She blew her nose.

"I jog here sometimes to look and call it in if I find someone." Camilla took a mint. "Everyone deserves to be found before the crabs get to them."

Ivy's stomach twitched in response and she sucked harder on the mint.

Then she sat on the rocks next to Camilla and waited. Camilla's friends left because they didn't want to talk to the police. Ivy realized, too late, that she should have asked them if they knew Shelby.

Camilla called her office to explain why she was going to be late. She gave directions to the person on the end of the phone about contacting a shipping supplier. Ivy could see why Shelby had hired her. Camilla kept it together and got things done in tough situations.

Ivy stared at the ocean, trying not to think of Jacko's body on the rocks. Because she'd killed him, one way or another. If it was a simple overdose, her story fee had paid for the heroin. If it was Mr. Linton or someone at Nyssa tying up loose ends, she'd led them to him by not being more discreet last night. Whatever Shelby had or hadn't done, Jacko was on Ivy's conscience.

A cormorant arrowed into the water and disappeared for so long she was sure that it must have drowned. Then its sleek head popped up carrying an ill-fated fish. The circle of life.

A familiar voice called from behind her. "Ivy?"

She turned to see Tristan picking his way across the rocks. The cuffs of his fancy suit weren't even dirty by the time he reached her. She looked down at her own wet pant legs.

"How?" he asked.

"OD," Camilla said. "Journalist?"

"What the hell are you doing here?" Ivy asked.

"I monitor the police radio for areas of interest to my clients," he said. "It's automated."

Camilla looked at him with interest. "Like with AI?"

261

"Excuse us for a moment." Tristan put a hand under Ivy's elbow and they walked a few yards away. "How are you feeling?"

"Responsible," she said.

"You're not," he said. "Either he injected his own death or someone else did. And it wasn't you holding that needle."

"Why do you suppose he ended up here?" She gestured at the waves, the rocks, and the nearby industrial business park.

"Maybe he was making a point to Nyssa or to Shelby or maybe this was just a peaceful place where he liked to get high," he said. "Don't go down that rabbit hole."

"I can see the White Rabbit from here," she said.

"You're having one hell of a trip," he said.

"If someone associated with Nyssa killed him, wouldn't they want him to be found far from their office?"

"If so, this place is a coincidence," he said.

"Or maybe someone was trying to make a point," she said. "That threatening Nyssa is a bad idea."

"You're not threatening anyone," he said. "Right?"

"Camilla over there knew Jacko and she said he talked about working at the lab. So maybe the other things he said were true too."

"Or maybe he knew how to tell plausible lies."

A police car rolled to a stop not far from Tristan's car.

"Excuse me?" called a police woman from the road. "Is this the right spot?"

"Yes," Camilla yelled back. She pointed toward Jacko's body, not visible from the road. "He's over here."

The policewoman walked over the rocks in the direction Camilla had indicated. She wore sensible shoes and a uniform. A short man in uniform was right behind her. Everyone converged at Jacko's body.

"You touch him?" the policewoman called back to them.

"Miss Corva checked for a pulse and then we called you," Camilla said.

"You should have left him alone," the policewoman said.

"He might have been alive," Ivy said.

"Except he wasn't," the short officer pointed out.

"Glad you're not an EMT," Ivy said.

Camilla snorted and Tristan shot her a warning glance.

"What about you?" The woman spoke to Tristan.

"I arrived later, to pick up Miss Corva," Tristan said. "I touched nothing."

"He didn't," Camilla confirmed. "Also, before I forget. Miss Corva threw up in the water, in case that's relevant."

Ivy felt like that was oversharing, but she didn't say anything.

The policewoman spoke into her radio in number codes that Ivy didn't recognize. Proof she didn't watch enough cop shows.

"I'll talk to this one, you take the other one," her partner said when she'd finished.

Ivy ended up talking to the woman. She introduced herself as Officer Finlay which Ivy's brain translated to Officer Friendly, even though she clearly wasn't.

She ran her through her lunch with Camilla, explaining that they'd met to discuss a story she was writing. Their walk along the beach until Camilla got a call and they found the body. Then Ivy told her that she knew the deceased and Officer Finlay perked up.

"You knew him?" she asked.

Tristan lightly touched her elbow and it was clear that he wanted her to shut up now, or preferably a few seconds ago.

"I saw him at Shelby Linton's funeral and I met him for a piece of pie last night," Ivy said.

"Why?"

"He's part of Shelby's story too, or he was. It was supposed to be about how she worked with people who are homeless."

"What time last night?"

Ivy gave her all the information, including that she'd slept at the airport.

"I'm sure there's video footage to show Ms. Corva was there all night," Tristan put in.

"I think he might have been mixed up with something at Nyssa. That he might have been dosed

264

with their product," Ivy said quickly. "And maybe that's why he was killed."

"Or the guy OD'd," Officer Finlay said. "Looking at his arm, his track marks. Sometimes the simplest explanation is right."

"Sometimes it's easiest," Ivy said. "Doesn't make it right."

"I've taken notes on all you said, and we'll be in touch." Officer Finlay seemed unconcerned by Ivy's words or her suspicions.

"Will you do an autopsy?" Ivy asked.

"We'll check for drugs, do a standard tox screen. See if he drowned." Officer Finlay looked down at the body. "But it looks pretty straightforward."

A white van with the words "San Francisco Medical Examiner" on the side pulled up next to the shore and turned on its hazards. A portly man got out of the front seat and Officer Finlay waved to him. Just behind him, Ivy watched Wendy approach on foot.

"Why are you here?" Ivy asked Wendy when she was close enough. Not the friendliest opening, but Wendy answered anyway.

"I came from work and saw the cars and stopped to see what was going on."

"Came from work?" Ivy asked.

"Nyssa's around the corner." Wendy waved vaguely to her right. "I went to see if I could get my personal stuff and feed the mice. But the feds had already sac'ed them."

"Sacked them?" Ivy asked.

"Sacrificed. It's what we call it. Killed them." Wendy sounded annoyed, as usual. "We could have gotten good data out of them. That's what they're for. Not getting dumped into an incinerator."

Wendy glanced over at Jacko's body with no hint of surprise or disgust. She was even more matter-of-fact about it than Camilla. Ivy imagined Wendy would be happy to sac him for his data. She felt downright sheltered.

"Who takes care of the mice usually?" Ivy asked.

"My postdoc, Martin Schmidt. He feeds them and sacrifices them when the time comes. Does the dissections. He's a genius at it."

"So you don't let civilians clean the cages and get rid of the bodies?"

"Not how science works." Wendy looked incensed. "We track those mice every second of their lives. Otherwise we can't be sure of the data."

Ivy pointed to Jacko's body. "That guy there said that Shelby hired him to clean out cages and get rid of some of the mice and replace them with new ones."

Wendy paled. She touched her right earplug, then sat down too hard on a rock. "Are you sure?"

Ivy shrugged. "He said so, but I don't suppose we'll ever know now."

"If it's true—if there's even a chance it's true— then all our data is useless." Wendy glared at Jacko's body like she wanted to kick it. "It's tainted."

"Have you seen the dead man around Nyssa's lab?" Tristan asked.

"Nobody unauthorized is allowed in. We have protocols and security."

Camilla spoke up. "He told me that he worked at Nyssa sometimes."

"Nyssa? Shelby Linton's lab?" Wendy bit off each word.

"I'm just the messenger." Camilla held up her hands.

Wendy switched back to glaring at Jacko.

"Years of my life," Wendy muttered. "At least Timothy's OK."

"He's out of jail?" Ivy asked.

"Paid a giant bail, but yes." Wendy looked at her hands. "I have to make sure my results aren't ever used. They'll have to start from scratch. If they ever start again."

She looked so forlorn that Ivy felt sorry for her, something she hadn't even thought possible.

"You can go now, Miss Corva." Officer Finlay headed toward the coroner's van. Over her shoulder, she tossed out, "But please don't leave town."

CHAPTER TWENTY

Tristan put his hand under Ivy's elbow and guided her away. "That's not legally binding. You can go whenever you want. In fact, leaving town is your best move."

"Running away as a power move," Ivy said. "Unexpected choice."

Her feet squelched when she walked and her pants were soaked to the knee. She must have gone all the way into the ocean to throw up, but she didn't remember it. She pulled her jacket closer and wished for Toomas and that nice warm ambulance.

"I know this might sound presumptuous," Tristan said. "But I have a washing machine and a shower."

"This is how horror movies start," she answered. "And thanks."

He chuckled in his Tristan way as a motorcycle zoomed past. A rickety old Kawasaki, it was a twin to the one Ivy had owned in college. This rider even wore a poison green helmet, as Ivy once had. The rider was a woman and the way she handled the bike, reckless but skilled, was familiar.

Ivy sprinted after her. She pounded down the street with Tristan at her heels asking questions. The bike slowed for a second, then sped up. Ivy redoubled her speed.

When she got close, the rider flipped her the bird and turned a corner. By the time Ivy got to the corner, she'd vanished.

Gasping, Ivy held onto a stucco-clad building. Tristan jogged up. He wasn't even out of breath. "What was that about?"

"The bike. Did you. See?" Ivy forced out the words between breaths.

"Female, normal height, riding a Kawasaki Ninja, black leathers, green helmet, dark hair," he said.

"Yes." Ivy looked frantically up and down the street, like the motorcycle would return.

Tristan looked at her. "And you decided to chase it because?"

She pushed off the building. "She looked like Shelby."

"She was wearing a full-face helmet," he pointed out. "And she had dark hair."

"I know that. But the way she rode and the way she flipped me off." Ivy pushed her hair back. Her hand smelled like sea water. "It seemed like her."

"That's a common grief response," he said. "When—"

She held up a hand to silence him. "Do you know where Timothy Shah lives?"

Tristan hesitated.

"I'm sure I can find out another way." She turned away.

"In Woodside," Tristan said. "I have his address."

"Is that too far for an Uber?"

"Unless you're richer than I think, yes." He looked back at his immaculate car and down at her wet shoes. "I'll give you a ride."

"That's kind."

"It's my job to keep you out of trouble."

She looked at the flashing police lights as they loaded Jacko's body onto a stretcher. "How do you think you're doing?"

"You're not helping as much as you could," he said.

Once she was in his car, she turned on the heat full blast and pointed it all at her feet. The car started to smell like seafood and Tristan cracked his window. She was glad to see that his politeness had limits.

"Once around the block, in case the motorcycle is still there?" she asked.

He looked like he wanted to argue, but he put the car in gear and circled the block. She spotted Nyssa's office, as Wendy had said, but no sign of the rider. She was probably miles away by now wondering why a stranger had chased her down the street.

"Can we check out the office too?" Ivy asked.

Tristan complied.

No sign of the mysterious motorcycle in Nyssa's parking lot. Was she wrong? As Tristan had pointed out, she hadn't seen the driver's face, or even any exposed skin. But her legs had known something when they took off running. Even though it made no sense, she thought it had been Shelby. Then she reminded herself how she'd thought that jogger on the bridge was Shelby too, and she hadn't been either. Grief did strange things to your head, as Tristan had tried to tell her.

"It could have been anyone," he said.

"Let's just go to Timothy's," she told him.

He used the same freeway that they'd taken to Kepler's. Golden fields rolled by on both sides of the pavement and blue sky formed a dome overhead. It was completely unlike the gray glass canyons of San Francisco.

No green-helmeted motorcycles here either.

"Are you certain that speaking to Mr. Shah is in your best interest?" Tristan asked.

She ignored him, like she did her conscience, bunched her coat against his window, and tried to fall asleep. Even with the smell and sitting upright, it was better than last night at the airport.

She woke up disoriented when the car crunched to a stop on gravel. Car. Man. Strange house. After her adrenalin kicked in, she recognized Tristan and a tasteful mansion designed with the clean lines and simplicity of a Frank Lloyd Wright house.

"Is that prairie style?" she asked.

Tristan looked over. "Good morning."

"It looks Frank Lloyd Wright-inspired to me." She wiped sleep from her eyes. "Let's go knock."

"And hope he doesn't have a dog," Tristan said.

"I'm good with dogs," she said. "I'll take point."

He was out of the car and striding down the walkway while she was still remembering how to open the door. Maybe she wasn't as awake as she thought she was.

Not that it mattered. No barking sounded when she caught up and rang the bell. It produced a deep tone very unlike the buzzing she was used to at Shelby's apartment. Based on the house, Timothy had more money than Shelby did. Didn't CEOs make more than CFOs? Ivy wasn't sure. And Timothy, being older, had probably had more time to accumulate his own wealth than Shelby had. Both were indisputably more successful than Ivy.

She and Tristan waited on the long front porch and she studied the woodwork.

"What kind of wood do you think that is?" she asked Tristan.

"Redwood?" He rang the bell again.

"Why are you here?" she asked.

"You asked me to drive you," he said. "Remember?"

"I mean in general. Why did you come to the beach to get me and then take me where I asked?"

"Your suspicious nature is useful." He paused and looked out over artfully arranged boulders draped with moss. "I'm here because you're my client and I signed a contract to protect you."

"And?" she asked.

"And my last client died while under my care and I'm not making that mistake again." His usually amiable face went stern.

"Or," Ivy said. "Maybe she didn't."

"Sure," he said. "Maybe her father and the medical examiner and the man behind that door were all wrong."

As if on cue, the door swung open and Timothy stood on the threshold. He looked very different from the man in the suit she'd watched being arrested at Nyssa's office. His dark hair was mussed and he wore jeans and a gray t-shirt instead of a suit. Dark circles had appeared under his eyes and his broad shoulders slumped. He was way more attractive this way and Ivy wondered if thinking this was part of some caretaker pathology she hadn't shown in the past.

"Mr. Walsh," he said. "And Miss..."

"Corva," Ivy filled in. "Ivy Corva."

"Apologies for forgetting your name. I've had a difficult few days." He opened the door and gestured for them to come inside.

Ivy wondered if he had any idea that she was Shelby's friend who he'd met at the funeral. Hard to fault him if he didn't. He'd been through a lot.

"I could make tea," he said. "My housekeeper is off today."

Ivy looked at Tristan, not sure about the protocol.

"Tea would be lovely," Tristan said.

Tristan slipped out of his shoes at the door, so Ivy followed suit. Her socks were still wet and, after a quick glance at the expensive rugs, she took them off and followed the men.

Timothy led them through the hall, past a living room with wooden Craftsman-style furniture to a large, modern kitchen done up in warm colors.

273

Like Shelby's, it was immaculate. Unlike hers, this one was cozy and inviting.

Timothy bustled around making tea while Ivy admired the wooden details. She'd never seen prairie-style furnishings outside of the internet, and they were a welcome change from all the blah modern stuff she'd seen lately. She wondered if Shelby had spent more time here or in her gray castle in the sky.

In short order, Timothy set a tray in front of them with green tea, sugar, and tiny round cookies with an almond on top of each one.

Ivy helped herself to a cookie and let the tea cool. The cookie tasted like butter and almonds and she could see herself eating the entire plate. Even the crunch was perfect. Timothy was clearly a guy who appreciated details. Shelby would have liked that about him.

"Is there a viable threat against me?" Timothy asked Tristan. "Is that why you're here?"

"What kind of threat are you expecting?" Ivy asked.

Timothy turned to her, mildly surprised. She couldn't decide if that was sexism or if he had forgotten that she existed. "internet crazies have been sending me death threats. They think I drove Shelby to her death."

"Did you?" Ivy asked.

Timothy blinked, drew in a slow breath and said, "No."

She took another cookie without feeling guilty. She was pretty sure this guy hadn't driven Shelby anywhere. Probably the other way around. "Why do people think that?"

Timothy glanced over at Tristan as if expecting rescue, but Tristan sipped his tea and smiled encouragingly. He was clearly the good cop in any good cop/bad cop scenario.

"Shelby and I worked together and we were...close," Timothy said. "We shared the same stresses."

"Not all of them," Ivy said.

Tristan cleared his throat. He was right. She wasn't here to needle Timothy. She was here to ask him questions.

"Tell me about that last night," she said. "The night Shelby died."

Timothy's shoulders sagged. "I was working late at Nyssa, like usual. We'd closed on a large round of funding and there were a lot of details to attend to. So I was knee deep in spreadsheets when Shelby called. She said she was on Golden Gate Bridge and asked if I could come get her."

"Did she do that often?" Ivy asked.

"Ask me for a ride? No. The situation was weird and her voice sounded off."

"Off how?"

"Tired, down." He took a sip of tea. "She was usually more commanding."

"What exactly did she say?" Ivy asked.

He closed his eyes as if thinking. "This is Shelby. I jogged to the Golden Gate Bridge. Can you come get me? I'm tired. Something like that."

"That was it?"

275

"She had to repeat it a couple of times because it was loud. Traffic goes right by the walkway. But, yes, that was it. So, once I knew what she wanted, I got in my car and drove straight over."

Ivy knew from his phone records that he had. "And then?"

"I got stuck in traffic behind an accident," he said. "Someone rear ended another car and smoke or steam or something was pouring out from under their hood. I was sitting there and I saw movement out of the corner of my eye and I looked up and saw her climbing that suicide fence."

"Are you sure it was her?"

Timothy's eyes widened. "She was wearing her white Gucci jogging suit. The one with the stripe. I'd seen it before."

"But that's just her clothes," Ivy said. "Anyone can wear clothes."

"It looked like her. Blonde hair. Her clothes. And later, later they said it was her who jumped."

"Did you see her face?" Ivy asked.

"She was too far away and it was dark," he said. "But everyone knows it was her."

"Everyone," Ivy said.

She asked more questions but didn't learn anything else. Then she let Tristan take over and discuss Timothy's internet threats. Compared to hers, his were like invitations to high tea. Apparently, driving Shelby to her death was considered a more minor offense than writing a book that devalued dicks. But she didn't say that because she didn't want to get into the suffering Olympics with Timothy.

So she listened and learned that Shelby'd had groupies because she was such a visible female CEO and they all hated Timothy. They blamed him for the company's financial woes. Technically, he was the CFO, so he had to be partially responsible, but so did Shelby and it seemed oddly sexist to take her actions out of the equation. Besides the Shelby-groupies, he had a lot of unpleasant emails from investors, potential investors, and people holding him accountable for taking away the world's chance to achieve immortality. All in all, his trolls were more interesting than Ivy's. Tristan counseled patience and not responding and got various emails forwarded to him for later analysis. She wondered how many blistering emails Tristan read in a day. He must have a strong constitution.

Instead of butting in, she ate all the cookies and drank all the tea. It wasn't exactly a meal, but it was better than nothing. And she felt hollow after throwing up her lunch.

Afterward she and Tristan walked out to the car side-by-side. Her shoes were still wet and a ring of salt had formed halfway up her calf. She was sure that she still smelled awful.

"Is that offer of a shower still open?" she asked.

Back onto the freeway they went. All roads lead to the freeway in California, Ivy supposed.

"Is Timothy Shah a client?" she asked.

"No, but I've analyzed communications for him in the past when they overlapped Shelby's," Tristan said. "There's no conflict of interest with you, if that's what you're worried about."

"I have a list of things to be worried about," she said. "But I guess I can take that one off."

"I'm sure you'll replace it with two other things," Tristan said. "I have faith in you."

She laughed. "Not wrong."

Tristan's apartment wasn't too far from Millennium Tower, so he must have been well-paid. She wondered what her protection was costing Mr. Linton, but was too afraid to ask. Tristan's building didn't rate a doorman, but it had a special key for the elevator and Tristan's alarm disarming process was as elaborate as she expected of him. Even after watching him, she had no idea how to turn it off.

"Do the crazies you deal with ever come after you?" she asked.

"Most of the crazies never come after anyone," was his non-answer.

The apartment itself was spare, but elegant, and his shower was great. She suspected he'd found some way to hack the low flow requirements that held Shelby's showerhead hostage because it nearly blasted her skin off. It was also gloriously hot and she felt warm again for the first time since seeing Jacko's body.

If this was a horror movie, Tristan would be coming through the door with a knife at any moment.

Enough of that. She stepped out and grabbed one of the towels he'd laid out for her. It was fluffy and smelled like lilac. He'd even left her a robe which also smelled of lilac. All in all, it was positively decadent compared to swabbing off her armpits at the airport.

After she cleaned up and brushed her wet hair, she sat on the couch in his robe, listening to the washing machine work on restoring her clothes to their former glory. But this time with a lilac scent.

"Tell me about Camilla," he said, setting down a tray on the coffee table. It had soup and toast so he must have noticed how she'd devoured the almond cookies.

"I'm fine," she said and then her stomach growled and they both laughed. "Campbell's?"

"Trader Joe's," he replied in a vaguely insulted tone.

While she ate, she filled him in on Camilla and her story of being cured of cancer by Shelby's help, and maybe also by her B12 shots. The soup tasted like chicken and ginger and was definitely a step up from the Campbell's soup of her childhood.

"Do you think she's credible?" Tristan asked when she finished.

"Yup." She dipped her toast in the soup. "She was ill and she got better. But she doesn't think her recovery was due to Shelby's shots either. That's just me wondering if they did. Nobody else."

"Can it be tested? Like in her blood or her hair or nails?"

"No idea," Ivy said. "Are you friends with anyone else at Nyssa? Like someone on the biological side?"

He shook his head. "I only worked with Shelby and sometimes with Mr. Shah if they received joint threats or threats against the company."

"I should have tried harder to suck up to Wendy," she said.

"So you were trying at all?" he asked.

The washer buzzed and he got up and put her clothes in the dryer. She settled down on his comfortable couch in his comfortable robe. If she wasn't careful, she was going to fall asleep right here. It was definitely better than his car or the floor at the airport. Her grading system for comfort was getting lower all the time.

She closed her eyes and saw the green-helmeted biker. What was it about that figure that made her think of Shelby?

Carefully, she replayed the encounter, second by second, in her memory. The rider slowed as she passed the coroner's van and saw Ivy squelching up toward the road. Her helmeted head turned toward them and then shifted to look past them at the police and crowd on the rocks. She couldn't have seen Jacko's body from that angle, but she must have known something was wrong.

Then she turned back to Ivy. Or Tristan, or maybe something right behind them. It was impossible to know because of the helmet. But Ivy felt like she'd been looking directly at her at the time and she wasn't going to discount that feeling entirely.

Anyway, when she looked at Ivy she took one boot off the foot peg, as if she thought about stopping the bike. Then she tossed her head, in a Shelby-like way, and accelerated away. Ivy replayed the head toss. She couldn't figure out why it felt like Shelby, but it did.

Then Ivy ran toward the motorcycle. The rider had clearly noticed that, because she rode away and flipped Ivy off. Head tosses and bird flips weren't considered a way to make a positive ID anywhere in the world. But who else would have chosen Ivy's old bike? Ivy's old helmet? Flipped her off? If those choices weren't coincidences, they led to one conclusion.

"Are you napping?" Tristan broke into her thoughts.

"Thinking." She sat up and pulled out her laptop. "I need to look something up."

He gathered up her tea cup and plate. "I'll wash up."

She searched for shelby linton sex tape and looked at the many links that led to Shelby's greatest humiliation. Several sites hosted the footage now and even more linked to them. Shelby's intimate moments were never coming back off the internet. Everyone on Earth could see her naked at any time and probably a horrifying number of them were doing that right this minute.

Including Ivy.

Feeling like a traitor, she clicked a link. Before she could mute it, Shelby's voice filled the room. Deep, sultry, and mischievous. Tears pricked Ivy's eyes and she hit the mute button.

But she couldn't stop watching. She cataloged details. The striped bedspread. The nondescript gray wall they'd called shades of institutional death. The white pillow where Shelby had placed the suicide note to her father a few weeks after this tape was made And then Shelby herself, naked on the single bed looking up at Gerald, the bastard who hadn't deserved her.

Ivy paused the video. She increased her browser size and dragged the scrollbar to focus on a single spot. A tiny birthmark shaped like a bell rested on Shelby's side. Ivy had seen it before, most

281

recently on a picture atop a giant easel at her funeral. The molecule tattoo covered part of it, but the rest was still visible inside a hexagon.

To be sure, Ivy searched the internet for a picture of Shelby in that white gown that she'd seen at her funeral. And found it. Shelby's whole life was out there on the internet. No private moments for her. Ivy increased her browser size and scrolled to view the same spot on Shelby's side. The birthmark was clearly visible there too. She clicked back to the tab with the sex tape.

Tristan spoke over her shoulder. "Is that—?"

"Yup." She pointed to his laptop. "Open up the autopsy photos. I want to see her side."

Tristan sat next to her on the couch and opened his laptop. His glance flicked toward Shelby, naked in Ivy's tab with a smile once meant only for Gerald and then he went back to work. He opened the report he'd shown her earlier and scrolled.

Ivy winced when he passed the picture of Shelby's broken face against stainless steel at the morgue. Mr. Linton could never have identified her from her battered face. Tristan stopped on the picture of Shelby's fully naked body. She looked so pale and thin and frail. Her skin was almost translucent. The word 'malnourished' popped into Ivy's head.

She reached over and zoomed in on the picture on Tristan's laptop, then leaned forward, eyes scanning the tattoo, that chemical structure that once pointed to Shelby's hopeful future. Her eyes stopped at the edge of a hexagon. She leaned in closer, inches from the screen, then looked back at the sex tape and the woman in the dress.

She knew the truth before Tristan drew in a quick surprised breath. She rocked back on the couch, her own breath stolen away too.

"No bell."

CHAPTER TWENTY-ONE

Ivy closed her eyes and slumped on the couch. Shelby was alive. She was out in the world, maybe riding motorcycles and eating food and having sex and planning for her future. And maybe injecting unsuspecting desperate people with an untried formula.

Tristan stood and poured a glass of scotch. The label said Highland Park and the number 15 so she assumed it wasn't cheap but she wasn't enough of a scotch person to know. He added a dash of water, swirled the glass and handed it to her. Then he followed the same procedure to pour one for himself.

A quick sip and the tastes of peat and smoke and a hint of citrus danced across her tongue. Another delicious thing way out of her price range. She sipped again, and noticed that Tristan wasn't sipping. He drank like a man who'd returned from the desert, and maybe he had.

He reached up and loosened his tie and undid the top button. He ran a hand through his hair and suddenly looked positively unkempt. She could see what Stephen saw in him.

"My job is keeping people safe. I'm good at it. I never lost one. Until Shelby." He grimaced. "I guess I didn't even lose her."

Ivy didn't know what to say, but that was fine because Tristan kept going on his own.

"How didn't I see this coming?" he asked.

"Unearned trust." She took a bigger sip of her scotch.

"I'm not here to trust my clients," he said. "I'm here to protect them."

He drew out the word protect and she could see how he meant every syllable.

"I'm honored," she said.

He finished his glass and poured another one.

"Why didn't she come to me?" He was facing away from her, but she heard the pain in every word.

"You would have helped her to fake her own death?" Ivy asked.

"We would have assessed the possibilities."

That wasn't a no. She took a second sip and held off on a third. Someone needed a clear head. Times were getting tough if that person was going to be her.

"And there wouldn't be an unidentified dead woman in the morgue right now," he finished.

Ivy took a tiny sip of the scotch. It was so good that it was criminal the way he was slugging it back. "I know one missing blonde in Shelby's orbit."

"Who?" he asked, surprised.

"Pat. Jacko's girlfriend."

"Jacko?"

"The guy lying on the rocks with a needle in his arm."

Tristan let out his breath in a whoosh. "Oh, boy."

He took a long drink and it became obvious that she'd be doing any driving for a while. With that in mind, she retrieved her clothes from the dryer. The scent of lilac enveloped her as she pulled on the warm clothes. She leaned into it. She needed all the flower hugs she could get right now.

When she went back to the living room, Tristan sat staring into his nearly empty scotch glass like it held the answers to the universe. Or at least to Shelby.

"We need to call the cops now," she said.

Detective Rodriguez picked up on the first ring. "Mr. Walsh."

Even if her tone was frosty, she still seemed friendlier to him than she had been to Ivy. Professional courtesy or cute chin dimple?

Tristan summarized what they'd discovered, pretty concisely, especially considering all the Scotch he'd downed.

"If the woman we released for burial wasn't Shelby Linton, this looks damn suspicious," she said. "Send me your evidence and I'll give it a look. See if we're looking at homicide."

Homicide. Ivy's shoulders inched up. But she could think of no other explanation for the body they'd fished out of the water either. That it could have been a random blonde who was the same size and shape as Shelby and with the same tattoo was impossible.

"One more thing," Ivy said.

"Miss Corva?" asked the detective. "Why are you on the line?"

Ivy was impressed that she'd recognized her voice. Those were good cop skills. "Shelby worked with a blond woman at a shelter called Margie's Second Chances. That woman was about Shelby's age and description and she recently disappeared. It might not be related."

"I'll follow that up," the detective said. "What's her name?"

"All I know is her first name, Pat, but I do know that she was in a relationship with a man who was found dead a few hours ago on a beach near the Nyssa office, allegedly via overdose. I don't know his last name either, but his first name is Jacko."

"I think you need to come down to the station and give your statements in person, Miss Corva and Mr. Walsh," the detective said.

Tristan agreed that they would and hung up. Ivy looked at him. His eyes were glassy from the booze.

"I'll drive," she said.

"Faster to walk," he said. "And I need to clear my head."

Before they left, he gathered together their evidence, taking screen captures of the sex tape, the dress photo, and the autopsy photos. He enlarged all three and circled the missing bell in red. He wrote a brief description and added links to all the source URLs. Then he zipped everything up and emailed a copy to Rodriguez, cc'ing Ivy.

"You do your homework," she said. Even drunk.

"I try." He closed his laptop.

"So, if someone does kill me with a plunger, I feel more confident that they'll get caught."

He smiled. "My job is still to keep the plunger away from you. Don't worry."

Then they headed out into a drizzly San Francisco December. The cold jumped right into her bones and settled there. Tristan looked impervious in his long gray coat.

"What about Mr. Linton?" She walked faster. "Who's going to tell him?"

"I'll tell him after we're through with the police."

"No chance for the police to accuse you of witness tampering?" she asked.

"I don't intend to do anything that would incriminate him," Tristan said. "Or get in the way of the police."

They walked a few steps before Ivy said, "Do you think he already knows?"

"If he does, I don't expect him to let on," Tristan said. "So we won't know for sure."

Neither one of them had an answer to that. They walked the rest of the way to the police station in silence.

This time, Detective Rodriguez came right out instead of making them wait in the long line with everyone else bearing a tale of woe. She offered coffee, which they both accepted and Ivy regretted as soon as she took the first sip. Stale, and it chased away the taste of the scotch.

Then Rodriguez separated them and interrogated them one after the other. Tristan went first, so Ivy spent her time sitting in a dingy interrogation room in a haze of stale coffee and looking at the pictures Tristan had sent her on his phone. They were as damning as they had been the first time she saw them, even more so with the circles. Shelby hadn't jumped off that bridge.

She was alive. That had to mean that she'd killed Pat. Maybe Jacko? Anyone else?

Maybe there was an answer that didn't lead there, but Ivy couldn't think of it. Why would Shelby do something like that? Yes, she'd have been publicly humiliated if she'd waited until the story broke, that much was clear. She'd have been discredited and unlikely to work again, also clear. But she could have licked her wounds, lived off her father's money, and maybe staged a comeback in a few years. Or lived the life of a spoiled rich girl. What were her options now?

She texted her suppositions to Anu, who was probably sound asleep and didn't answer. It did her good to at least pretend she was talking to her. The inner voice of Anu told her to stay calm, avoid drama, think logically, and be open to new information. Good advice, that.

Detective Rodriguez finally came into the room and sat across from her. She glanced down at Ivy's cup. "You barely touched your coffee."

Ivy suspected the detective wanted her to apologize for spurning the coffee so she went the other way. "How could you have misidentified my friend's body?"

"We trusted her father." The detective sat and opened a folder. It contained the pictures that Tristan had sent. "Walk me through this."

Ivy walked her through the day's events. Rodriguez seemed suspicious that Ivy had been on the scene when the police arrived to pick up Jacko's body and she also told her not to leave town. Ivy thought it was funny that people had been telling her to leave town practically since her plane landed and now they'd changed their tune. She didn't share this with the detective. Rodriguez didn't look like she'd find that funny at all.

Ivy found out that Jacko's real name was Jack Hannigan and Pat's last name was Nilsson. He had an arrest for dealing and one for petty larceny for stealing a guy's watch right off his wrist. Nothing violent. Pat had one arrest for solicitation.

The police were trying to get DNA samples to compare to the blood on file from Shelby's supposed autopsy, but so far hadn't had any luck. It would be weeks before they knew if Pat was the woman they'd cremated as Shelby. But they could get DNA from Shelby's father or her apartment to rule her out as the corpse they'd fished from the water.

"Where do you think your friend will go now?" Rodriguez asked.

"I'm surprised she's even still here in the Bay Area," Ivy said.

"If you did know, would you turn her in?" Rodriguez asked.

"Would you turn in your own friend? Without ever once listening to her side?"

They went around like that for a while and by the time she finished, Ivy was ready for dinner and a good night's sleep on the airport floor. And they'd both established that she had no damn idea where Shelby might be hiding.

Tristan waited outside the front door, looking at his phone. He'd put himself together before they went into the police station and he still looked immaculate, although he sported a five o'clock shadow.

"How'd it go?" he asked, without looking up.

"It was simultaneously the best and the worst police interrogation I've ever had."

"Newbie?" he asked.

"I've been deflowered now."

He smiled. "Do you feel safe here?"

"I did until you asked that question." Now she took in the people on the sidewalk, the cars zooming by, the dark street that led to the BART transit station. If her trolls or Shelby's were around, would she be any luckier than Jacko?

"Just keep up your situational awareness," he said.

An Uber stopped right in front of them and the driver called out, "Tristan? Like the opera?"

"My mom was a fan." Tristan opened the car door and she got in.

The driver was a young blonde woman with a beehive hairdo. Ivy was too tired to wonder about it.

"I'd like to go to Millennium Tower," she said.

"What?" Tristan climbed in next to her, forcing her to scoot over to the other side of the car.

"I want to see if she's been home. And I want to talk to Mr. Linton."

"I'd rather do that on my own."

"I bet." She wasn't even sure why she was being snarky, but she couldn't help herself.

The cab driver looked at Tristan and smiled like he was a frog turned prince.

"It's your account," she said.

"Millennium Tower," Tristan said. "We might as well get that out of the way."

CHAPTER TWENTY-TWO

Stephen was on duty and he let them pass unchallenged. The lobby seemed so much fancier after the airport, but at least it was warm.

She pressed the number for Shelby's floor.

"I thought we were going to the penthouse." Tristan's finger hovered over the button.

"You go where you want," she said.

"How are you going to get into her apartment?" he asked.

"I still have a key."

He raised an eyebrow.

"Shelby said I could stay with her when she first invited me, so until she asks for her key back, I can come and go as I please."

"Legally that seems a bit dubious."

"She can argue with me in court."

Into Shelby's apartment they went. It was cold and gray and tidy.

"Notice anything different?" Tristan asked.

"Soulless and immaculate," she said. "Same as always."

She wandered through the kitchen. The dishwasher contained her dishes and the ones Shelby had used on that last day. Everything else looked as if neither she nor Shelby had ever cooked here. The living room, too, was unchanged.

Tristan looked uneasily at the door. "I don't want to get caught in here."

"If Shelby catches us, she's in more trouble than we are." Ivy cruised the living room. No changes that she could see. The room had been and remained spotless.

The guest bedroom was exactly as messy as she'd left it. Her bed was still unmade and the towel she'd dropped as she'd hurried to leave with Stephen was still on the bathroom floor. No one had come in and cleaned up her slobbiness.

She took a deep breath and opened the door to Shelby's room. Her bed was perfectly made. Her closet doors closed. The carpet vacuumed in a pristine pattern. She glanced at Shelby's nightstand and stopped. The bag of licorice was gone.

Maybe it had fallen off somehow. She walked to the nightstand, checked the floor, under the bed. Clean carpet and a clear view through to the other side.

"Why are you on the floor?" asked Tristan from the door.

"You're a whiny person to take out on a stakeout."

"Or a borderline breaking and entering," he said. "Make a note of it."

She pointed to the empty nightstand. "When I left, there was a bag of salted licorice right there."

"House cleaner?"

"They didn't make my bed or clean the guest bathroom," she said.

He looked at the empty nightstand too, as if by looking at it they could see who had come and taken away the bag. But that's not how time worked, except in Ivy's novel.

"Anything else?" He looked hopefully at the door.

She gave in because there wasn't. "I'm ready for the next stop."

He waited in the hall while she armed the alarm system. She took one long look around before she closed the door. Then she locked it and dropped Shelby's key back into her backpack. She was keeping it until Shelby demanded it back in person.

In the elevator, Tristan swiped his card and pressed the button for Mr. Linton's penthouse. So Tristan had keycard access. A plastic reminder of his divided loyalties. She texted Anu telling her where she was going and then copied the text and sent it to Olivia with a notice that she'd call in an hour. Failsafes.

"I can read those in the mirror behind you," Tristan said. "Would you like me to do this on my own? You can wait in the lobby and I can take you home after."

"Trying to keep me contained?" she asked.

"Again, it's my job."

"You have at least two jobs here," she said.

"If they were to conflict, I'd do the right thing," he said.

"Which is?"

"Prioritizing the physical safety of both clients."

"So not sacrificing me if Mr. Linton asks you to?"

Tristan grimaced. "Not, not that. I'll protect you from that. And plungers."

"And, one time, a knife."

Tristan shook his head. "Amateur. You could have disarmed him with a wet noodle."

The elevator dinged and opened on a corridor with a single door. She hesitated.

"It might be unpleasant," Tristan said. "But I don't think it'll be unsafe. In my professional opinion."

"That's the kind of thing you would say if it weren't," she pointed out.

Tristan ticked off points on his fingers. "Detective Rodriguez can track you here via the Uber ride. You're on camera going into the lobby and into the elevator with me on tapes that neither I nor Mr. Linton can access or change. You sent out your safety texts to your friend and Olivia. And, finally, I'm on your side and I think I can take Mr. Linton if I have a little warning."

"Not entirely convincing," she said. "But I'm too curious not to go."

"That's a dangerous trait," he said.

"I know it killed the cat." She stepped out of the elevator onto a marble floor and rang the bell. It chimed out a song she didn't recognize.

Tristan stood next to her, his face a professional mask.

"Is that your meeting-the-client face?" she asked.

His lips quirked into a smile.

Mr. Linton opened the door. "What is it, Mr. Walsh? It's late."

"We have news for you. Good news."

Mr. Linton's eyes flicked to Ivy like he hadn't noticed her before. "Why aren't you in Estonia?"

"I missed my plane," she said.

"Out with it," Mr. Linton said to Tristan.

"I think it would be best to have this discussion inside," Tristan said. "Maybe while you're sitting down."

"There's nothing you can tell me that you can't tell me in the hall." Mr. Linton tapped his foot against the marble. He looked ready to close the door in their faces.

Ivy was sick of his attitude. "Shelby is alive."

Mr. Linton swayed and grabbed his doorframe. Tristan moved around to stand next to him, one hand out to catch him if he fell. Ivy felt guilty for jumping right into the news. Tristan would have softened it.

"Or at least we know that the woman who was identified as Shelby wasn't her," Tristan said.

"Maybe inside is a good place," Mr. Linton said.

Tristan kept close to him as they stepped into a hallway as gray and austere as Shelby's, except that this one was made up of high-end marble, not concrete. Mr. Linton led them into a huge living room with floor-to-ceiling windows facing the city. The Bay Bridge, Treasure Island, the sea, and a blanket of fog to soften the edges. Mr. Linton stared ahead, unseeing.

Tristan maneuvered Mr. Linton onto the couch, a leather crescent facing the window. The bridge's lights glowed white through the fog and it matched the couch.

Ivy looked around at the modern glass and leather furniture. What looked like a real Jackson Pollock hung on one wall. The art piece on the left half of the living room, by the grand piano, looked familiar too. A gaunt tortured figure made out of metal.

"I'll fetch you a glass of water." Tristan headed toward some probably vast kitchen leaving her alone with Mr. Linton and his art collection.

Feeling responsible, she went over and sat next to him. The leather felt cold against her jeans, but the couch was surprisingly comfortable.

"Is it true?" Mr. Linton whispered. The hope in his eyes brought tears to her own. Unless he was an amazing actor, he'd had no idea that Shelby was still alive.

"Yes," she said. "We're sure."

He covered his face with both hands and wept. His shoulders bobbed up and down and tears leaked between his fingers. It felt like an invasion of privacy to watch and she turned away to study the Pollock. Chaos and messiness, like her current life.

Then Mr. Linton grabbed her shoulders and pulled her into a hug so hard it knocked her breath away. She hugged him back, hoping Tristan would rescue her before she passed out. Eventually, Mr. Linton let her go and looked at her. Fear and hope filled his blue eyes.

"You're sure?" he asked.

She nodded. For a terrible moment, she wondered if it was possible to get café au lait birthmarks removed. Like maybe a laser treatment or something. And then she'd be wrong and Shelby would still be dead and she'd have broken her father's heart. Again.

Tristan returned with a glass of water that Mr. Linton drank in one gulp.

"Tell me everything," he ordered.

Ivy got out her phone and showed him the zoomed photographs of Shelby in her dress and the autopsy photo. She didn't mention the sex tape. He stared at the areas that Tristan had circled.

He touched it on her phone screen with one hesitant finger. "How could I have missed her little bell?"

"Everyone missed it," Tristan said. "Until Ivy."

"Thank you," Mr. Linton took her free hand in both of his. His palms were wet with tears. "You brought me back my baby girl."

Ivy swallowed. "I'm glad."

She didn't point out that they were no closer to Shelby than before. She had that much restraint.

"So." Mr. Linton looked at Tristan. "Where is she? Why hasn't she contacted me?"

"No one knows."

"Put together a team." Mr. Linton seemed to be coming back into his imperious self. "She must be found at once."

"I contacted Marcus and Allison," Tristan said. "We'll all be working around the clock until she's found."

"Contact hospitals. She must have been injured. Maybe she doesn't know who she is," Mr. Linton ordered. "She's alone somewhere."

Ivy didn't want to point out that Shelby's phone had called Timothy's from the bridge. That she had spoken to him from there, he had recognized her voice, and she had brought him to where she wanted him to be. That Shelby's jogging outfit was on the body of the woman who jumped. A woman who probably couldn't have afforded it. A woman who Shelby had murdered, either directly or indirectly. The cost of Shelby disappearing was this unknown woman's life. That was an irredeemable action.

Shelby wasn't lying around in some hospital because she'd had an accident. Whatever had happened, she did it on purpose. And she'd have come home if she hadn't ended an innocent life.

"We're looking into all possibilities," Tristan outlined a search plan. The initial steps were all about finding Shelby if she'd been in an accident. Team members conferenced in on speaker phone. Discussions were had. No one mentioned that Shelby must have left on purpose. It was a waste of time.

She wandered over to the window and looked out at the fog. Thicker than when she'd arrived, it had risen from the ocean and engulfed the Bay Bridge. Only a white glow told her where the bridge must still be. Like Shelby, it had gone undercover. Unlike Shelby, sunshine would reveal it again.

CHAPTER TWENTY-THREE

They weren't going to find her in the places they were looking. But where would they find her? Ivy had no better ideas to offer. Shelby hadn't told her about secret hiding places, remote cabins, or hideaway apartments. Olivia might think that her friend would have kept her in the loop, but she hadn't. Ivy was as clueless about where to look as Tristan's minions.

Almost reflexively, she pulled out her phone and checked Twitter. Still a Sarlacc pit, but it seemed less spiky than the last time she'd visited. A few defenders had spoken up and shared good reviews. Some people liked her book. Her publisher, she noted, seemed to have forgotten she existed. Maybe they were following Tristan's advice to not engage. Or maybe it was a sign of something deeper.

Restraining her urge to post, even though muzzling herself rankled, she closed Twitter and went to her email. That was a mixed bag. First she went through her daily death threats and violent messages and forwarded them to Tristan, although she imagined he'd be too busy looking for Shelby to analyze them any time soon. Finally, she moved them to the Trolls folder and tried not to think about them. This worked about as well as she expected. Troll voices whispered threats in her ear.

With those out of the way, she could see her real messages. One from @planula and a few others with B12 in the subject line. She should read them and forward them along to someone to deal with. Maybe Rodriguez could make something out of them.

Before she could read her messages, Olivia texted CALL ME

A little shouty and bossy. But it wasn't like Ivy had a lot of allies. She wasn't going to let this one go.

She waved to the men on the couch, held up her phone, and mouthed, "I have to take this."

Tristan and Mr. Linton didn't look up from their intense conversation about Shelby being injured or having amnesia or any one of a number of campy mirror-universe plots. No point in interrupting to tell them she was making the long trek down to the lobby, so she picked up her backpack, slipped out into the sumptuous hall, and called Olivia.

"The police called to inform me that Shelby Linton is alive." Olivia didn't bother saying hello.

"Why would the police call you if you're just her executive assistant?" Ivy scuffed her foot against the marble.

"Meet me downstairs in ten minutes. Stay in the lobby." And then Olivia ended the call. She was way more assertive now that she wasn't working for Nyssa anymore. Ivy wondered what her deal was. Still, the lobby seemed a safe enough place to meet. Hard to imagine anything terrible happening in the midst of all that Christmas cheer.

She turned back to tell Tristan where she was going, but realized that the door was closed and locked. She thought about ringing the bell, but she didn't owe him a detailed schedule of her whereabouts. She was an adult going to the lobby. She'd knock when she got back.

For now, she had to meet Olivia and play out the next scene in the drama that Shelby's life had become. Taking care of her friend was now her only priority, so she pushed off the shiny elevator wall and told herself to put on her big girl panties and deal with it. She glanced at her reflection in the bank of numbers on the wall. Her pep talk wasn't working. The face that stared back at her looked exhausted and bewildered and sad. Her face knew what was up.

Maybe she should go back up and wash her face and get a cup of Mr. Linton's tea and regroup. Come back down after she'd pulled herself together. Olivia wasn't due for a while anyway. But, if she did, Mr. Linton and everyone would see she was in a state and Tristan might even be sympathetic and that would drive her right over the edge. Best to grit her teeth and get on with it. Her life would still be in shambles in an hour.

The elevator doors opened onto the lobby and she stepped forward.

Four men in dark camouflage rushed at her. Each carried an automatic weapon. Her heart raced and her mouth went dry. She lunged for the elevator close door button. One man jumped inside. A thousand movie deaths flashed through her mind.

"Are you Ivy Corva?" The man's black helmet bobbed as he talked. It said Police.

304

"W-why?" Her throat was too dry to talk.

He yanked her out of the elevator and slammed her against the wall. Her sore nose throbbed in time with her sore shoulder and her legs gave out. The cop mashed her harder against the wall and she didn't fall.

"What?" she asked. "What?"

Detective Rodriguez must have sent them. This was about Shelby's reappearance. Or Jacko's death. She was going to jail for murder. She'd never get back to her cozy apartment. She'd never see Anu again. She should never have come here.

Her lungs ached and she forced herself to breathe. Her breath creaked in like it didn't want anything more to do with her cursed lungs. And then she started hyperventilating.

The cop mashed her face flat against the wall. He outweighed her by 100 pounds. He was a tank, a refrigerator, a block of iron. A bunch of metaphors. Trouble.

"Take us up to your apartment," he said.

"My apartment?" Her words came out muffled. She knew she sounded stupid, but she couldn't help herself. Her brain ran in little panicked circles.

"Let's go, Miss Corva."

"I don't live here." What would they do in the apartment? Interrogate her? Worse? None of them were women.

Across the room Stephen watched from the concierge desk. He looked as surprised as she was, and he picked up the phone. She hoped he was calling in a rescue party. That a rescue party existed.

A second cop stepped up and patted her down, hands hard and efficient. Weapons. He was looking for weapons. His name tag read Perry.

"Clear," Perry said.

The guy smashing her against the wall eased up, but not much. She craned her head painfully. His name was Adler. "Are you Ivy Corva? Can I see identification?"

She still couldn't move. "In the zipper pocket of my backpack, Officer Adler. My passport."

Adler jerked his head and another guy in camo and a bulletproof vest yanked out her passport. She didn't see his name.

"Where's your residence?" Adler asked.

"Tallinn, Estonia." She gave him her street address, like that would mean anything to a San Francisco police officer. "I have a current Estonian visa in my passport."

The other guy flipped through her passport. "Checks out."

"If you don't live here, why were you in the elevator?" Adler asked.

Ivy's fear was crowded out by anger. "This seems like overkill for riding in an elevator. What would you have done if I'd taken the stairs?"

A red-haired cop on her right cracked a smile and quickly replaced it with a stern expression. His last name was Cera and she already liked him best of the bunch, which wasn't much.

Adler leaned against her again. His forearm dug into the back of her neck. He wasn't into humor, she could see that. Only compliance would do.

"We've received a report that you're holding a hostage in your apartment," Adler said.

"Hostage?" She struggled to speak. Of all the reasons she had imagined them being here, that wasn't one.

"At gunpoint," clarified another voice from a man she couldn't see. "A child."

She closed her eyes to think and Adler leaned harder on her neck. Her lungs ached and her stomach told her it wanted to throw up. She couldn't breathe. When she opened her eyes, her vision was black at the edges. Was she going to die here? In a luxury lobby at the hands of four cops in bulletproof gear. Like an American movie.

And she wasn't going down like this.

She squirmed against Adler's hold and rasped out. "Can't breathe."

Adler didn't relent. He had her right where he wanted. Sadist prick. She looked wildly around and made eye contact with Cera.

Cera poked Adler hard in the side and he eased up a little.

She drew in shuddering breaths. The oxygen felt wonderful to her screaming lungs. Nothing else mattered but oxygen. Sweet, sweet oxygen.

Then her stomach heaved and she told it that now wasn't the time. Her heart raced and told her it might be. She wanted to sit on the floor and breathe and maybe throw up, but she wasn't going to get to do any of those things.

"Tell us more about the hostage." Adler's fingers dug painfully into her arm.

"No hostage." She pushed the words out her sore throat. "Got here three days ago."

Seventy-two hours, but it felt like seventy-two days. If this wasn't about Shelby or Jacko, what could it be about? Nothing made sense. This least of all.

And then it did.

She swore and Adler pushed her against the wall again. Apparently he didn't like profanity either. He seemed intolerant of a lot of things. Just a bundle of control issues and anger issues with a gun and a badge.

"I've been swatted." Her legs sagged in relief. "This isn't about me at all."

Cera moved in closer. "I beg your pardon, miss?"

She was glad he was being polite, but wished he'd started that when she was standing unarmed in the elevator or when she was suffocating against the wall. Better late than never though.

"This is an internet prank," she said. "Someone is angry at me."

Cera nodded to Adler. Adler peeled her backpack off her shoulders like he was afraid she had bombs in there. No mercy from Officer Adler. He was a believe-the-worst kinda guy. But at least he wasn't touching her any more. Stomach acid climbed the back of her throat and she took a step away from him. She scrubbed the back of her hand across her face where it had touched the wall and ran her hands over all the spots he'd touched as if that could erase the feeling of his hands on her.

To think she'd thought coming down here nearly naked and seeing Shelby's revenge tape was going to be the worst thing that would happen to her in this lobby.

"My name is Ivy Corva," she said, speaking slowly, and angry at herself that her voice was so shaky. "I'm a science fiction writer and my book has been generating a lot of nerd rage."

"Nerd rage?" asked Cera.

"I've had death threats. I was almost stabbed at a reading at Kepler's yesterday." That had been a lot less frightening than this. "Someone is using you to make a point."

The cops looked at each other. They didn't seem convinced. She had to make them see before they threw her up against a wall again or arrested her.

"Can I take my phone out of my pocket?" When they nodded, she pulled her phone out of her back pocket and opened Twitter. She gingerly held the phone out to Cera who had been watching the screen over her shoulder like she was going to use the phone to detonate a bomb or something.

"What am I looking at?" he asked.

"That's my face." She pointed. "And those are the tweets I've been getting."

He scrolled down and whistled. "Damn."

"I know," she said. "Believe me."

"Lessons from the Curie," he said. "You're that Ivy Corva?"

Her mouth dropped open and she nodded dumbly.

"I liked your book," he said. "Jasper's a badass."

"Th-thank you."

"We still have to look at your apartment." Adler was going by the book. He was going to make sure no nonexistent hostage was being held by one tiny science fiction writer in case those nerds were right. Under other circumstances she might have admired his relentless sense of purpose. Right now though, she kinda hated him.

"I'll take you up." When she rolled her shoulder, it popped. She looked at Adler to see if he was going to apologize for it. He wasn't so inclined. Her hands were trembling, so she jammed them in her pockets. She closed her eyes and did some yoga breathing. Let them wait while she pulled herself together. They'd taken her apart in the first place.

When she opened her eyes, Cera looked amused and the tension in the other cops had gone down a notch. Either they were starting to believe her or they'd joined in for the yoga breathing. Except for Adler. He was reserving judgment until the last possible second.

She took them up to Shelby's apartment, since that seemed like a better choice than telling them that she was living at the airport and they were free to search it all they wanted for their imaginary hostage. And then explaining that she was only here to talk to Mr. Linton about Shelby being alive and Jacko's murder. It felt like TMI.

She opened the door and went in to disarm the alarm with Adler inches away, gun up. Then Cera gestured and she went back out into the hall and stood next to him.

Adler nodded, and the others formed up around him. Adler first, then they fanned out like they were expecting more armed gunmen to pop up from behind Shelby's expensive countertop. She stood in the hall with Cera and wondered how her life had gotten so surreal.

Voices yelled "Clear!" from each room in vaguely disappointed voices. No armed gunman, no hostage, just boring gray decor. Clearly not what they'd signed up for. You'd think they'd be grateful that a child wasn't huddled at gunpoint somewhere in there.

"Does this kind of thing happen often?" she asked Cera. He seemed to be in charge of keeping an eye on her because he hadn't moved. His gun, she noted, wasn't drawn so maybe he didn't think she was a hostage-taker about to kill him. Or maybe he prided himself on his quick draw.

"Even once is too often," he said.

"Is it against the law? Does the caller get a ticket or something?" Some vengeance would be nice about now. Where was Batman when she needed him?

"Making a false 911 call is a crime," Cera said. "If we find them, they'll be fined, maybe go to jail."

"I want to press charges," she said quickly.

"You don't have to. It's automatic." He cleared his throat and looked at a spot over her right shoulder with an intense and anxious expression on his face.

Was he going to ask her out? Awkward, but who was she to judge when she'd asked for the number of the EMT back in Tallinn? She was calling him if she ever got back there. He was the best guy for thousands of miles.

"Yes?" she prompted Cera.

"Where do you get your ideas?" he asked.

Not the question she'd been expecting. Was that more flattering or less? Being attacked by a SWAT team gave her ideas, but she said nothing.

"I've been thinking about writing a book," he said.

She got herself together enough to say. "A police procedural?"

"God, no!" Cera looked so horrified that she laughed. "It's a science fiction story about squid-like creatures who travel through space in waterfilled spaceships."

"Like Cthulhu goes to the stars?"

"Exactly!" He beamed at her.

"Doesn't sound like ideas are your problem," she said. "That sounds cool."

Cera relaxed and readied himself for his next question. She assumed he was going to ask her how to get an agent and then how to negotiate a book deal, like she had good answers to either of those questions. Query and luck. But a longer, more optimistic version.

Behind him, the elevator pinged and opened. Tristan popped out all suited up and official looking with a determined set to his shoulders. She was happy to see a voice of sanity and reason who might even be on her side. He strode over.

"I'm Ms. Corva's lawyer," he said to Cera. He turned to Ivy. "Are you OK?"

"I got swatted." Was he her lawyer? At the very least, he was a lawyer which was better than nothing. She really ought to read that contract.

Tristan looked at Cera. "I can assure you that this is a misunderstanding."

"We figured that out." Cera didn't look happy to be interrupted.

"Then I assume you won't be harassing my client further?" Tristan had the right note of firmness in his tone. Ivy was again convinced that he must take vocal lessons and she liked his use of the word harass.

Cera snapped his mouth closed. "We won't be."

That was a relief.

The other cops filed into the hall. Adler's mouth was set in a mutinous line like a kid denied an ice cream cone and he glared at her like it was her fault. Her fault for not having a child tied up in the bathroom who he could heroically rescue. She resisted the urge to flip him off. This was the kind of situation where Tristan's policy of de-escalation paid off.

The other officers apologized like kids in Little League saying 'good game' only because the coach made them do it. Cera seemed sincere, but she assumed that was because he wanted something from her. Access to the glamorous world of being a writer. Complete with constant online harassment and now swatting. Who wouldn't want that?

Everyone looked at her like it was her fault they'd wasted their time and made asses of themselves. She didn't point out that it wasn't, but she did tell Cera to email her any questions he had about writing. Might as well get one of these guys on her side in case this happened again. She didn't see why it wouldn't since it worked so well the first time.

Then they trooped off to the elevator, trailing testosterone and dejection. The elevator looked small with all of them inside with their guns and gear.

"We'll get the next one," she said.

Tristan stood next to her and folded his arms. Together they watched the doors close. She wanted to collapse as soon as they did, but she held it together. Tristan had done enough already. He didn't need to deal with her being hysterical. Still, she leaned against the wall in what she hoped was a casual fashion and took another long breath.

"How'd you know I'd be here?" she asked.

"The front desk called."

"Point for Stephen," she said.

"Why'd you go downstairs at all?" he asked.

She wasn't liking his tone. "To meet Olivia Ajak from Nyssa."

"Special Agent Ajak?" he asked.

"Really?" Olivia wasn't what she'd seemed either.

"Yes," he said. "I checked her out when Shelby disappeared."

"So she was spying on Nyssa?"

"It would seem so."

Tristan wasn't a guy who answered questions with a yes or no, even simple ones.

She figured she wasn't going to get anything else out of him. "How's the search going?"

"The search really starts once we run out of avenues where she could be alive but unable to contact her father." Tristan's sculpted jaw clenched. Even he could get annoyed.

"So you think that she set everyone up too?" She was glad he wasn't fooled.

"It seems like the most logical premise, yes, but her father has to process his emotions first." Tristan's eyebrows did a squiggle thing that looked like sympathy. "He doesn't want to think his little girl could have done the things she did."

"She did," Ivy said. "I'm sorry, but she did."

"That doesn't mean it's not our job to help her," Tristan said. "She's a client and my job is to protect her."

"Even from her own choices?"

"Especially from those, Miss #Exowomb."

Ouch. Not wrong, but ouch. "Shelby's actions are a lot worse than picking a fight on Twitter."

"Nevertheless, she's my client and I'll stay at her side, no matter what."

She pressed the elevator button. "I'm glad you're on my side."

"Always," he said. "So please refrain from wandering off."

"I'm OK to go down to the lobby on my own," she said, deciding not to rise to that bait. "The sooner you find Shelby, the better for everyone."

"Except for Shelby."

"Maybe also Shelby." Or else she'd rained down bad things on a friend who might yet be innocent. Maybe something would come to light to show that Shelby was trying to save the world and unjustly accused. Which Ivy could relate to. Maybe bigger factors were at play here.

"Come right back upstairs after your meeting." Tristan sounded stern and like he thought he was actually the boss of her.

His phone bonged again.

"How many texts have you gotten since you came down here?" she asked.

"Twenty-seven," he said automatically.

Leave it to Tristan to count.

"I'm just going downstairs to the lobby. Stephen will be able to see me the whole time," she said. "They need you more than I do upstairs."

He studied her for a long moment. "I hope you're right."

CHAPTER TWENTY-FOUR

When Ivy got to the empty lobby, she thanked Stephen for calling in Tristan. Stephen seemed like he wanted to ask her a million questions, but luckily his phone rang and she slipped away.

Then she staked out two club chairs grouped around a coffee table next to the fireplace. She was now out of sight from the front desk, in direct violation of the claim she'd made to Tristan. Not that she cared. This was the most privacy she was likely to get in the lobby and she needed that. Of course, the walls were still made out of glass and everyone on the street could presumably look right in, but she tried not to think about that. It was always going to be an imperfect world.

She positioned one leather chair with its back to the glass wall, toward the fire, then sat down and let her carefully contained panic out of its box. She could have died. They could have shot her, suffocated her, or who knew what. Her trolls had escaped from under the bridge and had made an attack in her real life. As unpleasant as the experience had been, she had gotten lucky.

Her entire body shook. Adrenalin surged through her veins as her body caught up to her brain. The only way out of this was to let this move through. Breathe through the panic and come out the other side, a long-ago therapist had told her. Feel it and let it go.

She wrapped her arms around herself and rocked. A distant part of her hoped that Stephen wasn't curious enough to seek her out or a late-night jogger wasn't going to come strolling in or the person who had called in SWAT wasn't watching. But this was the space she had to work with. Slowly she stopped shaking.

Time to move to the next stage. Warmth radiated from the fireplace and she reached her hands toward it. She focused on smooth stones and warm flames and breathed in peace. The floor felt smooth and sturdy against her shoes. Strong and cold and clean. She breathed out stress. And breathed in peace. The chair supported her legs and back. It was soft and firm and clean and cushioned her in a safe embrace. Warm air tickled her skin and caressed her still damp hair. It swaddled her in safety. The soft sound of vaguely annoying Christmas music reminded her of the Tallinn Christmas market. Sleigh bells rang. Her senses were alive and she was safe.

Her heart was still convinced that she was being chased by a lion, but it had stopped pounding quite so hard. She took that as a win and kept breathing and concentrating on each sensation in her body. The belt around her lungs slowly eased as her chest rose and fell smoothly. Tension drained from her shoulders, leaving soreness where she'd hit the wall next to the elevator. Her nose throbbed where Jacko had punched her. The sensations of her body, while not all terrific, were real and grounded her in the present moment.

Ivy felt almost pulled together. She wasn't thinking about being slammed against a wall. Attacked by a plunger. Having her writing dreams extinguished. Or she mostly wasn't. When she held her hands up to catch the warmth, they no longer trembled.

She opened her eyes and studied the flames. They danced around the stones without any visible source of fuel. A strangely comforting freak of nature. Like Ivy herself.

Olivia arrived a few minutes later, carrying two Starbucks cups with a laptop bag slung over her shoulder. Her whole look screamed "this is going to take a while."

"I brought you a chai," Olivia said. "What happened to your nose?"

"Jacko." She took a sip of tea. Cinnamon and cloves rolled across her tongue. Not as good as Cafe Caffeine, but a good start. "Long story, but it happened yesterday."

"You're awfully pale. Are you OK?" Olivia sat and studied her. Her brown eyes held a lot more questions.

Ivy wondered what she'd looked like before her breathing moment. Stephen must have been too polite to say anything.

She explained about the swatting and Olivia assured her that there would be consequences for whoever had made the false call. Unless they called from a burner phone. Or a pay phone. Or via an internet service that hid their number. It sounded like the guy was going to escape pretty much unscathed if he'd taken basic precautions. Not. Very. Reassuring.

"Thank you, Special Agent Ajak," Ivy said before Olivia could list five more reasons how the caller could get away. "What are you a special agent for?"

"Mr. Walsh ran my name?" Olivia glanced toward the elevators like she expected to see Tristan coming down to join them with her entire life history in his hand. Which he probably would have done if he hadn't been so caught up in rescuing Shelby from herself.

Ivy raised her eyebrows and drank more tea. The cup felt so warm in her hands and the sugar and caffeine zinged into her empty system, turning on a few circuits on the way. Whatever this was, she could do it.

"FDA Department of Investigations." Olivia pulled a badge out of her pocket and flashed it at Ivy like it was going to explode on contact with air.

Ivy held out her hand and Olivia gave her the badge. It felt strangely heavy in its leather holder. The badge was gold and looked like FBI badges Ivy had seen on TV, except this one said FDA. Presumably it was authentic, unless she was in cahoots with Tristan and Ivy had been set up. But presumably then she'd have pretended to be FBI, since those badges had to be easier to fake and everyone had heard of them. Anyway, that level of paranoia was too exhausting to consider, so she decided to believe it.

"I didn't even know the FDA had a special branch," Ivy handed back the badge.

"How else can we keep the public safe from medical fraud?"

"Reform healthcare," Ivy said. "And regulate the price of prescription drugs."

Olivia tucked her badge away. "Above my paygrade."

Ivy held out her hand and Olivia shook it.

"Nice to meet the real you," Ivy said. "Finally."

Olivia pulled a laptop and a couple of folders filled with actual dead tree paper out of her bag. But she didn't open anything up. The folders sat on the table like angry accusations.

"Tell me about your friendship with Shelby," Olivia said. "Start at the beginning."

This was going to take longer than Ivy had thought. "A long time ago, my mommy and my daddy loved each other very much—"

"Skip ahead to college," Olivia said.

"For her sins, Shelby was assigned to be my college roommate." Or for her own.

Then she told Olivia about how they'd met and how long they'd known each other. And life in Pittsburgh and since. It felt like it was mostly useless information, but Olivia peppered her with questions so maybe it wasn't.

"Did Shelby strike you as a violent person?" Olivia took a sip of her drink. It must be cold by now.

"She turned her aggression inward." Ivy thought about the suicide attempt, but then about Jacko. "Mostly."

"Tell me about the suicide attempt." Olivia said like she'd read her thoughts, or at least the first part. "We have records from Carnegie Mellon."

No protecting Shelby from that humiliation either. Ivy ran through the events of that night on the bridge, including her own role and their friendship after. She highlighted the revenge porn and mentioned Gerald by name. Not that she imagined the FDA cared about either. Prosecuting offenders for posting sex with a minor seemed like it wasn't part of their remit. Or, in this case, probably anyone's.

"According to her phone records, she didn't call you often," Olivia said.

"We stayed in touch." Ivy felt defensive, although she wasn't sure why.

"Do you know that she called you more often than anyone in her life? Except for work colleagues about work-related activities."

Ivy stared. Shelby rarely called her at all. She had to have had more local friends, boyfriends, her father, anyone. "Since I don't have her phone records, how could I know who she called and when?"

The more she thought about it, the worse it became. Considering how little Shelby had called her, how often had she called her father and the others? Shelby had been more alone than she'd ever imagined. For years. And Ivy hadn't helped her or even noticed.

She'd assumed that Shelby's life was charmed and full and she didn't need her. They hadn't even seen each other face to face in four years, as long as they'd lived together in college. Ivy crossed her arms and looked at Olivia.

"I know you're protecting your friend," Olivia said. "That's only natural."

She thought of Tristan. "Sure."

"So I want to show you facts. See if it makes you more amenable to helping us." Olivia opened up the first folder and made her case like a prosecutor. She handed each piece of paper to Ivy after she finished explaining it and gave her a few seconds to verify before plunging ahead.

She'd accumulated plenty of proof of financial fraud against Nyssa, Timothy, and Shelby herself. Claims that Shelby had made to current and prospective investors that were flat out lies, and Shelby had known it. She'd even texted with Timothy about it, which looked like it'd be pretty damning to a jury.

According to Olivia's files, Shelby had lied about the company's fiscal projections, the number of scientists on their payroll, the findings of the computer models, their mouse trial results, the side effects the mice experienced, everything. And all that was assuming that Jacko and Shelby hadn't tampered with those results even more by replacing sick and dying mice with fresh ones. That would make things even worse than Olivia knew.

It looked like Nyssa had never been close to shipping their immortality drug or turning a profit. In the mouse trials, the drug was, at best, ineffectual and at worst dangerous. And Shelby had known it millions of dollars ago, but she'd kept going.

Ivy sat in a snowdrift of paper, barely able to listen as Olivia kept talking. Each sentence was crisp, efficient, and damning. Shelby and Timothy were going to be in jail for a long time. Or at least Timothy was. Shelby might never be found.

She wished she could question Olivia's evidence or her strong sense of moral conviction, but Ivy didn't have it in her. Nothing she saw contradicted what she'd found out for herself. If anything, her own conclusions were worse.

Then Olivia laid out what she'd found since Ivy called her yesterday. Ivy hadn't expected her to do much with Jacko's accusations so quickly, but so far, Olivia had found twenty-five people Shelby had injected with B12, and she suspected there were more. Olivia and her team had worked with Margie and other homelessness agencies. She had agents out canvassing people on the streets directly and every hour they kept turning up more and more victims.

Olivia's office had chemists running tests for traces of Nyssa's medication in the affected individuals' blood and hair. It would take days to get the results, but if those came back positive, they'd have a strong case that Shelby had been dosing people without their knowledge. She'd told some that the shots were B12, others that they were iron or multivitamins. None had signed a consent form and none had any idea what she'd actually put into their bodies.

Olivia left the worst for last. "Of the twenty-five test subjects, thirteen are already dead."

"But you're not sure it's from the drug, right?" Ivy wanted to hold on to that hope.

"Not yet." Olivia handed her another piece of paper. "Cancer killed ten. Suicide two. And one died in a car accident."

"Did she help anyone?" Ivy swallowed. "At all?"

"The remaining twelve subjects are in the best health of their lives. Some were ill before. Most were drug addicts. Every single one is clean and healthy now."

"That must mean a lot to those twelve."

"If it's related to the drug and not Shelby paying them for their silence, yes." Olivia took a deep breath. "Leaving out the car accident and saving the suicide for later investigation, almost half the people your friend injected are dead. Only one of them was known to have cancer before she injected them. Ten after."

"Camilla?" Ivy fought back tears. Shelby had killed innocent people.

"Yes, Camilla."

So they hadn't found a second person Shelby might have saved.

Olivia spread out photos on the table while she talked. Each one was of a person Shelby had injected. Their faces judged Ivy and found her wanting. If she'd paid more attention to Shelby, maybe she could have known, could have stopped this.

"It's still early stages in this part of the investigation," Olivia said. "But we need to find Shelby and stop her from doing more damage. I'd also like to get the names of others she's injected so we can help them, if that's even possible."

Ivy waved her hand at the mountain of evidence on the coffee table between them. "How long to get all this?"

"Two years, mostly undercover."

"But, as Shelby's assistant, you must have worked more than full-time already for Nyssa."

"Justice takes commitment," Olivia said.

"And obsession."

"Guilty," Olivia said. "In the beginning, I wanted Shelby to be innocent, just like you. I wanted her to be a hero working to save the world from death. Someone who was being picked on because she was a woman. A female CEO who'd overcome adversity to bring miracles to the world."

"She was trying, right?" Ivy's voice squeaked at the end.

"Whatever else she was doing, she was killing innocent people."

Ivy studied the pictures. Some were snapshots Olivia had gathered from family members and the internet. They smiled back at her, gamely trying to enjoy lives touched by hardship. The other photos showed people lying on a metal table, like the picture of the woman who'd died in place of Shelby. They were beyond anyone's help now.

"It would have taken us longer to put this part together if you hadn't called me." Olivia touched Jacko's photo. "Thank you."

"Why are you telling me this?" Ivy waved at the pictures. "What do you think I can do to help them?"

"Because you're the closest thing to a friend that Shelby has."

"She must have other friends," Ivy said.

"I've looked at her phone records, her emails, the visitor logs at her apartment building. She most assuredly doesn't," Olivia said.

Ivy thought of Shelby and then of Anu and the friends who'd showed up to her reading. Ex-boyfriends she was still in contact with, which was all of them. She had friends now, but back in college, she'd only had Shelby. And afterward Shelby'd had no one.

"Why does it matter that I'm her friend?" Ivy asked.

"Because if she reaches out to anyone, it'll be you."

"Or her father," Ivy pointed out. "Or maybe an ex-boyfriend."

"If she does reach out, will you tell me?"

"And then you come and arrest her?" Shelby wasn't getting out once they had her. She was what the law called a "flight risk." She'd already faked her own death and tried to flee once before.

"You'd rather she kept on killing?" Olivia gathered up her papers but left the photos staring at Ivy. "Injecting innocent people, some children."

"I don't want to be the one who turns the key in the lock and lets you throw it away," Ivy said. "She's my friend and she was trying to do something great."

Olivia tapped the picture of a nineteen-year-old girl who'd died of cancer after Shelby injected her. Ivy looked at her bright young face. Brown eyes, hair in neat braids, a shy smile. Gone. Somewhere, presumably, parents had waited for her to come home. They'd hoped and prayed and ached to see her again. And instead they'd identified her body on that table. Olivia had put the morgue picture next to the happy one, probably so Ivy would be haunted by the difference. And she was.

"I don't think she'll reach out to me anyway." Ivy stalled.

"But, if she does, can we count on you? You know that helping her is a crime."

Ivy wanted to sink into the floor and disappear. She wished she'd never come here. That she'd stayed in her snow globe drinking wine and complaining about trolls on the internet. But she hadn't. She'd flown straight into Shelby's mess. And she couldn't unsee these pictures. Couldn't unknow what she had learned.

But this was the prosecution's case. Their job was to paint Shelby in the worst possible light. What she saw here was spun to convict her friend. But maybe there was more. She hadn't heard Shelby's side. She didn't know what was true. Not without hearing from the defense. "I want to give her a chance before I condemn her."

Olivia shook her head. "Your loyalty to your friend is laudable. But it's wrong."

"Give me a little time to think it over."

"What is that time going to change?" Olivia asked.

"Everything? Nothing? If I knew, I wouldn't need to ask for it."

Olivia pursed her lips. "One more bit of bad news."

Ivy sighed. "Just one?"

"Nyssa's credit cards have been shut down and the charges questioned."

"How does this affect me?" But she already knew.

"Your ticket back to Tallinn has been canceled," Olivia said.

Ivy leaned back in her seat. She couldn't go home. Her credit card was maxed out. Her publisher wasn't going to pay her for the next book.

And she had no money to buy a ticket and no way of getting any. So now she was stuck in California until she could beg, borrow, or steal the money to go back and beg Liilia for her old job. The one she used to hate that had grown more appealing in its absence.

"The FDA might see its way clear to buying you a ticket back, if you cooperate," Olivia said.

"Thirty pieces of silver," Ivy said.

"Shelby isn't exactly Jesus," Olivia said. "Judas himself had a lower body count."

"Alleged body count," Ivy said.

"Can you call me tomorrow with your decision?"

It wasn't like she had anything else to do. "Yes."

Olivia gathered up the photos and slipped them into a folder. Ivy was relieved to see them go, and the guilt at realizing that was crushing. She was supposed to be a better person. She wasn't supposed to tuck the world's problems away and ignore them.

"I'm sorry this is happening to you," Olivia said. "I know it can't be easy."

"Easier for me than the ones she allegedly injected."

Olivia tossed the empty cups in the wastebasket and marched off with her laptop bag pressed close to her side. She'd sacrificed two years of her life to stop Nyssa and Shelby. To do the right thing. Olivia was on the side of law and justice, no matter the personal cost. Whose side was Ivy on?

Ivy watched her retreating back and longed to return to her old life. Before her writer's hopes were destroyed. Before Shelby brought her out here. Back to walking with the wolf in her arms and knowing exactly what she needed to do.

She sighed. For now, she needed to clear her head. Stand outside of Shelby's glass cage and think. Once she'd walked off some stress, she'd call up to Tristan and he'd help her figure things out. So long as Mr. Linton kept paying him for it.

She nodded to Stephen and went outside to pace in front of the building, staying where he could see her. She wasn't going far.

As she walked, she looked around the dark street. Her senses were on high alert, either from the SWAT team's visit or from Olivia's presentation. Nobody standing around with a plunger. Nobody on the sidewalk at all. Not even any cars.

She tried to push everything else to the back of her mind and focus on the next step: where she'd sleep. It felt good to have immediate and urgent goals, a solid priority. Shelby's apartment was the easiest option, but she was afraid of getting swatted again. And Mr. Linton and Shelby and who knew else had the keys and alarm code. Anyone could come in while she was sleeping.

What about Tristan? He might let her sleep on his couch. Presumably he'd be up all night searching for Shelby, so he wouldn't be using it. But did his lawyer safety protocols extend that far? Would there be a legal boundary?

If he said no, then Margie was her next best bet. She might know of temporary housing, like a homeless shelter. Ivy dreaded that idea. She'd gone from a luxury apartment to begging for a couch in record time.

Tomorrow morning she'd call Anu and see if she could help scrape together enough money for a ticket from her friends in Estonia. Then she'd have to hope the torture museum had more work so she could start paying them back. It turned out that having rich friends was way more expensive than she'd ever dreamed.

Without knowing why, she stopped walking. She glanced around, then down to the pavement. A motorcycle helmet sat in the middle of the sidewalk. Streetlight reflected off its poison green surface and a yellow sticky note was affixed to the visor. When she picked up the helmet, the note read Thanks for the licorice. Wanna go for a ride? xo planula

Shelby must have left it. Or told someone to leave it. She must have come inside to claim her licorice.

Ivy glanced back at the lobby. Stephen still looked down at his monitor and typed away, oblivious to Ivy's racing heart. If she went for this ride, he wouldn't even see her go.

Inside was warm and inviting and safe. It was where everyone would tell her to go. But it didn't have any answers for her.

She put on the helmet, but stayed where Stephen might see her, if he looked. The person who put the helmet here had to be close. A helmet like that would be snatched right up, wouldn't it?

Flipping up the visor, she scanned the street, waiting for Shelby or Shelby's agent. She thought about texting Tristan to say what she was doing, but she worried that Shelby was watching and wouldn't approach her if she took out her phone, so she waited, feeling as naked as she had back in that ambulance after the wolf.

Seconds later, a twin to Ivy's old green Ninja motorcycle rolled up and, in spite of her worries, she felt a pang of nostalgia for her college days. She'd had good times on that bike.

The female rider wore black motorcycle leathers and a helmet identical to the one that Ivy held in her hands. The rider's visor was down. Black hair stuck out the bottom of the helmet and hung to her shoulders.

She looked like Ivy herself, come to San Francisco via a time machine to help her out. Or maybe to kill her, like the Terminator. Not-Ivy gestured for Ivy to jump on the back of the bike as Ivy wondered which out-of-time visitor this might be.

Ivy shook her head and closed and opened her visor. She pointed to the rider's visor and raised her finger to indicate that the rider should open it. She wasn't getting on that bike until she knew who was driving. Maybe not even after.

The biker pointed one gloved finger at a wall-mounted video camera. Camera-shy. When she didn't open her visor, Ivy crossed her arms to show that she wasn't compromising. She looked back at Stephen again. Still typing.

The mysterious rider rolled forward a few feet until she was out of the camera's view. Ivy stayed where she was, visible to cameras and, with a little luck, to Stephen inside. Then the rider turned her head so the front of the helmet faced Ivy.

Ivy leaned forward in anticipation. She didn't know if she wanted the rider to be Shelby, or if she wanted her friend to be dead and beyond accountability for her actions. For everyone to be wrong about her.

Slowly, the woman raised her visor. She tilted her head back so that the street light shone on her face.

Shelby.

She looked the same as always. Same intelligent blue eyes. Same determined set to her shoulders. Same sardonic smile. Shelby gave her a thumbs-up. Ivy caught herself before she returned the gesture. Instead she nodded.

Then Shelby lowered her visor and became just another anonymous rider. She patted the seat behind her, invitation clear.

Frozen, Ivy stared. None of the scenarios where she'd imagined meeting Shelby again looked like this. Those scenes involved denial, remorse, apologies. In those scenarios Shelby wasn't smiling. She was suffering because she had made others suffer and she regretted her actions. She wanted to make things right. This Shelby looked like someone out for a pleasure ride.

Ivy's imagination was wrong, again.

Real-life Shelby patted the seat again and slowly rolled forward. The message was clear: Ivy better get on now or Shelby would leave her here in the rain with no answers.

Ivy's legs made the decision her brain wasn't ready for. They sleep walked over to the bike. Shelby shifted forward and Ivy sat on the back. The warmth of Shelby's body had heated the seat, a reminder that this was real. Ivy put her hands on Shelby's leather-clad hips.

Together, they roared into the California night.

CHAPTER TWENTY-FIVE

Shelby veered around a silver SUV at the last second and slid expertly through a yellow light onto Beale. Ivy gritted her teeth and clutched Shelby's waist.

The bike roared as Shelby gunned it. They leaped forward into the night. When Ivy looked over Shelby's shoulder, light reflected off the wet street. Any wrong move would spill them both onto the unforgiving pavement. Lights flashed by on both sides, so quickly she couldn't see where they came from. Her own wild ride with the Ducati seemed tame now. Shelby didn't seem to care if they lived or died. When you were already dead, what did you have to lose?

They hit Embarcadero going twice the speed limit, weaving between slower cars. Cold wind rippled against Ivy's jacket. Ocean glittered on the right and, for a split second, she wondered if Shelby intended to drive straight in, but she turned left and before Ivy knew it they were on the on ramp for I-80 East.

The freeway opened up a different set of options. Ivy didn't know the terrain, or Shelby, enough to make any guesses. She was as in the dark as she'd been when she tried to guess for Olivia. Her only option now was to wait and find out when they got there. She'd sealed her fate when she got on the back of the bike.

The freeway climbed onto the Bay Bridge. Earlier that evening, she'd seen the bridge from Shelby's father's penthouse, remote and beautiful. It was colder and scarier to be tearing along it.

The bike hit a bump and when Ivy tightened her grip around Shelby's waist one hand jolted high and she felt a cold lump on the side of Shelby's torso. A gun? Shelby twitched and Ivy's hand slid back down.

She thought about checking again, but there wasn't anything she could do about it and she didn't dare distract Shelby. They had to be going at least eighty. Sure, the bike could handle more, a lot more, but with cars weaving back and forth and concrete parapet walls on each side of the bridge, if Shelby made one mistake, they'd be a long red streak.

Metal supports flashed on both sides of the freeway and the upper deck blotted out her view of the sky. That deck carried thousands of pounds of bridge and cars a mere few meters above their heads. Hadn't the upper deck fallen down in an earthquake once? How stable was it, really? She laughed. Of all the ways she might die today, death by bridge collapse seemed the least likely.

Even through the adrenalin, she marveled at Shelby's daring. Any sane policeman who saw them cutting between lanes and weaving around cars would pull them over for reckless driving and Shelby's whole scheme would collapse. She'd gone through so much to disappear and hide, and now she risked it all to speed on a bridge. Anu wouldn't be impressed by that kind of recklessness, but Ivy was.

When Shelby veered over to the off ramp to Treasure Island, Ivy silently cheered. Hopefully this ride was coming to a safe end.

As they zoomed down the ramp, trees loomed through her rain-streaked visor. When Ivy turned her head to the side to let the wind blow off the raindrops, the city skyline in all its glory blazed on her left.

Shelby slowed to a positively sedate speed to pass an empty checkpoint booth with a sign for Treasure Island Naval Station. A quick turn later and they rolled to a stop on a beach facing San Francisco.

As soon as the bike stopped, Ivy slid off, then turned to face Shelby with shaking legs. She fought down an urge to kiss the sand.

Shelby lowered the kickstand and climbed off the bike too, movements slow and calm. Light reflected off her tinted visor. It could be anyone under there. For a moment, Ivy doubted that she had really seen Shelby's face before she got on the bike. Maybe, like everyone else, she saw what she wanted to see.

Hoping that the rider would follow suit, Ivy took off her helmet and shook out her hair. The other woman hesitated, then flipped up her visor. The helmet framed Shelby's familiar face. Ivy wasn't sure if she should be relieved or more worried than before.

Shelby took out a cellphone and pointed to Ivy's pocket. Ivy wondered if they were going to have this conversation via text and pulled out her own phone. Shelby grabbed it and tossed it into the ocean. Her lifeline to the outside world sank under the inky waves.

Ivy's heart jolted. No one could find her now. All she had was her wits and her faith in Shelby. They seemed like tissue paper shields.

"On top of everything else, you're littering." Ivy tried to sound calm.

"Desperate measures." Shelby grinned and looked not one bit desperate. Wind blew her newly black hair around her shoulders. Her leathers were clearly waterproof and she looked warm. Unlike Ivy.

"My bike. My helmet. Even my hair." Ivy wiped rain out of her eyes. "What's up, doppelgänger?"

"Why didn't you go straight back to Estonia?" Shelby asked. "My father would have paid for your ticket. Or Nyssa."

"I wanted to protect your legacy. Like a jackass."

"How's that working out for you?" Shelby unzipped her jacket and Ivy recognized the butt of a gun peeking out of a shoulder holster.

Ivy looked from the gun back to Shelby's face. "You didn't make it easy for me."

"I can see my house from here." Shelby pointed at San Francisco.

"Where is it, exactly?" Ivy glanced over at the skyline.

"See the one that looks like a giant penis thrusting proudly up into the sky? That's Salesforce tower. Millennium is right next door."

Ivy saw it now. If Mr. Linton had a telescope and Tristan looked right at this beach, could he see them here? Not that it mattered, because he didn't

338

and he wouldn't know where to look and even if he did and she waved for help, she was too far away.

She decided to get right to it. "Did you really inject all those people without their consent?"

"At least half of them will gain an extra twenty years of life. Maybe more. Could anyone else have given them that?"

Ivy wondered if that part was even true, based on what Olivia had shown her. "And the other half?"

"It varies, which makes interpreting the data a bitch," Shelby said. "Some get cancer, some don't seem to be affected at all."

"None of them got to choose to run that risk."

Shelby arched an eyebrow. "Like they aren't choosing death every day with a needle. They never really know what's in that either."

"They know they're making that choice. They choose to pay the price."

"If someone had done this work earlier, my mother would not have died. By the end she would have jumped at a shot that gave her a 50% chance of survival because it was better than the odds that the doctors could give," Shelby said. "A lot of other people would agree. Would you sentence them to death?"

"But—"

"What would you give for your parents to have survived?"

"My parents died in a car accident," Ivy said. "No injection could have saved them."

"I'm sorry," Shelby said. "Of course not. But think of all the children who won't have to lose their parents. All the people who are coming to the end of their lives and can have another chance. How much is too much to sacrifice for that?"

"But you're not the one making the sacrifice."

"I've given up everything to keep going with this work," Shelby said. "And I'm honored to make that sacrifice."

Ivy pointed at the bright dots of car headlights moving along the San Francisco waterfront. "Do you see those bright little dots, Shelby?"

"Nothing wrong with my vision."

"How much is each one of them worth?"

"You want me to say they're priceless, but they're not. Each one has a part to play in the world. Some might live and die so that others can keep driving forever." Shelby pulled the bag of licorice out of her pocket and offered it to Ivy, who shook her head. "Maybe in the fictional world you inhabit, you create all the rules, but here on Earth everything is a tradeoff."

"So, you traded off the lives of countless innocent people for your eventual success?"

"I wouldn't call fifty countless."

Fifty? Olivia had only discovered twenty-five. "I could warn them, if you gave me their names."

"Saving every puppy?" Shelby said. "That's so Ivy. But I can't give you those names."

Ivy gaped at her and tried to think of how to convince her otherwise.

"Look," Shelby said. "You've heard of the trolley problem, right?"

"I don't want to talk about trolleys."

"So, let's say you're driving a trolley and there's a switch up ahead that puts you on a different track. If you don't flip the switch, you run into five people on the first track. If you do flip the switch, you run into a single person on the second track. Do you flip it?"

Ivy thought she would probably choose to save five over saving one, but she wasn't going to tell Shelby that. "I don't know."

"You do, though," Shelby said. "And that's what I'm doing. I'm sacrificing a small handful of people to save billions. I'm not even sacrificing one billion to save five. It's way less than that. How can I stand by and let the trolley of aging take them all down?"

"You can't just kill random people."

"They're not random." Shelby took out another piece of licorice. "How long did you know I was alive?"

"When you flipped me off."

"It's really cathartic, flipping people off." Shelby smiled. "I couldn't resist."

"What else couldn't you resist?" Ivy said. "Killing Jacko?"

"A thoroughly unpleasant man."

"That's not an answer." But Ivy knew that it was.

Shelby took out another piece of licorice. "I love these things. They'll be hard to get where I'm going."

341

"Which is where?" Ivy wanted to press her about Jacko, but wanted to know where she was going more.

Shelby shook her head. "No spoilers."

Ivy stepped toward her and Shelby's hand darted up inside her jacket toward the gun. Ivy froze. Shelby didn't move her hand. Instead, she looked across the bay at her erstwhile home. "How many people have you told?"

"Told what?"

"That you saw me on that bike." Shelby's hand rested inside her jacket now and Ivy had all the answers she needed.

Ivy knew her life depended on her answer. "The police are doing DNA testing on the samples they took from the autopsy."

Shelby took her hand out of her pocket and Ivy relaxed, but only a little. Had Shelby been ready to kill her? Would she ever know the answer to that? Did she want to?

"Who will they find in your urn?" Ivy asked.

"A desperate woman eager to jump off that bridge."

"Is someone waiting for her to come home?"

Shelby shook her head. "And, before you ask, she begged me for the chance to make that money. It went to her daughter."

"How did you know she'd hit a pylon?"

"Physics," Shelby said.

Ivy pictured her calculating the poor woman's trajectory and instructing her on exactly where to jump, then giving her the Gucci jogging suit and sending her off to die. "So she's the one who called Timothy Shah from the bridge?"

"I called him," Shelby said. "I was waiting in that blank spot on the bridge for her to arrive."

"Standing there, waiting to send an innocent woman to her death. Not feeling an ounce of remorse."

"I did feel remorse. I still do." Shelby sighed. "I cared about her. But she was dying anyway and this was a way to make her death serve a greater good."

"The greater good meaning your escape?"

"No one else will carry on my work as well as I will, Poi. When I'm done, women like her won't have to leave their daughters."

"You monetized her despair."

"Technically, she monetized her own despair." Shelby pointed out. "I just helped her do it."

"How did you make her jump?"

"It's amazing what people who have never had money will do to get it." Shelby bit off another piece of licorice. "She wanted her daughter to have better chances in life and she knew I could pay for them."

"What was her name?" Ivy asked.

"Why do you need to know?"

"To tell her family."

"They won't care," Shelby said. "She lost her parents and her daughter. She was just a kid in the system."

"Like me," Ivy said.

Shelby winced. "None of this is easy."

"Are you going to pay her daughter?"

"Of course I am! I already did." Shelby pursed her lips in annoyance. "I set up an anonymous trust for her."

Maybe Olivia could follow the money to find her. Ivy took in a quick breath as it all hit her. Shelby had done everything she'd feared and more. She imagined the poor mother jumping to her death, hoping that her last act would help her daughter, but probably fearing that it wouldn't. The despair and terror she must have felt. Bile climbed up Ivy's throat and her stomach clenched. She hauled in a few breaths to calm down before she vomited all over the beach.

"You OK?" Shelby asked.

"Why'd you invite me to California?"

Shelby ate another piece of licorice. "I thought I had more time. To show you, really show you, what this work means to the world. That you'd want to help me carry it forward."

"Carry it forward where?"

"Somewhere else," Shelby said. "Somewhere safe from being shut down or running out of funding. Where the work can be completed. That's the only thing that matters."

"Where?" Ivy asked, but Shelby shook her head and chewed the licorice. "Outside the US?"

"Well outside," Shelby said. "That's all I'll say."

"I'm not a scientist," Ivy said. "I can't really help you."

"I can buy more scientists." Shelby swallowed. "I want a friend. Someone I can trust. That's a short list."

Her eyes shone in the streetlight and her smile was enough to break Ivy's heart. Olivia was right. Shelby didn't have anyone else.

Ivy pushed down her feelings and thought about Jacko, dead on the rocks, and the woman who'd jumped face first into a bridge pylon. "Trust is a two-way street."

"You're the only one I trust," Shelby said. "I don't want to do this alone."

"Wendy said your methodology means that you'll never know how close you are to success."

"Wendy is a blinkered fool more interested in statistical analysis than saving lives."

"Doesn't make her wrong."

"Think about my offer, Poi. Come with me. Never worry about money again. Help me to give humanity the greatest gift."

Ivy was afraid to tell her no, alone on the beach with a gun. "I don't know."

"Your life here kinda sucks," Shelby said. "Trolls and doxing and your canceled book deal."

"You know about that?"

"I saw your Kickstarter," Shelby said. "I could give you a million times what you're asking for. You'd never have to worry about money again. You could live a safe and comfortable life. Write whatever you want."

"Where?" Ivy asked.

"That's the part where you have to trust me," Shelby said.

"Give me a little time to think it over." Ivy's words reminded her of what she'd said to Olivia early that evening.

Shelby reached out and touched Ivy's shoulder, fingers brushing against her jacket. Ivy put her hand over Shelby's gloved one. She didn't know how long they stood that way, but Shelby moved away first.

"I'll give you twenty-four hours," Shelby said.

Before Ivy could respond, Shelby slapped down her visor, climbed on the bike, and roared away.

CHAPTER TWENTY-SIX

Ivy stared after her until the buzz of her bike faded away and left only the sound of waves lapping against rocks and the patter of rain on her jacket. Shivering, she sat on a rock and looked at the roiling ocean, one hand cupping her shoulder where Shelby had touched her.

This spot wasn't so different from where Jacko had died. She hoped he hadn't known he was never going to wake up. That he'd lost consciousness and slipped away. Not like the poor unfortunate woman who'd jumped from the bridge. She'd known as she was climbing that fence. When she jumped. And all the way down.

Ivy shook herself. Planula. That's what Shelby was calling herself. Planula was the word for a jellyfish larva. Ivy hadn't put the pieces together. She thought back to Shelby standing with her face suffused by the soft blue light of the jellyfish tanks talking about her dreams of saving the world. And now here she was, so disgraced that she had to fake her own death to escape from her crimes, which included murder. Just like the jellyfish, she was starting over. Which wasn't a good thing.

But what if she was saving the world? Who was Ivy to let that trolley slam into every person on Earth and make them age and die? What right did she have?

Her own dreams hadn't fared so well. Her first novel was a trainwreck and she was unlikely ever to publish another, at least under her real name. The copies she'd signed at Kepler's might be all that remained of her life's work when the internet was through with it. Who was she to judge Shelby? She hadn't changed the world either.

Hard to believe that their hopeful conversation among the jellyfish had led them both here.

Even with her book dreams shattered, the trolls weren't going away. They'd keep bombarding her with hate. The next SWAT team might be careless and someone would get hurt, probably Ivy but maybe someone else who was completely innocent. Or one of the guys with a plunger might catch up to her. And what for? She'd been loyal to her story, loyal to her friend. And it hadn't mattered. The world wasn't a better place.

It would be easy to walk into the ocean and never stop. Cold, for an instant, but warmer than when she'd saved the wolf. She could swim toward the city lights and, eventually, quietly go under into the darkness. She pictured water closing over her head, her mother's waterlogged jacket weighing her down, her helmet filling with water.

And then she let that vision go.

Giving up wasn't the right thing. Just like with the wolf, she'd fight until the last possible second. Writing the book had been the right thing, no matter what the trolls said. Her words and her vision were out in the world. Not like she'd hoped, but still there. She'd keep them alive as long as she could. And she'd write more. Maybe the kind people on the internet would reach out and repair the damage that had been done to her writing career. But even if they didn't, she would keep going.

Before that, she had to protect the innocent people Shelby intended to kill to reach her goal. No matter how much Shelby dressed it up in hopes of immortality someday, innocent people were dying by her hand today and there was no guarantee that their deaths, even if somehow justifiable, would ever contribute to a greater good. As Shelby's own father had pointed out, testing on unknowing victims would never lead to science that would be respected and accepted. Even if Shelby won, she'd lose. And so would those who died for her ambition.

She walked the length of the beach, eyes scanning for the familiar shape of a phonebooth. They belonged to a past without revenge porn, but also without GPS and constant connection to friends, family, and the vast community of the internet. Payphones were supposed to have become superfluous, but she needed one now. She'd been kicked right back into the analog world. Except there were no payphones.

Closed stores and restaurants lined the road. Cold rain drizzled and a sharp wind off the bay reminded her that her wet jacket was pretty useless. As she shivered, she wondered what her Estonian friends would think if she died of hypothermia in California. They'd definitely be unimpressed.

She thought of people who were homeless and had to endure this every day. Jacko and his Pat. Camilla who'd had to get through it while doing chemo and working. Ivy felt like a total wimp for even thinking of complaining.

Just when she was thinking about banging on random doors and begging for help, a siren whooped. A blue light strobed through the rain. Police. Her heart sped up and she whirled. She needed to run into the shadows and hide. Another SWAT team had found her. They were going to arrest her or shoot her. But her brain told her that they might also help her and it felt like her only good option. She stayed put and shielded her eyes against a bright light shone in her face.

"Miss?" called a man's voice. "Are you lost?"

"Yes." Her teeth chattered. "V-v-very lost."

The light moved to the path between her and a police car. It looked like an invitation. She knew it had to be warm in that car. That's how her night was going—jumping into a police car on purpose was her best option mere hours after she'd fought to keep from being thrown into one by a SWAT team. She took a chance and headed for the warmth.

Officer Mehta and Officer Washington introduced themselves and let her use their phone to call Olivia, then gave her a silver space blanket and a cup of coffee from Mehta's thermos. They put her in the backseat and turned their heat up all the way while they waited outside in the rain. They had waterproof jackets and little plastic shower caps over their police hats and seemed fine out there but it was still a nice gesture. So much nicer than the SWAT team.

In about twenty minutes Olivia showed up with dry sweatpants and a sweatshirt and a toasty warm Prius. She flashed her badge and the nice officers handed Ivy right over and went back on patrol, hopefully rescuing other cold unfortunates.

Ivy changed in Olivia's front seat, not caring that she was giving the neighborhood a show of her pale goose-pimpled flesh. After all, this was still less public than the ambulance in Tallinn. Olivia handed her a warm towel and after Ivy dried her hair she started to feel better.

"Here's a Thermos of hot tea." Olivia put it in her hand. "The top is a cup, but you can drink right out of it. I made it when you called."

Ivy poured herself some and took a careful sip. Piping hot, but not going to burn her tongue off. Perfect. She drank more. It tasted a little like apples and honey and a familiar earthy flavor. "Chamomile?"

"It's supposed to be calming," Olivia said.

Ivy sipped slowly, liking how warm it felt and being careful not to spill. It didn't seem to calm her down, but that was expecting a lot from a cup of tea right now. She'd settle for warm.

"How about I take you to my house for the night?" Olivia asked.

Ivy didn't have any better offers. "Thanks."

"I have questions for you."

"Whee," Ivy said.

They got on the Bay Bridge heading east and drove at a comfortable pace for a few minutes before Olivia spoke again. "What the hell are you doing out on a night like this in the middle of nowhere in the rain?"

"Sightseeing."

"Everything is closed." Olivia pointed out.

"I'd heard that the city never sleeps."

Olivia chuckled. "Your Mr. Walsh is about to call out a search party."

"He's very attentive," Ivy said.

Olivia handed Ivy her phone. "I told him you'd call him once I picked you up."

"He called you?"

"According to him, I was the last person to see you before you vanished. He sounded suspicious of my motives."

Ivy took the phone. "I feel like I'm getting a lecture from Mom and Dad."

"I got a call from a police officer in the middle of the night about you," Olivia said. "Your parents wouldn't lecture you for that?"

"Not even when they were alive." Ivy dialed Tristan's number and braced herself.

"Did you find her?" he asked in clipped tones.

"This is Ivy," she said. "On Olivia's phone."

"What. The. Hell." He sounded like someone trying hard not to yell, but the anger leaked through nicely in his tone so he didn't really need to.

She held the phone an inch away from her ear, just in case he decided yelling was the right idea after all. "I'm sorry I didn't call you. I didn't have my phone."

"You were supposed to be in the lobby. They have a phone there. All the time, there's a phone." He muttered something but she didn't quite catch it. Probably something about the phone in the lobby, plus profanity.

"So, you see, I went outside for a short walk," Ivy said.

Olivia chuckled and Ivy resisted the urge to flip her off. Tristan would probably kill her if she got kicked out of this car and then had to call him again from some stranger's phone. Or she'd die of hypothermia by the roadside. Shelby had left her with few options.

"A walk?" Tristan's voice rose on the end in a way Ivy could only describe as hostile and Olivia nodded from the driver's seat. They were ganging up on her, and they weren't even wrong. She'd been naive and stupid. Even the cars passing them on the freeway looked faintly judgey.

She plowed ahead. "And I saw a motorcycle helmet sitting right by the door to Millennium Tower."

"A helmet?" He sounded intrigued despite himself and Olivia spared her a quick glance before turning her attention back to her driving.

Ivy explained about how Shelby had picked her up and taken her to Treasure Island. Then she told them about their conversation and how it ended up with her alone with no phone. She cut the wandering around until the police found her and calling Olivia part short.

Neither one interrupted but if Olivia's expression was anything like Tristan's, they both thought she was the stupidest human being ever birthed. She was inclined to agree with them but that didn't mean they had to rub it in.

"Come back to Millennium Tower," Tristan said. "I'll put you someplace safe and from there we can figure out how to help Shelby together."

"Help?" Ivy glanced over at Olivia who looked back suspiciously.

"Speaker phone." Olivia had been fine with just Ivy's side of the conversation before.

353

Ivy shook her head and mouthed "No."

"My responsibility is to keep you both safe," Tristan said. "Can you concede that this goal will be best realized if I keep you both apart?"

Olivia pressed a button on her steering wheel and the phone's output went straight to the car's speakers. Ivy remembered too late that it was her phone.

"You're on speaker phone now," Ivy said quickly, so Tristan didn't say anything he'd regret.

"Hello, Special Agent Ajak," Tristan said. "Please bring my client to Millennium Tower. I appreciate you picking her up and I apologize for the inconvenience."

Olivia looked over at Ivy and then back at the SUV in front of them. "Is that where you want to go, Ivy?"

"Of course she does," said Tristan.

Ivy looked at the phone. She imagined Tristan on the other end, earnestly figuring out ways to help her because it was his duty. And while he was at it, he was figuring out ways to help Shelby because that was also his duty. He'd never turn Shelby into the police, and he'd do his best to make sure she remained free. Ivy respected his unswerving loyalty. A few days before, she'd shared it.

"Well?" Olivia asked. "Where to?"

"I'm going to Olivia's." Ivy ended the call before Tristan could respond.

CHAPTER TWENTY-SEVEN

While Olivia drove, she shot off a series of rapid-fire questions. Ivy's answers didn't make Shelby look better. By the time Olivia ran out of things to ask, Ivy was worried that she'd have to testify in court. Against Shelby. But she'd made her choice. Justice over loyalty. She didn't feel great about it, and she expected that to get worse.

Olivia kept asking while she switched to a smaller freeway and then exited onto surface streets so badly lit that Ivy had no idea where they were going. Oakland somewhere. Moraga Avenue. As if to distract her from worrying about ending up buried in a shallow grave in a wooded area, Olivia kept up the questions.

Then she stopped talking and Ivy stared out at darkness punctuated by streetlamps that illuminated only trees. Finally, Olivia pulled up to a ranch-style house. A eucalyptus tree so tall that Ivy couldn't see the top in the darkness towered nearby. The yard looked well kept and the house was newly painted in pewter green and black. How did Olivia find the time to keep her house so tidy while working full-time for Shelby plus running an investigation? Ivy was lucky if she washed her dishes every day.

"My wife's asleep," Olivia said. "Be quiet until we get to the kitchen."

Ivy gave her a thumbs-up and folded her silver space blanket. It crinkled and rustled as she tucked it carefully away in her backpack. After all, if she ended up on the streets, it might be the most useful thing she owned.

Olivia jumped out of the car and Ivy hurried after, inhaling the scent of eucalyptus. It was fresh and reassuring and, yes, a little bit calming. She wondered if Olivia noticed it anymore.

After fishing through a truly impressive collection of keys, Olivia found the right one to unlock the shiny black door. She darted forward and stood with one foot blocking the opening to keep something inside from getting out. Ivy slipped through the door sideways and a calico cat twined around her legs.

"That's Twinkle," Olivia whispered. "Don't encourage her."

Ivy ignored her and petted the little cat. Twinkle purred ferociously and blinked copper-colored eyes.

They all proceeded to a big and friendly kitchen, decorated in bright yellow with white stone countertops. The kitchen accents had a lemon theme and it all felt very cheerful and grownup. It was the opposite of Shelby's apartment and oddly also the opposite of Ivy's. Olivia closed the kitchen door and turned on the hob, also bright yellow.

Twinkle settled on Ivy's lap and proceeded to purr and shed fur at a prodigious rate. Ivy absorbed the restful cheeriness against her will. Her shoulders relaxed and her neck cracked when she turned it from side to side.

"When life gives you lemons." Ivy waved one arm at the lemon accents while petting the cat with the other.

"Exactly. What kind of tea do you want?" Olivia asked. "Chamomile again? Peppermint? Decaf English breakfast?"

"You have quite a selection." Ivy pointed to the decaf English breakfast. At least it would taste like it had caffeine.

"Jill's a doctor," Olivia said. "She's anti-caffeine in the afternoons, so we have herbal tea coming out our...ears."

In a few minutes she set a yellow teacup and a plate of warm pizza rolls next to Ivy.

"I keep them hidden at the back of the fridge," Olivia said. "For emergencies. Don't tell Jill."

"Deal," Ivy said.

Twinkle put both paws on the table and looked at the pizza rolls. One paw crept toward the yellow plate.

Olivia deflected Twinkle's hopes. "She can't eat any. It'll make her puke red all over the carpet."

Ivy didn't ask when she'd run that particular experiment. Instead she put the cat on the floor with an apology and guiltily devoured the first roll. Warm and salty and tasted like tomatoes. Definitely not something she'd consider related to a pizza, but it was hot and it was there. Like that one German guy who walked into Murphy's at closing. Hopefully the pizza rolls would be easier to get rid of.

"Shelby gave you twenty-four hours to think it over," Olivia said. "Did she say how she'd contact you?"

"Not even a hint." Ivy ate another roll and caught a little orange paw before it snagged the last one.

Olivia looked thoughtful while Ivy finished the pizza rolls and had a good long sip of tea. She finally felt warm and dry and safe. That probably meant that something horrible was coming. Twinkle jumped onto her lap and sniffed the empty plate suspiciously.

"If she contacts you electronically, there's not much we can do to track her location," Olivia said.

"Well, I don't think she'll be calling. One phone is on its way to Estonia and the other one is in the bay." RIP phone, she added to herself. I barely knew you. She settled the cat on her lap and got back to petting her.

"Would she be reckless enough to meet you in person?" Olivia asked.

"She did it once." Ivy thought about Shelby's driving on the bridge. "She might again."

"Why do you think she wants you to go with her?"

"She said she wants someone she can trust."

Olivia raised a skeptical eyebrow. "That's probably what she told the woman who jumped off the bridge."

Ivy looked down at her hands.

"I'm sorry," Olivia said. "But you shouldn't take her words at face value."

"What else would she want me for?"

"Where do you think she's going to go?" Olivia ignored the question.

"She's not giving up on her research. So she has to go somewhere where she can continue it."

"That's nowhere in the United States," Olivia said. "Obviously."

"China?" Ivy thought aloud. "Or Taiwan? Someplace with no extradition treaties with the US. With good research labs."

"We put her on the no-fly list," Olivia said. "Maybe we'll catch her that way."

"She can still drive. Or catch a private plane."

"Or ride out of the country on a unicorn," Olivia said. "We do what we can."

"I think you have to be a virgin to ride a unicorn."

"Unicorns do a hymen check?" Olivia said and they both laughed.

They sat in silence for a moment and then Ivy yawned and Olivia led her to the guest bedroom where Ivy brushed her teeth and put on a pair of flannel pajamas provided by Olivia. She'd expected lemons, but instead cheery yellow ducks decorated the flannel. Twinkle seemed to like them and the two cuddled up and went to sleep.

The next morning Ivy awoke alone to the smell of coffee. Based on the light, she'd slept in, for the first time since her arrival. Maybe she was through her jetlag. That must mean it was time to go home.

She stretched, thought about going back to sleep, but instead got up and padded into the kitchen. Hiding wasn't going to help anyone. Time to face the day.

Olivia stirred oatmeal on the stove while talking on the phone. The homey smell of cinnamon filled the kitchen. Olivia tilted her head toward the table to indicate that Ivy should sit.

Ivy sat and looked around for Twinkle, but the little calico had gone about her own business. She was probably outside enjoying her day and not working to betray her oldest friend. Or maybe Ivy was projecting her emotions on the cat, just a little.

Olivia plunked a cup of coffee in front of her and put a phone next to it. Then she set out two yellow bowls of steaming oatmeal and big spoons next to a ceramic pitcher of milk and a bowl of brown sugar. Ivy added both, then started eating like it had been years since her last real meal. It tasted reassuring and hearty. The oats and cinnamon practically exploded with healthiness and tasted nothing like the oatmeal cardboard she'd eaten at Shelby's apartment.

"Do you think she's really leaving the area in twenty-four hours?" As befit her no-nonsense demeanor, Olivia ate her oatmeal with precise movements and no added sugar.

"Maybe?" Ivy sighed. "I guess I'm not much of a Shelby expert."

"You're all we have," Olivia said, not contradicting her.

"I feel sorry for us." Ivy had already engulfed her oatmeal while Olivia still worked stolidly through her bowl. "We could do better."

Olivia slid the phone across to her. "Check your email. Maybe there's a message from Shelby."

Obediently, Ivy logged in. Her publisher wanted confirmation that she knew they'd dumped her and weren't going to pay her. She wasn't going to bother sending them that. Let them wait for it.

361

And why did they even need it? She made a mental note to think about that later.

A couple messages from angry trolls, but fewer than yesterday. Maybe Tristan's de-escalation strategy had worked. Or maybe they'd moved on because they'd gotten what they wanted: her digital annihilation. She'd obediently muzzled herself and it hadn't even helped in the end. They'd won and she'd lost. Maybe she should have kept drinking wine and fighting with them. Following protocol, she forwarded the messages to Tristan and moved them to the Trolls folder.

Speaking of Tristan, he'd sent her two emails. One last night requesting that she call him immediately. He'd sent it after she basically hung up on him so she kinda knew what that was about. The second had arrived an hour ago and told her that the knife guy from Kepler's was also the @allspermmatters guy, so that was a bit of good news. He was still in custody for pulling a knife on Tristan. One less violent guy with a knife looking for her had to be a cause for celebration, right?

Off Olivia's impatient look she said, "Nothing from Shelby."

"What about that one from Mr. Walsh?" Olivia pointed to it. "He'd be a good go between for Shelby."

Ivy didn't think he'd be helpful, at least not intentionally. He didn't want Shelby to get caught and face justice. She called him anyway.

After a polite good morning, she asked if he'd heard from Shelby.

"I haven't," he said. "As a lawyer, I must caution you against speaking too freely with Special Agent Ajak."

"I have nothing to hide."

"If I had a nickel for every client who mistakenly thought that." He paused. "I'd have a nickel for every client."

Ivy laughed. "Nobody is a good judge of personal risk?"

"Lots of folks are better at it than you," he said. "So don't get cocky."

Ivy thought of her email from that morning. "Can I send you a couple emails from my publisher about pulling out of my book contract? Are they allowed to do that? I'm thinking maybe they have to pay me off but are conveniently not mentioning it."

"I can take a look," he said.

Ivy thanked him and broke the connection.

"So, he didn't say she'd strolled right in and was waiting for us?" Olivia asked.

Ivy shook her head, wondering how Tristan planned to find Shelby. He probably had better ideas than she did. Hopefully Olivia did too.

Olivia delivered the last bite of oatmeal to her mouth. "I'd hoped we'd get lucky and pick her up for something else. But I think we have to go to Plan B."

Ivy took a slow sip of coffee. Hot, but not too hot, and smooth and strong. "I hate to ask."

"I follow you for the next twenty-four hours." Olivia checked her watch. "Sixteen hours. Along with a small team."

"How small?"

"Big enough," Olivia said. "If Shelby comes near you, we pick her up and your part is over."

Ivy doubted that. "Nobody gets hurt, right?"

"We'll exercise as much restraint as we can." Olivia studied her over the rim of her coffee cup. "Injuring her would only make her less compliant and sympathetic to the jury."

CHAPTER TWENTY-EIGHT

And that's how Ivy found herself standing in front of Shelby's apartment trying to look casual. She watched passing cars and listened for approaching motorcycles and worried that Tristan would come strolling by and start an argument. So far he hadn't, but her bait hadn't hooked Shelby either. She'd talked to the lady with the sweater dog about knitting. She'd nodded coolly to Todd at the front desk who she'd last seen watching Shelby's revenge porn, which made him look rightfully nervous. And she'd handed out all the dollar bills in her wallet to passing people who were homeless. At least the weather was good.

In case Shelby made her ditch her phone again, Olivia had insisted on sewing a tracking device into the lining of Ivy's jacket by the right pocket and Ivy had to stop herself from fiddling with it. She also wore a recording device that Olivia was monitoring, presumably from inside a van somewhere, if Ivy's television watching experience was accurate.

"It's been long enough," Olivia said in her ear. "How about you walk to Margie's?"

"Sure." Ivy ambled down the street trying to act like she was just out for a normal walk on a normal day. But her steps felt awkward and she didn't know what to do with her hands. She stuffed them in her pockets and let her index finger touch the tracking device.

Still Shelby didn't come. Ivy reached Second Chances and went inside to talk to Margie.

A harried looking white-haired woman told her that Margie had called in sick before she bustled off. Not sure what else to do, Ivy walked to the bulletin board. Someone had taken down both her messages, the one to Jacko and the one asking about B12 injections. Olivia or someone else? A new notice was tacked up in their place. Printed out on crisp, white paper, it looked like Olivia had hung it and then ordered it to never get dirty. It also asked about injections. Two of the phone number tabs on the bottom had been ripped off.

Ivy went back out to the street and leaned against the stucco wall where Jacko had stood smoking. She watched an old man push a shopping cart down the sidewalk. The right front wheel was broken and he had to jerk it every few steps to straighten it out.

"Can you spare a dollar?" he asked and jerked the wheel straight.

"I can't." She wondered if Shelby had sent him to deliver a message.

"Not even a single dollar?" He tucked long white hair behind his ears.

"Not even enough to buy my own lunch." Ivy was out of American money. "I'm sleeping on a friend's couch. Or at least I hope I am."

"How about a cigarette?" he asked.

"I don't smoke." She wondered if she should get close and pretend to be giving him a cigarette.

The man rolled his eyes at her utter uselessness and left. No message to deliver. As she watched him push his cart further on its stuttering journey she wondered what had led him here.

Her phone rang.

"Tristan here."

"Yup." Ivy looked up and down the street. Nothing out of place. And if Shelby was following her it wouldn't be weird to take a phone call.

"What are you doing right now?" he asked.

She hesitated, then told him. Predictably, he wasn't thrilled.

"You're standing around waiting for a woman who you know is armed. A woman who will probably be angry with you when she realizes that you're trying to catch her? A woman who may or may not be a killer."

"Sort of." Exactly that.

"Let's call this your 'waiting to be killed' plan," he said.

"I was thinking of it as my 'waiting to save others' plan."

Tristan sighed like a man searching for patience. "Do you have a vest?"

"I have on a shirt and a jacket," she said. "Why are you giving me fashion advice?"

"A bulletproof vest." He pronounced each word carefully, underlining that she was an idiot.

Ivy felt like she ought to have figured that out, or Olivia should have. Her call waiting beeped.

"I have another call. Be right back."

"Who is that?" Olivia asked.

"Tristan. He wants me to wear a bulletproof vest."

"Too bulky," said Olivia. "Shelby would notice right away. It might scare her off."

Ivy went to the other line and explained that to Tristan.

"If it scares her off from shooting you, how is that a bad thing?" he asked.

"I'm sure Olivia knows her business and this is the right decision." Ivy wasn't sure.

"Where are you going next?" he asked. "I can wait there and give you a vest. You can put a sweater over it. It's so cold out today that it'll look natural."

She could put it all on and see. Maybe he was right.

"I'm going to head over to Embarcadero," she said, like she had a plan. "Walk along the ocean and see if that draws her out."

"I'll be inside the ferry building." He hung up, presumably to head off to find a bulletproof vest and an innocuous-looking sweater. She appreciated his thoughtfulness. Someone ought to be looking out for her.

Olivia texted her. Embarcadero is fine. Vest isn't.

Ivy thought about flipping off her phone but decided that wasn't the best way to motivate Olivia to take a bullet for her. Instead she headed toward the water feeling like there was a giant target on her back and also vaguely insulted that no one was shooting at her. Did Shelby not even care anymore?

About a mile later the ferry building came into view. She admired its white arches and checked that the time on its clock matched the time on her phone. It was two minutes slow. Analog time.

Her phone buzzed.

"I see you," said Tristan. "Come inside."

Olivia texted No!

The exclamation mark looked stern. And there she was, caught between the two of them.

Before she got to the ferry building, a red streetcar stopped nearby and, on a whim, she jumped on. She didn't want to fight with Tristan or Olivia. Her phone buzzed immediately.

Walk

It was too late to get off though and Ivy was getting fed up with Olivia's bossiness, so she sat down and rode. It felt nice to sit down. She was starting to think that Shelby knew what she was doing and this was going to be one long disappointing day.

She got off the streetcar and texted her location to Tristan and Olivia. @ Pier 37

Tristan texted back immediately. Meet at ice cream store behind the aquarium at Pier 39

She admired his flexibility, but she still didn't know about wearing that vest.

Olivia texted. Don't get on another train. Or bus

"Sure," Ivy said so Olivia could hear. She strolled along to give them time to catch up. Tourists jostled her, stopping erratically to pose in front of random objects for selfies. It was like they had a set number of photographs they needed to take each day and they were working their way joylessly through the list. Nobody stopped long enough to actually look at what they were photographing.

Most wore San Francisco-themed jackets, like they'd all discovered how cold it was going to be after they arrived. She couldn't exactly blame them, since she'd made the same mistake, except she hadn't been able to afford a tourist jacket so she'd had to opt for freezing instead.

Her jacket. The vest and a sweater would never fit under her leather jacket. And the jacket was probably what Shelby would use to spot her. She'd have to turn Tristan down.

The thought of that made the back of her neck itch. It felt like someone was watching her. But, of course, someone was. Olivia and her not-too-small team and maybe Tristan. Maybe Shelby had a different plan for contacting her.

For the tenth time, Ivy stopped to check her emails. Nothing from Shelby. Maybe being out on the street was the wrong approach. Maybe Shelby had left a clue in her apartment. Maybe Ivy should go back there and see.

She hesitated in front of the Aquarium of the Bay. She was at Pier 39, where she could find the ice cream store and at least try on that vest. A giant painting of a great white shark swam above her head. Pictures of jellyfish covered one wall with orange bells and red tentacles and gelatinous arms. Even though they were much larger, they reminded her of the jellies she'd seen during her trip to the Pittsburgh aquarium. Something only Shelby would know.

"Do you think she might want to meet me in there?" Ivy said aloud.

"Why?" said Olivia in her ear.

"Because jellyfish are important to her." Ivy knew it sounded lame.

Before Olivia could respond with something snarky, a Kawasaki Ninja motorcycle jumped onto the sidewalk and skidded to a stop next to Ivy. She flinched away and tourists scattered like pigeons.

The rider was a man with long dirty blond hair wearing a leather vest. She'd never seen him before. The man dropped the bike onto its kickstand.

"Take it, Ivy!" he shouted, then sprinted north up Embarcadero.

Ivy looked at the poison green Ninja he'd left behind, engine running. She should have brought her helmet.

Olivia spoke in her ear. Let us catch up. Stall

Ivy was inclined to agree. She sauntered toward the bike, looking around for Shelby. She didn't see her, but there were so many people she probably wouldn't have seen her if she was two feet away.

And then she heard it.

The deep, throaty call of the Ducati, slowly fading away to the north.

"I have to go, Olivia," Ivy said. "I hear her bike."

"Wait," Olivia said in her ear. "We need to stay close to you."

Ivy threw one leg over the Ninja. As she did, she pictured Tristan standing at the ice cream store

371

holding a now-useless bulletproof vest. Imaginary Tristan looked pissed off. She silently apologized.

"Try to keep up!" she yelled to Olivia. "I hear her ahead of me and she's almost gone."

And then she chased the sound.

In the mirror, a guy in jeans and a black San Jose Sharks windbreaker sprinted after her. Presumably, he was one of Olivia's men. If so, he was never going to catch her.

Then she aimed for a bright red helmet retreating a block away, its growl barely audible under the noise of cars and pedestrians. As she closed in, she recognized the Ducati cutting through a river of cars. The leather-clad rider dodged from side to side. Shelby. She must have freed her motorcycle from the tower's luxury garage. Or maybe she had another one. Or a dozen. She'd defrauded investors of enough money to buy a fleet of Ducatis.

Ivy poured on speed and the Ninja shot ahead into the traffic. Wishing she'd brought her helmet, she wove between a cab and a cable car, hoping that they both stayed in their lane. She cleared them with a hand's breadth to spare on each side. The cabbie laid on his horn and she risked taking a hand off the handlebars to flip him off. Shelby was right. It felt cathartic.

Olivia had to have a car or something. She'd catch up. Maybe that white van Ivy had imagined was right behind her. A quick glance in the rearview mirror turned up zero vans.

Ivy slowed, but the Ducati didn't and the gap between them widened. If she didn't speed up, she'd lose it forever. She gave up on a rescue from Olivia and focused on following Shelby.

They shot past Pier 41 and rode right next to the bay. Without the high stakes, it would have been a great ride. Ocean breeze in her face and the road ahead full of obstacles to be avoided. Of course, without the stakes she never would have done it. They had to be breaking a million traffic laws. Including not wearing a helmet.

"Passing Pier 41!" Ivy yelled, hoping that would help Olivia.

Accelerating through a red light, she followed Shelby toward Pier 45. She hoped Shelby would drive out onto the pier. If Olivia was fast, maybe she could trap them out there and move in. Ivy tried to remember if there were multiple entrances and exits. But she was no Google Maps, so she wasn't sure.

Not that it mattered because at the last second Shelby took a hard left. Ivy leaned to keep from crashing and followed.

They turned onto a busy street. Ivy hadn't had time to read the sign so she didn't know what it was called. Not that it mattered because Olivia could never catch up. Cars and buses and SUVs jockeyed for position. People pushing shopping carts or pulling out their phones to take pictures packed the sidewalks.

"Left on some street," Ivy called.

Then Shelby opened up the Ducati and it charged forward. The Ninja had no choice but to follow. Ivy hoped that Olivia was still behind them somewhere. At least she was tracking her GPS locator. She'd catch up eventually. She had to.

With gritted teeth, Ivy wove around cars behind Shelby. At night, this kind of riding had been dangerous, but by day it was suicidal. A driver in a black SUV hammered his horn and she didn't blame him. She shot around his side and swerved in front of a VW bug who slammed on her brakes and beeped a cute little toot. Ivy kept her eyes forward. She wouldn't last much longer without wiping out.

Then Shelby cut left into a pedestrian-only park and Ivy followed. She lost hope of Olivia catching up. No cars allowed here. No motorcycles either for that matter. At this point, they'd only catch Shelby if some park ranger pulled her over for driving on the nature trails, maybe by flinging himself under her wheels. Unlikely. She gritted her teeth and followed.

"We're in a park. Pedestrian-only." She called to Olivia like it was going to matter.

Families and dogs leaped out of Shelby's way as she sped down a walking path. Shelby swerved hard around a stroller that Ivy hoped was empty. She followed and didn't even have time to check.

And on they went. She had no more time to think about Olivia or anything else. Avoiding obstacles and keeping Shelby in sight took all her concentration. Her shoulders hurt from yanking the bike around. Or maybe from being clenched up on account of fear of death. Ahead of her Shelby cleared the path with considerably more finesse.

And then they hit the Golden Gate Bridge heading north. Ivy was grateful that they were weaving between cars instead of people. At least if they ran into them the innocents inside would be spared. An international orange line streaked by on her right.

Where were they going? Was Shelby staying up north? In college she'd talked about hikes in the redwoods and staying at her grandmother's cabin. She should have thought of that this morning when she was talking to Olivia.

Wind tore through her hair and her eyes watered. She shouted, "On Golden Gate Bridge. Family cabin?"

She hoped Olivia could hear her and that her words made some kind of sense. At this point, Olivia would only arrive there after things were over.

Then Shelby accelerated the Ducati and Ivy fell behind, losing ground. Shelby's bike had a bigger engine and she could ditch Ivy whenever she wanted. But she didn't want to. She'd let Ivy catch up to her again, maybe once they got off the bridge.

Then the northbound traffic stopped cold. Ivy swerved into the space between lanes and kept going. She hoped no one would open their door. She had nowhere to go and if she hit one, that would be the end of everything. At least she wouldn't have to feel guilty about not wearing a bulletproof vest.

The Ducati growled a few yards ahead. Then it, too, slowed and stopped.

She looked past the Ducati to the end of the bridge. Two police cars were parked sideways, lights flashing. Next to them stood at least a dozen officers. Olivia had called in reinforcements. She and Shelby weren't going to be able to drive off the bridge that way.

Shelby must have realized it too. Her Ducati jerked to the left and wove in front of parked cars to reach the barrier that separated the northbound lanes from the southbound ones. She was going to try to head back into San Francisco.

Slowly, Ivy followed. The concrete barrier that separated the lanes looked almost three feet tall. Shelby pulled her bike into a wheelie and headed for it. Ivy could tell that she'd never be able to get over it, not without a ramp and a better run up. Even if she did, the southbound cars were parked, too, and Ivy imagined another row of police waiting on the San Francisco end.

"Don't!" Ivy yelled even though she knew Shelby couldn't hear her over the Ducati's roar.

The red Ducati raced up the barrier and hung in the sky for a moment like Icarus. Then it too crashed to the ground. The bike bounced off the side of a semi truck and Shelby flew off the side. She skidded under a Prius and the Ducati lay still by the truck.

Ivy ditched the Ninja and ran toward Shelby's fallen body. The truck driver opened his door and climbed down, swearing. Ivy was close now.

Shelby stumbled to her feet. She tore off her helmet and hurled it at Ivy. Ivy dodged to the side and held up a hand to ward it off. Pain jolted through her wrist.

Swearing, Shelby limped for the sidewalk. Dark hair streamed behind her in the wind.

Ivy followed, cradling her arm against her chest. The truck driver shouted something, but she didn't slow to listen. She didn't imagine it was useful.

"Ambulance!" she yelled, hoping someone, especially Olivia, might call one.

Placing both hands on the railing, Shelby vaulted over the fence and onto the pedestrian walkway. She landed with a groan and stumbled forward. It looked like her ankle was injured.

When Ivy broke into a run her wrist throbbed with each step.

A man jogging with a golden retriever stopped next to Shelby.

"Are you OK?" he asked.

"Get the fuck away from me!" Shelby yelled.

The man backed up, hands in the air like she was going to shoot him. The guy had good instincts. His dog stood between them, growling.

Ivy climbed over the fence a lot less gracefully. Her right wrist was messed up. Maybe broken, maybe sprained, but definitely not happy.

"It's OK," she called to Shelby. "It's going to be OK."

Golden retriever man looked at Ivy.

"Just go," she told him. This would be easier without an audience. "Keep people back."

He shrugged and stepped away, waving at the bridge pedestrians to move. Ivy gave him a quick thumbs-up with her left hand and turned back to Shelby.

"I just didn't want to go alone." Shelby trembled and stood on one leg, the other held off the ground like it hurt to stand on.

When Ivy walked slowly toward her, Shelby stumbled back a step.

"You're not alone," Ivy said. "I'm right here."

Out of the corner of her eye, she watched uniformed cops converging from both sides. They didn't have much time.

"We're right back where we started." Shelby hopped to the outside fence and leaned against the chain link. Waves glittered behind her back.

Ivy sang the first few lines of the Beatles' song 'Long and Winding Road.' Shelby's shoulders inched down.

"I was so close," Shelby said.

"I know," Ivy answered, although she didn't know anything. "We can figure this out."

Shelby looked right and left, taking in the police.

"I wanted a good thing," she said. "You know it was good, right?"

"Sure." Ivy was almost close enough to grab her. She could hold her until the cops came.

But Shelby must have read that in her eyes because she turned and jumped onto the chain link fence. With one quick movement, she pulled herself up out of Ivy's reach.

Ivy stepped up next to the fence. All she saw was the drop and the waves impossibly far below. She'd never been afraid of heights, but her legs told her that she didn't want to go up on that fence.

"Don't make me come up there!" she said, like the angry mother of a toddler.

Shelby inched upward. It was slow going with her injured leg, but she wasn't giving up.

Ivy ignored her common sense and climbed onto the fence, hoping it wouldn't collapse and fling her into the ocean. She held on one-handed with her toes jammed in between the links.

"We don't have to do this," she called up to Shelby. "We can still come back down and face whatever happens together."

"Come down," called a familiar voice.

Ivy looked and there was Tristan. He had a bundle under one arm that she assumed was her bulletproof vest. He looked out of breath and about as angry as she'd imagined.

The chain link rattled as Shelby kept climbing. The fence curved inward near the top, and she was having trouble getting onto it. Tristan dropped Ivy's vest, then ran over and stood under Shelby.

"Let go," he called. "I'll catch you."

Ivy gave him points for trying, but Shelby shook her head. Her injured leg was giving her trouble. Ivy sympathized. Doing this one-handed was nearly impossible. Still, she forced her good hand to unclench and lifted one leg up and jammed it into a higher position.

The fence shook as Tristan jumped onto it. Would it hold all this weight? What was it designed for? Ivy pushed herself up with her legs, toes searching for gaps in the chain link. This would have been easier barefoot, but she couldn't even imagine how she'd get her shoes off here. She kept going.

People shouted from cars and wind lashed her face, but she only had eyes for Shelby. Tristan passed her easily. Two working arms and legs were a winning combination.

"We got this," she yelled to Shelby. "Come down."

Tristan grabbed for Shelby's leg, but she swung it away. He pulled himself up closer and reached again.

Shelby took the gun from under her jacket and shot at Tristan. He let out a gasp and peeled off the fence. For a second, he hung from one arm, chest arching backward. Shelby shot him again. He fell past Ivy and landed on the walkway with a meaty smack.

"What the hell?" Ivy clung to her section of the fence with one hand and glared up at Shelby. "Tristan cared about you."

Shelby hauled herself up to the top of the fence. The curve slowed her down.

"Don't." Ivy pulled herself up further, trying not to think about Tristan and Shelby's gun and the ocean and everything. She just needed to grab hold of Shelby and hold her long enough for the police to finally arrive. She could do it.

Shelby pulled her legs in close, but Ivy was almost there.

"We can get through this together," Ivy yelled. "Wait for me."

Shelby lashed out with her good leg and caught Ivy in the shoulder. Ivy's grip failed and she fell. She landed hard on the concrete walkway and white-hot pain jolted from her injured wrist. She struggled to breathe. Her chest hurt. Had Shelby shot her too?

Unable to move, Ivy watched Shelby climb atop the fence. Far above her, silhouetted against the blue sky, Shelby raised one black-clad arm and flipped her off. Shelby held her arms out like she was about to take a bow, then pushed off the fence and fell backward.

Ivy's chest ached and she struggled to pull in air. Someone hauled her into a sitting position.

"You got the wind knocked out of you," he said. "You're OK."

"Tristan?" Ivy's voice and air came back. She drew in another breath and struggled to her feet. She staggered to the fence and looked down. Nothing but green waves and painful white light reflecting back at her.

Her knees buckled and she slid down onto the concrete again. With a groan Tristan collapsed next to her. The cops were close now, Olivia sprinting near the front of the pack. She wondered how Olivia had managed to close down the bridge and get here so quickly. Federal stuff.

"Are you OK?" Tristan asked.

"Shelby shot you. How are you—"

"I was wearing a vest," he said. "Like a normal damn security consultant."

"You knew she'd shoot you?" She looked up at the fence like she expected Shelby to still be there.

He took a deep breath and winced. "I hoped she wouldn't, but hope is a fragile flower and Kevlar blooms eternal."

She cradled her arm against her chest and tilted her head up to look at the spot where she'd last seen Shelby. The empty sky didn't care.

CHAPTER TWENTY-NINE

This time Ivy showed up early for the funeral with her arm in a cast. Either the helmet or the fall had broken her wrist. She wore a black suit from Olivia's closet and drove Olivia's car. Olivia wasn't attending. Gravestones surrounded Ivy like whitecaps on the sea that had taken Shelby.

Alone, she walked across the field of carefully tended grass. She halted at the grave of a child adorned with a small lamb. Four years old. Next, she lingered next to an angel left for the beloved mother who had made it to seventy-nine. The mother had endured decades of grief. If Shelby had lived, maybe there would have been no more graves like this. Or maybe there would have been more of them.

When she arrived at the Linton crypt, she pulled on the door but it was locked. She wondered if the other woman's ashes still rested next to Shelby's mother's. Maybe the mystery woman and Mrs. Linton had bonded in the intervening days. They'd both left daughters behind too soon.

She stood awkwardly and felt like she should say goodbye to Shelby while they were alone, but Shelby wasn't here yet.

"I'm sorry," she said aloud to the crypt and the grass and the rows of graves. "I didn't see another way."

Only the wind answered.

Tristan arrived next. He was impeccably dressed in a black suit with a black armband and walked slowly across the field. Shelby's second shot had broken two of his ribs. Kevlar might bloom eternal, but it wasn't a magical forcefield.

"How are the ribs?" she asked.

He shrugged and grimaced. "I'm sorry for your loss."

"If she hadn't come back for me, she wouldn't be lost." Her broken arm ached.

"Others would be lost instead," he said. "And many more of them."

He lifted his arm, winced, and dropped it over her shoulder. She leaned against him.

"No vest today?" she asked.

"I'm trusting you. I figure, as a European, you probably don't even own a gun."

"Guilty." She stepped away and watched him slowly lower his arm. He'd done all he could to keep them both safe, but things were still awkward between them. "Do you blame me for turning Shelby in?"

"You did what you thought was right," he said. "Shelby made her own choices. There's no reason to shoulder all the guilt for how things turned out."

"I can take all the guilt. Even one-armed." She lifted her cast.

They stood for a few moments looking at each other awkwardly.

"Congratulations on the Kickstarter," he said finally.

She felt warm inside. "I didn't know so many people would step up and help."

"There's more good than bad out there, even in my job," he said. "I'm excited to see what you do in a book about an immortal race corrupting human creativity while searching for redemption."

"We can all use a little redemption sometimes," she said.

"I can help you with security if the book's reception all goes wrong," he said.

"To hell with that." She looked over at the crypt. "I'm going to let it all hang out this time. No regrets. Maximum arguments and angry hashtags."

"That's one approach."

"I'm not letting them silence me," she said. "I'm going to be angry and loud and then I'm going to harness the forces of good against them."

"OK." He straightened and drew in a quick breath. "That might not work every time."

She searched for Mr. Linton, but he still wasn't there. "How did you get to us before the cops?"

"I tracked the Ducati using its anti-theft device and had a friend meet me at the end of the bridge with a bicycle."

"Nicely done, Mr. High Tech."

"I arrived in time to get shot and knocked off the fence," he said. "Super useful."

"I was glad you were there with me." She blinked. "After."

Together they watched Mr. Linton and the priest walk across the field of graves. Mr. Linton carried another urn, this one a burnished bronze, darker than the last. She guessed he'd given the previous urn to the police. The thought of him pouring the ashes into a box to reuse the original urn was awful and she was glad to see he hadn't.

"Thank you for coming," said Mr. Linton when he reached them.

"Of course," Ivy answered and Tristan nodded.

And then a stripped-down version of the last service began. No posters of Shelby smiling down at them. No other mourners. No flowers. Even the priest hurried through his spare eulogy. Someone must have briefed him on keeping it short.

After a brief moment of silent prayer, Mr. Linton handed Ivy the cold urn. It felt surprisingly heavy in her good hand and she curled it against her chest one-armed. Mr. Linton unlocked the crypt and beckoned to her.

As before, Ivy followed him in. The flowers she'd seen at the first funeral were gone, except for a sprig of lavender in a dusty purple vase.

"She would have liked the lavender." Ivy had nothing else to say. She'd used up her stock phrases at the first funeral.

He held out his hands and she put the urn into them, feeling like she should say something, but not knowing what. Carefully, he tucked it into its alcove, polishing the nameplate with his cuff. He stepped back, then reached over and repositioned the lavender, as if moving it close enough for Shelby to smell.

His movements were slow, his back hunched. He'd aged so much since they'd last stood here. Back then he'd laid his daughter to rest with a different set of memories.

Ivy leaned closer to look at subtle patterns etched onto the surface of the urn. She recognized the molecular structure of the drug that Nyssa had sought to bring to market. The molecule Shelby had tattooed on her own side. She remembered how Shelby had called her that day.

"I did it, Poi!" Shelby sounded ebullient, almost drunk.

"It what?" The phone had woken Ivy up and she was not in the mood. Tobias, a guy she'd been seeing for a couple of months groaned and rolled over. She sympathized.

"I got a tattoo. Wait, I'm texting you a picture."

"Just a minute," Ivy whispered.

She slipped out of bed and padded into her living room, then checked her text messages. Shelby had sent a picture of her torso. A bunch of chemical symbols covered one side and her bell-shaped birthmark peeked out of a hexagon. Her pale skin was red next to the blue lines, so the tattoo hadn't yet healed.

"What's that?" Ivy yawned.

"That's my molecule!" Shelby crowed. "It's the drug that's going to change the world."

"Really?" Ivy looked at it more closely. It did look like something she vaguely remembered from high school chemistry. "And it's a tattoo?"

"Did I wake you up?"

Ivy laughed. "You did. But tell me about this tattoo."

"This represents forever. Children never losing parents. Parents never losing children. No one dying before their time."

Ivy plopped down on her windowsill. It was summer and pale blue light reflected off the stone buildings. Imagine a future where people could last as long as the things they built.

"Tell me more," Ivy said. "Tell me more."

Back in the crypt, Ivy ran her index finger over each line, imagining the pain that Shelby must have felt when this was tattooed on her body, and the despair she'd known when she realized that she was taking her precious molecule to a watery grave.

Mr. Linton cleared his throat. "Another company bought her formula."

"They did?" She had stayed off the internet since the accident.

"It's confidential, but I thought you'd want to know."

A pale blue ray of hope shone in her imagination. "Will they carry on her work?"

Mr. Linton smiled. "They're calling the new company Lemniscate, after the infinity symbol, and they'll start from the beginning, but using Shelby's molecule. This time with tightly controlled research methodology."

"She would have been glad of that," Ivy said.

"The world will be glad of it," he said firmly and she heard a note of pride in his voice. "Immortality didn't come in time for her, but it's not too late for you."

Like the jellyfish, Shelby's idea had been battered and forced back to its earlier state. Now it would, hopefully, grow up and swim free again. Like the jellyfish who had inspired it.

ACKNOWLEDGEMENTS

This novel was a long time coming. I'm very grateful to be back writing again. Thanks to Joshua Corin, Sharon Linnae, and Maxwell Cantrell for all their editing advice and support while this book was taking shape. To James Rollins who offered encouragement from the earliest stages. To Peter Salmon for a masterful copy edit. To Sabrina for excellent reader advice and patiently listening to several versions of various parts. But most especially to Toby for being there to hold my hand and push food under the door while I was working. You make it all possible. Finally, a giant shout out to all my readers who've been waiting far too long for another novel.

ABOUT THE AUTHOR

New York Times and *USA Today* bestselling author Rebecca Cantrell has published twelve novels in over ten different languages. Her novels have won the ITW Thriller, the Macavity, and the Bruce Alexander awards. In addition, they have been nominated for the GoodReads Choice, the Barry, the RT Reviewers Choice, and the APPY awards. She lives in Hawaii with her husband, son, and a slightly deranged cat named Twinkle where she listens to too much Christmas music.

Made in the USA
Las Vegas, NV
19 January 2023

65900106R00229